WHAT WAS PROMISED

TOBIAS HILL

BLOOMSBURY CIRCUS
LONDON · NEW DELHI · NEW YORK · SYDNEY

First published in Great Britain 2014

Supported using public funding by

**ARTS COUNCIL
ENGLAND**

LOTTERY FUNDED

With the assistance of a grant from the Arts Council of Great Britain

Bloomsbury Circus is an impprint of Bloomsbury Publishing plc
50 Bedford Square
London
WC1B 3DP

www.bloomsbury.com

Bloomsbury Publishing, London, New Delhi, New York and Sydney

A CIP catalogue record for this book is available from the British Library

Hardback ISBN 978 1 4088 4090 0
Trade paperback ISBN 978 1 4088 5096 1

10 9 8 7 6 5 4 3 2 1

Typeset by Hewer Text UK Ltd, Edinburgh
Printed and bound in Great Britain by CPI Group (UK) Ltd, Croydon CR0 4YY

MIX
Paper from
responsible sources
FSC
www.fsc.org
FSC® C020471

For Kit Fleet Hill

Cities give us collision

Ralph Waldo Emerson

1948

(So Now Where is Our Reward?)

1. SPRING

Why do things smell more in the cold?

This March still keeps one foot in winter. Last night the fog had ice in it – you couldn't see it but you felt it, prickling your nose and cheeks – and the fog still lingers now, with its vinegary crocus smell of London docks and factories.

Why are the smells so sharp? It's because the cold is dangerous. Even now spring is here, the cold can go to the back or chest. This weather can take a man, and these people, the survivors, they know what danger is. How they cried, when the bombs came down! They'll remember it all their lives. The early risers sniff the air, the organs of their senses prick; their bodies are on tenterhooks.

In Columbia Road the barrowboys are setting up the market stalls. It's Sunday, and Sunday is flowers ... but flowers are still hard to get, so these days there are other trades. A rabbit on the sly. Laughing Boy, with his pills and Fairbanks smile, and a stranger with a mynah bird you could learn French off of in a month, and a woman with four puppies that leap and flop and writhe like trout.

Thank God, now the fog is lifting. London comes clear under it. Rubble and waste ground. Crenellations of chimneypots. A mile and a half away, the indestructible St Paul's.

And now, at last, the punters come ... though too many are here to look. Only the lucky few will buy.

'Nothing worth selling,' Michael Lockhart says, watching them all with his gas-blue eyes, 'and no one left worth the pitch.'

'Bollocks to that,' says Rob Tull, as he sets out his blooms. 'Don't listen to Mike,' he says to the rest, 'it only ever rains on him.'

The costers loosen their throats, Ted Frost outshouting Michael and Rob Tull outshouting both of them. Alfred Shrew, the wreath-maker, is making up a crucifix. Business is quickening, though not as quickly as they'd like. Michael leans on his horse-head stick and waits for the world to come to him. His look says: I've family to feed. Come, spend. Nothing you give will be too good for me and mine.

Laughing Boy stamps his feet. Michael dickers over pennies. The runners fetch them jugs of tea. Come dark there'll be nightbarrow-men, their stalls decked out in lights, and Noakes and Judd, the market mastermen, thickset and flush, counting their cuts. Eating fat blackmarket meat, each in his accustomed haunt. And at midnight there'll be a ghost –

Not yet. The sky's still brightening. The churchbells are only just beginning. The birdseller peers in longingly as he reaches the Birdcage, and a boy stops short and goes around him. He is a slight thing, the boy, with poor clothes and a poor face. Surely he matters as much as anyone does, though no one looks at him twice.

'Such colours!' somebody says, in earshot of the boy in the mill-ing crowd. 'Columbia Road must be the gayest street in London. Still, we can't eat flowers, can we? Where next, Club Row or Petticoat Lane?'

'Not yet,' says her friend. 'Don't let's go yet, I do so need some gaiety.' And on they pass between the stalls, with Frost and Tull and Michael Lockhart crying out their hearts to them.

'Lemon trees, ladies, lemon trees, ever so ladylike, just add your G and T ...'

'A bunch for a shilling, freesias, a bunch for a shilling, roseys, two bunches ...'

'Have a look at them, girls, have a look at these, look at the SIZE of them, four for a bob –'

'She's touching me, Mike, she's TOUCHING me, ooh, tell her to stop, Mike, tell her, she's digging her nails into me, she wants her posies so bad –'

'Oh, I'm not, I'm not!'

'LiliesliliesLILIESlilieslilies'

'Two bob! Perfume! Two bob! Sweet pea! Say two bob! Perfume!'

'– Beautiful flowers, put that in your garden it'll come up like *that*, it's all Wedgwood blue, it's beautiful, it'll *smother* itself, this will, who wants it? Where are you? I'm not going to muck about, six plants, three bob, where are you? Who wants it? There it goes ...'

'WHO WANTS SERVING?'

'Oh, I don't mind'

'NO SECONDS, ONLY THE BEST! Just you wait your turn, ducks. I've only one pair of hands, dear, if I had more I'd be in the circus.'

And Rob waggles his elbows, like a chicken.

★

Poor clothes, poor face.

The boy goes on, south and west, down Club Row and Commercial Street. Every car is black as a hearse. There is the

5

cidery smell of dung. Already, ahead of him, he can hear Petticoat Lane: Sunday is the day for it.

He walks like a man with a train to catch, but there is no train and he isn't a man. He is just a boy, though he is small for his age.

An old woman in a worker's cap shoves past as if he isn't there. The boy shudders but doesn't stop. The noise of the Lane draws him on. The sounds are like a fairground, or a streetfight, or an accident.

Now it opens out around him. Goulston; Strype; Cutler; Cobb, Bell Lane, Wentworth, Old Castle; the great market's streets connect like the limbs of a living thing. Here and there land lies bombed out, but the market abhors a vacuum, growing to fill any unfenced ground.

It isn't what it was, this place. Six years of war, nine of rationing, and everywhere feels the pinch – even Petticoat Lane, where it used to be you could buy anything. No meat on show, no sweets in sight, no bread or butter above board. No clothes but hand-me-downs, unless you know where to look. No fat on anyone: all lean. Even spuds are on points now. All the more reason to do your best, then, to make a proper show of it. Everyone likes a show . . . still, it's not the place it was.

Sunday clothes and day perfumes. Yardley mixing with the smell of the Bell Lane slaughter houses. Bill Dove, the Eel Man, works his knife and board. Mrs Peacock guards her mushrooms. Solly Lazarus, the shy watchmaker, mends a worn-out Ingersoll, fish-eyed behind his spectacles.

The boy knows all their names.

He has come into Middlesex Street, still called Petticoat Lane by all but the authorities. He sits on the steps of a boarding house and peers down at the crush of people. He looks as if he is looking for someone, though no one would ever find anyone here.

He sees:

Percy Webb, the tic-tac man, on lookout for the food inspectors;

Mr Wolf Witch, the Russian spy, yanking hairs out of his nose;

S. FLAUM BIRD SEED 1d/PINT

A wedding dress, two guineas, once owned by One of Quality;

The Banana King, ten foot tall, a black man with a blackened crown of precious foreign fruit, only for those with special rations;

A woman, dire skin and bone, with two babies in a pram, and on a blanket, at her feet, a bottle of fizz, a celery vase, and a slice of old, old wedding cake, set on a silk handkerchief.

The boy gets up. Idly he scratches the sores on his arms. It's cold even in the sun and he has been sitting still too long.

'We can come again,' he says, as if encouraging a friend, although there's no one with him. 'We can try another time,' he says.

He starts towards Liverpool Street. He checks people as he goes, gazing into faces, but nothing he sees in them alters his own. He doesn't look panicked, as a lost child might. He is cautious but determined, like the scavenging sparrows, or the better of the beggars who work the crowd around him.

'Smell that?' he asks. It is apple fritters. His stomach cramps at the tang of them.

He has stopped to watch the fritter seller when he hears snarling and a cheer. Limbs press around him as he moves towards the commotion. A hatless man with cockerel hair is selling off a pair of lurchers. The dogs have turned on one another. A woman in a seal-skin coat laughs herself red in the face.

'Who wants them?' the hawker says. 'Who wants the useless fuckers? A crown for the pair of them, and you can dash their brains out right here.'

'Two bob on the bitch,' a man says, and someone else, a Welshman, 'Four on the little fellow.'

'Done. She's the measure of him.'

'She's all bark.'

'Stroll on. He won't last.'

Elsewhere the money is already coming out. The crowd don't know where to look: they're drawn to both fight and coin. The boy sees the whites of eyes under the brims of hats.

All of a sudden the bitch is hurt. She growls in outrage. When she shakes her head she leaves blood in the dirt. The second lurcher circles her. He is smaller, quieter, but he won't leave her be.

'He's only a little thing,' the boy says, though no one listens to him.

'Blast you!' someone says, a docker in the oily lounge suit he wears for work all week. The Welshman grabs his arm.

'Four bob. Fair's fair.'

'Leave off, will you? They ain't done yet.'

'I'll bet on her,' the boy says, and this time the men hear him.

'Alright, son,' the Welshman says, 'what are you in for? Make it quick.'

He only has one piece of money, a paper note. He shows it. 'Ten bob it is,' the Welshman says, and he spits fast and shakes on it.

'Ten bob, you say?' the docker laughs, and glances down at the boy and his cash. 'You'll be in for a hiding and all,' he says, but he's only half-watching, and the Welshman not at all: his eyes are back on the fight.

'She's done,' he says, with certainty.

'She's down!' echoes the woman in the sealskin coat. 'Oh, look at her, poor thing, she's down!'

The boy looks. The man with cockerel hair is prising off the smaller lurcher. The bitch lies panting on her side. There's not much blood in the end.

'Now then,' the Welshman says, and the docker pays up, muttering all the time that it smells like a twist to him.

'What about us?' the boy says. 'What do I get?'

'Get?' says the Welshman. 'You don't get a thing. You pay up. The bitch lost, didn't she?'

The boy thinks about it. He gives the Welshman his money.

'It wasn't really mine,' he says. 'It was a man's, but he didn't need it no more.'

The Welshman doesn't reply. The crowd are all looking the same way. A policeman is coming up Middlesex, parting the onlookers with one hand, the other resting on his truncheon.

'Come along, then,' he says. 'Move on, all of you.'

But they already have, the hawker and the Welshman among the first to melt away. Soon only the boy and the dog are left.

He squats by the animal. He reaches out and touches her. Her head moves of its own accord. Her eyes are slits. There is a smell to her as if something has broken inside. A shiver runs up her flank.

'Soon you'll be dead,' he whispers.

Someone says, 'It will be a mercy.'

The boy looks up. The Russian spy is there. He's poor but he never looks sick. He has an old officer's coat. He's wrinkling his nose at the smell of the dog.

'Hello, Mr Wolf Witch,' the boy says, and Wolf Witch stops wrinkling and frowns.

'Do I know you, boy?'

The boy scratches. He shakes his head.

'But you know me. How's that?'

'My friend told me. You're the spy.'

'Ha,' Wolf Witch says. 'I heard that one too.'

'Aren't you, then?'

'You think a spy would dress like this? Spies know where to get new suits, and more flesh on their bones.'

Wolf Witch pats his trench coat like a man looking for his pipe. The boy is sorry for him: it's a shame for Mr Wolf Witch that he's not a fat spy in a new suit.

'My friend,' the boy says, 'he's got the names for everyone.'

He only says it to be nice, but Mr Wolf Witch laughs!

'Then you must be friends with God.'

'Don't you believe me? Ask me. Go on.'

Wolf Witch nods at **S. FLAUM**.

'That's too easy,' the boy says. 'I can read.'

'Who am I, then?'

'I told you. Wolf Witch.'

'*Wolfowitz.*'

'That's what I said.'

'Suit yourself. The Banana King?'

'Clarence Malcolm, from Jamaica.'

'The Jew watchmaker, there?'

'Solly Lazarus.'

'Bravo. You've a knack.'

'It's not a knack. It's Solly, and his missus is called Dora. He's foreign, like you.'

'*Pff*! Not at all. Solly is a different foreign. You know them, Solly and Dora?'

'No. I told you, my friend gets their names.'

Mr Wolf Witch tuts. He eyes the street. The policeman has moved on a way, but the crowd makes room around him. He's a sergeant, an older man, and not so often on the rounds these days, though Wolf Witch knows him well enough.

'The copper?'

The boy cocks his head. He didn't look at the policeman before, being so busy with the dogs.

It's Mr Wise, someone whispers. *Dick Wise, from Quilter Street. And his sweetheart was called Susan, but he called her Sukie when he was tender –*

'Your friend isn't so clever now,' Wolf Witch says when he gets no answer, but the boy doesn't grin or blush at the jibe.

'He is. I just don't want to say.'

'A boy who keeps things to himself. Maybe you'd make a better spy than me. A bit more flesh, it wouldn't hurt you neither.'

The boy says nothing. He is thinking that some names matter more than others. Some are like butter or meat. You don't give those things away, you keep them for yourself. Dick Wise is a name that might matter.

He'll keep it for later, then. When he's alone with himself he'll work out what to do with it.

If you're lost, ask a policeman. That's what the boy used to be told. But things aren't like they used to be. You have to be cautious, now, you have to mind yourself. You can get in trouble with policemen.

A noise comes out of the dog and the boy strokes its head. Its tremors are weakening.

'I bet on her,' he says. 'I thought she'd have the other one. He was only small.'

'Small like you,' Wolf Witch says. 'Smart like you. Small and smart is useful things. You wouldn't bet against yourself, would you? You should have known better, shouldn't you?'

The boy gets to his feet. His face is a state, Wolf Witch notices, dirty even for a child's. It is seamed with grime. It makes him look for all the world like a weary, wizened old man.

'I'll know for next time,' the boy says, and he walks on.

★

Evening. In the dusk the markets are almost beautiful. As the light goes they're picked out in oil lamps and coal braziers, and here and there an old naphtha flare, hissing and sparkling.

A bomber's moon is rising. Rob Tull wheels his barrow home. He thinks of Michael Lockhart as he goes. The way Mike looks at them all, costers and punters alike, as if none of them are fit to spit for polishing his boots. Mike's one of those young men who thinks the world owes him a living. Well, he'll find out, won't he? He'll wise up soon enough. London will knock the corners off him, it'll snuff the pride out of his eyes, and Rob won't be sorry when it does. They'll get on well enough once Mike learns his place. *Chin up, mate*, he'll say, then, *Might get some sun today. We mustn't grumble, must we?*

Two empty deepsunk rooms. A wing of kipper under a plate. Rob sits down and lifts the plate. 'Nothing worth selling,' he says to the kipper, 'and no one left worth the pitch.'

Elsewhere, others eat better fare. At the Birdcage public house, in the private room upstairs, Cyril Noakes, the masterman, is mopping up his pudding with a slice of good white bread.

'Get out,' he says to the barmaid, who has brought up the slice, and who, until Cyril spoke, had been doing her best to smile, lingering in the hope that the handsomer of the men (the one with the stick and the gas-blue eyes) would ask for something for himself, or – even better – smile back through the sediments of smoke that dim the room's dark fittings and the features of both men.

The barmaid gets out. She shuts the door behind her.

Neither the man nor the masterman speak. Muted by doors and stairs, the churning of voices reaches them from the saloon bar. Cyril finishes the bread. His plate is clean enough to eat off.

'I don't like it when they smile,' he mutters. 'I can't be doing with that. If they look happy it means they aren't working hard enough.'

Michael Lockhart holds his tongue. He knows his gaffer, and others like him. Cyril doesn't want agreement. He only explains himself to share his modicum of guilt. It would be impertinent not to acknowledge that in silence. Michael understands the etiquette of full-blooded men, the small ethics of their small talk. To speak now would be to snub the glimpse of weakness that Cyril has offered, in the vain hope of Michael Lockhart's fellowship. And that would be foolhardy.

Michael will be nobody's fool.

The masterman sits back. There's nothing left, Michael thinks, for him to stuff in his gob, but there he's wrong: there's still more bottled stout, and a case of cigarettes. Cyril fills their glasses, offers the case, and lights up a fresh one.

'I always liked this place. The thing about it is, it's peaceful. I come in here on Sundays and I get a whole room to myself. I don't get that indoors. Sundays there's eighteen in my kitchen, all my boys and their little ones. Or now it's the dining room, and Sunday clothes on all of them. As if that makes it any better. Talk about a monkey house, it isn't in it. But here ... listen. Peace and quiet. That's all a fellow wants, isn't it? This is my own little corner of heaven.'

When Cyril grins, smoke escapes his teeth. The confessional moment has passed: he is at ease with himself again. 'How are your girls?' he asks, avuncular, and Michael thinks, *Skin and bones*, but 'Growing up,' is what he says.

'I always wanted girls.' Cyril points his lit ember. 'Your older one,' he says, 'Floss. She takes after you. Same look. Spirited, ain't she? You ought to keep an eye on that.'

These people, Michael thinks. These London men – women too – who see fit to tell him his business. So puffed up with unearned worth, they are, so full of themselves it's a wonder there can be any room left for the shit they spout. 'I don't see the harm in spirit,' he says, and when Cyril only shrugs, Michael gets the takings out and puts them on the table.

'Not bad,' says Cyril. 'Better than Rob. Better than Ted, and he's been with me since before. Too polite, that's their trouble. You could all do better still, with the spring blooms here.'

He leaves the money where it is. It isn't going anywhere.

'No joy with the other line?'

Michael grimaces: it is the nearest thing he has to a smile. He reaches for his winter coat, mantled over his chair, and brings out – with a jeweller's care – not flowers, but other bright things. A phial of Guerlain's Shalimar; two signet rings; a medal in its satined case; a Merchant Navy sweetheart brooch; a French peach in a handkerchief; a pair of kidskin driving gloves; a three-gill hammered hip-flask; a rope of mussel pearls; and a folding knife, small as a little finger, one pearly side inscribed, *MISS MILNE.*

Michael quarters the goods unequally. 'Blossie,' he says, as he tidies up the lion's share, then puts names to the others. 'Adam. Luke. The rings from your foreign boy.'

'Leveret, his name is. He's neat hands,' Cyril says, but Michael says nothing. He doesn't care to learn their names.

Cyril goes through it all, muttering and figuring: his neat-handed boys will get their earnings later, round the back of the pawnbrokers in Earl Street. He swigs the flask and makes a face. He pushes the medal away. *For Gallantry in Saving Life*, it says, and there is a name, too, *Hubert Loughlin*, in tiny letters round the rim.

'No call for that,' Cyril says.

'I told him as much.'

'Blossie, was it? I'll have a word. That's more trouble than it's worth. It's always the best boys go too far. What's this, a penknife?'

'Fruit knife.'

'Looks like silver.'

'Sheffield marks. It's nice work.'

Cyril looks up quick. 'And what would you know about that?'

'I know a good thing when I see it.'

'Do you, now? Well, it might be worth a bob or two.'

Cyril takes the money like a diner who has saved the best until last. He rakes it up, counts it out, pockets his cut and pushes the rest – a third of the take and a fence's tip – back to Michael.

'That for last month. More next, if you keep it up. You're turning out alright, Mickey. You're coming along. It might be you could handle a bit more responsibility. You could square things with the boys yourself, if you know what you're doing. I wouldn't miss them hanging round the shop. I get all kinds in now. It gives the wrong impression, the boys. There'd be extra in it for you. What would you say to that?'

'I wouldn't say no,' Michael says.

'No promises. You better know what you're about, I won't straighten it with you if you pay over the odds. Well, we'll try it. See how you go.'

'Mr Noakes,' Michael says, choosing his words one by one, 'I can do more for you, if you'll give me the chance.'

'Well, aren't you the squeaky wheel tonight?' Noakes says, and looks at his watch. 'You won't say no to a game, either? Same place as last time. Same crowd.'

'I'd be delighted.'

'No hurry. Not throwing-out time yet. See off your drink, why don't you? A shame to let it go to waste.'

And he opens Miss Milne's knife, admires the tiny blade, and cuts a flank off the peach.

★

Downstairs, a small woman sits alone in the Birdcage's saloon. Her name is Dora Lazarus: she is the Jew watchmaker's wife. Dora is promising herself she isn't going to talk too much.

She talks when she's nervous. She thinks when she's nervous, too. Sometimes she talks to herself, and sometimes her thoughts fly away from her. When she's happy she sings and doesn't think of anything. Solly teases her about it. *Dora is singing,* he says. *She must be kissing or cooking.*

She isn't singing now. This isn't where she belongs. What will people think of her, alone in a public house? The Birdcage is full of men. Not quiet men like her Solly, but loud ones, like those he works with in Petticoat Lane; like the Banana King, Clarence Malcolm, though really Clarence is good as gold. Besides, the Lane is not the Birdcage. There is fresh air in the Lane – there is room to shout – there is something to shout about! A market man has to shout because who would buy if he didn't? Who would know he was alive? The shouting makes him what he is. He shouts the words his father shouted in the streets before the war. That is a *useful* kind of noise.

Even Solly shouts sometimes. Dora has seen him try. *The right time, all the time!* he shouts. He isn't very good at it. He's too shy for shouting.

Now there are men looking at her. Dora can feel it. Some of them she knows by sight. They are her neighbours, she supposes, from the Columbia Buildings. She wonders what they think of her, coming here, into their place.

She wishes they wouldn't look.

And why is it called the *Birdcage?* Dora had a birdcage once, with a pretty bird in it. The people in the Birdcage are not pretty birds. There are so few other women: Mrs Joel the publican, and a barmaid who looks pale and two old ladies in a corner. One of them has a pint of beer. And all the men are talking, smoking, drinking, laughing, singing (not like birds), making noise with their boots and glasses, elbows, tables, and the piano (which is full of sour notes). All at the same time!

It makes Dora wish she could shut her eyes. It makes her want to talk and talk, until the men are all drowned out or fall silent or just die around her. She wouldn't care if they did.

'I don't mean that,' she whispers, and bites her lip.

She says nothing after that. She sits with her handbag in her lap and waits for the stranger to come back.

The Birdcage was the stranger's suggestion. Dora wanted to object, but she couldn't think of anywhere else. They might have met at Bernadette's, their only mutual friend, but Bernadette has gone to Camden to cook for her brother-in-law. And a park would be too cold, and – also – it might seem romantic. And after dark the parks are locked. On Sundays everything is locked. The only things that are unlocked are the drinking places, and the churches, and the hospitals.

The barmaid comes to wipe the table. Dora turns away and looks longingly out of the window. The glass is frosted, except where lettering is cut into it: Dora looks through the letters.

There is a boy out there, a poor boy in poor clothes, looking through the same letters into the saloon's light and warmth. Their eyes meet and Dora smiles. She thinks, I want to be out there, and you want to be in here.

The boy doesn't smile back. The glass distorts his face: it fractures and doubles him.

When she breaks his gaze she finds the stranger standing over her.

'There you go, Mrs Lazarus,' he says, and he puts a glass in front of her and sits down with his own. 'Cheers!'

'Cheers,' Dora says.

The stranger drinks off half a pint without even stopping for breath. The muscles of his throat work. He's younger than she is. His name is Thomas. Bernadette says he's a good boy.

'You must be thirsty,' Dora says, and wishes the words back before they're even out of her, so that they trail off on *thirsty*, but Thomas smiles a nice smile.

'Sorry about that. We don't get much aboard, you see. Water, water everywhere. It were better in the war, but there's precious much chance of anything now.'

'I see,' Dora says, although she doesn't quite, Thomas's accent is strange to her, and besides, it doesn't matter what she says: Thomas has been distracted by the need to stand aside. Two more women have come in, seeking shelter from the coarseness of the public bar. Silver shines on Thomas's coat as he finds his seat again. He wears a badge, Dora sees, its metal buffed to a high polish: a crown and knotted rope embracing two letters: *MN.*

'How's Bernie, then?'

'Bernie?' Dora asks, but she is stupid with nerves: he means Bernadette Malcolm, of course; they have nobody else in common. 'Oh yes, Bernie is very well! We are neighbours here, and my husband is friends with her husband. He is a Banana King, except there are few bananas, only for children and women with child. They are market sellers together, in Petticoat Lane.'

'I know, she wrote to me all about it. She's lovely writing, you know, look.'

Thomas gets out a paperback, opens it, removes a picture post-card. On one side are four Scenes of London. On the other Dora can make out his name and rank, *Thomas Cowlishaw, Leading Steward*, written in faultless copperplate under the King's post-marked head.

'Got a proper schooling out there, didn't she? Always told us she were brought up British. Writes better than what I do. Shame she weren't around tonight.'

His voice is full of admiration. Dora has to smile. Thomas catches her eye and blinks.

'I'm not soft on her.'

'Oh no! Dora says, 'No –'

Thomas takes another drink. When he puts down the glass his ears are scarlet, but he meets her eye again and smiles.

How brave, Dora thinks.

'Well, if things had been different. Mostly it were men only we had out of Montego Bay. She made a change, her and her fellow and the little shrimp. Is he well, the lad?'

'Jem. He is not a shrimp now. He's going to be tall, like his father.'

'Right. Still, we had a laugh.'

'She told me that,' Dora says. 'That you had a laugh.'

Thomas busies himself putting the card away. 'She says in there you need a favour.'

'Oh,' Dora says, 'yes,' – but she frowns. The favour has been a long way from her thoughts. She is drinking with a handsome man, looking at a handsome man. She has been *enjoying* him . . . as if she has come to the horrible Birdcage for her own enjoyment. She is not here for the joy of it! She is ashamed of herself, that she could have forgotten that.

'Something taking, she says?'

'Yes; no,' Dora says, 'well,' and she clutches at her handbag. 'Bernadette told me that you are sailing east, sometimes?'

'For my sins. Not much of a swap for the old route. Give me the West Indies any day. We're back up the Baltic in the morning.'

'I need something taken to Danzig.'

Thomas shakes his head. 'No Danzig any more. Gdansk, they call it now. Because, you know, it being Polish.'

'Yes, of course,' Dora says. 'Gdansk.'

She retreats into her chair. Her heart is going too fast. Like her thoughts and words when she's afraid, it is running away with itself. But Thomas is talking too much too, his cheeks a little flushed with drink. A young man ashore, hitting his stride.

'It's Russians we're taking, Russians in and us lot out. There's Scots still there, don't ask me why; the Germans had them all locked up. To be honest with you I could do without Russians on board. Politics, that's all it is with them. It's all tommy rot to me. Jerry's got nothing on them. I've heard they're locking it *all* down soon, their share of Germany, Poland, the lot. It's them makes the rules there now. Nothing goes in, no one gets out, that's what the lads are saying. Next thing you know we'll be at war with *them*, and that'll be short and sweet, won't it? One mystery bomb and bang! We'll all be cinder.'

Dora opens her handbag and takes out the photographs.

There are four of them. She has more at home, but even four would be a loss. Four is the maximum that she can bring herself to relinquish.

'What are those?'

'My family.'

Thomas puts down his drink. His rubs his mouth with finger and thumb, as if cleaning it. 'Right,' he says, finally.

He cocks his head at the pictures, then turns one. 'This is good. Your father, isn't it?'

'Yes.'

'You take after him. He looks well-to-do.'

'He is a doctor,' Dora says, with a spark of pride. 'His name is there, you see? It's small, I hope you can read it.'

'*Gottfried,*' Thomas reads, '*Rosen.*'

'Gottfried Rosen, yes. And here, my mother, Sophia Rosen. My little brother, Hermann. And here, this is all of us. You see me, there? This is in the street where we live. I have written the address on the back, here. Third floor, 41 Jopengasse. And this tower, here, this is St Mary's. This is a, what do you say? You can see this from anywhere.'

'A landmark,' Thomas says. 'You won't have seen them for a bit, I suppose.'

'Not since we came here,' Dora says. 'Not since before.'

'You'll miss them, then,' Thomas says, awkwardly, and Dora says that yes, she does, awkward herself: what can it be but awkward, when one gives the only answer to a question that need not be asked?

'I don't know where they are,' she says.

Thomas doesn't look surprised. His brow is furrowed in thought. It makes him look older. The saloon's electric lights reveal the scalp under his hair.

'You'll have written to them?'

'Yes, but I don't hear from them. Not for seven years. Of course I think they must be dead. It is a long time now, so probably . . . I see the news, about the things the Germans did. But sometimes I think, perhaps they are gone away. So many people, you know, it is just that they are not where they were before. No one is where they belong. Perhaps they went away and never heard where we are, either, if they never read my letters.'

'Mrs Lazarus . . .'

'Dora,' Dora says, 'please.'

'Dora. What are you asking of me?'

'I want you – I am asking you – please, to take these to Danzig – I mean Gdansk – and ask people. Show these to people. My father is a doctor. People know him in Danzig. *Gdansk.* In Jopengasse. If there is nothing there is nothing, but I must do what I can. I have to know. I can pay you, look, I have money, here –'

She is still going through her handbag when Thomas takes the photographs. He gets the paperback back out, takes the pictures, one by one, and stows them away, with the card of Bernadette's.

'Oh thank you,' Dora says.

'Put your money away, won't you?'

'Thank you.'

'I'll do my best.'

'Yes.'

'I can't say more than that.'

'No, of course not.'

She thinks, Oh God, I'm going to cry, but then Thomas stands, and she takes the chance to look down and gather herself.

'Let's have another, love.'

'No, I can't,' Dora says. 'I can't, I must get back.'

'Next time, then. When I bring you news.'

'My husband thinks it's foolish. My coming here. My asking you.'

'What's foolish about it?'

She looks up at him. 'The hope,' she says.

★

'Soon the anchor was short up; soon it was hanging dripping at the bows; soon the sails began to draw, and the land and shipping to flit by on either side; and before I could lie down to snatch an hour of slumber the Hispaniola had begun her voyage to the Isle of Treasure . . .'

Camden Town. The Banana King's wife is warming up saltfish and rice. Next door she can hear her man hammering, and his brother reading to her boy.

22

Bernadette Malcolm hopes the neighbours don't complain. It's late to be cooking and hammering, on the Sabbath of all days: but it's cold again tonight, Neville already has a chest, the window sash is broken and he won't fix things for himself. So her Clarence has to do it.

Out of the panes beside the stove Bernadette can see a bit of churchyard, the trees around the gate lit up in a wash of lamppost light. Cars are parked up for the night. This is a decent neighbourhood. Neville's rooms are let to him through a friend he flew with in the war. Neville doesn't keep it up but it's a good place for him. Bernadette doesn't want the neighbours talking.

It isn't Neville's fault it's late. It's wrong to blame him, but she does. The saltfish is still cold and the gas thin as a ghost. They should have eaten hours ago! But Clarence got in late from Petticoat Lane, and then there was so much to bring – soda, rags and vinegar, and the food she's made for now and later, and cord and nails for the sash – and then the buses were so slow . . .

Bernadette aspires to have a sunny disposition. When she thinks it – *sunny disposition* – she sees a painting of herself, done like a Ministry of Food poster. The painted Bernadette is giving out handfuls of sunshine (golden-rayed, unrationed, pure) to the grateful crowds around her, with cheerfulness, and dignity. But cheerfulness, she finds, is hard to do with dignity, and worry ruins both. Like this, today: the too-late eating. Clarence hammering.

Worry makes Bernadette fierce. Her worries harden her.

She thinks, Camden is too far. On Sunday nights, leastways. I'll tell Clarence for next time. Neville is a man, isn't he? So let him look out for himself. Her boy should be in bed by now, not having his head filled with pirate stories.

'*Come away, Hawkins, he would say; Come and have a yarn with John. Nobody more welcome than yourself, my son. Sit you down and hear the news. Here's Cap'n Flint — I calls my parrot Cap'n Flint, after the famous buccaneer — here's Cap'n Flint predicting success to our v'yage — wasn't you, Cap'n?'*

Neville has a fine voice, even with the chest: a singer's voice, rich and tender. He used to sing plenty back home. He led the morning hymn each day at Elementary School, where he was Principal and Sir, even to Bernadette Jarrett and to his own little brother. He sang at St Andrew's Methodist, where he was churchwarden. He was singing there the Sunday morning Bernadette saw Clarence again, for the first time since childhood: Clarence Malcolm, grown into a man, sixteen years old and nightwatchman at the Frome sugar factory. She was fifteen that summer. Mama had allowed her home from boarding in Green Island. It was Clarence who turned her head, but it was Neville's voice that others turned to, then. Neville's voice was the kind the old parishioners would call The Backbone of the Congregation.

He has no congregation now. Bernadette has tried with him, found him a chapel close by, but Neville ducks her questions. Bad enough that Clarence has to work Sundays to make ends meet, but Clarence says his brother won't even step inside a church. And Neville never sings.

Make do and mend, people say. But what if some things can't be mended? What when they are too far gone?

It's not far. She knows that. How can she say Camden is far, when they've come — all four of them — five thousand miles, home-town to mother country? This Sunday visit, this isn't far, for family. Neville is never better than when he's with her boy.

'Ah, she's a handsome craft, she is, the cook would say, and give her sugar from his pocket, and then the bird would peck at the bars —'

There is a drumming: Neville pecking the chair-arm with his fingers.

'*– And swear straight on, passing belief for wickedness. There, John would add, You can't touch pitch and not be mucked.*'

'Pitch?' she hears her boy say. 'Like black?'

Neville laughs. 'No! Not like that.'

'It don't make sense,' Jem says, and his uncle coughs, once, twice.

'*Doesn't* make sense,' Bernadette calls. 'Boy, I don't know what they teach you in that school.'

'Doesn't,' Jem says, dutifully, and – just as good – the hammering stops. It's giving her a headache.

Clarence comes into the kitchen. He's trying to tread quietly, to soothe her with his quietness.

As if there's an ounce of quiet in him! The man doesn't know himself. It's as if he's never seen the faces when he walks into a room – in London, England or Glasgow, Jamaica or anywhere in between. It's as if he doesn't understand the way he fills the little kitchen, six foot six of displaced air and manpower.

'I hear you,' Bernadette says. 'Creeping.'

'Who's creeping?' Clarence says. 'I heard some rumour about food in here. I'm working up a hunger.'

'Well, you'll just have to work it up some more.'

'What is it, ackee and saltfish?'

'No ackee,' says Bernadette. 'As if you didn't know already.'

'Saltfish without ackee. Like fish and chips without the chips,' he says, and puts his arms round her.

Bernadette feels herself lean back into his strength. She can't stop herself. The movement is like gravity. 'It's your fault,' she says.

'My fault? How is it *my* fault?'

'If you want ackee,' Bernadette says, 'you should be the Ackee King.'

That makes him laugh, and she laughs too. Clarence's laughter is like that, you can't hear it and not join in.

Bernadette unwinds his arms. 'Have you fixed that window?'

'Soon.'

'Now! Can't you see I'm busy?'

'Ackee King,' he says, and goes.

She can joke about it now, his work. That's a good thing, she supposes. Not that their life is all laughs, now. Sometimes her man might as well be the Ackee King, when he goes down to meet the train and there are no bananas to be had, nothing to buy, nothing to sell for all the money or coupons in London.

Still: when they arrived, in Neville's wake – cabin class; they are decent folk – and found Neville the way he is (no help in finding Clarence a job, and a job to look after, himself), well, that was a harder time. Clarence is a proud man. To fight for King and Empire, and then to come and ask for a living, and to have to live on your wits alone – to have to make work for yourself, and to make nothing that will earn, until you make yourself into the Banana King . . . to take your blessed strength and height and put a crown of fruit on them, on the body you sent to war – like you were a clown, or a joke, or a fool – like you were a blasphemy –

Bernadette was angry for him. She was ashamed for him. But Clarence was never those things, and his feelings, like his laughter, are infectious.

Bernadette remembers the first time she swallowed her shame, and went with Jem after chapel to watch his father make their livings. Clarence was so pleased to see them. He bought them tea from the market runners, then he put on his banana-hand crown as easily as a clerk puts on his collar. He seemed to wear it as if it never weighed on him at all. When people laughed, he laughed back. He never lost his smile or temper. And so he has kept his pride. Because he is a gentleman. Clarence is a gentle man.

It has to be a good thing, for a man to keep his pride. Even if the English see nothing but the sin in it. Even if England hammers down the proud.

Now the food is almost ready. No ackee. Bernadette misses it. It's foolish, but some days she misses that more than anything. The taste of ackee fruit: its dirty, oily ripeness. Last summer Clarence found her some, as a treat, but the sea had got into it, it smelled of salt and engine rooms and Bernadette didn't like to eat it. She made a show of being pleased, but the truth was it made her want to weep.

Never mind. There are worse things than no ackee and a bit of saltfish. A bit of ackee and no saltfish – that would be worse! But saltfish isn't hard to get just now, and Bernadette has onions and tinned tomatoes. The smells of Neville's lodgings – the sour sweat and fear – are retreating like shadows in sunlight. The rooms are sweetening.

It is going to be a good meal.

★

Midnight. In Columbia Road the flower market's rubbish makes middens of the gutters. By the bomb site end the scraps have been swept into heaps taller than children. Big Ben tolls, miles away, across the City, along the river.

Here are Michael Lockhart's daughters, hiding in the willow-herb. Wrapped in matching Blustons coats, cardies over bony knees, they are looking for the ghosts of airmen. This is Long Debris, their place, where by day they play Cowboys, Spacemen, Trolls, Tarzan, or build their dens, or spy on roomless lovers or beggars' bonfires. Beyond them is the Devil's Punchbowl left by a rocket attack. Sycamore and aspen have populated the depression, but the moon is bright tonight and everything is visible.

Their mum has been calling for them, but now she's gone back in. The girls are crouching side by side, snug as a pair of owls, Iris thinks. But owls eat mice, and Iris likes mice.

She shivers.

'Floss,' she says, 'I'm cold.'

'Stop talking then, it makes it worse.'

'Aren't *you*?'

But Floss is never cold. It's like the Banana King says: Floss is a right little trooper.

'It's midnight,' Iris says. 'I still don't see anything.'

'He won't come if he hears you.'

'You don't know that, you're just saying. You never saw a ghost.'

'Shush, will you!' Floss says, and Iris shushes.

The mist is coming down. Way across Long Debris there are still lights on here and there, in the tops of the Columbia Buildings, and down towards the water fountain someone is out walking, whistling the gloomy hymn about those in peril on the sea. But London has finished for the night, there is no one else about, and the mist makes even the few lit windows seem desolate and remote.

'Floss?'

'What?'

'Dad might be home by now.'

'Fat chance. He's seeing his masterman.'

'Mum is, anyway.'

'Are you scared?'

'No,' Iris says, but her voice is shivery. 'Floss?'

'*What?*'

'I am scared.'

'It's alright, Iris.'

'It's not.'

'It is. I'm here, aren't I?' Floss says, and puts her arms around her sister. Wraps her up and kisses her.

'Whisper,' she says into Iris's hair (which smells of biscuits, or warm milk). 'I don't think he'll hear whispering.'

'I'm still cold, though,' Iris whispers. 'Do you think he's coming?'

'I don't know. Jem swore he saw him. It wasn't just one of his stories,' Floss says, though she likes Jem's stories, if it comes to that, and half of her hopes it is.

'What do we do if he does come?'

Iris feels her sister thinking.

'I think we should observe him,' Floss says, 'and probably make notes. Then tomorrow we'll tell a policeman.'

'Is he bad, then, the Airman?'

'He might be. Anyway he's German.'

'Is he still German, if he's dead?'

Floss doesn't answer that. She's thinking of the things Jem told her. The Airman crawling out of the pit. Wet. All wet and black. *First he burned and then he drowned.*

Her teeth want to chatter but she doesn't let them, locks them tight. Iris would feel it.

'He was a bomber,' she says. 'Shot down on his last raid.'

'Was he bombing us?'

'Silly. Who else would he be doing?'

Floss lets go of her sister, stands up and hugs herself. The mist is starting to gather over the sunken ground. There are no ruins here except one stump, a chimney-breast that uselessly withstood the blast. Beyond the stump is jungle, and the cellar of the house it once served. Over the years the pit has flooded partway. Floss can see the water through the mist, black and still.

'Floss?'

'What?'

'If he's still German, is that what he talks?'

When Floss sighs her teeth chit-chatter. 'I don't know!' she says, too loud, disappointed at her own weakness.

'I'm only asking,' Iris says. 'It's only that I won't be able to talk to him if he does. I mean I don't know any German. Do you?'

No answer. Moon-shadows in the mist. Then, '*Schnell*,' Floss says, and Iris giggles, breathless with cold, fear and excitement.

'*Schnell, schnell!*'

'*Gott in Himmel!*'

'Oh God!'

'What?'

'I saw him Floss I saw! He's there!'

Iris is on her feet. She huddles into Floss, burying her face in her sister's coat. Floss stares over her, down into the shallow crater.

'I don't see anything,' she says. Her voice is shaking, but not as much as Iris is. 'Iris, there's nothing there.'

'There is!' Iris says. 'There was. I want to go home now.'

'But I haven't *seen* him yet –'

Iris raises her head. Her face is serious.

'Let's go home,' she says, and takes her big sister's hand, and goes.

★

Mary Lockhart waits up for her girls. Mrs Platt from next door has come in to sit with her. Just in case, as Mrs Platt says. Just to see out any trouble.

'Like animals,' Mrs Platt says, 'and the girls go worse than the boys. It's ever the same with the wars. No old man to whip them into line. They all get into mischief, they get away with murder, and then they've got the taste for it. Like beasts. Not that Alf was much for whipping. Where's your Michael, then? Working nights?'

'When he must,' Mary says.

'On a Sunday, too. Not that I'm a churchgoer.'

'Won't you have another, Mrs Platt?' Mary asks, and the old woman puts out her cup and keeps on talking, perpetual as St Paul's.

'We had a horse when I was a girl. His name was Dusty . . . no, it was Dash, Dusty came *after* Dash. Mr Jones used to stable him for us, in with his dairy cows, that was how gentle a horse Dash was. Then one day Jack was out with him – this was my brother Jack, he passed in the first war – and it was getting dark, so Jack is pushing it, and isn't there someone in the road, why there is, some old drunkard, weaving about in the dark, and Dash goes right over him. Spurns him. Head broke open. Well. The thing is, after that, Dash was never the same. Like a different animal. Bit just for the joy of it. He had the smell of blood, you see, he had a taste for it. Jones wouldn't keep him no more because he kicked one of the cows and all the milk was off for days.'

Mrs Platt drinks her tea. 'And that was why we got Dusty. Any more biscuits?'

'Sorry,' Mary says, and her neighbour sighs and mutters.

'Well, they was only arrowroot. What time is it? I heard midnight.'

'Yes, it's late,' Mary says, but too quick. Mrs Platt sets her chin. She isn't going anywhere; and just to prove it, she leans over and strokes Mary, like a cat.

'I'll stay, I will, don't fret. At least until they're in their beds. They'll be back soon.'

Mary goes to the sink and starts putting away. Where do all these chipped things go? She doesn't care, she just needs to be doing. Mary tries with Mrs Platt, but the old woman never fails to rub her up the wrong way. Still, you have to try your best. What are neighbours for but this, for troubles? If Mary can't bring herself to be grateful, she can still manage to be civil. Mary was brought up properly: she knows how to bite her tongue.

'I know they will,' she says. 'They're sensible girls.'

'Of course they are. Well, the little one is. Not like that Irish lot upstairs. Six girls – they sleep them in the parlour. The fellow beats them raw and it makes no odds to them. You can hear them all the time, in Irish, but you know they're talking back. The mouths on them, cheeky little chits! I don't know one from the other and I don't want to. It's a pity the way things have gone. When I was a girl we used to play out all hours, we used to know everyone by name. Now it's all bomb sites and strangers everywhere, everyone's cut loose and floating around where they don't belong. Not *you*, dear, I don't mean you, I mean at least you're English, ain't you? It's the foreigners and tinkers. You heard about the man they found? The foreigner with all the cuts?'

'Yes,' Mary says, 'I heard.'

'Cuts all over. Bacon Street. Not far,' Mrs Platt says, and she gets to her feet. 'I've just got to go in the corner. Where is it? Oh, don't worry yourself. Same as ours, isn't it?'

With her neighbour gone Mary leans on the board. She pictures Mrs Platt, in the dark, taking a wrong turn, hitching up her skirts and pissing over Michael's bed. Well, then she'd get what she deserves. She's like the horse she talks about. Hungry for disaster.

He had the smell of blood, you see, he had a taste for it.

She pours herself more tea and sits. She's calm. She's not frightened, whatever Annie Platt would like. Worried? Yes. She heard about the man with the cuts – found by the dustmen in Bacon Street, half dead and too drunk to know it – but the gossip is that the man might have been living rough. That would be less worrying. The troubles of beggars are not those of other people.

In any case, her girls won't have gone as far as Bacon Street. They'll stay in sight of home, Mary's sure. The adventure will be Flossie's idea, and Floss might find trouble, but Iris is sensible.

Iris is Mary's girl. Floss is her father, to the bone.

Mary looks up and sees there's a new crack in the ceiling. It makes her stomach turn. In the pantry, yesterday, she caught weeds growing in. She pulled them through by their green hair and found they had even put on flowers. Little strings of violet stars, trailing out into the sun. Pretty things, doing their best; but Mary doesn't lack for flowers, and she felt sick at the sight of those.

The Columbia Buildings are falling down. Mary wonders if they'll have to leave. It's one bomb did the grave damage, a big one, early in the war. It came right down the air shaft of the shelter, the official one that lay under the old market square. There were forty died down there, though others were pulled out alive. Mrs Platt was one of them.

Of course she was, Mary thinks. Mrs Platt would find a way out of an atom bomb.

A blessing, Michael calls it. Mary wishes he wouldn't say it so plain, but it's true for them. Where would they be, if not for that bomb? Michael saw their chance and got them in quick. They're the lucky ones to have a roof at all. Where would they live, if not here? They might be as wretched as that man in Bacon Street. They might still live apart, Michael in his Old Street lodgings, her and the girls still cheek by jowl with her Aunt Kate in Birmingham, living off sour charity. Waiting for Michael to make their fortunes, to find the gold in London's streets . . . though gold's only in stories: Mary's streets are Michael's, and those are only paved with flowers.

Or silver. Mary has seen the silver, and other things. But she doesn't ask.

The latch clicks and she jumps up. She's quick into the hall, but Mrs Platt is there before her, wiping her hands on her skirts.

'*There* you are! Your mother's been so worried. I don't know what you two were thinking of!'

'Thank you, Mrs Platt,' Mary says, and the girls troop past in general silence, Floss head up, Iris head down.

Mary has them all back in the kitchen, is doing her best to be stern while the girls clean their hands and faces, when she sees that Iris has been crying.

'Dirty as a coal miner,' Mrs Platt says, and Floss looks up, wet and feral.

'I'm not!'

'Mrs Platt,' Mary says, 'you've been a help.'

'I'll be going then,' the old woman says, grudgingly; but she does. Alone with her children, Mary touches Iris's blotched face.

'What's this for?'

'She saw a ghost!' Floss says, but Iris shakes her head.

'It wasn't.'

Mary cleans her child. She had the water warm, but already it's cold in her hands. 'Of course not,' she says, 'there's no such thing.'

'There is,' Floss says, 'she saw it in Long Debris! You did, Iris, didn't you?'

But Iris won't say. Only later, when they're both in bed, when Mary is kissing them in the dark, does Iris lean into her neck to whisper muzzily.

'It wasn't.'

'What, love?'

'It wasn't the ghost,' Iris says. 'It was smaller than him.'

2. SUMMER

On the first it is dry. A watercart goes laying the dust.

On the second, third and fourth, it's wet. The costers are crestfallen hawks, the tarps fat ponds of rain.

On the fifth, the Jew watchmaker plays chess with the Banana King.

Just as they do most Saturdays, weather and families permitting, Solly Lazarus and Clarence Malcolm climb up to the fifth floor laundry (where no one much goes anymore – the cant of the Columbia Buildings is appreciable up here), and set up the table and chairs, the board and pieces and the ash-tray, out on the old drying balcony. Clarence has brought apples. Across the bombstruck wasteland that runs a zigzag east of them, Solly can see his wife. She's tramping through the rubbishy grass, her basket – hooked over one arm – full of a froth of elderflower.

Clarence whistles, Solly waves, and Dora waves back up at them. Clarence is glad to see her there. He's hoping she'll give him an edge.

When Clarence takes a piece, he slams his own on top of it – 'Ha!' – so that the board and table shake, and sometimes (the floor being what it is) the whole thing goes teetering over, both men wailing and catching at it, and all the pieces sliding south, so that they have to start again.

When Solly thinks he has a clincher, he grips his pipestem in his teeth, smiles around it – 'Aha!' – and moves his piece extra slow, his goggle eyes darting up to make sure Clarence is watching, so that they'll both remember his genius for posterity.

Now it's Solly's turn. Clarence blows a Gold Flake smoke ring. He says, 'Bernie was talking.'

'You're trying to distract me, Clarence. Don't think I don't know.'

'It's true, though. Someone knows a council man, says they're going to turf us out.'

'Just talk,' Solly says, 'those council men, they like the sound of their own voices.'

'Let's hope.'

'They must have better things to do.'

'Let's hope that too.'

Solly's hand wavers. It was with his help that Clarence got a place in the Columbia Buildings. And if the Buildings are condemned? Solly will find rooms somehow – he'll be more Jew or less Jew, as landlords and circumstances require – but what will Clarence do? There are coloured fellows in Notting Hill, and some in Stepney, but they live bachelor lives, and if Solly knows Bernadette she'll have nothing to do with them.

Another thing: if what Dora says is true, it's no time for the Malcolms to be without a roof over their heads. Solly scratches the birthmark on his scalp. 'It's too hot today,' he says.

'Hot! This isn't hot, this is nice. Jamaica, now, that's hot. Melt a man down like chocolate.'

'Have it your way. This someone, did she say when?'

'No.'

'Well,' Solly says, and moves a knight with some reluctance. Silence rules on the balcony.

'So!' Solly says, too loudly, as Clarence ponders, 'Bernadette looks well.'

'Plenty well.'

'Dora says so too. Dora says she glows.'

'Bernie always glows.'

'I am making an implication.'

'I know what you're making,' Clarence says. 'Gossiping like an old woman.' Then, with a kind of shyness, 'It's true.'

Solly claps his shoulder. They shake hands over the board. Downstairs a wireless is talking up the Olympics.

'My sunshine woman,' Clarence says. Then, '*Ha*!' he crows, and the board shakes like an earthquake.

When they're done Solly goes down and pours himself a drink. He doesn't like to drink in company. He is excited by others, invigorated by them, and often fearful of them. With others he likes to keep his wits about him. Six days a week, in the Lane, he wears his wits like best clothes. Now there is no one to see him.

He stands and sips in the sun-thinned gloom and thinks of Clarence Malcolm. He has never known a coloured man before, not to call a friend. He has never needed many friends, but one is a good thing to have – and Dora gets on with Bernadette, so that's two. Better still.

Neither he nor Dora has ever moved in wide circles: small ones in Danzig, smaller here. *House mice*, his father used to call them. If they lived in Whitechapel it might be a different story, but

Whitechapel has too many godly Jews for Solly's taste. Solly has no truck with gods. No, they fit in better here.

After the war – before he got a proper license in the Lane – Solly traded on the hoof, roundabout Club Row. He knew the other costers, he was on first-name terms with some, but it was never more than that. And then, one day, Clarence arrived. Solly got down there late – Dora had needed him to queue – and there was Clarence, looking to Solly like his own self multiplied: twice as tall, twice as foreign and twice the looks as well, he doesn't mind admitting it. Clarence Malcolm, fresh from Jamaica, astride a crate in the rain, knees up to his armpits, playing chess with poor Ben Weir, the cascara salesman with the stutter.

Solly watched him beat Ben hollow. His game was unconventional: Clarence played like a boxer, waiting for the overreach, the lazy guard, the opening. Solly plays a different chess – all guns blazing, is his way – but there were lessons to be learned, he saw, in Clarence's idling aggression, his velvet-gloved ambushes. A cute game, that was what it was. When Clarence won he grinned and stretched in unconcealed delight, slapped the drops off his fedora, turned to Solly and boomed, *You got legs like a Coldstream Guard, standing there all this time! Sit down, man, come, come. Tell the truth, now; are you partial to the sport of kings?*

That chess should have thrown them together, two such different fellows. That they should share, not a love for music, or some other worthwhile thing, but this boyish passion; really, it is ridiculous. It is remarkable.

Still, it's hot, whatever Clarence says. Solly takes off his tie. He opens the window. He wonders where Dora is.

All around the kitchen stand the paraphernalia of her craft: the buckets, the fraying sieve, muslin, a small jar of tartaric acid, and a big one of precious sugar; the rations she's saved all spring, plus the extra meant for summer jam.

Dora makes cordials. The elderflower is the best. It's Solly's favourite, and for Dora it entails tier on tier of happiness. Happiness in the picking, in the making and the drinking.

He looks forward to the smell of it. The smell is alchemy. At first Dora's cordial will be nothing but muck and water. It will smell of the pharmacist's acid and the anodyne sweetness of sugar. Then one day they'll wake up, one or the other or both. They'll cough and sigh, and there! Instead of the smell of themselves – instead of Solly and Dora – there will be the elderflower. Its heady scent will fill their rooms. It will be the smell of summer itself. The English summer, that begins with the elderflower, and ends with the berry.

Solly frowns. He thinks, But what's wrong with the smell of us? Why wish for anything more than Solly and Dora? Aren't we lucky to be alive? Aren't we young, and in love?

Not so young any more, whispers the imp inside his head, which (he hardly knows it) speaks with the voice of his mother. *Not so much of the genius. You smell of beer and no money. You smell like a refugee, Solomon. You smell of childlessness.*

Solly clicks his tongue. The drink is souring his thoughts. He likes the way it loosens him, but he's never had the head for it.

What he needs is some music. He takes the drink into the lounge, turns on the wireless, grumbles over the dial until he finds a vein of jazz. Then he dances – little hops – around the room, past the one-bar electric fire, the bookcase full of paperbacks and Dora's photograph albums, the workshop table with its watches and orphaned parts – all the way to the easy chair, where he collapses gratefully.

There are letters on his table, but they don't look new to Solly. They'll be old news, Dora's hoardings, brought out to be read again. He swipes a postcard off the top.

NOTHING is to be written on this side except the date, signature and address of the sender. Erase words not required. IF ANYTHING ELSE IS ADDED THE POSTCARD WILL BE DESTROYED.

I am (~~not~~) well.

~~I have been admitted into Hospital~~ {<small>Sick
for operation</small>} ~~and am going on well~~.

<u>I am going to be transferred to another camp.</u>
I have received your card dated *19th September, 1944*

                                       Signature
                                       Solomon Lazarus

                                       Camp Address
                                       Onchan,
                                       Isle of Man
                                       Internment Camp.

Date *12th October, 1944*

'Oh, this?' Solly says to the room. 'Yes, I remember this.' And he nods; not happily, only backing up the words, as if some authority has asked him to confirm his statement.

He remembers Onchan Camp. The boarding house room he shared with a procession of other men – Jews, Hungarians, Italians. The beauty of the view from their window across the island. Douglas town in the rain, or the castle in the sun, and always the green or gold of gorse – even, on clear days, a hint of Port Erin, where the women's camps were, and where – the Italians said so – the Finns swam naked in the sea.

He remembers leaving Dora. They'd been in England six months. Dora, pregnant, nineteen years old, weeping on the platform. The night train to Lancashire. The transit camp, two thousand men, with twenty buckets and no chairs. Then Liverpool, the crossing, the Steam Packet heading into a storm, all of them sick or sleeping, one or the other, taking turns. And when they came into Douglas he woke, and the first thing he saw was the flag of Man, the triskelion, its three legs so like a swastika that for a wild moment he thought he'd been betrayed. He thought he'd been given back into the hands of the enemy.

It was morning, and the sky was white. The soldiers lined them up like soldiers, all along the wet quay, the whole crazy muddle of them – the London waiters, the Oxford professors, the buskers, tramps and vicars, and Ferracci, the opera singer, and the Germans and the Jews, and the man who had a Scotty dog, and the man who had brought a fishing rod – and with sixty others Solly was led up to Onchan, on the cliffs above the town. They kept him until Onchan closed, then sent him on to Mooragh.

Dora, weeping on the platform. That stayed with him a long time: then it was lost to him for years. It was as if he'd worn away a snapshot kept in a wallet. That was harder. To not remember Dora weeping was worse than remembering.

It won't be long, he said to her. He didn't know it was a lie. In the end it was five years. The war for him was nothing but the view from the cliffs of Onchan. It was all echoes and distances. The long draw of ships' horns, the *ha-ha*-ing of gulls, the echo of a football struck by men wasting their years in play, the rumours of other men killing and killed far away. The dust-pocked newsreels of Hitler, the crowds rising to his gesture like flowers to the light. The disbelieving whispers of things still inconceivable.

And Dora's war? Well, he'll never know. He knows what she has told him, which is only what can be fitted into words. He knows they lost the child, a boy, and that they'll never have another. He knows how desperate her hungers have become for the things she lacks most – not food or clothes, or friends or neighbours, but parents and children; for family, above and below and around her.

41

He knows he wasn't there when it mattered most, and that, return-ing to vacancy, he is no longer enough to fill it. The Dora he left weeping isn't the Dora he came back to. What else can he know?

Solly puts the postcard back. He turns off the wireless.

★

Some said "no" and some said "yes". Some said they could but go and see, and anything was better than little supper, less breakfast, and wet clothes all the night. Others said: "These parts are none too well known, and are too near the mountains. Travellers seldom come this way now. The old maps are no use: things have changed for the worse and the road is unguarded ..."

Someone is calling Jem Malcolm's name. He's so deep in his book that at first the voice seems miles away, and when his head comes up he blinks like a boy coming awake.

'Jem,' he hears, 'Je-em,' his name drawn out into a singsong.

It's Floss, and he smiles, listening: he knows exactly where she is. She's in the depot yard – which used to be a market square – by the old market arcades, where the council keep concrete and timber and the spindlemakers is. If you stand just there and call just right the square works like a megaphone. Floss found it out with him. It's wizard.

'Jem, where *are* you? I know you're there. Are you there, Jem, are you? Jem!'

Soon some old lady will come out and ask what all the racket is. Floss Lockhart, she'll say, I see you down there, yelling. We'll have no more of that today. This is a nice neighbourhood. You go lark about somewhere else.

Doesn't he want to lark with Floss? Oh, he does, but the book won't let him go. If he stops reading now something might happen to it. A thief might find his hiding place. A bomb might find Columbia Road, like the one that blew up Japan. The book and everything will burn with the power of the sun, and then he'll never finish it.

His specs are slipping. He'll have the National Health 524 Contours soon: these are just market hand-me-downs. He's tried the 524 Contours. They hurt, but that was because they weren't properly prescribed. His mum said they looked intelligent. She's going to queue for them all hours.

Jem pushes the hand-me-downs back up. He wrinkles his nose to keep them there. His gaze drifts to the pages.

They asked him where he was making for, and he answered: "You are come to the very edge of the Wild, as some of you may know. Hidden some-where ahead of us is the fair valley of Rivendell where Elrond lives in the Last Homely House. I sent a message by my friends, and we are expected."

Jem bows like a monk over scripture. His knees are capped with fine white dust; but he likes the smell up here, which is of ancient wood and stone, and soap suds and all clean things.

This is his best hiding place. Once upon a time there was a laun-dry below him, but it was forsaken long ago. No one comes up this way any more – only sometimes, on days off, Dad and Mr Lazarus. But they don't know the hiding place. All they notice is their game.

Mr Lazarus has prescribed specs, but they're not the 524 Contours.

'Jem,' Floss says one more time, but she's losing steam, she'll give up soon and look for someone else to play with.

He gnaws his lip and reads faster. He'd really like to go with Floss, but he has to get to Rivendell. It's dim in the hiding place, though, the sun gets tired creeping in the gaps where the slates have gone, and outside it's so bright and warm ... and if he goes with Floss he can make up his own stories. He could make up one like this. Not with a sissy hobbit – Floss won't like that – Jem doesn't like the hobbit either – but with dark trees and waterfalls, and the great heavy faces of trolls.

Jem likes telling Floss stories. He makes them up ahead of time. She likes the frightening ones best, so he's got good at frightening. Stories like the German airman. Floss was all for that. No one listens to Jem like Floss. He loves the look she gets when she believes in him.

Floss will believe most anything.

Sometimes she worries him. Jem worries about lots of things, but not all worries are the same. The worrying he does for Uncle Neville gets into him like a London winter, a bone-deep cold that makes him shiver; but the worry he has about the bombs is a heat so fierce it's hard to breathe, and those he has for himself are mostly furtive things, little noiseless creatures that infest all his imaginings, his thoughts and stories and dreams.

With Floss it's like a tide. The worry for her comes and goes. Sometimes it swells up so high that fear is what it really is ... she frightens him, then, like her father, Mr Lockhart, whose face is pulled down on one side, as if the wind changed on a game, and who looks at Jem so hard but never says a word to him. And then the worry for Floss will ebb away again. They'll be having a lark and Jem will wonder what he ever worried for.

Sometimes he doesn't understand her. She'll do something that makes no sense, and after Jem will ask her why, and Floss will say, *Oh Jem, you don't understand*. But he knows he doesn't understand – that's why he asks her *why*. But Floss says he doesn't understand, as if that *is* the answer. And then they just go round in circles.

She's pretty. Jem thinks so. Most of the time it doesn't matter and then sometimes nothing else does. People will give her things just because she looks that way. Once a lady in Bacon Street bought her an ice – and one for Jem (*She thinks you're pretty too,* Floss said) – and once a man in a Homburg offered her a ticket to the Electric Theatre. But Floss said, *What about my friend?* And the man shook his head at Jem, and Floss said, *I don't want to, then. And I think you're rude. And I don't talk to strangers.*

But Floss, Jem said, after, *you did.*

Other times she just gets wild. Then their games go bad. It always comes up out of nothing. It doesn't give Jem time to think. It's only later that he stops and knows he's gone astray.

One time they made a girl give them her hat and money. It was only farthings. Floss told her that Jem was Dick Turpin, the famous boxer and highwayman. It was her money or her life. Floss wore the hat halfway home, then threw it in an alley. She said it had nits. Another time, in Kingsland Waste, she stole a rubberstamp. She nicked it from Mr Instance, the rubberstamp engraver with the wart. She hid it in her mouth. After they got away she spat it into Jem's hand and her tongue was blue. The stamp said HENRY WILTSHIRE, ESQ., FARRIER, 9B LAVENDER WALK – but backwards, like a secret message in a secret agent story.

'Klaw Redneval,' Jem whispers. It would be a good name for a troll.

'I'm going, then!' Floss yells. 'I'll go to Long Debris without you!'

He listens to her leave. He chews his lip and turns a page. At first he still thinks of her – wishes he could be with her – but soon Jem is gone, too. He is in other times and worlds. Nothing – not Floss or Uncle Neville or the worry of the bombs – can ever reach him there.

There were many paths that led up into those mountains, and many passes over them. But most of the paths were cheats and deceptions and lead nowhere or to bad ends; and most of the passes were infested by evil things and dreadful dangers.

★

Michael is receiving goods. Noakes's man unloads the pots and together they haul them inside.

He doesn't talk much, this man. On Saturdays he brings potted plants. On Sundays he comes back with cut flowers and blooms, and once a month – more, when trade's brisk – the shaving goods Michael shifts six days a week in the Roman Road. Nine loads a month, and hardly a word. Sometimes they share cigarettes, but even that's more smoke than talk. The man could speak Latin at home for all Michael knows or cares.

Michael approves of him.

One of these days he won't need Noakes, his dour man or his neat-handed boys. He'll buy as he wishes and earn for himself. He's a fellow of his own already – not that Noakes will hear of that – and if one man will obey, why not others? For now he'll do as the masterman asks, but it grates on him to serve, and to serve a man like Cyril Noakes – thick wits, small mind, no more thought than where the next meal's coming from –

Michael's patience is wearing thin, and under the thinning patience lies the raw flesh of his pride. Still, all things in good time. He'll move on in the world. He'll be his own master one day. It can't come soon enough.

He goes back out to the truck, brings in the last rose columbine – the pot tucked under one arm, his weight on the horse-head stick – then rests. He's short of room. The lock-up is already crowded with greenery and hard goods – straight and safety razors, leather strops and honing stones – and he'll need a cool spot for the blooms. The pots will sell or they won't, but it's the flowers that draw the crowds, the blooms which are the dazzlers.

He stretches – his shoulders crack; the pots are awkward work for him – and sees his younger one. She's watering the lavenders, half hidden in the greenery. She whispers as she waters, and smiles as she whispers.

What is it she's whispering? Who does she think she's whispering to? It's time Mary put a stop to that. The child has a head on her shoulders but too many fancies in it. What age is she now? Too old for make-believe. As she waters each lavender she hunkers down, nuzzling into the green, like a cat into a hand.

When Michael was Iris's age he dined with silver at his father's table.

He thinks, again, of Miss Milne's knife. It's not much to be dwelling on. It was only a little thing. Still, he liked the work. The scales good pearl throughout, well cut. No piqué, no carvings of grapes or hunting hounds, no excess: only the silver cartouche with the owner's name engraved on it. All skill and little showmanship, the one proud flourish hidden along the flat of the blade: a wild cornucopia of vines and passion flowers. Michael found that forgivable. Pride's no sin when work's well done.

The marks were hard to read, but he has a knack for them; even his father would give him that. On Miss Milne's knife they were worn thin – the blade being pure soft silver, the better to resist the tarnish – but the insignia was Aaron Hadfield's, and the work maybe Hadfield's own: a name worth something in itself, and the piece more than a century old, made in Sheffield, the City of Steel.

It reminded him of Birmingham, that knife. The Lockhart workshop in the Jewellers' Quarter. The voices of his father and Graeme and Christy, before the war, his brothers' banter and their father's songs rising and falling as they worked together. The life which he was meant to have and which he has been cut off from.

He would have kept it, if he could – the knife – but it came through Noakes's boys, not Michael's private man. Word might have got back. It's nice work, not that Noakes will know it. Noakes will let it go for a song. Noakes wouldn't know nice work if you walked up and sheathed it in his throat.

'Daddy,' Iris calls, 'look, I made room for us! Now we can put more flowers in. Isn't it good?'

'Aye,' he says, 'good,' and the dear child smiles up at him, for all the world as if his words are payment made in silver.

★

This is the day when the Lane rests. On Saturdays alone, Middlesex and its dependent streets lose their rush and noise. The fight goes out of them. They become frail and thin, like fields where a fair has been and gone.

Columbia Road isn't so worn. Its market only lasts a day, and so it lives a separate life. Paul Jones makes his round, door to door, out and home to the dairy in Ezra Street. The Birdcage and the shops are open. Passersby peer in their windows. Now and then one goes in, blinking in the blue fluorescence.

Other markets take their place. Club Row and Spitalfields, Whitechapel Waste and Kingsland Waste, the Broadway and the Roman, and half-ruined Watney Street, where Bernadette fans herself with Wells's *The Invisible Man* at the stall – two pitches long – of Mr Nothing-Over-Thruppence.

'Vanishing cream, Mrs Malcolm?' Mr Nothing says, and Bernadette has to laugh, light-headed, the girl in her three months' old and there to stay, so *there* already she feels like she might stay put forever: there's no vanishing her away.

(Sybil, Bernadette calls her: Sybil Malcolm, after her own mother; even if, as yet, this Sybil is only a dream of a child, a slip of a girl coiled in bliss, without fear or hunger.)

'No!' she says, 'no, no,' and she leans gingerly against the sun-warm spread of wares, the scented soap, the exercise books, the elephants carved from Authentic Alabaster. 'I want some reading, for my son.'

'He's on to novels now, is he? My, but he's a quick little fellow. It'll be the grammar school for him. That one you have, that's a page turner. My clients speak highly of it. See how he goes on with that one. Bring it back when he's done and we'll choose him out another.'

Bernadette opens the book. *But what devilry must happen to make a man invisible?*

'I don't want him frightening himself,' she says. 'I don't want him losing sleep. Do you have something educational?'

'Bottles of ink,' Mr Nothing says, and again, 'bottles of ink,' so that Bernadette laughs some more: he sounds so like the parrot in Neville's pirate story. 'Ten thousand words in every bottle, and *every word* an education! Or, now, there's this by Mr Orwell, calls itself a fairy story. Very intellectual man. Or here, this is good old Strang. *Round the World in Seven Days.* This is the one for him.'

'I'll think on it.'

'Thruppence a read, for as long as he likes –'

'I'll *think* on it,' Bernadette says, and Mr Nothing tips his hat and twinkles.

'I'll keep it for you, Mrs Malcolm. I'll put it by until you say so. You'll come by later, now, won't you?'

Flatterer, Bernadette thinks. Charmer, sweet-talker, honey-tongue. But Clarence honeys his words, too, when he puts on his crown. He's sweet enough in his old fedora, but no one's sweeter than the Banana King.

Towards Shadwell she slows again. A coster is selling Scotch Bonnet peppers. Peppers! Bernadette has never seen them in London: their strangeness jars her pleasantly. It's like finding a flock of parrots wheeling around Trafalgar Square.

The coster is a small island man. She asks the price of the peppers – too dear for such withered things, and who will buy them, here? – just to linger by their blaze of colour. It makes her think of how different her daughter's nourishment will be – of how pale and scant it is, even now – and of the markets back home, too: but then she chides herself. Bernadette, she thinks, your home isn't there any more. It's here, fair old London Town.

She thinks of soursop. A hot, hot day, and the sweet-sour juice of June plum. Scallions and sorrel and the red rags of the ice sellers. The grater cake her nursemaid bought her, year after year, from the Green Island Grand Market on Christmas Eve. The first time Mama took her beyond the western parishes, all the way to Kingston; the markets she saw there. Redemption Ground and Queen's – which the poor folk called Chigger Foot – and Jubilee – which they called Solas – and Coronation – which they called Duppy – oh my gosh, all the names for everything! And all the small-time higglers, selling anything under the sun, higglering and higglering all the way up Orange Street.

Duppy Market, though . . . she never liked that name. Coronation is much better. Duppy was what they called it, still, because they went and built it on a graveyard.

She doesn't want to think of duppies. They'll turn her thoughts onto Neville. The things Neville says on his bad days. Instead she narrows her eyes and thinks of Redemption Ground, willing the memories to flood her again. A hot, hot, *hot* day . . .

But it's hot here, too, in Watney Street. What's the difference, really, between Watney and Redemption? The noise is the noise and the dust is the dust. What is there for her to be missing, here? The markets are the same. Ackee and June plum she'll always crave; but the crowds of people of all types, and the neediness, the gaudiness, the rituals and the higgling – whatever they want to call it here – those things are all the same in Solas Market or Petticoat Lane or Whitechapel Waste or Chigger Foot. And the sweet-talk and the dazzle, that make even common things seem otherworldly and foreign.

The market is the crossroads: wherever you go, it's the same. Any place you wash up on God's earth. Yes, thinks Bernadette, and that's why I like it. Because in the market everything is lately come. Everything is foreign, and so nothing is foreign. No one is out of place here. They come up weary from the docks, and when they see this place, they know they're nearing home again.

East of the pepper stall the wastes are parked up with cars. A man stands on the roof of one, shouting at the passing trade. He doesn't have a coster's voice but he's building up a crowd. He has papers in his hand. He shakes them as he shouts and they flicker in the sun.

'Excuse me; what is it he's selling?' Bernadette asks the man beside her, but he runs his tongue under his lips, as if he means to hawk.

'Foreign muck,' he says, under cover of his moustache, and then suddenly raises his voice to roar at the man on the car, 'You ought to be locked up!'

The man on the car turns to them. He's in shirtsleeves but the car is hot: the sweat is running down his cheeks. His eyes search for his adversary and find only Bernadette.

'You say so, do you? Then name my crime. Name the punishment for free speech in a free country. I'll tell you what I've learned, freely.

I've read the writings of great men, and I say it's the high hats need the locking up! If someone wants blaming it's them! I say we've had enough, you and I, of unearned privilege. Yes, and empty promises –'

She has her hand to her chest. She can feel her heart's quick-time, but as she moves away a woman catches her eye and Bernadette finds herself sharing a smile.

'What a lot of noise!' the woman says, and Bernadette says yes, it is, and she stops with the woman and her friends, safe at the back of the crowd, more grateful than she can say for the small spark of empathy.

She waits there, catching her breath. She can hear the costers behind her and the women and men all around her, a dizzying whirl of voices, and the man on the car still raging above them.

'Is this what we fought for and won? Is this – this waste – is this what was promised us? Fathers and mothers, sons and daughters, have we not all done our duty? Have we not done all, all and more, than was ever asked of us? So now where is our reward?'

'– PARSNIPS, lily-white PARSNIPS, sweet ONIONS and pearly BARLEY, they'll make you a broth that's better than BRANDY –'

'I'm not a fiddler, am I now? No one can call me that. No, I put myself about. I'm not a grafter, fair enough, but no one can call me idle –'

'– I told him, I'm right browned off. Alright, he says, I'll take you out. We'll go up west and live it up.'

'– I'm too expensive for wages, is all.'

'And did he?'

'Didn't he just! He wasn't getting out of that!'

I want to go, Bernadette thinks. I want to be home. But home is here, now, isn't it? Isn't it fair old London Town?

'No,' she says. 'Home is my children.'

'Are you alright, dear?' someone says, and she nods and flaps her hand.

'It's passing,' she says. 'It'll pass.'

She peers homewards, through the crowd . . . and there is Mary Lockhart, Mary from the Columbia Buildings, at a stall of china-ware. And Mary has seen Bernadette, is looking back at her; is looking through her and away.

Bernadette blushes in the sun. She has too few friendly neigh-bours – Dora, upstairs: that makes one. Another friendly face or two would make the rest easier to bear. The coldness of these people! Look at this woman now. Beforetimes, Bernadette has caught the way Mary watches her boy. All she does is watch, as if Jem might steal something; as if he might be stealing just by breath-ing London air. Bernadette has heard the edge in Mary's voice when her girls play out with Jem. The worry when she calls them in. And her fellow is worse, with his limp and his stare and the chip on his shoulder. Mary's fellow is trouble. There's violence in the man, just waiting to get out.

As if their girls are anything, thinks Bernadette (the coldness reaching her own heart). Them with their pokey faces.

When she looks again – ready to scowl – Mary is already gone.

'What did you wear, then?' says the woman who showed her a kindness, but she isn't speaking to Bernadette, of course; only to her friend.

'My New Look,' says the friend. 'We took the bus to Selfridges. Then it was tea at Lyons and then the Marble Arch Pavilion. I drew some looks, I can tell you. The old man didn't half have a fit!'

Bernadette draws her summer coat around her. She raises her chin and starts for home. She has forgotten the book that Mr Nothing keeps for her. The man on the car is still shouting behind her.

★

Dora is scrumping elderflower, basket on one freckled arm. Or is scrumping only for apples? Perhaps it's a harvesting; but no, harvesting is things like corn. She has an irritating feeling that elder might just be a picking.

I don't care, she thinks. I am scrumping my elderflower.

Her English is getting better. She remembers how shameful it was when she and Solly first arrived. It made her feel such a fool. And it made the people seem dull, when all they spoke was gibberish. The first thing she decided, then, was that people talk too much to say even the smallest thing. But then her English improved and she had to admit to Solly that she'd been wrong. It was just that things sounded smaller, in gibberish.

Her basket is full of elder – creamy plates of flowers, laid down in springy layers – but they weigh next to nothing and Dora can squeeze in more. On her way she found nasturtiums and sorrel, but she'll pick them going home, for freshness. Jones's milkers only graze the plot he's fenced, and Dora has never met anyone else foraging in summer. The English are foolish that way. They'd rather go without than eat any wild thing, except the nuts and berries that any child knows.

She's saving the best tree till last – an old one, with one split trunk, that must have stood in a garden long before the houses fell around it – but she hasn't got that far. Dora is still close to home, where the waste isn't so wild and the elders are still young.

She'd better hurry, she thinks. She's been having such a good time that the sun is already past noon. She'll have to put some vim into it if she means to finish before dinner.

There is a sound and she looks up. A small boy is walking by, from the south side fence into the ruins. His cheeks are tanned with dirt. He's dressed as if for winter: sweater – shirttails poking out – and a duffle-coat, all mucky and too small for him.

'Good morning!' Dora calls (but the morning has gone, hasn't it? Oh well), and the boy slows and peers at her.

'Hello,' he says. He stands on one foot, scratches an ankle, then walks on into the ruins, upright as a City gent. All he needs are a brolly and bowler.

How funny, Dora thinks; but then it isn't, really. It's nothing to smile about, a little boy so poor and dirty.

She goes back to work on the elder. It's best picked on sunny days, but there have been few this year, and Dora has left it late. Some of the flower heads are thin, the green showing through, and the rest are full of bugs, but Dora doesn't mind them; they don't mean her any harm. Each time she cuts a head, she shakes the creatures free – gently, so as to keep the pollen – then bows to smell the flowers.

Now she has stripped the young trees bare. She starts towards her best elder. She is wading through weeds and buttercups (cups but no butter, she thinks) when someone whistles, far off, and she turns and sees Solly and Clarence, high above her in the distance. Solly waves, and she waves back.

The waste basks in the heat. Long Debris, the children call it, and it does run for a good way, winding between houses and yards, but the bombing here was meant for the docks, and there's no pattern to it. Only where the rocket struck is the waste much wider than a handful of tenements. Elsewhere, here and there, buildings still stand in the jungle. Dora stays away from them. Sometimes there are people in them, beggars or tinkers or lovers, and they shouldn't frighten her – they mean no harm, either – but still, they make her wary. Besides, the buildings are all condemned: most are burned out or have fallen in, or are no more than right-angles or single monolithic walls, leaning or bulging, their bricks topped with buddleia.

Dora goes deeper. It's greener here. The walls are suntraps and rubbish traps. She's getting near the sunken ground – the old elder is close to it – but she doesn't like the smell here, which is of cats, and worse.

She's thinking of the noise through the walls. This month new people have moved in next door, a young plasterer and his wife with singsong Liverpool voices. They've been nothing but nice to Dora, but she finds it hard to talk to them. At night she can hear them doing it. She knows Solly must hear it too.

Going at it like animals, Mrs Platt says, though Dora doesn't see how she can hear them, three flats away, and upstairs.

It's offputting, the sound of them. Their pleasures embarrass Dora; their joys shame her. She is not a prude. When they first came to London it was the same for them – worse – with the old lady next door, Mrs Gash in Cable Street, who banged on the wall and shouted horrible things (*In out, in out, all fucking night!*).

Dora isn't ashamed of the act of love. But it has been hard with Solly, in that way, ever since he came back. Still she loves him, but it has been difficult. In that way.

And in other ways, too, it hasn't been easy. There is too much that Dora can't explain. She hasn't kept things from Solly. She has told him what she can, about the bombs, night after night, and the fires; and the boy she lost, stillborn, and what the doctors said about the chances of another. She has told him how alone she was. How, when things were at their worst, she blamed him for her loneliness.

Sometimes the telling is not enough.

Well, but that's enough of that. Other people have suffered worse. They've all had their wars. Chin up, is what people say. *Onwards and upwards,* Solly says, when he's pretending to be a plucky Englishman. *Shining uplands, and all that.*

She clambers over a low wall, and there is her best elder. As it is every year, the injured trunk is heavy with flowers. It looks romantic, in the ruins, like a tree in an old tapestry. Dora knew it would.

She has put her basket down, is reaching to cut the first head, when she sees the man. He's lying in the willowherb, not far beyond the tree. His beard is creamy yellow. He looks as if he's been asleep, but his eyes are open now, and on her.

'What are you doing here?' he says. 'What are you doing here, with scissors?'

He has a newspaper in the crook of one arm. Dora can see a bottle inside it. His coat is open; under it he wears a suit with a peppercorn waistcoat. The suit is shiny with dirt. His trousers are undone, and his shirt is pulled up round his belly. The flesh there, and the flesh of his face, is red from the sun, and unwrinkled. He's all baby fat, as if some pressure fills him up from the inside.

He gets up slowly on one elbow. Oh, Dora thinks, but he looks just like St Nicholas.

'Scissors,' he says again. 'There's no call for that. I won't touch you. What do you want with me?'

'Nothing,' Dora says. 'I'm scrumping. I mean I'm cutting.'

The man holds up the bottle. 'Have a drink with me.'

'No,' Dora says, 'I don't want to.'

'Drink with me. Why won't you? I saved it for you special. Put away your scissors, I won't touch you. Oh, it's you again.'

He's squinting past Dora as he ends, and she turns and finds the little boy beside her.

'Go on, Maurice,' the boy says, but the man frowns and rears up.

'What is it now?' he yells.

His anger is that of a sick man. The boy steps closer. 'It's alright, Maurice,' he says. 'It's clocking-off time now.'

The man screws up his face at the sun. 'Is it already? Oh, ruddy hell. If it's clocking-off, then it's time to go home.'

The boy helps him to his feet. When he has his balance, the man pats the boy, gestures at them both – not rudely; it's more of a salute – then starts off towards the Hackney Road fence, his voice rambling through the undergrowth.

'– Good day to you, good health to you. Sleep well, won't you? . . .'

Dora turns to the boy. She takes a breath. 'Thank you,' she says.

The boy doesn't reply. He only stands, watching her. 'You rescued me,' she says, but the boy shakes his head.

'Maurice wouldn't hurt you.'

'No,' Dora says, 'of course not' – too quickly, because she doesn't want to think about what Maurice would have done. She busies herself, finds her purse, and takes out tuppence. 'Here you are,' she says, and when the boy takes the coins she smiles, to leave it there.

She turns back to the elder, picks up her basket, and starts to cut. The man frightened her, but Dora does what Dora does with so many frightening things: she doesn't think about it, and soon the trembling goes out of her arms. Everything is well again.

Except the boy is still there.

She can feel him, behind her. He hasn't gone away. After a while she begins to watch from the corner of her eye. He has sat down behind her, on a low, crumbling wall.

It makes her awkward, as she picks. The truth is that it annoys her. She wants to forget the drunkard, but the boy won't let her do it. Once she looks around, certain that he's watching her, but he isn't at all. He's lying on his back, asleep or gazing up into the blue. She can't be sure: his face is turned.

I'm a selfish woman, Dora thinks. He made the man go away, and all I did was pay him off, like a dustman or a salesman. That wasn't gracious. It was brave of him. And I've no right to mind him being here. It's not my home he's in. And even if it were mine, he's just a little boy. Let him be near me, if he likes.

She glances at him one more time, and he's looking at her.

In Danzig, in her childhood, Dora had a bird in a cage. Her father bought it for her. It was a tiny cocky thing, unafraid of anything. Each afternoon her mother would put it out, on top of the old courtyard well, down behind their apartment; and every afternoon, the neighbours' cat would come and sit by the cage. It would curl up there, its eyes full of adoring hunger.

That's the look she sees in the boy's eyes.

It's only for a moment, and then it's veiled, gone, and he's only a little boy again, lying on a sunny wall, watching her pick elderflower.

Still, it's unnerving, and so is the secluded silence that falls around them. Dora doesn't like silences, especially not when she's with strangers. They make her think of the rockets in the war, the ones that you could be sure would miss only as long as you could hear their engines.

Once she drops her basket. Some of the flowers come bouncing out, and in the nuisance of picking them up she makes up her mind to talk again. At least that will be better than this quiet.

She says, 'Do you play here alone?'

'Yes.'

'You shouldn't. It's dangerous here.'

'You're here,' he says then, and she has no answer to that.

She dusts off the fallen flowers. There is the sound of bees, and a scrapmonger's bell and cry, somewhere back where people live. She cuts another flower, and then there's no more room in her basket, and she has the best of them. Her morning has been spoiled, but at least she has the elder.

'There,' she says, and dusting off her hands, she smiles at the boy. 'Finished! And now I'm going home. Thank you again.'

'It's alright,' the boy says, with a wretchedness that gives her pause.

'Aren't you going home too? It must be time for your dinner.'

He shrugs, puts his hands in his pockets, and stays seated like that, shoulders still up. Like a little old man hunched against the cold, Dora thinks; and just like that, she remembers him.

'But I know you,' Dora says. 'Don't I know you? I've seen you before.'

'In the Birdcage,' the boy says, and Dora laughs.

'Yes! That was you, wasn't it? I was inside, and you were outside. It must have been cold,' she says, but the boy shrugs again.

'It doesn't matter now.'

'I don't really go there,' Dora says. 'To the Birdcage. That was my only time.'

She doesn't know why she says it, but the boy nods as if he forgives her. He gestures at her basket. 'What's that?'

'*Holunderblüte*. You call it elderflower.'

'Can you eat it?'

'No, but I make a drink with it.'

'Like in the pub?'

'Not that kind of drink. Like lemonade. But I think this is better.'

The boy nods. He wipes at the dirt on his cheeks. 'I like lemonade,' he says.

She wonders if he's slow. He seems a bit that way. His face – except for that one look – is so often expressionless.

'Do you live nearby?' she asks, and when he nods again, 'Which side?'

The boy kicks his feet together, bouncing the worn canvas of his shoes. After a while, he says, 'I live here.' And he points – along the line of his wall – towards the sunken ground.

'What do you mean?' Dora says, but her voice is weaker, now: she has an inkling; she isn't sure she wants an answer.

The boy bounces his feet again, looking by turns at them and at her. Then he jumps off the wall and begins to trudge off, down towards the sunken ground.

'Wait,' Dora says, 'wait –'

When she catches up with him he's standing by the flooded pit. The water is rank in the sun. It smells of sewage and decay.

This is silly, Dora thinks. I don't like this any more. And she is going to tell him so, she has already turned to speak, when … is there something there?

Down the hole, above the water, she sees a slit of darkness. She can make out bricks, burned bricks, and, to one side, the black foot and angle of a timber prop. There is a bit of cellar there, or a shelter. The owner of the house might have dug another chamber, for the neighbours or the servants. Now the roof is almost collapsed, and nothing is left but a last bit of space.

Dora goes closer. She squats down in the weeds. The space is not as small as she'd thought. As her eyes adjust she begins to see shapes deep inside. Huddles. Nothing moves. She thinks they must be heaps of blankets or old tarpaulins.

'Oh,' Dora says. 'You poor boy.'

She puts out her hand, but he shies, the way an animal would duck away from an insect or a blow.

'It's alright,' Dora says, 'it's alright, I didn't mean to touch you.'

And then for a while she says nothing. She stays, squatting by the hole, with the boy standing beside her. He doesn't look at her, but neither does he move away.

He's little, Dora thinks. He could be seven or eight, younger than Bernadette's boy, but his looks are somehow older. It's hard to tell, with the dirt and scars. She thinks perhaps he's small for his age.

'This is where you live?' she asks finally, and when the boy nods, 'For how long?'

'I don't know,' he says.

'Alone?'

'Yes. It's mine,' he says, and cuts his eyes at Dora, as if she might mean to take the pit from him.

'What's your name?'

'Pond.'

'Just Pond? Don't you have another name?'

'Moon.'

'Moon Pond? That's a strange name for a boy! It sounds like a Chinagirl,' she says, and – just for a second – the boy's face wrinkles in amusement.

'Not Moon Pond,' he says. 'I'm just Pond.'

'But Pond is a family name. You must be Something Pond. Don't you remember your first name?'

He shakes his head, then wipes his face.

'I've looked for it. I've looked, but I haven't found it yet. It's hot today.'

'Yes, isn't it! Very hot. Pond,' Dora says, 'are you thirsty?'

But he only shrugs his shrug: a practised, dumb equivocation.

'Or hungry?' she asks, and is glad when he nods.

'Mostly,' Pond says.

Dora stands. She brushes herself down. A thrill runs through her. In her mind something has been decided.

How extraordinary, she thinks. How mad. It is so unlike her, this decision, it is such a brave and sudden thing. But she wants to do it, she needs to it, and she will: it is hardly even a choice. Her mind has been made up for her.

'Well,' she says, 'you know, I have food at home. There's enough for three. If you'd like to come and have something with me . . .'

The boy, Pond, examines her. It's more than watchfulness. His face is expressive again. His eyes are green and narrow.

'What is it?' Dora asks, and smiles to encourage him; but Pond's eyes stay the same.

'Three,' he says.

'Oh yes!' Dora says, 'well, because there is my husband.'

'What's his name?'

'Solly,' Dora says, and she thinks, My God, what will Solly think? But Solly loves her, doesn't he? That has never changed, however hard things have become. Solly will do anything for Dora.

'And I'm Dora,' she adds, 'Dora Lazarus.'

The boy looks her up and down. He nods, as if content with what he sees. 'What kind of foreign are you?' he asks, and Dora blushes and blusters and laughs.

'What a question! Well, I'm German. And also Jewish.'

'Those are nice names,' Pond says.

'You think so? Really I'm Isidora. And Solly is really Solomon.'

'Like the king,' Pond says.

'But you're clever,' Dora says. 'Where did you learn about the king?'

'In books.'

'You have books?'

'Not now,' Pond says, and takes her hand. He, too, has come to a decision.

3. AUTUMN

After school they go out to play: Jem, Floss, Iris and Pond.

Their numbers make them brave. They've come clear across Long Debris, but this is where the Troll bridge is. You can't play Troll anywhere else.

The bridge is made of brick and wood. The wood is old railway timber. Once the bridge was bricks and stone, but that was in another time. There's a field beside the bridge, with chickens in a chicken run and one drayhorse, all ribs and hips, with its nose in a bag.

The horse is still. A lane goes under the bridge and into the trees, blue as slate in the evening light.

An old lady with a terrier peers at them as she goes by. Floss smothers a giggle in her fist. Maybe Iris will make her a troll!

Troll was Jem's game first. It was his idea, but Floss made the rules. This is how it goes:

One hides. He goes under the bridge, down in the lane where the echo is. That one's the troll. The troll calls *Who goes on my bridge?* Then it climbs up as fast as it can, and it waits. It listens to the bridge: no looking. When it hears a child it jumps out and shouts, *Troll!* If no one's on the bridge, the troll has to go back, down in the wet where the echo is. But if anyone's on the bridge, then they turn into trolls.

Then all the trolls hide under the bridge. They climb down where the echo is, and they all call out together.

Who's the troll?

Iris is. Her face peers out, a sad imp. 'I don't want to be it,' she calls.

'Well, you are,' Floss calls back. 'It's decided. You have to do it now.'

It would be better if it was one of the boys. It would be best if it were Pond. Then Floss would win for sure, the way she did before Pond came. And Iris's a bad troll. She's too scrawny for climbing, and sometimes she gives up and plays alone with her made-up friends.

They start. Jem is caught first. Sometimes, Floss thinks, he plays to lose. He just likes them to like his game. He wipes his specs and sighs and climbs down to where Iris is. They whisper for a bit together: then,

Who goes on my bridge?

Their voices mix with the echo. It becomes one sound, like that of the markets. It's all one voice in the end.

Pond always waits too long. Floss is braver than him. She doesn't run – that's a mistake – but she goes first, crafty, crabwise. She's hardly on the bridge when there's a splashing and Iris pops up. 'Troll!' she shouts, but Floss won't have it.

'Cheat. You weren't in the echo place. You have to go back down.'

Iris does. They start again. This time Pond goes with Floss, but just behind. He shadows her. Floss twists round and glares at him.

Go away! she mouths, and he backsteps, like a dog, keeping his eyes on her. He's chicken. He's just like the people he lives with now, the watchmaker who works in the Lane but never shouts like a real coster, and his wife, who's even shy of Iris.

Still, it's Floss who's caught.

Who goes on my bridge?

It's just Pond now. He's so quiet. He waits. He waits. He waits.

One more crossing and the trolls have lost; but it's hard when there are so many of them. Jem pokes his head out early, grinning madly. He shrugs and clambers down. He's getting tall: the climbing is easy for him.

Who goes on my bridge? the voice says again.

Pond creeps out. He ghosts forwards. He puts a foot on the timbers. The wind catches a newspaper and it flutters like a broken wing. He's alright. He's almost there. He's so careful. His body is sure.

A man is walking up towards him. Under his cap his face is dark. He whistles as he comes. Pond stands still as stone. His sores itch as the man passes. His feet aren't a child's feet, and the trolls don't come for him. The man is halfway across the bridge when he stops whistling. He slows and stops. He peers back at Pond.

'You alright there, chum?'

'*Troll!*' Floss screams behind them. '*Troll!*'

When they're done they sit together, dangling their legs.

'Jump,' Floss says to Pond. 'I dare you.' And he looks down from the parapet as if he really might; but then he shakes his head.

Jem tosses pebbles. The air smells of rain. Sweat is drying on their skins. The cold will get into them soon, the hunger will sharpen in them, and then they'll have to go. Down by the trees the horse whinnies.

'When I'm rich,' Floss says, 'I'll own a horse, and I'll feed it proper. And I'll own a swimming pool.'

Jem scoffs; he can't help himself. 'People don't own pools.'

'I will when I'm rich. And it won't have water in it.'

'What then?'

'Golden syrup.'

'You'll drown in that.'

'I won't. I'll dive in, and there'll be a big golden dent, and then a bubble with me in it, and then I'll chew my way out.'

'Brill,' Jem says, all admiration.

Iris looks at Pond. 'Are you an orphan, then?'

They all go quiet, listening. No one talks much to Pond. Iris tries to be nice, but Pond makes her timid, as he makes Floss jealous and Jem shy. Ever since summer Pond has been with them, but he isn't one of them. A fourth is useful – good for games – but Pond is no one's best friend. No one has him round. No one asks him about the things the grown-ups murmur amongst themselves, the things children aren't meant to hear but do, the frightening things that are at the root of all their envy, shyness, and timidity.

'I don't know,' is all he says, after all that waiting, and Floss huffs and stares away.

'But Mr and Mrs Lazarus,' Iris says, 'they're your parents now, aren't they? So you're not an orphan any more.'

'He is so,' Floss says. 'He still is. Once you're an orphan you stay one forever.'

'Do you? But that's cruel.'

Jem says, 'Is it true you lived in a hole in the ground?'

'It is,' Iris says. 'We saw him. I did see you,' she says to Pond. 'I thought you were a German ghost, but you weren't. That was just one of Jem's stories.'

'I saw you too,' Pond says.

Jem shivers in the fading light. The horse whickers again.

'What was it like, then?' Floss asks, 'the hole?'

The way he looks at her is the way he looked when she dared him to jump. There is an eagerness in him. There's a second when he looks as if he might dare to do something. In the end, though, he just shakes his head again.

'It was my place,' he says. 'But I don't need it any more.'

A spot of rain darkens the parapet. A woman hurries past with a parcel of Friday fish and chips. They all catch the smell of it. Jem thumps onto the bridge.

'Race you for a chip,' he says, and they do. They go racing through the rain.

★

'It's too much!' Mary exclaims.

'It wasn't so dear. Noakes knows a man.'

'That's not what I meant.'

'I know what you meant.'

'But Michael –'

'It's what we deserve.'

'People will look.'

'Let them. Go on, get in,' Michael says, and Mary does.

She tries not to touch anything. She's in the driver's seat. The car rocks gently under her. The smell of its insides is strong. Leather, oil and cigarettes: money, men and potency. Outside, people dash through the tail-end of an autumn shower.

Mary puts a hand on the wheel. Her wheel. The wood is warm. It has the polish of good furniture. She closes her fingers on it.

Michael used to pick her up in his old man's Hampshire, early on, when they were all still speaking. Once, too, when she was a girl, someone took her for a spin, her and half the kids in the row inside or hanging on. She has been in cars before. This is different.

She begins to look around. The roof is lined with padded satin. Near the back it has sagged, but she can patch that up. There are dials beside the wheel, and a clock set flush under glass. There is an ash-tray that shuts by itself, and a glove compartment that opens with a click and closes with even less than that, as if gloves are an indiscretion.

All these things, Mary thinks, fitted together so perfectly. Somewhere a man crafts each of them. It should cost the earth, to buy the work of so many men.

'Budge up,' Michael says, 'I'll catch my death out here.'

She can hear the enjoyment in his voice, but when she looks up his face is as it always is, at all times except when they make love: as handsome and unyielding as the face of a soldier carved in stone. He gets in clumsily as she moves over, stowing his stick between his knees.

They sit together, side by side. The last of the rain taps at the roof.

'Do you like it?' Michael asks.

'It's like being in a tent.'

'What does that mean?'

'I don't know.'

Michael rolls down the window. Outside, two women are going past. One is young and sad; the other has thickened with age, but is still the prettier, with curls and rosy cheeks like those of a soapbox child. Neither of them looks at the car.

'Oh shut up, duck,' the rosy woman says. 'Come along and have a drink and forget it.'

Michael watches them go. He rolls up the window again.

'I made a mistake,' he says.

'Wait. Let's just sit awhile.'

'I can take it back.'

'It feels so private,' Mary says. 'That's what I mean. It feels like a place of our own.'

'Do you like it, then?'

Mary reaches for his hand. 'Take me somewhere,' she says, and Michael frowns, but his eyes are smiling.

'Where?'

'I don't care. Anywhere.'

'What about the girls?'

'Not yet,' Mary says. 'Just us.'

★

A trace of her is still on him – her fertile, musky dirtiness – when Cyril calls for him. Michael wears it out with him, under his clean shirt and shave. It gives him pleasure to know that no one else will know it's there; all of them, and the whole city, being sunk in the stink of themselves.

They drive. Michael would walk, if he could – the nights won't stay warm forever, and it does him good to stretch himself – but the choice isn't his to make.

It's not yet late, but it's dark out. The street lamps have been off all week. The route is lit by their own car and by those few others that pass.

There are three of them this evening. The third is Cyril's man, whose name (Cyril says it) is Oscar, and whose voice has the same laconic coldness Michael has heard before, but which he under-stands now as the echo of a northern country.

'Here,' Cyril says, and tosses Michael a bit of paper. Only by the proportions does he know it for a pound.

'Spending money?'

'Swan might be in. It's time you met the old bugger. Buy a round if you get the chance. Go easy if we have a game – and don't lose it to Swan if we do. He isn't one for flattery.'

What do you care? Michael thinks. What business is it of yours how I play my cards? But he knows, though he cavils at the thought.

Cyril is Alan Swan's man, and Michael is Cyril's ... for now. A pound says he is. If Michael goes down well with Alan Swan, he'll do them both some good. And they both want to move up in the world, don't they? They all want to get on.

'He's not the man he used to be,' Cyril says, speculatively.

They get out of the car. 'You and all,' Cyril says to Oscar, and to Michael, 'I'll want the change back after.'

They're down on the basement steps when a drunk goes past above them. He's singing to himself – some mucky music hall song – but Michael knows the voice. He glances back as Cyril knocks. It's Wolfowitz, huddled in his ratty trench coat. The old man slows, waits, goes on.

Does Oscar look up, too? Michael can't be sure. It's gloomy in the basement yard until the club door opens, and by then Wolfowitz is gone.

'In before the lock-in,' Cyril winks, and they duck inside.

If Michael were to speak his mind, he'd say that Cyril's gentlemen's club isn't worth the epithet. There are two girls, but neither cares much for the drudgery and both are always tired under their pancake and peroxide. There are a few card tables and no shortage of drink or men; and that's that, as far as entertainment goes.

Cyril leads the way, past the snugs, into the warmth, where an old man sits with company at a stained baize table.

'Alan,' Cyril says, and the man peers up.

'Cyril. I was just talking about you.'

'This is Michael, Alan. The young fellow I was on about. Mickey, this is Alan Swan. You can shake his hand, he won't bite.'

'Mr Swan,' Michael says. 'Mr Noakes speaks highly of you.'

Alan Swan cocks his head, like the dog who hears His Master's Voice.

'Brum,' he says. 'Birmingham born, but a bit of something else at home. I wouldn't be at all surprised,' he says, raising his tumbler to half-mast, 'if you had a touch of Scotch in you.'

'A good trick,' Michael says; but Alan doesn't like the answer, any more than Michael likes the acuity. The old man lowers his glass.

'Oh, it's not a trick, Michael. It's a skill. It never does harm to know who you're dealing with. Michael what?'

'Lockhart, sir.'

'Lockhart, of Birmingham,' Alan says. He nods, twice – as if the act unlocks and locks a file in his pale skull – then smiles benignly. 'Well, sit down, sit down. We're not at war now, there's no need for formalities. What will you have, Cyril?'

'Just a mild for me, Alan, and the same for Oscar.'

'Michael?'

'I'll have what you're having.'

'Ah,' Alan says, and smiles his brand new false Health Service smile.

There are three other men at the table. Alan introduces them. Michael listens to their names and shakes their hands in turn. None of them matter.

As they settle there's a lull in the talk. Michael props his stick between his knees. One of the girls brings the drinks. She smiles at Michael as she sets them down, meets his eye and lets hers linger. What was her name? Noakes told him once, Fay or Faith or the like. A clean girl, a picker and a chooser, with a room of her own upstairs. Michael lays aside the thought for later.

'That stick,' Alan says, 'that's a shame to see, a young fellow needing that. A war souvenir, is it?'

'An illness,' Michael says.

'I hope you don't mind me asking.'

'Not at all, Mr Swan.'

'I find it never hurts to ask. Did you see much action, Michael?'

'As much as I wished for,' Michael says, but Alan won't let it go as easily as that.

'Norman, here, he was in Malaya. Won himself some decorations. Only got back last year. A long time gone, weren't you, Norman?'

Norman shifts in his seat, as if he might escape attention. 'It's done with now,' he says.

'So it is,' Alan says. 'And you, Michael? How was it for you?'

Michael tries his drink. He wants another bland reply – truth and lies both being risks – but it won't do to stall too long, and nothing comes to mind except passing thoughts of the girl and the more nagging recollection of Wolfowitz, up in the dark.

Something's come up, he thinks. Well, it looks like I need to have words with him. If it's now then it's none too soon ...

The men are waiting for him. Too late, now, to play it safe.

'The war was inconvenient,' Michael says, 'most of the time. Some of the time it was an opportunity.'

Two of Swan's men go still, he sees, but the third wipes at a smirk. Alan widens his pale eyes.

'Home Front for you, was it? Not much call, I suppose, for the lame to go marching off to war.'

'I was never much for marching.'

'I take it,' Alan says, 'that you're not much for King or Country, either?'

'I've done as much for them as they've done for me.'

Alan waves away his neighbour's fit of smoke.

'An opportunity, you call it. Well, it was. A lot of people hungry. A lot of them going short. Desperate, some of them. And you took your chances where you could. What did you get your hands on, I wonder? Nothing too steady, I suppose, or you wouldn't be shifting Cyril's goods now. Salvage off the bombings, was it? There were tidy pickings there. You wouldn't be the only one.'

'A bit of that,' Michael says, 'now and then.'

'And selling underhand. Not that I'm saying you were a spiv,' Alan says. 'Not that I'd call you a horrible name like that.'

'I don't mind what you call me, Mr Swan,' Michael says, and the old man's steady gaze flickers in ... something. Interest or amusement.

'Norman here, he learned all kinds of things in the war. A handy man in a tight spot, that's what we know we've got in Norman. What do we have in you, Michael? An education, a trade?'

Michael shrugs. 'Silversmith's apprentice.'

'Not much call for that, these days. Takes too much money to make money. Not a lot of good to us. Still, Cyril tells me you've been useful, down the markets.'

'He knows what he's about,' Cyril says, like a salesman. 'He's a hard worker and all. Come rain come shine, isn't it, Mickey?'

'I was asking Michael,' Alan says. 'Michael, how are you finding things?'

'I can't complain,' Michael says.

But Cyril won't shut up. 'Just bought himself a nice little car. A family number.'

'Earning more than your missus can spend, eh?' the smirker puts in, and the cougher rises and gets in another round.

Michael says, 'It's not as busy as I'd like. There are the wrong kind of crowds.'

'Wrong kind?' Alan says. 'I thought barrowboys liked crowds. The markets would get a bit gloomy without them. Cyril's lads would get gloomy, too, if everyone stayed tucked up at home. What kind's the wrong kind, then?'

'Too many selling, not enough buying. Not enough brass. Too many foreigners,' Michael says, 'shoving in.'

'Ah,' Alan says again. 'That kind of crowd.'

The drinks are set down. Alan pours his dregs into a fresh tumbler of malt: his hand is unsteady. The chat around the table is breaking

74

up into small talk – the Hammers game against Argyle, the blacks causing trouble up west, the boys from down Ratcliff way, who pulled a job on Alan's patch and won't be trying that again, not in a hurry, all of them looking three years in the face –

When Alan speaks again his mildness cuts through the voices.

'Ever been on the sea, Michael?'

'Why?'

'Jetsam and flotsam. If you'd been at sea you'd know the difference.'

Michael swirls his whisky. Cyril laughs tightly. 'You're on a hiding to nothing, Alan,' he says. 'I don't reckon Michael takes well to lessons.'

'Well,' Alan says, 'do you know?'

'I couldn't give a tinker's shit,' Michael says (choosing his words, like stepping stones), and some of those at the table smile, and some raise an eyebrow and lean back, but Alan stays just where he is, and his face hardly moves at all.

'I don't suppose you could,' he says, 'but I'm going to tell you anyway. Jetsam's what gets cast away when there's no place left for it. Flotsam's what comes off the wrecks.'

Michael swallows his drink. He can feel its fire in his gut. He says, 'I'm the flotsam, am I?'

'That's right,' Alan says. 'And they're the jetsam, all of them. All the spicks and yids and nignogs. But it all ends up the same. It's all shit on the beach at the end of the day. From where I'm sitting, up on the prom, I can't hardly tell the difference. The only thing I care about is whether any of it's still alive. I want to see it crawling, up out of the muck. If it crawls then I can use it. Are you still crawling, Michael?'

Michael looks away first. The horse-head stick rests by his hand. He draws his eyes away from it and lets his gaze rest on the table, where it can do no harm. Where Alan mixed his drinks a spill has darkened the baize. Elsewhere there are older stains, dim isles and continents.

Like a map, Michael thinks. Like the atlas of a greater world.

'Mr Swan,' he says, 'I'll seem young to you, but I'm past the age of crawling. I learned to stand on my own two feet a good long time ago.'

Cyril coughs into his hand. Alan smiles a third time. His false teeth gleam like wet ivory.

'Did you?' he says. 'Well, standing will do. Standing will do just as well.'

★

Afterwards, in the street, Cyril slaps him on the back.

'You play it fine, don't you?'

'Here's your change,' Michael says, and he takes out the note.

'What? Keep it,' Cyril says. 'Keep it, Mickey, you earned it. You're a plucky fucker, I'll give you that. You sail too close to the wind with Alan, you'll end up like those Ratcliff boys, or worse . . . Christ, but his face. I'd pay guineas to see it again. I'd put it up and frame it. Who's got a smoke left?'

Oscar does. Cyril's eyes are bright, like a man whose dog has come in first.

Cyril gets out his flask. He offers it to Michael, then shrugs, sucks, bares his teeth, and tips a toast to the street. 'Long life,' he murmurs. 'Here's to a long life with plenty of trimmings. Oscar?'

Oscar takes his drink.

'There, well,' Cyril says, when his smoke is done, 'may as well call it a night.'

'I'll walk,' Michael says, 'if it's the same to you.'

'Good idea. Work off some steam, your missus will thank you. It's chilly, though.'

'Not to me,' Michael says, and Cyril chuckles in the dark.

'You're like my boys,' he says. 'You don't feel it yet. I envy you. You've got your life ahead of you, Mickey, and look at you! You're on the up. Well, mind how you go – I don't want you getting into trouble.'

Michael watches the car pull off. When it's out of sight he starts eastwards. He has a fair stride, stick or no, and it won't do to wait on his man; still, it's asking too much to expect Wolfowitz to match him, and he tempers his pace.

He's left Clerkenwell behind before the old man draws level. 'Wait,' Wolfowitz hisses, 'wait!'

They stop for him to catch his breath. Michael looks east and west. The street is dark enough.

'Well?' he says, and Wolfowitz spits thick matter and stares at him, hands on knees.

'What are you doing, running away like that? I'm sixty-three years old. I stand out in the street like a nag while you drink whisky inside and then you make me chase you home. You should be thanking me.'

'How do you know it was whisky?' Michael asks, and Wolfowitz grins painfully.

'I can smell it. It smells nice.'

'It's Alan Swan's whisky,' Michael says, but Wolfowitz waves away his caution.

'They didn't see me.'

Michael finds a step. The flag is cold under him. 'Best keep it that way,' he says. 'I hope this is worth it.'

'What else was I supposed to do? Don't show yourself round

mine, you say. Wait for me to come round yours. Stay off Columbia Road and the Roman. If something comes up, what can I do?'

Back in the day, before the war, Wolfowitz worked for Swan. It didn't work out for the best. Still, Alan Swan's enmity is Michael's opportunity. The old man makes them both good money.

'You can use your head,' Michael says. 'If Swan hears you're still working his turf he'll see to it you're back inside before you know it. If he hears you're working for me I'll break your hands myself.'

'Michael,' Wolfowitz says, 'don't talk like that.'

But Michael says nothing more. A chill silence falls in the street, and it is Wolfowitz who ends it.

'Dick Wise stopped by. He's a sergeant at Leman Street, used to live round your way –'

'I know who he is. I didn't know you were chums.'

'So that shows what little you know, eh? Dick Wise is a good friend of mine. A good friend, not like some.'

'Let you off, did he?'

'He's a soft spot for me. Sometimes we help each other out.'

'What help did he want this time?'

'Nothing,' Wolfowitz says, sullenly. He straightens and brushes down his coat. 'Just something for his girl. I chose him out a bracelet, nothing special, you wouldn't have got much for it.'

'And what do we get for our bracelet?'

'Dick says to take things slow. His men are all stirred up. A day or two, they'll be crawling all over the place. They found a man, done like that one in Bacon Street, back in the spring. Cuts.'

'Dead?' Michael asks, and Wolfowitz clicks his tongue.

'Of course dead! The police don't budge if not, do they? It's no news being alive, is it?'

His voice has risen. Michael gets up. 'I'll walk you home,' he says.

'Don't do me any favours.'

They come onto Old Street. Wolfowitz walks along in silence. Now and then he tugs his coat like a bird ruffling its feathers. Michael is glad to see it. The old man needed ruffling.

'Alright,' he says. 'We keep our heads down. You'll lay off the streets, keep your hands to yourself. How long for?'

Wolfowitz shrugs. 'Might be a week. Dick can't say more than that.'

Michael gets out the pound note. He can see the old man watching, his eyes hungry in the gloom. He takes it quick when Michael offers it.

'Obliged,' he says, and then nothing else until they reach his lodgings.

Michael looks up at the building. The windows are thick with grime, or broken or boarded up. Here and there, light comes through rakes in old blackout paint.

'There's a young fellow in your room now,' Wolfowitz says. 'He was a tank gunner in Africa. He's that kind who seems to miss it. Fighting drunk all hours. A nasty piece of work.'

'No change there, then,' Michael says, but Wolfowitz shakes his head.

'Michael. You're better than you know.'

They wait while the old man fumbles with the latch.

'They found him up by your manor,' Wolfowitz says, 'the man.'

'Where?'

'That stretch of waste by you. Dead a while, Dick says. Still, you'll look out for your girls, won't you?'

'I look out for my own,' Michael says, and adds a goodnight, and turns for home.

★

Clarence is underground. He sways out of time with those around him. They all rush onwards through the darkness.

No one is smiling except Clarence. His eyes are lidded and his smile is crooked (*You smile like a pirate*, his boy says). The folks around him hold on tight, they set their feet and their faces to say nothing, but Clarence leans into the sway and his face says everything. He almost looks as if he's dancing.

He's thinking of the trick of chess. The trick – or so he thinks today (and why not this morning, when Solly had him licked in ninety?) – the trick is to be asking questions. As long as you keep asking you don't have to be answering. And answers? Well, you might not have them. The Answerer on *Twenty Questions*, he always knows the secret, but that's just a parlour game for every manjack with a wireless. Chess, now, that's the sport of kings. In chess no one holds all the answers. And that's why you want to be asking the questions.

Next Saturday, Clarence thinks. Next Saturday *I'm* doing the asking.

He's not made for the Underground. He has to stand bowed so deeply that his backbone aches. It's better if he can sit and sometimes, as the train heads northwest, seats come up near enough to take; but Clarence lets them pass. He's young and strong – he could stand all year – but the truth is, he chooses to stand because elsewise folks will look at him. He takes the ache over that look.

This country, Clarence thinks. It wants you shy. It wants you humble. For any gift you're born with it wants you to apologise. But what should he be sorry for? And how can he ever be shy? People have been looking at Clarence ever since he was eight years old and started to put on his height. The more they looked the higher he got. The looking *up* – oh, he likes that. Those looks are all awe and laughter. They feed his pride. They make him stand taller.

The look he'll get if he sits down, that's different. That's the English look. There's nothing you can do about it; the English look's too sly for that. It flits away if you try to meet it. It's a fly on your back if you try to catch it. But sooner or later, if he sits, someone will cut their eyes at him, and their look will be accusing, as if Clarence has taken something that was never meant for him.

His grandfather was Scottish. Clarence gets his height from him. He used to tell Clarence and Neville stories of London and the Highlands. Clarence would like to see the Highlands, one day, but London is the place for him.

London is the place for big men, the old man used to say, ruefully, as if he hadn't measured up himself. But isn't Clarence a big man? A big man needs a big city. If Britain is the mother country then London is the mother city. Clarence loves it for its might and clamour. The war has worn it down, but it'll haul itself up again. Clarence can help, he knows he can. Isn't he strong enough?

The English, though . . . if they spoke their minds then Clarence could talk to them. But the English don't speak their minds, not in company. Their minds are hush–hush, like their homes. An Englishman's mind is his castle.

I fought for my country, Clarence wants to tell them, when they give him that look. But he never does. It wouldn't be true anyway.

At Camden Town he surfaces. It isn't far to Neville's place and he's early, so he wanders. After the Tube it feels fine to stretch his legs and breathe easy, and there are costers on Inverness Street, fruiterers and mushroom men, with stragglers towards the Lock, Greek fly pitchers and jumble sellers, a Caymanian he knows by name, and a chestnut roaster down in the mouth, hankering for colder weather.

There's not much warmth in the day, but Clarence takes off his hat and walks with that in one hand and, in the other, a bag with a banana and some dumplings Bernie has made. It's something to have dumplings again. The week that bread came off the ration Bernie cooked up a fete.

'Hey, Nine,' the Caymanian calls, and Clarence stops and talks a bit. Not overmuch – the island men mostly keep each to their own, like the English, Irish and Scots – but the Caymanian knows Kingston and he always has some news from home.

King Nine Hand is what the boys call him. They all make with these names, the new boys, Lord this and Admiral that. Clarence has no time for Lordships and Admiralties, he's too old for vanity, but the boys went and named him anyway, just like the costers did. Nine Hand is from the time Clarence heard the Moresby, the banana reefer, was due in early at Southampton, and going down to Waterloo to wait for the banana train he was first in line for the best haul London had seen in months. For once the porters had no call to send him off empty-handed, but the Irish crew that was on that night always sold him short when they could. Instead of no bananas, they told Clarence there were no crates – the whole greasemonkey gang of them all trying to wipe the grins off their faces, with crates piled around them. So Clarence bought the biggest bunches they could fetch, all the fruit he was licensed for, two monster nine-hands, and hoisted them up and carried them off as if they weighed nothing at all – sixty pounds on each shoulder, like the spoils of war. He hardly got them home, and they put his back out for days, but the story got around.

It's not a bad part of town, Camden, with the narrowboats in their company colours, bright diamondbacks and gaudery out of another time. Clarence has looked into settling here, but Inverness Street is too small, pitches are hard to get, and the place has its own banana king. Bernie isn't keen, besides. She likes the Columbia Buildings, which are grand old things, alright. And Neville vexes her.

Quarter past one by the timber yard clock. That's a good time for Neville. He worries over numbers, now. The big ones trouble him.

Clarence cuts back through Inverness and on, southwest to St Mark's Square. He rings and leans by Neville's bell. An Indian child on roller skates labours past the steps, alone. Two men move among the ruins of St Mark's. They are tearing down burned stones, leaving of the bombed church only that which remains sound. Clarence looks beyond them and for a moment his spirit fails. Despair fills him.

The sky is dull as a dead hearth. The sun is desolate. It gives nothing away: no light, no heat, no strength or comfort. Clarence's boy knows, by heart, the true distance of the sun, its tens of millions of miles. In England that's how it feels. And the people, too, they feel the same.

They come on him sometimes, these moments. Moments are all they are. Clarence has learned to live with them. He has the measure of them. Look: he rolls his shoulders – on he goes. A man should have pride in himself. It's what Bernie expects of him. It's what she looks to him for.

Clarence is her sun.

The door opens behind him.

'What time is it?' Neville asks, dustily, and Clarence smiles and turns.

'One and some.'

'Fine, then,' Neville says, 'come on up. Come in, come in.'

★

On Neville's dining table sit:

An open tin of Kiwi black;

A Tate and Lyle treacle tin with one last scrape still left in it;

A pair of shining, shoehorned Oxfords;

A wrapped nub of Nutter fat;

A jelly the colour of cement;

Three yellowed stacks of cuttings, one taken only from *The Times,* one from the picture magazines, and the last – yellowest of all – from *The Jamaica Gleaner* and *The Barbados Advocate*.

Clarence stands over the table, looking down at everything.

'Neville? You making jelly?'

'What?'

'What's this jelly here?'

'Don't talk nonsense,' Neville calls through. 'That's what folks call donkey.'

Clarence pokes the donkey. 'You eat any of this thing yet?'

'What does it look like to you?'

'Looks like you went and made the worst jelly I ever saw.'

Neville comes stalking in. He's better when he's worked up. He looks more himself again. Besides, Clarence has been working him up for thirty years, and he isn't finished yet.

'There's nothing wrong with it,' Neville snaps. 'It's *donkey*, it's not required to win any beauty contests.'

'Good thing too. So, when did you start on all this cooking?'

'I get hungry, I cook just fine. Any tomfool can follow a recipe.'

'Looks like you put grout in it.'

'That's oats – don't poke it, man. My God. Why don't you go make some tea?'

'Who, me? You're the chef.'

Neville makes the tea. Clarence pulls out the dining chair – there's only one: Neville's rooms are furnished with one of each necessity – and leafs through the cuttings, listening to the intimate succession of water, kettle, match and flame.

'Are those bananas I see in that bag there?'

'Dumplings from Bernie. Might be a banana too, if you got coupons for it.'

'I have coupons for teaching little brothers manners.'

'Not so little.'

'Coupons! How's that boy of yours?'

'Not so little neither.'

'Still reading, still growing?'

'That's all he does.'

'Working hard? He better be ready for that examination. Any nephew of mine has the mind for grammar school.'

'Let him be, he's got a year still. He made another friend. You know Solly took in a boy? His wife found him living rough. Had some foxhole to sleep in.'

Neville spoons the tea leaves. 'Sounds like trouble,' he says. 'Listen, do me a favour before you go. Check my bed for bugs. I think I got some bites. They got so bad downstairs the folks sit out on the steps half the night.'

'I'll check.'

'Silverbacks, too. The other week one fell on my bed. They smell bad, those things.'

'I'll check,' Clarence says.

He glances up from the cuttings (*"Windrush" Settlers Sing "Calypso"; How an Atomic Bomb Works; The Flying Miss Coachman Takes Gold*) and peers into the kitchen at his brother. A big thin figure of a man – too tall to fly, the air force said, but gave him his chance in the end – in braces, stooped over the ring. The clothes mangle inside the door, the draining board heaped with clothes, the tea caddy perched beside them.

Orderly, ordinary things. It looks like a life that works, Clarence thinks, a life that goes on. Lonely? Alright. A bachelor's life, like that of most island men in London, but nothing worse than that. Nothing broken or past mending.

But he's wrong. He's overlooked the burns, the pinched, pink skin which discolours Neville's hands. He's ignoring the clothes. The heap of washing is all dark. There are shirts in the pile, collars and vests and underclothes. None of them are white. Clarence doesn't know where Neville gets these things – Bernie says he must dye them himself – but Neville won't wear white any more. He says it would be dangerous.

He's still thinking of Neville when he turns back to the cuttings and comes face to face with himself.

There is his regiment. There's him, four years younger: Neville has him circled. Clarence is standing to attention. He remembers doing it, the thump in his chest and the crick in his neck.

He's down at Parade, one of many, but the tallest in the ranks: perhaps that's why the photographer has let the shot fall on him.

The crowds are heady in the sun. His family are in Kingston for him: Clarence looks for them, but there's sweat in his eyes under his cap, and all he sees are papers fanning, higglers selling, faces cheering. The Carib Regiment is leaving for Virginia. They'll be trained in America, and then they'll be sent to do their duty, to fight for King and Empire.

Clarence feels a heat rising into his neck and cheeks. His eyes fall across the words.

> . . . Its ultimate destination is, like that of any other fighting unit, unknown, but on whatever field, it is determined to acquit itself worthily. To fight in the common cause, alongside forces not only of Great Britain and the British Empire but also of America, is to have been admitted into the wide comradeship of arms. The activities of the

**1st Caribbean Regiment will be followed with the keen-
est interest by all within the West Indies. They take with
them the fullest confidence of those left behind, and
they hope to prove worthy of that confidence.**

In Virginia they were told nothing. They listened to old news
and rumours. The Allies had crossed into Europe. The Americans
were moving out. And then, finally, they were on their way, the full
twelve hundred men of the Caribs; Jamaicans, Trinidadians,
Guyanese, small islanders.

When they boarded ship again the word was they were bound
for Normandy. Already, then, they were sick of the sea and bored
past time of the months of waiting. Restless at night, gambling or
praying. Fearful of the pitchblack decks. Sitting on their bunks,
intent. Boys making something of themselves: dead men or
damaged men or old men, but men. Young islanders and mainland-
ers in the oily dark, waiting and wanting: waiting to reach their
destination, wanting to be part of something. *The wide comradeship
of arms.*

They never saw Normandy. The troop ship docked at Naples.
Italy had already fallen. For six months they trained for war again
at the foot of the Vesuvius. Then they were assigned as guards,
escorting German prisoners down to Port Said. And then?

And then they trained for war some more. They marched into
the desert – where the hulks of Italian tanks still stood like ancient
ruins – while a thousand miles north Hitler made his final stand.
And then?

And then the war was done. None of them had ever seen it.
They had not been wanted. Or had they not been trusted? Had
someone played a joke on them? Or a trick? Yes: a confidence trick.
They had been sent in confidence, but no confidence had been

placed in them. They had promised their lives and found them unwanted. They were sent home safe and sound, but shamed. They were left still waiting.

'You should be glad,' Neville says at his shoulder, and Clarence looks down at his hands and sees the cutting is still there, intact, not crumpled and torn. He had thought it was.

He folds it and puts it back where it belongs.

'Don't tell me what to be,' he says. 'You don't know. You had it different.'

'I did,' Neville says, with a sick man's calm. 'I died,' he says, and sets the tea down on the table.

★

Solly and Pond are flying kites.

The Tower is behind them. The bridge is east of them. There are Saturday crowds, and tugs and lighters on the Thames, and a black police launcher, nosing down into the docklands.

If the kites come down the river will foul them, but Solly won't let them fall. When Solly makes a kite, it does what you want it to do, it doesn't bilk you, Solly tunes it like a watch: a kite that Solly makes you, that's a kite you can trust. And he's brought the boy where the wind is best. There's always a breeze along this stretch, smooth as glass over the deep water. It thrums along the strings.

Solly grins around his pipe. 'Alright?' he asks, and the boy nods, his solemn face upturned, watching the diamonds lift above them.

He doesn't talk much, the boy. Oh, he talks to himself, some-times, but doesn't Solly do that too, when Dora leaves him to work alone? Let the boy keep to himself – Solly doesn't mind. Let him talk to the world when he's ready. Where's the sense in hurrying him? Let him speak when he's something to say. Dora says he's catching up at school, the teachers tell her he's quick, and he has friends in the Buildings. The boy is coming along. Besides, chitchat is overrated. Solly's too chatty himself. People listen to quiet men. Perhaps the boy will grow up to be a man people listen to.

Solly doesn't like his name.

Pond: what does it mean? It's uneasy, a name like that. He should have a proper name – a boy's name – an English boy's name, John or Henry. And after that name, Lazarus. If they're going to take him in, they should do it properly. He's told Dora, several times, and the Food Office are pestering them – the school and hospital too – but she isn't listening. Solly has told her how it'll be. The other kids will needle him, and that'll be just the start. A name like that, it causes problems.

So far he's been wrong, it's true. People ask the boy his name, and he tells them. *Pond*, he says. *Pond*, they say, *pleased to meet you, Pond*; and they shake his hand, all smiles. They make allowances, as if he's a well-bred foreigner.

Solly knows what's going on. You don't have to tell him: he knows what Dora's afraid of. If they make him Something Lazarus, they'll have to do it legit. They'll need a new birth certificate. There are official channels, here, but official channels have no faces: you can't reason with channels; and channels have little love for foreigners called Lazarus. What if the channels decide to take the boy away from them?

As if they would. As if they're crying out for war orphans, or runaways, or throwaways – whatever the boy is. Those channels, besides, they've got enough on their hands. They're hardly going to quibble over one less boy on the street, are they? No, Solly thinks (champing his pipe between his teeth), no, all being equal, the channels should be *paying* him.

(Chance would be a fine thing.)

No point pushing it. Dora loves the boy. And the boy calls himself Pond, so let him be. Oh, let him be. Things will work themselves out in the end.

★

'It's poetry,' Jem says, and Floss turns the book in her hands, as if it might be hiding something. A mousetrap, a silverback.

'Have you read all this?'

'Just bits. My mum rents me books. This is an anthology.'

'You're brainy, aren't you? But you're not canny.'

'What's that?'

'Pond's canny, like my dad. You're brainy, like Pond's dad.'

'What are you?'

'I'm the one who decides.'

They're at Jem's place, in his room. Jem has his own, where Floss and Iris have theirs. Floss's mum doesn't know she's here. She's going to need a lie for later.

She flickers through the book. 'Look,' she says, '*Goblin Market*!'

'That's good, that one,' Jem says, but Floss wrinkles her nose.

'Goblins are for children's stories.'

'You like stories.'

'Well,' Floss says, 'perhaps I'm growing out of them' – and then, seeing Jem's face fall, 'Anyway, goblins aren't scary, they're not like your ghosts and trolls and that. You're not afraid of goblins, are you?'

'No. I'm scared of duppies, though.'

'What are they?'

'They're like ghosts. In Jamaica they don't get ghosts, they get duppies instead.'

Floss nods: ghosts she can still respect. 'Do duppies haunt people?'

90

'Sometimes. The bad ones do,' Jem says; then, in a rush, 'The bad ones, they dress in white, that's how you see them coming, and if a bad duppy comes after you, you have to draw an ex in the dirt. Then the duppy stops to work it out, because ex is ten in Roman, and duppies, after they die, they forget all the numbers after nine.'

'Well,' Floss says, 'I think that's tosh. Why would they just *forget*?'

Jem reaches for the book. 'I'll read it.'

'No, I will,' Floss says, holding on doggedly, and she does.

> *Curious Laura chose to linger*
> *Wondering at each merchant man.*
> *One had a cat's face,*
> *One whisk'd a tail,*
> *One tramp'd at a rat's pace,*
> *One crawl'd like a snail . . .*

'My dad's the cat.'

'Which one's mine?'

'Yours is the one with the tail. Pond's is the snail.'

'That's not fair.'

'Alright then, he can be the rat.'

> *The whisk-tail'd merchant bade her taste*
> *In tones as smooth as honey,*
> *The cat-faced purr'd,*
> *The rat-faced spoke not a word . . .*

It's nice out, Jem sees. Dusk is coming down and the streetlamps are on. After a week of shortage they look special, like Chinese lanterns laid on for a festival. Inside his mum is boiling clothes, their steam ladening the air.

She never tasted such before,
How should it cloy with length of use?
She suck'd and suck'd and suck'd the more
Fruits which that unknown orchard bore;
She suck'd until her lips were sore –

Floss shuts the book. She purses her lips.

'Don't you like it?' Jem asks.

'It's alright,' she says, and turns to him, her legs crossed on the coverlet. 'What's the best thing you ever tasted?'

Jem thinks. 'One time, when I was hungry, Mrs Lazarus – Pond's mum – she told me how in the war they had to hide in the dock warehouses. A bomb came down and everything caught on fire. She said they had to run away through burning butter and treacle.'

Floss laughs. 'But you never tasted that!'

'I know, but I wish I could. What about you?'

'My mum says I had turkey once for Christmas, but I don't remember, I was just a tot.'

'Don't you really like the poem?'

'Your stories are better,' Floss says, and Jem beams. 'Tell me one. Tell me one about the duppies.'

'No. They're not meant for stories.'

'You can go in my car.'

Jem thinks about it – he'd love to go in the car – but he has to shake his head.

'Why? You like making me stories! I don't mind if it's scary.'

I know that, Jem starts to say, but it's no good, he can't explain. He'd have to tell about Uncle Neville, who thinks he was killed in the war. And the whole point of frightening stories is to make real things less frightening, isn't it? But a duppy story won't do that.

Duppies will do the opposite. He wishes he hadn't mentioned them.

'Don't you want to go in the car?' Floss asks, and Jem takes off his Contours.

'Your dad wouldn't let me, anyway.'

'Oh,' Floss says. 'I don't know.'

They sit in awkward silence. Floss looks out at the streetlamps. 'Flip. What time is it?'

'They only just come on,' Jem says, not wanting her to go. 'We could play out, it's not too late. We could find the others and do Troll.'

Floss grins. 'Alright,' she says, and jumps up. They make for the door, Floss with her coat halfway on.

'Where do you think you're going?' Jem's mum calls from the kitchen doorway. Her shape is heavy and new.

'Out to play,' Jem says, 'can I, Mum?'

'Who's that with you?'

'Me,' Floss calls. 'It's Floss, Mrs Malcolm.'

'You both best get home right after,' Mrs Malcolm says, and they bomb it.

Jem goes and knocks for Pond. Floss runs upstairs and gets her sister. They meet up in the square. Foursquare and hollow around them, the Buildings are full of noises: the clinking of chipped dishes, the tinned songs of the wirelesses, and the men out on the balconies, smoking, twilit, asking how the missus is and what each is getting for supper.

'It's going to rain tonight,' Iris says, 'I heard it on the weather.'

'Smart alec,' Floss says, but Pond looks at the sky and does up his duffle, and Jem looks down and sees he's forgotten his in the rush for freedom. Oh well, rain won't hurt.

'Where are we going?' Pond asks, and Jem says, 'Troll. Last one there's it!'

They pelt across the square. Jem has a yard on Floss. He risks a gigglish look back. He doesn't see the man ahead – coming in through the arch that gives onto the street – until he bundles into him.

'Watch it, can't you?' the man mutters, tall and grim in the dark of the arch, and Jem's laughter dies in his throat. It's Mr Lockhart himself.

'Dad!' Floss cries, hot on Jem's heels, 'it's us, look! How was the Roman? Did you make a packet? Did you fleece them?'

Iris comes up, breathless. Michael catches her by the arm. 'Ow! What did *I* do?' she squawks.

'No playing out tonight,' Michael says. 'You two are coming in with me.'

'That's not fair,' Floss says, 'is it, Iris?'

'No, and you're hurting,' Iris says, though he hardly is, it's only the indignity.

'I won't tell you again,' Michael says; and to the boys, none too kindly, 'Off with you, the pair of you.'

'Sorry, mister,' Jem mumbles, but Pond steps up by Iris.

'You're hurting her,' he says.

They all go so quiet. They can hear the Buildings in the hush, their small tea-and-supper sounds. Michael takes his hand off his younger one.

'What was that?' he asks, and the boy has the sense not to answer, but neither does he step down.

'It's alright, Pond,' Iris says, her voice high. 'I'm alright, look! I didn't mean it, I was just being awful silly.'

Pond looks at father and daughter. He hardly understands, and seeing that Michael barks a laugh. 'Get on home,' he says, and gives the boy a push.

He isn't rough about it. His temper is in check. He only means to have done with it, but the light is dim and the child off-guard: Pond stumbles back and falls. And there behind him is the dark boy's mother, Mrs Malcolm, darker still in the dusk, with her son's coat over her arm.

'Shame on you,' she says.

'Mind your own business,' Michael says. 'You mind who you go judging.'

Bernadette comes on. She is afraid of Michael Lockhart – she admits it to herself, freely – but she has the pride not to show it. 'Shame,' is all she says again, and she touches Pond, just on the shoulder, like a child playing a game; and gently, though her eyes in the dusk are fierce. Like a cat's, Pond thinks.

Little more is said between them. Lockhart mutters something gruff, and off he goes with his girls while Bernadette shepherds the boys. At her door Pond stops. She thinks she'll have to have him in, but 'Thank you, Mrs Malcolm,' is all he says, very formal.

'You're welcome,' Bernadette says, and still stern, 'You stay out of his way, that man.'

'I will,' Pond says, and goes.

'Bed,' Bernadette says to her boy, and Jem does as he's told, cowed, no fuss, though it's still early. She lets him read to get him calm, and after she puts out the light she can still hear him whispering, reciting in the dark the lines he's learned by rote, as if poems were protections.

> We must not look at goblin men,
> We must not buy their fruits:
> Who knows upon what soil they fed
> Their hungry thirsty roots?

★

Outside the rain begins. Under the streetlamps the pavements teem with it. Inside, Dora sings to her boy.

Unter Yidele's vigele

Shteyt a klor-vayse tzigele

Dos tzigele iz geforn handlen

Dos vet zayn dayn barur

Rozhinkes mit mandlen

Shlof zhe Yidele, shlof.

'What does it mean?' Pond asks.

They are in the kitchen, Pond in the tub, Dora washing his hair by the light of the paraffin lamp. The electrics are out on their floor tonight, and something or other is broken, too, in the Columbia Buildings Baths, as something or other often is these days: so Dora must heat the kettle on the gas and wash her child herself.

Not that it's a chore. Not that she minds doing this. Dora has catching up to do.

'Oh, well, it's just a song,' she says. 'It's silly, it doesn't mean much. My mother sang it when I was small. It says that, one day, you will go work in the markets, like your father. You'll sell raisins and almonds and be a wealthy man. You like it?'

Pond thinks. He nods.

'Sing it again,' he says. So Dora does, running water through her fingers, running her fingers through his hair.

'There!' Dora says. 'All rinsed. Let's get you dry before you catch cold. Up you get, hutch-plutch!'

Pond finds his feet. He looks ahead, chin up, over Dora's crouched form. Even now that he is hers he rarely meets Dora's gaze, let alone the eyes of others: he is animal-like in that. He looks towards the window, the courts and ruins beyond made indistinct by the dark and rain and the patterned glass, the pale suds creeping down over his imperfect skin.

There are new bruises on his shoulders, but they don't worry Dora: boys will be boys, she thinks. Worse to her is his eczema. The worst sores have infection in them. The doctor tells Dora so, but it's not so bad, it's not forever, they have a paste for it.

He has hair around his thing. Dora doesn't look at that. It doesn't frighten her any more, but she skirts it with her eyes, in much the same way that Pond skirts the dangerous faces of others. The first time Dora washed her boy, her hands froze when she saw that growth. The organ seemed, then, not to belong to him. It seemed part of a man, shadowed, glabrous. It had no place on the body of her boy.

Now she is used to it, almost. Pond is what he is. He is as Dora found him. She couldn't have found him sooner, could she? Dora cherishes what she has. What can she be but grateful?

She wraps the towel around him. 'We have boiled eggs for supper. And your father is getting chips and scratchings and gravy, too, if they have any to spare. Isn't that nice?'

'Yes,' Pond says.

'And when you're dressed we can try those shoes. Your father was clever, he got them just for mending a clock and they're almost new, but if they don't fit yet we can put them away, can't we? You'll grow into them. Do *you* know any songs?'

For a moment she thinks he hasn't heard her. She is about to let it go (and why even ask? He is not a boy for songs) when she feels Pond straighten under the towel. He begins to sing.

> *Pack up your troubles in your old kit-bag*
> *And smile, smile, smile.*
> *While you've a lucifer to light your fag*
> *Smile boys, that's the style.*
> *What's the use of worrying —*

'Don't stop!' Dora says, but it's too late, he has.

'My mum did that one,' Pond says, 'but I don't remember what comes next.'

Dora sits. The towel is round Pond's bruised shoulders. His head is bowed. If there was a light heart in him he'd look like a boy playing at knights, but there isn't and he never will. Never playful, nor even boyish. He looks more like an old man than a boy, an old man worn to meekness, frowning at some irretrievable memory.

You must miss your mother very much. She almost says it now, as she has almost done many times. But better not. Better not to hear the answer.

How she wishes she could tip his chin and raise his eyes into the light! But that, too, Dora does not do. She is afraid he might flinch at her touch, now that he has drawn back into himself. She closes her hands on themselves and leaves his face in shadow.

The front door slams. 'Horrible out!' Solly calls. 'Hello? Where's everyone gone in here?'

Dora says, 'I think I know the rest. We could try it together. We could sing it for your father.'

'Alright,' Pond says.

They begin the song again, softly and imperfectly, in the half-light of the kitchen.

★

'I don't know why we play with him,' says Floss. 'He's not normal. It's not a *normal* name, is it? You didn't half give him a fright.'

Her dad is eating. He's got the same tea Floss had: hot pot. She's staying on his right side now, good and washed and dressed for bed, where Iris is tucked up already, mumbling to her made-up friends.

'Floss,' her mum says, 'let him eat.'

Floss tries. She stands at her father's shoulder. *Music Hall* comes on the wireless, soft, that being the way he likes it. When he's done he takes out a Benson and Hedges. He only smokes the best.

'You look like an actor in the pictures,' Floss says, and her dad smiles at that. He doesn't, really, but Floss knows that's what he means. Even though he's hardly finished eating he smiles for her, because he likes her best. Whatever trouble there is, Floss is his favourite, she knows. And he is hers.

When Dad was young he had a stroke. A stroke is like an awful shock. It's why parts of him don't work and why he didn't go to war. That's why Granddad cut them off. Because Dad didn't do his bit, even after Floss's uncles died. There was an argument. Dad called the war a fool's errand, and Granddad could never forgive him.

Floss liked her granddad. He used to give her Scottish shillings. She has a silver rattle he made for her christening.

Cut off. Like when you trim the blooms. You cut away the dead wood, the spent petals, stems and leaves, so that the punters see only the good. But Dad isn't dead wood. Even though he got cut off he's still well, he's never spent.

Mum sits down. 'Now, Floss,' she says.

'I didn't do nothing!' Floss exclaims, but her mum *tsks*.

'Your father and I've been talking. I know you won't like it, but I'm telling you and you tell your sister. I don't want you going on the waste ground any more. You're to stay off, both of you.'

'What, Long Debris?'

'All of it. No climbing fences. And never you mind why.'

Floss sulks, but her heart's not in it. 'For how long?'

'Floss,' her mum says, and her dad stubs out his cigarette.

'It can't be forever.'

'No, not forever.'

'So how long, then? A week?'

(And her voice has changed, though she doesn't know it. It's hard and sure, now; it's the voice Floss uses with the other children. She sounds as unyielding, now, as her father, when he dickers a bargain.)

'How *long*?' she says again, but it's her dad who answers.

'You've been running wild,' he says. 'It's time you were growing up.'

'It ain't fair.'

'You'll do as you're told,' he says, and Floss knows by his eyes she will.

'Bed now. And tell your sister,' her mum says, as Floss grates back her chair.

The bedroom is all dark but for where light creeps in from without. As her eyes get used to it she can make out Iris in the gloom. She's talking to herself, sitting the way she always sits when she's playing her made-up games, with her head on one side, like a waiter. 'What?' she says to the air. 'Oh, I don't suppose so.'

She starts when Floss gets into bed. 'What did they say?' she asks, in her normal voice.

'None of your business,' Floss says. 'Come *on*, will you, what are doing, just sitting there, muttering?'

When Floss gets in, Iris does. 'I was waiting for you,' Iris says. 'Is Mum coming soon?'

Floss sighs. 'Who cares?'

They lie side by side in the darkness. 'We're not to go in Long Debris,' Floss says at last, bitter.

'It's not Mum's fault,' Iris whispers. 'I think something bad happened there. I saw after school, there were all policemen –'

'Who cares?' Floss says again, '*I* don't.'

She's tiring now. It makes it hard to brood. She rolls into Iris's flank. 'I heard you,' she whispers hotly. 'Talking.'

'I wasn't,' Iris says. 'Anyway, I'm allowed to talk to him.'

Him is Semlin. Semlin is Iris's made-up friend. She's had him for a long time, just as long as they've lived in London.

Floss says, 'What does he look like, then? Is Semlin handsome?'

Iris giggles. 'Of course not!'

'Well, what does he look like, then?'

'He doesn't look like anything,' Iris says, and yawns. She is falling into sleep; the softness of it dulls her sister's malice.

'I can't see him,' Iris murmurs. 'He's not *real*.'

As if it's Floss who is making things up! As if Semlin is *her* friend. She can feel Iris, shifting into sleep beside her.

'If he's not real,' Floss whispers, 'then why's he called Semlin?'

'Because that's his name,' Iris says, with the false simplicity of dream. And then they're both asleep, one on the heels of the other.

★

EXTRA FOOD EXPECTED FOR CHRISTMAS
MORE TEA AND SUGAR

Mr Strachey, Minister of Food, stated at Westminster yesterday that there is an expectation of extra rations of tea and sugar for Christmas this year. There will still not be as much sugar as there was last year, although it is hoped there will be more tea.

Rather more poultry is anticipated. Fresh fruit, except apples, should be available, and at the beginning of December there may be another small allocation of dates.

———

BORSTAL FOR £60 ROBBERY

Three boys, GEORGE EDWARD KNIGHT, 16, labourer, JOHN RONALD KNIGHT, 16, labourer, and JOHN ROBERT YEOMANSON, 16, driver's mate, were at the Central Criminal Court yesterday sentenced to three years at a Borstal institution after pleading "Guilty" to two charges of robbery, and one of breaking and entering a dwelling-place and stealing therein. The RECORDER, Sir Gerald Dodson, expressed hope that they would be detained for the full period of time.

It was stated that the three lads had escaped from an approved school. While lodging at a Maltese Café in Pitsea Street, Ratcliff, they broke into a house at night at Shoreditch and attacked the male and female occupants, threatening them with an iron bar, and robbed them of £60 and various articles.

―――

MAN'S REMAINS ON BOMB SITE
BELIEVED KILLED MONTHS EARLIER

The remains of a man were found at 11 a.m. yesterday in the flooded cellar of a condemned building near Columbia Road, Shoreditch.

The remains were discovered by Paul Jones, dairyman, of Ezra Street, one of whose milkers had strayed into the condemned building. The remains were taken to Leman Street Police Station where a *post mortem* examination indicated that death occurred between three and four months ago. The cause of death was likely blood loss caused by multiple lacerations made by a sharp instrument – possibly a knife. In a statement to the press to-day, Police-sergeant Richard Wise, of Leman Street, stated that the remains have been reasonably well preserved by the enclosed cellar and the water in which they lay.

The three-storey Georgian house where the remains were found had suffered considerable bomb damage during the war. The man was about 5ft.8in. tall, and wore a covert coat, an overall suit and a knitted brown waistcoat. Police-sergeant Wise stated that the man is believed to have been living in the derelict building or in its environs. Officers from Leman Street and Scotland Yard were examining the bomb site to-day.

This is less than half a mile from Bacon Street, where Gerd Visser, an unemployed seaman of no fixed address and a native of the Netherlands, was found unconscious having been attacked and wounded in a similar manner in March this year, but there is no evidence to connect the two events.

★

A boy is walking down the road. He is slight. No one looks at him twice.

He is going home to his old home. Sometimes he still returns to it. It's hard because it's dirty and Dora hates dirtiness. He wants to do what Dora likes but sometimes he has to do this. He has to check if it's still his. He has to look at the things that matter. He likes to sit in there, or lie ever so quiet where the clay has taken his shape. So sometimes he visits, and then he goes back to Dora and Solly.

It's true that he has Dora and Solly. They want to be his mum and dad. They've given him room in their own home. They give him kites. It has happened perfectly, like you see on gravestones: *Gone to a better place*. But you never know. Be careful. Sometimes people change their minds and sometimes their hearts. Sometimes they pass on. The boy has gone to a better place, but neither places nor people last forever.

If he could keep his old home he would, but other things always want it. It's a good place, a place he's fought for, but now he'll have to let it go. Already his smell is fading. When his smell is gone something will come, the rats or a fox or a bad man, and then the only home he'll have will be with Dora and Solly.

That's why he's visiting now. Pond is collecting his things.

It's Sunday, early morning, meagrely lit and mizzling. Pond moves through the flower market's fringes, towards Long Debris's southern fence. There are policemen there today, big blue men in ones and twos, but they're as slow as Jones's milkers, they don't know where they're going any more than cows do, they don't know the ways like Pond does and they don't see him duck the fence and edge into the jungle.

He comes to the pit. The ground is damp around it. He takes care climbing down because his shoes are almost new, Solly got them for him special, but he can't help muckying them.

Inside he shuts his eyes. He never used much light in here – he learned how it could make men come – but he knows it all by touch. Nothing is missing but his smell is thin. It makes his throat clench even so. It never used to do that.

There is a cat smell, too. There was one that used to visit, with fine fierce eyes, like Mrs Malcolm's. He'd let it sleep with him. It would press right up touching him. It used to let him stroke it. *I could eat you,* he used to tell it, but he never did.

He takes the things that matter from the best high shelf. There are two piles of newspaper, the ones that were for keeping warm and the ones he kept to wipe himself, and he wraps the things in a clean sheet, like a parcel of fish and chips.

It isn't a small thing, to leave. He'd like to stay. He'd like to lie down for a while, but he knows he should go. He puts the parcel in his coat and climbs out of the pit. The sun is getting stronger, and he stands and looks around, so that he can remember it. He won't come again.

'It was our place,' Pond says, and Moon speaks like a echo.

It was our place, but we don't need it any more.

Pond thinks of Iris's ghost, and Jem's story of the Airman. Iris and Floss up in the March mist, two whispering girl-soft strangers. It's funny, because there was an airman. It was a long time ago. The man came down in the night. He was on a parachute like a big white moth. He was still moving on the ground, but Pond didn't go near him, and in the morning he wasn't, and people came and took him away.

Now there are police in the southern ruins. Pond skirts around them and goes north. When he comes out of Long Debris again he's up on the Hackney Road. Two big boys are smoking in the shelter of a telephone booth, and one of them looks his way, but they don't really see him.

He heads southwest. By Diss Street another copper is standing by the fence. He has a friendly old face with a beard. Pond knows him, has thought about him ever since spring. His name is Dick Wise.

'What have you got there, then?' Wise asks, and he nods at the bundle in Pond's coat. 'Fish for breakfast, is it?'

'No,' Pond says. He wraps his arms around his bundle. 'My things,' he says, 'the ones that matter,' and Dick Wise laughs an easy laugh.

'Well, they're the ones to hold onto. You keep them safe, son,' he says, and looks away as if Pond has already gone.

He hasn't, though. He studies Wise. 'You used to live here,' he says, and Wise glances at him again.

'How's that?'

'You used to live here, before the bombs. In Quilter Street, with your sweetheart. Her name was Susan, but you called her Sukie. Only she died, in the war.'

Sergeant Wise stares at him. He starts to say something, and stops. His cheeks blush above his beard. 'Do I know you?'

'You used to,' Pond says. 'You did when I was small. You knew my name, most probably. Don't you remember it?'

Dick Wise says nothing. He goes on staring at the boy with the narrow green eyes. 'It's alright,' Pond says. 'I don't either.'

'Lost it, have you? Your name?'

'Yes,' Pond says. 'I've looked for it all over. My friend, he told me you might know it. My mum, my old mum, she told me that if you're lost you should ask a policeman. He'll help you find your way. Will you?'

Wise frowns. His face still looks friendly, but it's only because he's old and his skin has grown into that shape, like the clay in the hole, which keeps your form after you're gone. His eyes aren't smiling any more.

'Go on,' he says. 'I've work to do. I don't have time for your games, sonny. Away with you, now, I don't want to see you again.'

Pond goes. It's not far home. When he comes to the Columbia Buildings he goes through to the depot yard. One half is taken up with stacks of sacks and stacks of timber with a barbed wire fence around them, so you can't steal anything before the council makes its houses. In the other half are parked one car and one van. The van is the spindlemaker's and the car belongs to Iris and Floss; they're the only motors owned by all the people in the Buildings.

Long ago a rich lady built the Buildings. Dickin was a famous man and he put her up to it. She did it for the Shoreditch poor. She meant the depot yard for their market, but the Shoreditch poor didn't like it, they liked the streets the best, so that was where the market stayed. Thank you very much, they said, but we know what's best for us.

Pond's old father told him that. Pond remembers the words, but not the voice of the man who said them.

He takes the stairs up the north block. Not the eastern one, which is where his new home is. It's best not to take his things there. He's always tried to keep the things that matter good as new, but Dora won't like them all the same. Pond has found somewhere else for them.

The stairwell is always dark. There's an echo in it, but Pond goes quietly. At the top there used to be a laundry, but no one comes any more.

There are good hiding places here.

Above the stairwell is a hatch. There's no ladder, but the arch is almost like steps, so long as you never look down.

The attics are dusty and dim. Here and there the sun comes through. There are things forgotten under tarps and little broken windows and places where the tiles are gone. Pigeons are crooing in the eaves. Pond wipes his shoes. He crawls inwards. It's mostly dry up here, and sometimes the light is warm when the morning ends and the afternoon begins.

He sits up against a beam and takes the parcel from his coat. The hiding place is under the boards. He unwraps the newspaper and looks at the things that matter. There are only four: a map of Shoreditch and Bethnal Green from *The Illustrated London News*, the remains of his siren suit, his kangaroo cloak – with pockets, for when the bombs come and you have to get up quick-smart – and his knife.

When he's finished looking he wraps them up again. He puts the parcel under a tarp. 'Safe as houses,' he says. His things will be waiting for him here whenever he needs them again. He should go home to Dora, now, but for a while he lies and drowses, with dust and sunbeams in his hair, listening to the world outside, the men and horses and motor cars, and the dogs, the women and the children. Just listening.

4 . WINTER

Five days and nights of smog.

The air tastes of old batteries. Columbia Road is a cloud forest. The great water fountain looms like a cenotaph. In the Lane the costers do their best, but the crowds don't linger and they spend only if they must. A woman buys a twopenny bloater. A man buys a winter coat and walks away in it.

With December the weather breaks. The sun drinks up the mist. All week the days are bright and blue, but the nights are cold with a vengeance.

On Saturday, first thing, Mary goes shopping with the girls.

The queues first. Get them done with. Mince and liver, lard and sugar, vests and knickers. Cold hands on the ration books (*DO NOTHING WITH THIS PAGE UNTIL TOLD WHAT TO DO*). The butcher's line is four shops long and mealy-mouthed with Chinese Whispers (hock, chops, giblets, brisket). Floss bites a hole in her glove ('What did you do that for, silly girl?' 'Because it had a *lump* in it!'). Then the markets. Four grey heads of cauliflower, ten grey pounds of potatoes.

Leeks for soup. Chestnuts for stewing. Skate for frying. Seven dabs — old and grey as the rest — and a decent bit of red-spot plaice for Michael. The women pressing up around them, reaching in to pinch the fish, searching their flesh for tenderness.

Oats and milk. Dried milk. Dried eggs. Tinned fruit. Tinned music drifting down from Bessie Pretty, the Long Play Lady. The girls are carrying. Iris has her face squinched up. Her arms are thin as strings.

A woman goes past with a pram heaped up with parsnips and sprouts, and a baby wrapped up in the middle, jolly as a Christmas chicken.

They stop inside a telephone booth. Mary checks her list.

'Done?' Floss asks, and Mary nods. 'Can we have a treat, then?'

'Well, you've been good. What is it this time?'

'Mr Izzard,' Iris says, dreamy. 'Mr Izzard and his Three Wise Birds.'

It's the wrong way, and her feet are numb, but Mary lets herself be led. The girls are merry to be in charge. The peddler is by the Underground, and he has a dustbin brazier. Mary warms her face and hands — the pleasure is unspeakable — while her girls fuss around the cage.

The Three Wise Birds are canaries, dyed pink, blue and green. Inside their cage, one wall is lined with rows of wooden pigeon-holes. The pigeonholes have varnished doors with doorknobs made of matchstick ends.

Both girls want the Pink Wise Bird.

'Not a problem, ladies! Not an issue. He's wise enough for the both of you,' Mr Izzard says, and he leers at Mary as she pays.

Mr Izzard leans over the cage. His face is sunken as smoked meat. He murmurs to the pink canary; he clicks his tongue at it. It looks as cold as Mary is, but it cocks its head at its master's mouth. It hops to the pigeonholes and takes a paper from one, rolled tight as a dog-end.

'This one's got your name on it,' Izzard says to Iris. 'A little bird told me,' he says, and he drops the scroll into her hands, then does it all again for Floss.

'You too, Mum,' Iris says, but Mary says no. It's money down the drain and it's past time they were home.

Get ready! Iris's fortune says. *Good luck comes in great big bunches!*

'Look!' she cries, 'great big bunches! What's yours, Floss?'

But the wise bird hasn't been fair. *An oath made is a debt unpaid* is all that Flossie's says, and what's that supposed to mean? It must be Mr Izzard's fault, he must know what the birds will pick, he must like Iris better. It's rubbish, Floss doesn't want it. She humps her bag along, as if four cauliflowers and a proverb are the burdens of martyrdom.

They haven't far to go, but the girls run out of puff at the bottom of Columbia Road, and Mary has to leave them there with half the bags, bickering. She's got the first lot into the square, is catching her own breath again, when she sees that there are people gathered under the balconies.

Death, she thinks: it looks like a death. There are men in the knot, drawn out from their work, and their voices are lowered. Mary recognises one of the spindlemakers, and the Jew, the watchmaker who took in the troublesome boy. He's peering at the eastern block. That's his building. Mary's too.

It can't be Michael. Michael will be out at the Roman Road all day. He never comes home before dark. Michael won't slacken for anything.

Mary prepares herself. She goes up to the watchmaker. He's wringing his hands. He stares at her with his goggle eyes.

'Mrs Lockhart –' he starts, but Mary cuts him off.

'Who is it?'

'It's Mrs Platt,' says the spindlemaker, and Mary thinks, Oh, thank Christ. Thank Christ it's her, and none of mine. But the spindlemaker is still talking.

'They put the bailiffs on her. Rent unpaid, that's what Dick Wise says. He went up to talk to them, but it's all in order he reckons. They've got their papers alright.'

'She oughtn't have opened up to them,' a woman says. 'It's too late once you open up. You ought to lock your windows, even. You would have thought she might know better. What are they doing now? Can you see them?'

'Just sitting,' the watchmaker says. 'All morning they are just sitting. What are they waiting for?'

'That's what's they do,' the spindlemaker says. 'First they take inventory, then they get comfortable. You've five days before they clean you out. Bastards don't want you running off with the goods, see. Like bloody great vultures, aren't they? Bloody great bruisers in their bloody great boots.'

'They're all piss and wind and that's all they is,' the woman says, but Mary has already turned to go. Her relief is ebbing away, leaving behind a residue of unease. Mrs Platt is her own neighbour. By rights that should mean something, and if it hasn't – if Mary has never cared for Annie Platt – well, then it should matter now. In Birmingham, Mary was brought up to know what neighbours are for.

She takes up her shopping and climbs the stairs. Outside her door she leaves the bags: the next door down is Annie Platt's.

There are two men sitting on the step. Both of them are smoking. They don't look like bruisers. One is stocky, with little shoes, and the other is hardly more than a boy. They look up at Mary quietly, steadily.

'Can I go in?' she asks.

'Ma'am,' the stocky man says, and he takes off his hat and stands aside, courteous as an undertaker.

Mary steps past them. The flat is dim. She can make out Annie in the lounge, standing by the mantlepiece. The old woman picks up a china thing – a little shepherdess – looks at it in the gloom, and puts it back in its place.

'Mrs Platt?' Mary says, and Annie raises her head.

'Oh, hallo dear,' she says, cheerily. She's in a duster coat and slippers. She has no stockings on. Her legs are white as talc. She looks around the room.

Mary asks, 'Are you alright?'

'Oh *yes*, I'm alright,' Annie says, and smiles. 'I was just looking for something, whatever it was. I don't suppose it matters.'

The girls, Mary thinks. I need to get them home. But she's here, her unease has brought her in, and she can't just leave like that.

'Why don't we sit down,' she says, and notices for the first time that the dim room is crowded with chairs, as if Annie is hoarding them against rationing: a stack of churchy straight-backs, two pink wing-chairs with matching antimacassars, a stool, a pouffe, and a settee with an ancient knitted cover, faded as old heather. There's hardly room for company.

'Yes, *why* don't we?' Annie asks. 'And we could have a cup of tea. I bought a pennyworth yesterday. I offered those men a pot but they wouldn't even have it standing. The caddy's in the pantry. Only they might have taken it already. Do you think they have?'

'They haven't taken anything. They won't. You've time to find the money, and then they'll leave you be. Didn't they explain it to you?'

Annie goes to the window. She stands in the light that comes through the nets. 'Are they out there now, are they?' she whispers.

'Mrs Platt –'

'Where anyone can see them.'

'Annie, listen to me. You've five days. Can you get the money together? Is it much?' Mary asks, but the old woman isn't listening. Her hand grips the nets.

'They're scoundrels. With Christmas coming. After everything I've done for my country. They're brutes, oh they are. I can't bear it. It's shameful. I won't stay. I been here since I married, and now everyone's dead, they don't know who I am. Well, I won't stand for it. I'll be gone tomorrow if they lay a finger. How *dare* they! How dare they?'

But Mary doesn't know how, and she has to go for the girls. She finds them halfway up the road, dragging the bags between them, and by the time she gets them in and warm, Annie's door is locked shut.

The bailiffs stand aside again. They flank her while she knocks and calls. Like hounds, she thinks. Big silent hounds, the kind that are the most dangerous.

When she gives up – as she steps back – her glance falls on the older man. He's not looking at her. He's standing with his pipe in his mouth and his hands deep in his pockets, smiling up at the blue sky, as if he finds it beautiful. For a moment Mary hates him, and then he nods – feeling her eyes – and the men sit down again, and she sees that they've been playing cards, and that she's trodden all over them.

★

Dora, Bernadette and the boys are eating potato crisp sandwiches, the boys sandwiched between their mums, the four of them on wooden seats, in a blue tobacco smog, watching the stars converse in a distant firmament.

'*You sent for me, sir?*' says a shooting star. It twinkles as it speaks.

'*Yes, Clarence. A man down on earth needs our help.*'

'*Splendid! Is he sick?*'

'*No, worse,*' says the brighter star. '*He's discouraged. At exactly ten-forty-five PM tonight, Earth time, that man will be thinking seriously of throwing away God's greatest gift.*'

'I don't think they're really stars, I think they're angels in disguise,' Jem tells Pond, who nods in grave agreement.

'*Oh dear, dear! His life! Then I've only got an hour to dress. What are they wearing now?*'

Jem beams at his mum. The pictures light him up. He's a star himself, or a firefly, like Donna Reed when she's around James Stewart. The pictures are Jem's own heaven.

'Mum! That one's called Clarence!'

'Hush up now,' Bernadette murmurs, but the woman in the row behind grabs her chance, leaning in between them to hiss, 'Do you *mind?*'

They settle down. Dora takes mouse-bites of her sandwich, so that the crisps won't crunch. Jem wolfs his down and looks at Pond's, which Pond has held untasted since the film began. Pond's eyes are on the silver screen. In spirit he's inside its world, where the star-angels are now gone, and in their place a boy is falling through a sheet of river ice.

The film was Dora's choice. She's sure she loved it the first time, when Solly took her out, and she's told Bernadette so; but now it worries her. She doesn't remember it being so *fierce* as all this ... she hopes it's the film she thought it was.

She glances down at Pond. He gets nervous, just like her, but he hides it better; a stranger would never notice it. Still, he looks all right. She's worrying too much again. She should enjoy herself. It's nice to be out with Bernadette, and to be able to treat her – it's such a late thank-you, this, for the meeting with the sailor, Thomas – though Dora did give her a jar of cordial, but there's no harm saying thank-you twice – not that she ever heard from Thomas ... anyway: her boy looks happy. His face is purely peaceful, as if he's sleeping with his eyes open.

Bernadette is thinking of Neville, and God's greatest gift.

It's a sinful thought. She's had it before. She thinks of going to Camden and finding Neville passed away. They break in and the gas is on. The evil of the thought is that it comes on her like an idle daydream. It's a sorrowful dream – in it Bernadette is sorry – but there's something in her, even so, which blossoms with relief to think of the pipe's covert hiss, to picture Neville at rest. There is that hard part of her which is glad to find him proved right: dead at last.

She remembers the day she arrived in England. Neville wasn't there to meet them. They looked up and down the docks – Jem, seven years old, sat waiting on the trunks – but he hadn't come for them and in the end it was the boy from the boat, sweet Thomas Cowlishaw, who was their Good Samaritan, who took them onto the boat train, saw them to Waterloo, and put them on the Underground that led to Camden Town.

They should have known beforetime, that's what Bernadette thinks now. The letters should have made it plain that something had gone awry. But they were younger then, younger than the three years it has been, and so caught up in themselves, busy with their hopes of life in England. Busy with Jem, busy with themselves. If they noticed Neville writing less, well then, letters went missing, didn't they? There was a war on and Neville was fighting it. Flight Sergeant Malcolm was a busy man himself: Flight Sergeant Malcolm would get news to them when he could.

It had been Neville's idea first, England. After he went across himself – giving up his headmastership and paying his own way to fight – Neville told them to be ready. The war would soon be over, and then England would need plenty of hands on deck. London would be hungry for men. *Have your bags packed,* he wrote. *You will do well here.*

And then for years his letters glowed with proof of how well a man could do. Neville had joined the Royal Air Force Volunteer Reserve: Neville had been promoted. Ground staff, flight staff, NCO. Neville Malcolm, of Glasgow, Jamaica, was flying his own

Lancaster. Ten operations, twenty, and the home parishes all talking him up. Neville was their war hero.

Later – when their bags were packed, their minds made up, their plans laid – later the letters changed. Neville's worries crept into them. He'd been having headaches. He thought it was the cold at altitude. He didn't want to write about his good fortune any more in case pride came before a fall. He didn't want to jinx himself. And then there was an accident. Neville never wrote of that. The news reached them, oh, a long time after, from the family of a Montego Bay airman, injured himself and writing home. Neville's bomber had come down in a wood near Lowestoft. Two of the crew had been killed, but Neville had made it out of the fire alive. The Montego man wrote that an angel must have watched over him. Neville had come through it with broken ribs, a strong concussion, and hardly a burn on him.

That man knew nothing, Bernadette thinks. Not a thing. Nor did I.

It was dark when they had got to Camden. They were all bone-tired. Jem was swaying on his feet. There were children playing out in the road like those of the poor folk back home. No one answered Neville's bell but there were people on the steps, the door was open, and they went up. They found Neville's door unlocked. A dog was howling outside. They opened the door and there he was, just sitting in the dark. He was rocking back and forth, and when he turned to look at them his face had an old man's beard, and his eyes were white.

Neville? Clarence said. *Is that you?*

Don't come in, Neville said. *Don't come in here. This is where the dead live.*

'It's a good picture, Mum, isn't it?' Jem whispers.

'Yes,' says Bernadette. 'A good picture.'

'*Well,*' James Stewart says, '*You look about like the kind of an angel I'd get. Sort of a fallen angel, aren't you? What happened to your wings?*'

'*I haven't won my wings yet. That's why I'm an angel Second Class,*' Clarence says, and when Jem smiles up at her, Bernadette smiles with him, and the baby kicks inside her.

★

Solly works. Not that he wants to. It's Saturday, his holiday. God has nothing to do with it – a man needs a holiday, that's all.

At least he isn't missing anything. This picture Dora likes so much, *It's a Wonderful Life*, well, Solly's seen it. Nothing to write home about. Schmaltz. Too much religion, too much of angels and salvation.

He might have talked to Bernadette, he might have liked that, it's true, but Dora would have shushed him, then. And they took the boys along with them, and he's had his game with Clarence, so there's nothing to do now but work or twiddle his thumbs. If they come back soon they could all still make a day of it, but in the meantime Solly has a watch that won't fix itself, and the owner is a busy man, the kind of gent who needs what Solly offers: the right time, all the time.

Is Solly that kind of gent? An all–time–right–time man? Pull the other one. He might have been something once. In Danzig, before they left, he was training for the law. His father was a judge's clerk. Solly might have gone one better if things had been different. He might have amounted to something by now.

The spring they left, 1938, anyone with eyes and ears was getting out however they could. The Eastern Jews went back to Poland or sailed for Palestine, and the German Jews – Solly's Jews – they got on whatever ship would take them, the longer the passage the better. Everyone going their separate ways, to Sweden or Britain or

118

further – Canada, America, Argentina; a dam-burst, the Old World emptying into the New. And Danzig soon falling to ruins behind them, all the bustling streets, the pretty gables and bright awnings, the crowded promenades and waterfronts, all of it left for dead.

Eyes and ears and a bit put aside; that was all you needed. Only the poor and the fools would have stayed. But Dora's father was neither, and where is he, now? Surely dead with all the rest.

It'll pass, Dr Rosen used to say, when Solly was trying to change his mind. *These things come and go. Think of it like Baltic weather – one day one thing, the next another. These things people say against us, Solomon, these things they do . . . they are not sensible. Sooner or later, people always return to their senses,* Dr Rosen used to say, over *Goldwasser* and cigars, in the parlour on Jopengasse.

Solly misses him. He misses Danzig itself. He thinks of it especially when he takes the boy to the river. It's the waterfronts that bring it back.

At least they're alive, Dora and him. At least they've got each other, and London . . . well, London will pick itself up. But the Law? Well, the laws are all different here. All that learning Solly did, it's no more use here than his High German. The only learning worth a schilling is that which his grandfather gave him when he was just a boy: how to take a watch apart, tune it, and put it back together.

It's not forever. This thing he does, it's not a life; it's only work, and it could be worse. There's still time – isn't there? – for Solly to better himself again. If this is all in the meantime, well . . . it could be worse, it could be meaner. At least he has Dora. At least he does something he likes.

What he likes best are the times like these, when you don't even think. Your hands remember what to do. It's as if they touch the watchwork and turn into clockwork themselves. When all you do is *do*, you don't have time to dwell on things. Like their families, all far-flung or missing. Or like the bailiffs they put on Mrs Platt: since he sat down to work Solly hasn't thought of them at all.

It's a nice watch, this one. A Lindbergh-Longines. It makes a change from the Ingersolls and suchlike Solly usually sees. A man brought him the Lindbergh on Thursday: a Pole, but one of the good ones. Not a peasant. An educated man. Things must be looking up, when people like this come to him. To work on a piece like this, it's a privilege.

It's a better watch than Solly will ever wear himself.

He's still at it when the postman comes. Solly pops the loupe out of his eye and bustles to the door, blinking. There's nothing for him but one for Dora. Solly stands in the hall, squinting at the envelope. It has an Edinburgh mark, but he doesn't know the hand. It isn't an impressive one.

Never mind. Dora likes getting post, it always perks her up, and a perk for Dora is a perk for Solly. He takes the letter through, pops it on the mantlepiece, and forgets all about it. It will stand there until Monday morning, when Dora will come across it while she's dusting. She will sit down alone, in Solly's chair, and her hands will shake as she reads.

'*Now some music for you,*' the wireless says. '*This morning we have the great pleasure of welcoming back Mr Jack Simpson and his sextet.*'

'Morning, Mr Simpson!' Solly says, in his best flamboyant market English, and turns Jack up a notch.

★

Evening. Mary waits for her old man.

It's late. There are few other lights still on in the Columbia Buildings' Neo-Gothic blocks and towers: soon hers will be the last.

The girls are fast asleep. On the wireless the Home Service has finished: all that's left is the end of the Third Programme. Still, she doesn't mind sitting up. There's something soothing about it, a comfort to be kept to yourself, like the softness of a worn house-coat. Mary has always been waiting for Michael. She waited sixteen years for him to find her. She has done this before, other nights, and will do so again. So much of her life will be spent waiting.

She doesn't get enough of him. He works so hard for them, all day, and his nights, too, are often spent in the company of men. Tonight the lack of him is keen. The flat is hollow with his absence. The kitchen hems her in. Mary thinks, It's worth any wait to have him mine, but I spend too much time in this dratted room. She almost wishes she was back out in the grey and the cold with the girls at her heels. She does wish that.

The Third Programme ends. The anthem plays out into silence. The window has misted up. The last lights are uneven stars.

On the kitchen table: an ash-tray (hers); a covered plate; two glasses; a bottle of sherry wine. Sherry is too sweet for Michael's tastes, but it's all she has. Besides, she likes it herself. She pours one now, to settle her nerves.

He comes in a quarter shy of twelve. He kisses her fast – brush of dank bristle – and splashes water on his face.

'What's the occasion?' he asks, straightaway, without even seem-ing to have glanced at the bottle, and Mary shivers.

'Do I need one?'

He turns, leans on the washboard, and laughs – one of his rare, gruff laughs – but he doesn't say anything. It is she who goes on. 'How was it, out?'

'Same as ever. Old men flashing their money around, young men begging for it.'

'I kept supper for you. It's plaice,' Mary says, and he comes and sits. Mary pours the sherries. Michael raises his, peers through its citrine. He is in good spirits, and she's glad for that, grateful that the night has sweetened him.

'What are we drinking to?' he asks.

She doesn't know. She hasn't thought. 'You choose,' she says.

'Health and wealth.'

'No,' Mary says, 'let's drink to us,' and that's what they do.

She takes another of his cigarettes and smokes it while he eats. He dines slowly, as always. Food and drink, smoke and love: her man takes them all the same way, curbing his natural appetites. She wants to talk, but she waits. Michael is like a dog with his food. It won't help to interrupt.

'How was Cyril?' she asks, when he's done, and Michael wipes his mouth. He likes Cyril no more than Mary does, the few times she's met him. A cocksure, shifty little man.

'Cyril was there,' Michael says. 'It was Alan Swan's invitation.'

She has heard of Swan. He's respected: not respectable. Feared. Should she be worried, that he's courting Michael? Mary doesn't judge on rumour; rumours are all she's heard of Swan. You don't know a man until you meet him. Besides, Michael can look out for himself.

'He wants to meet you,' Michael says, and Mary starts at the thought-echo.

'Why?'

'Wants to know us better. He's keen on family, likes family men.'

'Does he like you, then?'

'He will,' Michael says, 'When he meets you and the girls.'

'Oh no, Michael, not the girls!'

'It might get us in his good books. They're good books to be in, Alan's. I wouldn't be surprised if he put some work my way himself.'

'Cyril might have something to say about that.'

'Cyril's no fool. He's Alan's man too.'

'You never told me that.'

'Well, he is, at the end of the day. If Alan went over his head, Cyril would know to hold his tongue.'

Mary begins to clear. She doesn't want the girls meeting Alan Swan and Michael knows it. Mary will do what she has to, she'll put on a pretty face and meet the men Michael deals with, all those they both despise – the respected-not-respectable men, the fences and spivs and mastermen – but her girls will have nothing to do with that world. Mary won't have it.

'There's no hurry,' Michael says. 'You've time to think it over. Alan mentioned the new year. His house. A good spread, I shouldn't wonder.'

His *house*, Mary thinks. She says, 'But what will I wear?' and Michael laughs again. He pushes back his chair and comes round by her.

'All things being well,' he says, 'We'll find you something better than cinders.'

'I mean it!'

He puts his rough cheeks down by hers. She can see the cruel curve of his mouth, the part which has lacked all volition as long as she has known him; the single sign of weakness which is, for her, a part of him. His hands go to her waist, her ribs, running up under her breasts. Her finest hairs rise where his fingers pass.

'You could go in mourning,' he murmurs, 'you'd still be the sweetest lass there.'

They kiss again. Not briefly, this time. Her throat is curved back to him.

'Not the girls,' she says, and he sighs.

'Not the girls, then. Let's go to bed,' he adds, when he lets her go; and she wants it just as he does, but he feels her hesitation. 'What?'

'I had something to ask you. It's about Mrs Platt.'

He frowns, not comprehending, nor much pleased not to. 'They put the brokers on her,' Mary says, 'did you hear?'

Michael doesn't answer. Slowly he goes back to his chair. He sees what's coming, Mary knows, and he doesn't like the look of it. His eyes linger on the sherry, her inadequate sweetener, and she winces.

'I'd like to do something for her.'

'What's Annie Platt to us?'

'She's our neighbour, isn't she? At home, we looked out for our neighbours. We did.'

Michael nods. Their talk has taken a turn for the worse, and his mood turns quickly in its wake. 'You did,' he says. 'You and yours.'

'What's that supposed to mean?'

'What have they got to show for it? They're poor as they ever were. Hopeless, the lot of them. They've no call to be giving charity, to neighbours nor strangers. What's charity done for them? And mark me, this is London now, we're not in Birmingham now. No one has time for neighbours, here, no one looks out for us. We owe no favours.'

It strikes home. It's true in its way, all of it. Mary has said as much herself, of her family, all of them still in Ladywood, going nowhere, the lucky ones – the ones not bombed out – grafting to make ends meet in the threadbare rooms and houses they were born into. But she has started on Annie now, she won't sleep easy if she lets it go, and Michael won't let it drop if she does. Better to try and make a fist of it, to soldier on.

'Annie's alone. She's no children to look after her –'

'You reap as you sow. If we're talking of children, now, it's time we did something about those boys.'

'What boys?'

'The urchin,' Michael says. 'And the darkie. The girls are growing up. They should know not to play with them.'

There is a glint in his eye. Mary has roused him, has stirred the fighter in him, who always argues this way, like a maddening boy or a brawler, ducking her points, jabbing with words. She presses her hands into her lap.

She says, 'I'm not talking about that now. I'm talking about Annie.'

'You should,' Michael says. 'You put a stop to them running on the waste, you can put a stop to this. It's high time.'

'They're just children, Michael.'

'I don't want them mixing. I want the best for them.'

'I know you do, and so do I –'

Still they keep their voices down. It won't do to wake the girls.

'You used to be dead set against them. The darkie and all his kind.'

'I'm saying they're just children. Wait until they start new schools, they'll go their own ways, then, you'll see. They won't need us telling, they'll understand what's best. It can wait, love, but Annie won't. She doesn't need much to put it right. It wouldn't be much, I'm sure –'

'It won't have to be anything. You've never had a good word to say about her, why would you want to help her now?'

'Oh, *Michael*! Why do you always have to be so hard?'

His eyes widen for a moment. I've hurt him, she thinks, surprised. There is injury in his eyes; and then it's gone, snuffed out, and she knows she has only angered him.

He stands. Mary rises with him. 'I'm sorry, love. Please don't be cross with me,' she says, and she puts her hand on his arm, but she takes it away when he looks at it.

'You've the housekeeping,' he says. 'Give her that if you must. I'll make it up.'

She nods, but Michael doesn't see her. He's looking round the kitchen – the cracks in the ceiling, the grease on the glass – as if he feels its meanness, and fear uncoils in her.

'Where are you going?' she asks, almost before she knows he is; perhaps before he knows it himself.

'Out,' he says.

'I'll wait for you.'

'Do what you want,' Michael says, and he takes his mack from the hook.

★

On Sunday they awake to snow. It's nothing to write home about, as Solly would say, but here and there the wind makes something of the fall. Along the south side of the square it's deep as the cream on country milk.

The snowball fighters take to the streets before the sun can thaw them. Packs of them snipe and scuffle between the water fountain and the flower stalls.

'Throw that anywhere near here,' Rob Tull yells at Jem, 'I'll thrash you into Christmas!' And he brandishes a holly wreath until the boy scuttles off, all done up for chapel in his too-short Sunday clothes.

Pond and Iris crouch together. Iris's not much use at throwing, but they're both ace at not getting hit. They're hiding behind the car in which the bailiffs sit. Floss streaks past, bellowing, with snow-melt in her hair.

'What are they doing?' Iris whispers, and Pond peers through the car's back window. One bailiff is reading the racing edition. The other is watching the Columbia Buildings.

'They're waiting, aren't they?' Iris says, and when Pond nods, 'They're waiting in case Mrs Platt decides to make a run for it. The bloody bastards.'

Pond looks down at her. 'You shouldn't say that.'

'I know,' Iris says. 'Sorry. They make me want to spit, though. Rotters. And I don't see why they need a car. It's not as if Mrs Platt is going to run. It's not as if they'll have to chase her, is it?'

'No,' Pond says.

Iris goes up on tiptoes beside him. She inspects the brokers. The thin one tips up his hat and scratches behind his ear. The fat one licks his pencil and turns a page.

'They look like Laurel and Hardy!' she hisses. 'You wouldn't know they were rotters. They look just like anyone.'

'Anyone can be rotten,' Pond says.

'But if they're just like anyone, then it's not right to hate them, is it? I wonder what they're called? I think the thin one's Mr Doe, and the fat one's Mr Dear.'

'Those are good names,' Pond says, and smiles.

Iris lets go of the car. She squats. She takes her mittens off. Her hands move furtively.

'Pond?' she says. 'Pond, look here. I think they dropped something. It's bailiff equipment.'

Pond hunkers down beside her. Iris brings her cupped hands between them. 'See?' she whispers, and she opens her thumbs – as if she holds a butterfly – and there is the snow, blue-white, packed and scalloped by her fingers.

'It's Mr Doe's snowball,' she says, and gulps, looking at Pond in wonderment.

He darts back as she goes for him. She shrieks – she goes to throw – but Pond is too quick for her. He's away, up and running. Iris races after him.

Already the crowds around them are turning the white back to grey. Pond goes at a dog-trot, feinting to stay clear of Iris, cautious with his footing. The sun is out, bright in his face. In Club Row a lone Sunday cheap-jack is calling out the prices of bird sand and cuttlefish bones. It's a nice day. Pond is still smiling. Iris is calling after him.

'Wait ... Pond, wait for me ... It's not fair, your legs are too long ... Pond, will you *wait?*'

On the corner of Wentworth Street he slows. He doesn't have to, he could run all day in this dazzling light, but he stops anyway. He knows what's going to happen, but he doesn't mind, it won't hurt at all.

Iris comes up panting. She leans on him to catch her breath. She risks a look at him, titters, then crushes Mr Doe's snowball against his duffle-coated chest. There's not much left to crush. Her hand is crab-clawed from clutching it.

'I got you!' she crows. 'I *got* you I *got* you!'

They pull themselves together. Iris's fingertips are turning blue. She puts her mittens back on, but her teeth are chattering, and the sun is going behind the clouds.

'We could get tea,' Pond says.

'I haven't any money. Have you?'

'No, but Solly's pitch is down there.'

Iris puts her hands under her arms. 'It would be nice,' she says.

Solly has two customers, and a very important repair to finish, but being busy makes him cheerful, and he gives them a halfpenny each, brushes Pond down and sends them packing. They save one halfpenny for later and share a mug of tea by the seller's brazier.

'Why do you still call him Solly? He's your dad now, isn't he? You should call him Dad properly.'

'I know,' Pond says. 'I do, sometimes.'

'He's a nice man, isn't he? He sounds so foreign, but he's alright when you get to know him. You must be glad he's your dad. I am. You make all the games better,' Iris says, and blows on the tea. She bathes her face in its steam. 'I hate feeling cold. It's the worst thing there is, worse than feeling hungry, even. Don't you think so?'

Pond thinks about it. 'Some people, they don't like being alone.'

'Oh,' Iris says, 'yes, Floss hates that. That would be the worst, for her.'

The tea is finished. They trudge homewards up the Lane, through the wet and the clamour, past Jem's dad's pitch and the Pound Note Man and the hot sarsaparilla seller.

'You must have been cold all the time,' Iris says, 'when you lived in Long Debris.'

'Not always. There were fires. The men make them in the houses.'

'Weren't you afraid of them, the men?'

'Some,' Pond says, 'when they were drinking. Mostly I kept away from them. I had my place.'

'You were alone, then.'

'No,' Pond says. 'I wasn't never alone.'

They have come up Bishopsgate and back into quieter streets. The snow still lies white in the alleys, virgin on the yard walls. Iris looks at Pond. All of a sudden she is shy again. When she says what she wants to say it all comes out in a halting rush.

'I know why. I know why you weren't alone. It's because you had someone with you always. I do too. I have a friend, a made-up friend. He's called Semlin. I know he's made-up, really, but I do so like having him. And you have someone, don't you?'

Pond doesn't answer. His face has stilled. His sharp eyes cast one way and the other. He starts to walk faster. Iris jog-hops after him.

'You don't have to tell me, I don't tell people either, but I know you've got one, a friend. I saw you whispering to him. You don't do it as much as I do, only sometimes when we're playing Troll, or things like that. Pond? You're going too fast.'

Pond stops. He doesn't speak. Iris takes his hand.

'Mine's still cold,' she says.

They come up to the Birdcage. Mrs Joel, the publican, is salting her pavements. Iris can see her dad, standing up a little Christmas tree for a lady customer. She lets go of Pond's hand.

'I have to go in now,' she says, and Pond nods. He doesn't look at her. 'Call for me later, if you like.'

He shrugs; the old shrug, inarticulate and meaningless. Only as Iris starts off does he look after her. He frowns.

'What's he for?' Pond asks, and Iris turns, with the market's Christmas picture – trees and holly, wreaths and berries – all behind her.

'I don't know. He's just for playing, or when I'm lonely. What's yours for?'

For a moment it seems that Pond won't answer: then he starts, as if woken. 'He looks out for me,' Pond says, and Iris smiles, as happy as if her father had praised her.

'Call for me later, then?'

'Yes,' Pond says, and he stands there, hands at his sides, until Iris is gone.

★

Mary is calling through the letterbox.

'Annie? It's me, Mary from next door. Are you there?'

She's trying to call quietly; quietly enough that only Annie will hear. There's no one on the walk – only two little mites out playing – but someone will be listening, one walk up or down. Someone always is, in the Columbia Buildings.

'Annie, dear, the men are gone. There's no one out here but me.'

Right, Mary thinks, that's it. The letterbox is so cold that her hands feel like they'll freeze to it. She's made up her mind when the door opens in her face and there is the old woman, grinning.

'Har,' Annie says, 'har har. Bit fresh for them, was it? Serves them right. Bloodsuckers. I hope their balls drop off.'

'Can I come in?' Mary asks, and Annie nods craftily.

'Oh, *you* can, yes. You come in where it's warm,' Annie says, but she looks out both ways as she shuts the door.

It is warm, too. Annie has a fire going. Mary follows her back into the lounge. There's a battered old suitcase on the settee with a few things in it; stockings, photographs. Annie riddles the coals.

'There,' she says, and perches on one of the straightback chairs; all of them, Mary sees in the firelight, painted with the chipped brown gloss of classroom desks or church halls.

'Are you packing?' Mary asks. 'Are you leaving, then?'

'I told you I would,' Annie says, and waves at Mary, as if she's standing in the way of a pictures screen. 'Sit down, won't you? Sit down on that nice armchair there.'

Mary sits. She watches Annie rise and fold more clothes into the case. There is a flush in her cheeks that wasn't there yesterday. She looks well. She looks so well that Mary wonders if it can be healthy.

'Where are you going to go?'

'Pontefract,' Annie says promptly. 'I've a nephew there.'

'But what about your things? All your things?'

Annie waves an arm at her again. 'Oh, things!' she says, and her voice drops to a mutter. 'I don't give that about things. You can take them or leave them, can't you? That's what makes them just things, they don't matter. I don't hold that against those men, not when it comes to it. Let them take what the landlord's due. It's just that I won't be made an exhibition. If there's anything left when they've finished, well, you might send it after me.'

'But you don't have to go,' Mary says, 'do you? Your nephew, couldn't he pay them off?'

'I won't be made an exhibition,' Annie says again. 'I wouldn't ask. I wouldn't want him fussing.'

Mary takes out the notes. They're in an envelope, with a few half crowns. The housekeeping, and a bit she's saved in the years they've been in London.

'What's that there?' Annie asks sharply, before Mary has put the envelope down, even, and she knows it's useless. Annie stands over her, the fire behind her, a pinny in her hands. 'I don't want your money. Put it away,' she says.

'But you could pay them, Annie! You could stay.'

Annie cackles. 'Put it away, girl. I don't suppose that'll keep me anywhere. I've eight months' owing. Besides, I won't take charity.'

She goes to the mantlepiece. She picks up the china shepherdess and brings it over to Mary. 'Here,' she says. 'I want you to have this.'

'Oh, no –'

'You want to do something for me, you'll take that. I'll be cheer-fuller, knowing you've got it and they don't.'

Mary is still frowning at the figure when Annie kisses her. A whiff of Ponds and powder. 'Anyway,' Annie whispers, 'I owe you for all them biscuits. Now off you go. I've a lot to do. I'm tired already, and I've things to do.'

When she lets Mary out she locks and chains the door behind her.

★

Edinburgh, Nov. 30th 1948

Dear Mrs Lazarus,

I am very sorry that I cannot tell you any more than that which follows. It seems to me no better or it might be worse than nothing but I am conscious of your being waiting. It would be better all round if I could have got down to see you but it is now more than eight months since we spoke in the Bird Cage and though we dock in Edinburgh six hours hence and in Liverpool thereafter there will be no time ashore for me to do more than send you this letter. Then it is the Argentine for us and no shore leave on home soil till Christmas when I will be needed at home by my mother who is not in the best of health. Therefore I am writing to you.

In Gdansk (Danzig) I spent a day ashore in April and a second in May. I hoped to return there this winter but with things the way they are, the Russians more and more our enemies, I do not think I shall be able. It seems I might have writ to you sooner and for that my apologies. I had hoped to find out more and something more definite by which you might put your mind at rest at last.

Be that as it may I did what it was you asked of me viz. looking for your family and asking of them and showing the people your photographs to as it were "jog" their memories. On my first leave it seemed to me I would be no earthly use at all for the language is a trouble and the people too are not much inclined to helpfulness. Their own lives are on the whole pretty grim and the city casts London in a fair light being in a terrible way itself as you may know first from the Germans but in the main from the Red Army who drove out the Hun with poundings day and night.

On this first leave I did find the street you wrote of by way of the church you said to look out for but no one in the houses would speak with me at all and the street and the church were both in a sorry state with the great church floor all broke up by soldiers turned grave robbers and its roof all burned away and the tower like to fall with bricks all melted together from the fierceness of the fire that took it. Jopengasse was not much better but the house of your family still stands all excepting the top floor and the wash house by the courtyard.

On this visit I did speak to a lady at the City Hall whose name if you should wish to write is Mrs. A. Belova though she is not the most friendly of women. Mrs. Belova is Russian. She does however have some English. She told me that there were still Jewish people getting out of Gdansk up until she reckons the winter of 1941 at which time the Germans locked the doors. What happened after that she says there is no record of but the Russians are all for making the most of the evils of the Germans as they do now of our sins whatever they may be. From Mrs. Belova I did ascertain that there is no one in Gdansk now who goes by the family name Rosen.

In May we docked at Gdansk for a second time. Already then our official dealings were cooler and laggardly & I had less time ashore than I would have liked & went straight to Jopengasse determined to find something for you. There had been some rebuilding there & enough in the way of mending to see them at least through this winter. There was a new roof of sorts on No. 41.

I went into the house. In the four floors were five families or couples as well as a pack of boys who I think were not family but who insisted they were. All these people were Polish and spoke that local kind of Polish which they call Kashubian & all were suspicious besides & not happy to speak to me.

On the third floor where your family were are a family of three & one of six named KULASH and MISHKA though I cannot vouch for my spelling of these. Between these two families there was but one man of working age & from my enquiries roundabout I understood that these families had been in the house three years & come from nearby in Poland though nobody could or would tell me where. As best I can make out most of those in Gdansk now are in much the same boat, the only others being Russians most of whom are soldiers. I met no one with anything like a German or Jewish name.

The man of these two families was called Thomas Mishka & at length I persuaded this other Thomas to sit & talk with me in those bits of French & German we had in common. I showed your photographs to Thomas who recognised nothing of them excepting the house he lives in himself & which he says was empty of all but the pack of boys when he moved his folk in.

Then Thomas spoke with an old fellow who said he knew your father

& mother. This old fellow who would not give his name was certain he had spoken to your mother in Gdansk in the midst of the war. He could not tell us in what year that might have been exactly & when Thomas asked this old fellow about the whereabouts of your family he only shook his head & said nothing for a long while & then something which Thomas would not at first convey. Later however Thomas told me that this man had said that all the Jews of Gdansk were taken away into the forest and that they all died there.

However this is wrong of course since many left such as yourself. I tell it all to you as it was told to me since it is the nearest thing I have to an answer for you. Still it is my own belief that this old fellow spoke in ignorance. I do not think it possible that so many people could have been led into the forest as he says. I am not sure there is any need to put trust in this account.

I am very sorry that I have no more to tell you than this. I wish for your sake that I might have gone back to Gdansk again but I do not think it likely now & besides we are on the beef run all this winter & spring.

I enclose your photographs. I have kept them as well as I could but there is a spot of rain that fell on one whilst I was showing them about Jopengasse.

My fond wishes to you and Mr. Lazarus and Bernie and to her boy.

> *With regret,*
> > *Thomas Cowlishaw,*
> > *Leading Steward,*
> > *M. V. Lough Erne.*

★

Jem is dancing from foot to foot in nothing but his Contours and his lime flannelette bathing trunks. Clarence is stripping down, folding clothes into his basket, hat off last to crown the pile. Pond is sitting listening to the myriad sounds of water: the echoes of the foot baths, foot slaps, plunge baths, rain baths, the gush of taps, and – from the pool – roars and squawks and gibberings that sound nothing like boys or men, but like the voices of the creatures in the stories that Jem tells.

'Dad,' the boy beside Pond whispers, 'Dad! It's the Banana King!'

'So it is,' Dad says, with his trousers round his ankles. 'Pity you ain't got a pen, you could've had his signature,' and he winks at Jem, friendly as you like, since the King himself pays no attention.

Now they are ready, the three of them lined up on the slatted bench: there are queues here, as everywhere. 'How much longer?' Jem complains, and Clarence rolls his eyes.

'What are you in such a hurry for, Nature Boy? And what you got your specs on for? You got dirt on them needs bathing? You just be patient, like Pond here. You could learn a lesson or two from him.'

Jem takes off his specs. The changing room blurs to a congelation of male forms, pink and grey and pallid, squatting, stretching, smoking, sitting. A centaur resolves itself into a tall man kneeling with his shirt halfway over his head.

'*Forty-one to forty-six!*' the Super calls, and the autograph boy and his dad hoist their baskets and go splashing out of sight. Jem slumps down next to Pond.

Pond keeps his towel to his groin. For Dora and Solly he comes here. He doesn't like the baths. His body isn't like that of the others. It is scarred and rashed, and thinner, harder, more naked, as if he has shed more than others in the act of changing. He doesn't like the changing room, with the weed-green stripe in its tiles and its reek of strangers. He doesn't like the reek of himself. He can smell it now, coming off his armpits and the dirty things between his legs. He never used to notice it. Now he does, and he knows it's wrong. People say so. He shrivels into himself.

An old man lingers in the foot baths, withered and troglodytic. His belly is a purse of flesh that droops over his trunks. Pond looks at him and sees what he will become.

He doesn't like it here. He only comes for Dora. And Dora is crying so much and he doesn't like that either.

Jem wraps himself in his own towel. It comes complimentary, like the trunks, but you have to give them back when you go. If you buy Second Class tickets then the soap's complimentary, too, and you can go in the rain bath, but Pond's dad got them soap from the Lane, three old green slivers of it, one for each of them. This evening the three of them are

~ *Third Class Bathing* ~

~ *Gentlemen* ~

It says so on the tickets.

'Is your dad working tonight, then?' Jem asks Pond, but Pond is down in the mouth today, he just shakes his head and looks at his feet, and then the Super calls their numbers, and they have to hurry on.

Pond is in Cubicle One. He locks the door and takes off his trunks. The bath dwarfs him. He washes quickly, with the soap, the way Dora taught him. But the water he sits in is dirty itself. There is grit and muck between his toes. There is a film on the top that ripples as he moves.

'More hot?' yells a man, and the Super yells back for his number.

'Seven, *sir*!' the man shouts, the way a soldier would do it, and men laugh up and down the rows, because it is a joke.

'Get away from the taps, then,' the Super grumbles, and there is a gush of water.

Pond thinks, you're supposed to clean yourself, but this place is just as dirty as we are. All we do is sit in the water and put on the dirt of one another. It makes us all like soldiers, all in the same uniform.

For a while he stops washing. He sits with the warm water up to his chin and scratches and waits for the Super to call time. Then he thinks of Dora crying, and he stops scratching and starts to clean himself again.

When Dora cries it makes him tremble. It makes everything sick and wrong. She was crying when Pond got in from school. At first he thought she was laughing. For a long time she locked herself in the lav and Solly sat outside the door and whispered to her. He told Pond they'd just have to wait. It's all because of a letter. What the letter said was worse than nothing.

'You boys alright there?' Mr Malcolm calls.

'Alright, Dad!' Jem calls back, and then there is a silence, into which Pond says, 'Yes,' his voice too small, but only one man chuckles.

'Can I have some more hot too, please?' Jem shouts, but the Super shouts back that he's had enough already; and then it's time to get out, and Pond rises from the water, the film of soap coming with him, drawing off and coating him, a second skin made from the skins of the men of the Columbia Buildings.

★

Come better days – and they will come – Michael will miss the Roman Road. It's a sorry market and no mistake, the punters hang-dog or hard-bitten, the costers hawking tat, and the wind never letting up this Monday, the sixth of December, the cold coming straight out of Russia, the East Wind whistling down the arse-end of London, raising hair on the costers' necks, whipping the punters home along streets that smell of gasworks and the cooking of

Indians who live out their lives as surreptitiously as rats in paltry basement rooms.

Michael will miss it, for all that.

Mary is upset with him. It hurts him. It riles him, that she should call him hard – as if hardness were a fault – when all he does, he does for her. Still: onwards and upwards. Here's the good ache of work in his arms, the clout of money in his pocket. He is taking coin, turning a profit, and soon enough the winter dark will soften the unsightliness around him. The lamps and braziers will be lit, and there's beauty to any market, then.

London loves the man who loves his business. Michael is that man. It makes some fellows small, London, it dwarfs and belittles them; but others rise to it. Others brace themselves against the city's push, shove back, grab what they can and thrive. Michael hates indignity – the indignity of poverty, and that of answering to men with less spine than himself. He chafes at those things, but not at the hardness of London.

It has been a surprise to him, but he has begun to like Cyril's East End markets, for all that he's meant for better. They're lands of opportunity, mucky though they are. There's a freedom about them. Certainly he loves freedom.

It has been a fine year for him. He has kept his temper with Cyril Noakes, and Alan Swan is his reward. He has done well out of Wolfowitz, and Wolfowitz likewise of him: there's no need, anymore, to sell his old friend's pickings underhand, at the stalls, where Cyril might get wind of them from any one of his boys. Now Michael pays off the lads himself, he's free to pass his own man's goods along with the rest of them. Cyril buys what Michael brings him each month, gladly and none the wiser.

Four o'clock. The dusk is gathering, but it's not yet dark. Off west, homewards, a chink of sunset remains. *Between the dog and the wolf*, Michael's father used to call it, this last scrap of twilight. For all Michael knows he still does.

A man buys a jar of stropping paste. Michael sells a Gem Damascene, an imitation silvertip, four wraps of safety blades. An old Scouser with the shakes comes to have his cutthroat honed and Michael does it and takes the tuppence owed without a word: business is business. At the next stall Len Ramshaw parcels up chitterlings for Father Bright. 'Excuse me, I was before him,' a punter complains, and the butcher doles him out a look. 'Right you are,' he says, 'but the difference between you, see, is he's a vicar, and you're a cunt.'

John Children, the Dogfight Man, stops by as he does every month for the Vitalis Dressing he applies – without noticeable effect – to his wayward cockerel hair. Blossie, Cyril's best lad, comes with two cigarette cases in silver and ivorine and Michael pays him in the alley by the library.

Blossie is a tall boy-man, going on fifteen, with a disappointed look that serves him well, Michael hears, both with money and sweethearts; but Michael isn't fooled by faces, and he pays the boy his due, no more. Blossie fingers his profits.

'Swan's here for you,' he says, sourly, and, at Michael's prodding, points out the car, an export model, drawing looks down by the Roman's end.

'Running errands for Alan now?' Michael asks.

'I'll run him the Derby, if he pays me,' Blossie says, and Michael tips him to mind the stall, liking the lad when it comes to it; he reminds him of himself.

'Michael,' Alan says warmly, when Michael stoops beside the car. 'How are you keeping?'

'Busy.'

'Michael Lockhart, man of business. Family well?'

'Well enough.'

'Well enough, and not a word wasted. You're not much for small talk, are you? That's what I like about you. You're thrifty and you don't do smarm. Well, get in.'

Michael gets. Alan is sat beside him; another man is up front, one of those from the club whose names Michael never cared to learn.

'Norman's taking us for a spin. I thought you might enjoy the Austin, being a driver yourself. Say what you like about you Brummies, you know how to build a car. What do you think?' Alan asks, and gestures at the saloon's fixtures and fittings, all of which are dense, deluxe: even the windows look inch-thick, like plates of lead crystal, hushing the market's raucousness as Norman draws them out of it and into Cambridge Heath Road.

'Very handsome, Mr Swan,' Michael says, and Swan *tsks*.

'Now then, I'm asking for your honest opinion.'

Michael weighs the odds. 'It's too proud. A car like this stands out. It's liable to get you noticed.'

'Ah,' Alan says, and smiles, his teeth lit by the electric lights of the showrooms on the corner. 'That's my boy.'

For a while they drive in silence. By Three Colts Lane the driver, Norman, turns his head to watch for traffic, and Michael sees his eyes – anxious, probing – and recalls him as the man who came back late from the war, the one who was a long time gone off East.

Norman here, he learned all kinds of things.

'The thing is,' Alan says, 'I don't mind the notice. You move up in the world, you draw attention, it's only natural. You have to learn to live with it, you have to take pride in standing out proud, you'll find that out soon enough. You remind me of myself at your age. Pride and ambition; those are the qualities that get you places, and you've got them in spades, Michael. How's that old man of yours?'

For an instant Michael thinks Alan means his father, and then he knows he does not, and his heart sinks in the dark.

'No need to worry,' Alan says. 'A spot of business on the side, it shows initiative. More than a spot … well, that's where problems start. What's his name, now? There's a Wolf in it.'

'Wolfowitz,' Michael says, unwilling.

'I never took to him myself. I tried to do business with him. But too much trade on the side, that was his trouble, too. Too independent-minded …'

Alan's gaze drifts away, out towards the advancing night: he looks disappointed with it. Michael keeps his mouth shut. There's enough rope here to hang himself, if he doesn't guard his tongue.

'He was always good at his work, it's true. And he must be getting on by now?' Alan asks at last.

With gratitude Michael takes his cue. 'He's not young. He's come round to doing what he's told. All he wants now is a living.'

'And I like you, Michael, so I'll tell you what. I'll do you both a favour. We'll keep him on, above board. You'll have to keep him straight with us, and you'll have to sort it out with Cyril. I don't suppose *he'll* be best pleased, but tell him it's all squared with me.'

'You won't regret it,' Michael says, but Alan gestures, waving off the whole problematic business.

'I've some work for you, too, by the way, if you're not too independent-minded yourself.'

Michael licks his lips. He doesn't answer straight off, though it's an effort not to. He composes himself. This is what I'm here for, he thinks, and this is what I've waited for. This is what I've earned; a chance with the likes of Alan Swan.

'It's driving,' Alan says. 'Just a bit of driving.'

'Norman can drive,' Michael says, curtly crestfallen, and Alan grins again.

'Don't be like that, Michael, we all have to start somewhere. You'll be with Norman this time out, but I want you in the driving seat. This time tomorrow, if you're not too busy.'

'Where?'

'Isle of Dogs. Millwall.'

'In this?'

'Oh no,' Alan says, 'no, this won't do. There's a van at Limehouse. Norman can show you. He'll come for you tomorrow.'

They turn into Mile End, going east, shadowing the Roman Road. Alan is watching Michael. The old man looks hungry himself.

'And when we get to Millwall,' Michael says, 'what do we do there?'

'You drive,' Alan says, softly. 'That's all you do, you drive. Norman will take care of the rest. You're not afraid, are you, Michael?'

It is a moment, just a moment, before Michael shakes his head.

'I didn't think so,' Alan says. 'Cyril gets afraid. That's the trouble with men like Cyril, they're too fearful to make a mark. A small beer drinker, that's Cyril, a small beer kind of man, always has been, always will. But you're not like that. You asked for Scotch, bold as brass. That's what you meant to show me, wasn't it, Michael? That first night in the club? You've ambition, you've pride, that's what you had to say for yourself. You want to leave your mark on the world. I didn't have you wrong, did I?'

'No,' Michael says. 'I'm your man.'

Alan pats him on the knee.

'Good boy. Norman,' he calls forward, 'it's time we were getting back. We don't want to keep Michael from his business.'

He works on after they've gone. There is still business to be done, and he thinks only of that until the crowds thin out to nothing. He glances at the library clock, then, and sees that the hours have flown: he's stayed longer than he intended.

He has taken down the tarp, is boxing up the strops and blades, when he looks up in the lamplight and sees Mary, standing there.

'I thought I'd see you home,' she says. 'It's a cold night to walk alone.'

'I was feeling it,' Michael admits, and she comes up and kisses him. Her own lips are chilled. Her cheeks are red. She's beautiful as the day he first saw her, laughing at him amongst her friends, ten years and a lifetime ago, in Ladywood, in Birmingham.

★

'Mrs Malcolm? Bernadette Malcolm?' the Sister calls, her smile thinning when Bernadette raises a hand, though it's no great loss, a smile like that; there wasn't much sunshine in it to begin with.

Somewhere a baby is crying; and there is something wrong with the sound, an incredulous distress that hiccoughs for breath now and then, but persists, on and on, echoing down to the waiting room along barely lit corridors, through wards of peeling wartime paint and governmental linoleum; there is apprehension in that voice, a lonely terror of exist-ence, that puts Bernadette's nerves on edge, so that one hand grips Clarence's quite fiercely as she smiles up at the nurse approaching them: a proper smile, that lights her eyes, despite the nerves and the pain that comes and goes; Bernadette shows them all how it's done.

'Can we go in, Sister?' she asks, but the nurse shakes her head.

'Not today, dear, unless it's urgent. We're very busy, Bernadette; we see so many these days, with the National Health, but Dr Rogers did tell me he's space for you on Sunday. Noon. It's kind of him to offer, not all of them hold with Sunday hours, but babies don't keep the Sabbath, do they? At least the sun has come out, see? We should count our blessings, shouldn't we?'

'Air,' Bernadette mutters, when the Sister is out of earshot, and Clarence bends down to hear. 'I said get me up, I want air.'

'You wanting to lose your seat for it?' Clarence whispers back, and it's true that it's standing room only around them, the only mercy for Clarence being the cavernous ceiling, where tobacco smoke collects out of reach in stained corners.

'I'll come Sunday,' Bernadette says. 'I want to be out of this blessed place.'

Out they get. They do a turn round the grounds, where pigeons pick over the lawns, or huddle in the coppiced planes with their grim amputations and witch-broom branches.

London churns around them. It's as ugly as it's ever been this winter, its jams and crowds, its ruins and clearances – the first sign of rebuilding – all grey as newsreels in the long, revealing light of a sun already falling.

'Lord!' Bernadette exclaims, and Clarence clutches her arm more tightly at the sound of the name taken in vain.

'What is it? What?'

'No,' she says at his mistake (he is looking her up and down in alarm). 'I just miss it. Home.'

'Here is home,' he shrugs. 'We come this far together, what else can it be?'

'I know that,' Bernadette says, 'oh, I know that really,' and she takes his hand and squeezes it, to let him know she's alright.

As they come back round to the front gate she stops and looks up into his eyes. He's still a handsome man, her faithful giant. He's a fool to have come down to the hospital with her when he should be working – he'll be out late because of it – but Dora was poorly, so here he is, all done up in his Sunday suit, gawky as a boy in his best, the look on his face so worried and that face still strong despite it; still strong enough that she can draw succour from it.

She gazes beyond him. There is a narrow view of the river there, and before it, of one almost beautiful thing: the Monument, with the sun twinkling off its fiery golden summit.

'Let's walk there!' Bernadette says, but Clarence tuts.

'You get that far, I'll be carrying you back.'

'Don't you kiss your teeth at me. You think I can't do it?'

'Alright, woman,' Clarence says, 'don't say I didn't tell you so.'

Carefully they make their way down. When Bernadette was young she had a picture that she loved, of London couples by the Monument, but it's no picture when they get there. Where did the beauty go? Bernadette cranes her neck. The square in which the pillar stands is full of dustbins crammed in doorways and laundry on balconies, and a lone drunkard coiled under papers.

She winces as they turn to go. 'It kicking?' Clarence asks, and she nods.

'Digging her heels in. Don't want to go nowhere. Not out here,' she says, wistfully, glancing round one more time: she wishes she weren't here herself. The wind cuts cold in the square's shadow.

'Let's go home,' she says. 'I can last till Sunday.'

'You so sure it's a girl,' Clarence says, as they turn for home.

'You better hope I'm not dreaming,' Bernadette says, 'because I'm telling you, I'm set on Sybil.'

He laughs at that, *ho! ho!*, and Bernadette laughs with him, but her heart's not in it. The name makes her think of Mama, and Mama leads her on to home again.

It is still Home, on a day like this more than most, when the wind cuts cold and the child struggles inside her, as if it knows it is coming to a new beginning and fears it. It is an idyll, Jamaica, like the best days of childhood: always out of reach behind her, whatever other places she and her man make for themselves, whatever they tell themselves, however far they have come, or go.

★

Michael is driving to the end of the world.

Some nights, in the war, when Mary and the girls were still half-way safe up north, Michael and Wolfowitz would come down to the Isle of Dogs. It was the old man's idea, and Michael still owes him for that. There were rich pickings to be had in the wake of the bombings, rich enough to make London worthwhile, though it was nervy work, with the Germans always drawn to the Island – the river's great meander the plainest of landmarks – and the fires smouldering and bringing down roofs, and the dockers and firemen on the lookout for looters, though Wolfowitz always insisted they weren't that. Salvage, that was all they took. Salvage from the wreck of London.

It was a broken place then, the Island, and it's still broken now, as Michael drives through the dusk; so marred that it's surely past mending. The wharf cranes loom immobile over the docks, gaunt as guns, and south of them, where the Thames closes round the neck of land, the darkening streets of Millwall are barely lit, barely wanted, with God only knows who marooned in the timber-propped terraces, and the roads all mud and country ruts, with grass and reeds growing up around the woodpiles, and here and there a sign of erst-while wealth, a custom house or shipwright's office, fallen into disrepair since the heyday of the docklands; and what new buildings have gone up ramshackle, gone-tomorrow things, and the smell of mud always on the air, and no sound but the sound of gulls.

Norman looks this way and that and says nothing. Michael likes a quiet man, but he doesn't like the man beside him. Twice, since Limehouse, he's spoken up himself to break the uneasiness of their silence. *Makes Shoreditch look handsome*, he said, as they came down into Millwall, to which Alan's man said nothing, and later, when Norman pointed them east, towards the old Mudchute batteries, Michael asked in so many words what they wanted with the place; but Norman only swung his head, looking at Michael unblinkingly with his anxious eyes.

Nerves, Michael thinks. It's nerves that make a man talk too much, as he has. Only Norman is nervous, too – sweating with it, despite the cold – and he says not a word.

There's something broken in him. Michael can feel it; can smell it, almost, coming off him with the reek of his sweat. There's something in Norman that echoes the world around them. Michael wants nothing to do with it, that thing (the war is past; he has escaped it, even if Norman has not), but here he is sitting beside it, driving it to its destination. It's too late now.

'We're here,' Norman says just then. 'Stop here,' he says, and points Michael to a stretch of buildings, a warehouse with an office outhouse, the office old glazed brick but the warehouse new-built or rebuilt, thrown up out of makeshift timber, with no lights on and a hoarding up front:

McEACHAN BROS.

METALWORKERS

METAL BROKERS

is all it says.

Norman gets out of the van. He walks towards the office, tries the door, stands back. He rolls a cigarette and lights it, peers up at the pockmarked building and around. When the cigarette is spent he hawks, comes back to the van and leans by Michael's window.

'Lend us that,' he says, and gestures towards the horse-head stick, close at hand, stood in the footwell of the seat.

'What for?'

'Door's locked.'

Michael regards his stick, then Norman. 'You won't be jemmying it with this.'

Norman smiles. He reaches across Michael and takes the stick out through the window. He does it quickly – Michael is too off-guard even to speak, even as the ferrule clacks cold against his cheek in passing – but once he has what he wants, Norman waits. There is a pause in which Michael might act – Norman allows him time – and only when it is clear that Michael will do nothing does Norman's smile fade, as if Michael's submission disturbs his momentary happiness. He nods and turns and goes back to the office.

Michael doesn't watch. He sits looking at his hands. He checks his cheek. The bone aches, but the skin is unbroken. He hears the sound of breaking glass, the first report loud, the rest muffled, and when he looks that way again, one of the office windows is staved in, and Norman is gone.

There are stones, he thinks. He could have found a stone or timber. But it was the stick he wanted, to test me, or to bruise me.

No one comes at the sound of the glass (who would come, in this desolate place?), and Michael's thoughts begin to wander. He thinks of the stick. It is his father's work, made for him when he was sixteen, when the stroke took him. It's good work, that horse-head. His father fashioned gold and bronze, now and then, but he was always most at home with silver.

He thinks of the stroke. Why recall that now? But there it is: the smell of oranges. The smell and taste of oranges, cloying at first, then overpowering. When he came to he was lying on his bedroom floor. Hours had passed – the light had gone – and Graeme was there with him, murmuring comforts, lifting him.

He was still half a boy. *A warning from God*, the doctor called it, and what earthly use were such words? And why in God's name think of it now?

And then the war. Graeme and Christy cheered off with the rest of them. Michael left behind, like the crippled boy in the story who couldn't keep up with the piper. He hated the war for that, well before the news came back of Christy, missing at Dunkirk, and then his death, and then Graeme gone the same way; gone and dead, not dead and gone.

The war made plain to all and sundry his redundancy. It made him pitiful. How bitter he grew then. And the bitter arguments. His father, telling him to leave the house and never to come in it again, on the day of Graeme's memorial.

Powerlessness. What else links those times and this, but that? Norman may be broken in mind or spirit, but his body is whole. He could break Michael as easily as he might break the horse-head stick (*More easily than that,* a small voice whispers in his skull. *The stick is sound*). It is powerlessness that Michael recalls, here, so far from anywhere.

He hears a sound then, a queer cry, and when he looks he sees a light has gone on in an upstairs window. How long it has been there he doesn't know, and it goes out soon enough. When Norman appears again – stooping out the door – he has a carpet-bag in one hand and the stick in the other. He props the stick by Michael as he gets in beside him, and in the dark it looks to Michael as if the horse's head is wet.

'Drive on,' Norman says, and Michael starts the engine.

★

'You woke me up,' Floss says. 'What are you doing?'

He is bent over the sink, shirtsleeves up past his elbows. His teeth are gritted. He is scrubbing at the stick in his hands, its head under water.

'Go back to bed,' he says, and Floss sighs and does. She dreams of silver horses, racing through orchards full of green and blue and apples.

★

Wednesday, dark and early, the last flakes of a night of snow still twirling down as soft as smuts.

Mary hangs clothes, pegs in her mouth, steam-ghosts rising between her hands. Bits of conversation drift across the balconies.

'What do *you* want?'

'A stick of wood. I haven't a bit of fire in the house.'

'It's a hundred pound you'll be wanting next. Look, the sun's coming up.'

'Oh, I know, but it's this cold, it's gone right into me.'

'Go on, then. Door's on the latch.'

'Ta, love. I owe you one.'

'*And wipe your feet!* Not half, she don't. More like all the trees in Essex.'

How hard London is, Mary thinks. All these years after the war, and all it seems to get is harder.

Still, maybe nowhere else is better. Maybe the war was really the end, and none of us knows it yet. No one sees that everywhere is going on the same way, the whole world getting harder and harder, until it just cracks apart and takes us all with it.

Don't think rot.

At least she has Michael and her girls. And at least they still have their own place, cracks and all, and look – new clothes on the line. It's like Michael says, when it comes to it: they need to look out for themselves. They're alright, and that's what matters.

She hears a sound down in the square. She glances down into its well, and there is Annie, walking away through the snow.

From up high the old woman looks childlike. The view fore-shortens her, and her suitcase is too big for her, so that she limps, weighed down like an evacuee.

The square is still in deep shadow. It is all shades of grey; the snow, the depot yard, the car and van, and Annie Platt, hobbling too quickly for comfort towards the far arch: holding her hat and peering to see the street beyond; looking for the brokers who have not yet arrived for her on such a cold morning.

'It's been five days,' Mary murmurs, but then she remembers that it hasn't: only four. Annie is getting out to Pontefract with a day to spare.

As Annie reaches the arch, Mary almost calls her name, wanting her to wait, needing to go down and . . . what? Urge her back? Take her in? Well, at least to say goodbye, to wish her well up north. Mary is poised to shout; but she holds back. All she does is raise an unseen hand, and then Annie is gone.

Later, Mary tells herself that she did the right thing, after all. How Annie would have hated shouting! Everyone hearing her name. Everyone at their washing lines, looking down at her, there in the snow with her battered case. Mary knows she's right about that. She tries to find comfort in it, but all she feels is shame.

★

'I'm going to get a watch. Not a market one, a real one. It's got Roman numbers.'

'Wizard.'

'What are you getting?'

'I don't know, really,' Jem says; and really he doesn't want to know. What Jem likes best is the not knowing. The best bit is the waiting, the potential of mystery; the perfection of the gift unopened.

'I shan't wear it to school,' Floss says, her voice and torchlight coming back to Jem dimmed by the attics' clutter. 'It's a ladies' watch. I'll only wear it on occasion. I should think it'll last me years and years,' she says, and sneezes. 'Gosh, it's filthy up here! Why didn't you show me before?'

Jem shrugs, not that Floss can see him: they've only his torch between them, and she's crawled away with it. Its dusty light dithers between beams and tarp-clad heaps of tiles and slates and other, obscurer things.

Why didn't he show her the attics before? Because they're his secret place. Only today she's been so down. That's why Jem brought her now, but he doesn't tell her that. It'll only remind her to be glum again.

Her dad yelled at her at breakfast. Floss told him coming home from school. Jem didn't tell her he was surprised; not that Floss's dad would yell at her, but that she should mind so much, because her dad looks like a man who would yell at people all the time.

Except he doesn't, Jem thinks now. Mr Lockhart looks like a man who never needs to raise his voice to anyone. He cows people just by looking. And Floss is his favourite. She always says so.

I didn't even do nothing, Floss told him. *I was just talking. I wasn't even talking to him! I was telling Iris my dream. It had apples in it, and horses.*

'You should have shown me this ages ago. We could have made up games for it. It's a bit late now,' Floss mutters, and Jem squints up into the gloom, jarred out of his contemplation.

'Why is it late?'

'Well,' Floss says, 'we'll have new schools soon. We might end up at different ones.'

'So what? We'll still be friends,' Jem says. 'Won't we? We'll still live together.'

'I suppose. My mum says the Buildings are falling down. We might all have to move away.'

Her voice is some way off now, and moving farther. Jem shivers. He only really likes it up here when there's daylight coming in. Now it's dark outside, and he recalls how big the attics are, with crawlspaces and crooked corners he's never explored.

'Don't go too far,' he calls. 'The torch might go. Floss?'

'I'm here,' she says, though the light is obstructed, or else Floss is saving it. She's brave if she is, Jem thinks, but then he knew she was. Or maybe she can see in the dark. Maybe Floss eats all her carrots.

'Jem, how long do you think it'll last?'

'Not long. It's hard getting batteries, it only takes number eights –'

'No, dopey, I meant my watch.'

'Oh,' Jem says, 'well, you could ask Pond's dad.'

'Don't you know?'

'No. They last a long time, watches.'

'What will you be when you're old?'

'I don't know.'

'You don't know anything today. You should think about it. You'll have to decide in a year or two, else someone decides it for you. What do you like doing?'

Being with you, Jem thinks, but he daren't say that. 'Mum says I'll grow up tall, like Dad. I could be like him.'

'What, a Banana King?'

'Why not?'

Pfft, is all Floss replies.

'What's wrong with that?' Jem asks. 'I like the markets. You do, too.'

'They're alright. I'm going to do better. People will talk about me on the wireless and in the papers. You'll read all about it. Oh!'

'Floss?'

Stillness. Scuffling. Jem stands up, arms outstretched.

'Floss?'

'It's alright,' she whispers, close again. 'I'm here. Look, I found something.'

'I can't look, can I? You've got the torch,' Jem grumbles, but Floss is already crawling up beside him, he can perceive her greater darkness, can sense her as she kneels.

'I was saving it. Here,' she says, and bathes them in light.

She has a package in her hands, a bundle of yellowed newspaper. As soon as she has handed Jem the torch she sets to unwrapping, impatient as a child at Christmas.

Don't, Jem wants to say, *wait, Floss, it might be dangerous*. But it's too late, she's already opened it.

'It's just rags,' Floss says. 'Spit! It's just a load of old rags.'

She sits, kicks the soiled clothes away, and out of them falls the knife.

It's a straight razor, the bone handle stained yellow. It looks ancient and fine, like so many things from before the war.

The blade comes cleanly from its fold. There are flowers of rust along its spine, but someone has left it oiled and its troughed flanks are unblemished. It has kept its edge. It nicks and nibbles at the whorled ridges of their fingertips.

Floss hisses. Jem's eyes go wide.

'You cut yourself!'

She sucks her finger, peers at it. 'Look, it's just a bit of blood,' she says, and offers Jem the knife. 'Now you.'

Her face is spectral, uplit. He knows what she wants him to do. 'I don't want to,' he says.

'Go on. It's like one of your stories. We found it, so it's a sign: we're meant to do it. It'll be our secret, even if we have to move somewhere else. Go on! It doesn't hurt.'

Floss takes the torch, Jem the knife. He squeezes his eyes tight. Presses. Blood wells around the blade.

'Ow!' he whispers. 'You liar!'

'Don't fuss,' Floss says, and takes his hand. She presses her finger to his, like a seal to wax. 'There. That's a promise.'

Afterwards, when the knife is hidden, after they have climbed out of the attics' dark, into the cold blue steel of the evening, Floss talks and talks. Jem is glad about the knife, then, seeing how happy it has made her.

'Making things up,' she says. 'That's what you like doing. You should make up things for people.'

'Like games.'

'Or stories, you're good at those too. I could be a famous writer and you could write my books. Or lies! You could lie for stupid people.'

'No, I wouldn't want to do that,' Jem says.

'Why? You'd be doing them a favour.'

Only days later, too late, does he think to ask what the promise was.

★

'Mrs Lockhart,' says the well-fed man, his hat already in his hands. 'Sorry to call late. You're looking well. Is your husband – ?'

'He might be,' Mary says.

She has never liked Cyril Noakes. Now – as he runs his eyes over her – she likes him less than ever. She could do without Cyril tonight.

'Well, if he is, may I – ?' Cyril asks, and Mary takes the bar of her arm from the door.

Michael is in the kitchen, but she gets him up and puts them in the front room: Cyril is company, and besides, Mary is glad to have space to herself. These last two days Michael has been hard to bear, too grim and so bleak: so grim that the girls have become wide-eyed around him; so bleak that Mary is almost afraid for him.

She can get nothing out of him. It isn't the business with Annie, that's all done with now. This is more than that, and there's less anger in it. Is she to blame herself? And if not her, then who?

She makes tea for Cyril Noakes.

'Very nice,' Cyril says, peering around when he and Michael are settled. 'I do like a nice front room. Some of the lot who move in now, they just don't make the effort. Not like you, Mickey, you've never been short on endeavour. You've made your own luck. Is that a new stick?'

Michael sits uncomfortably in the unsoftened parlour chair. The new stick leans between his thighs. The other is out of sight, out of mind.

'If it's about the old man,' he begins, but Cyril tuts.

'Don't worry about that. You slipped that one by me, eh? You had me going. But Alan told me all about it. That's nothing to worry about.'

Cyril ducks at his tea. Somewhere upstairs, a wireless or record player sings too brightly.

'Chilly, isn't it?' Cyril says, rubbing his hands. 'We could do with a little fire in here.'

'What is?' Michael asks, and Cyril stares at him.

'You what?'

'What is there to worry about?'

Cyril puts down his cup and saucer. They give an awkward clatter. 'It's Norman,' he says. 'It's, well. Mickey, it's Norman and his missus. Not that she's his missus, she's not that soft ... still, it's her and Norman, that's why I'm here. That and the man, McEachan. You'll have seen about him, in the papers.'

Michael says nothing. He has seen the newspapers; has seen, too, the policemen on the streets. The Millwall man is in a bad way.

'He wasn't meant to be there,' Cyril says. 'Alan told me to tell you that, and he's sorry for it. There wasn't meant to be no trouble. McEachan's alright, mind you, don't believe everything you read – he's got a sweet bump on the head, he's not up to much talking, but he's not as bad as they're making out. It's Nancy who's the worry. That's Norman's missus. They used to be sweet, but not so much since he came home. It's worse when he's on edge, and the things he does for Alan, that puts an edge on things, I'd imagine. Six of one and half a dozen, it always sounds like with them, but six of one from Norman, I wouldn't want to be on the end of that. I don't suppose she does, either. She ended up in hospital this time. They took her in last night, up Bethnal Green Infirmary. She almost lost an eye. She's two boys with him from before. It's always been a nasty business.'

'What's it to me?' Michael asks, and Cyril meets his look and flinches.

'The police have been in with her. I don't know if she asked for them, but they was called. Nancy's been talking, that's what Alan hears. He cares, and you should and all, because this time it sounds like she might have had enough. And Norman talks to her. He tells her things he shouldn't, then he tries to beat it back out of her. And even if he didn't this time, she'll know he was working Tuesday. She'll have read all about it, and she knows the things Norman does. You, well. You know what he does.'

Michael gazes down at the table between them. It's an occasional table, finely inlaid. Mary laughed when he got it. He picked it up for a song in the summer, knowing she would like it, knowing it would tickle her. It was a good deal any way you judged it.

An occasional table! she said. *It sounds a bit high-born for us. What does it do the rest of the time?*

By God, he's tired.

Cyril is reaching into his jacket. He brings out an envelope and puts it down on the table.

'This is from Alan. Something for the job, a bit more to tide you over, and there'll be a cut for you later. Alan means to see you right, you and yours, whatever happens. Meantime, he says to keep your nose down. Go about your business, same as normal, but only the market trade. The boys come to me for now. Your man too. You and me, you and him, we all steer clear of each other.'

'Have they talked to Norman?'

'Not yet.'

'But they will.'

'They might,' Cyril says, 'And Norman Varney's a funny fellow, isn't he? A fucking bunch of giggles. He might keep his mouth shut, he might behave, or he might own up. Christ knows, he might try and pin it all on you, Mickey. Whatever he does, you don't know me, I don't know you, and God help us if we ever did business with Alan. If anyone wants to know where you get your flowers and blades, it's Oscar, and he'll say the same. Oscar's clean. You, me and Alan, we're there for each other afterwards, but for now it's each man for himself. That's how it works. It's for the best. Alright?'

Michael nods. Cyril sighs.

'It's a different way of business, Alan's. He's a harder take on things. I never liked it. I never meant you for that.'

'I knew what we were about.'

'I never said you didn't. I ain't saying you went in blind. I almost wish you had, but I don't take you for an innocent. You might think yourself a hard man, Mickey, but I'm sorry you got mixed up in it.'

Michael nods again, accepting the rebuke, ever so gentle as it is.

'Was it just for the profit?'

'How's that?'

'The fellow, McEachan. Was he something, to Alan?'

Cyril shakes his head. 'If he wasn't before, he is now. Get some rest,' he says, then stands, his voice rising. 'Thank your lovely wife for the tea. It was good to see you, Mickey. Look out for yourself, won't you? Onwards and upwards, that's the way. Never mind the downs, and we'll all meet up at the top.'

★

£1,200 GOLD ROBBERY

MAN GRAVELY INJURED

A man who entered the premises of J. G. McEachan and Brothers, metalworkers and brokers, in Marshfield Way, Millwall, late on Tuesday, attacked the owner, Mr. McEachan, with a stick, and having forced Mr. McEachan to open a safe, stole silver bars and gold wire valued at £1,200.

Mr. McEachan, 64, a widower, was asleep on his premises when he was woken by a noise. He confronted an intruder who struck him with the stick and demanded the safe box be opened. Having complied, Mr. McEachan was struck several more times and lost consciousness, not being discovered until the following afternoon, when he was taken to hospital with grave head injuries. On Thursday Mr. McEachan was able to speak briefly, and the police were called, but his condition has worsened since.

Police are pursuing other lines of investigation. A van has been impounded by police officers at an auction mart in the East End where second-hand cars are sold. In addition to the attacker of Mr. McEachan, a second man, the driver of the van, is being sought for questioning.

★

'Found your name yet, have you?'

'My dad wants to call me Henry.'

'I thought you'd lost him and all, your dad.'

'I've a new one now.'

'That's right, the watchmaker. Good news gets around, you see? And we keep our ears to the ground. Bible name, isn't it?'

'Lazarus.'

'Lazarus, raised from the dead. Funny, the names people end up with. Funny old thing to lose at that, a name. Still, all kinds of things get mislaid, when there's a war on. People, too.'

'Yes.'

'You've scrubbed up well, at any rate.'

'I have to wash all the time.'

'I should think so. Don't forget behind your ears. Where you living now, then, Henry?'

'I'm not Henry yet. I'm up there.'

'The Columbia Buildings, is it? I always liked them, handsome things. It's a shame the bombing got into them. Come back here in ten years, this'll all be gone, lock, stock. That's what the depot yard's for – knocking it down, building it up. It'll all be concrete a mile high, and all of us buried in it. How are your neighbours? Making friends, are we?'

'Yes. Iris, Floss and Jem.'

'Floss Lockhart, that would be. You'll know her father, then?'

'Yes.'

'And how is he?'

Silence. Almost silence. Far away, someone is out playing. It's hard to tell the game from here. It could be almost anything, Bulldog or Grandmother's Footsteps, Robbers or Kiss Chase or It.

'He's not my friend.'

'Well, no. He's a bit big for the likes of you.'

'He's nobody's friend. He shouted at Floss.'

'I'm sure he did. She takes keeping in line, I hear.'

'He's got a new stick.'

'Has he?'

'I liked the old one better.'

'What was wrong with the old one?'

'I don't know. It had a horse on it. It was a good stick.'

★

Sunday, they come for him.

It's Alfred Shrew who sees them first. Business is good, the best in weeks – even those who should know better forget their thriftiness for Christmas – and the police make slow headway through the throng: big men muffled in heavy cloth, four of them, six of them, with Dick Wise in the vanguard, shepherding through the crowd.

'Heads up,' Alfred says, and Michael follows his gaze, lays down the holly in his hands, collects his stick and steps back through his firs like an actor into the wings.

At the arch of the Buildings he looks back. The police are out of sight. By the Birdcage he glimpses their van – a Black Maria, as if he's as good as a prisoner already – and playing by it, his younger one and the orphan boy, in amongst their friends. There is snow in Iris's mittens, snow in her hair. She is pretty as the mother she has always taken after.

He turns, loses his footing as the bad leg takes his weight, rights himself. Useless body! Already he is panting. Where is he going? He wants Mary, but she's no good to him now, nor is he any good to anyone. Go anywhere, he thinks, but not to those you care for most.

He makes it to the car. The handle is ice, snow has climbed the wheels, but there's petrol in the tank and a can in the boot. I'll start north, he thinks: Start now and think about stopping later. His hands are clammy, they work slipshod at the starter, but luck's on his side, the engine fires . . . and there, now, are the police, coming on in ones and twos, shadows in the arch.

'Oh no, you don't,' Michael whispers. 'You can't have the likes of me, you bastards.'

The wheels slip. They grip. The car brushes a man – strikes him a glancing blow; there is a yell, the thump of a greatcoated shoulder – then he is through, and the market all around him.

A whistle starts up its shrill screaming. Michael wrestles the wheel, veers around the frozen water fountain. The car fishtails, corrects. Faces – hundreds, it seems – turn to him, pale flowers to his sun.

Faster! The car balks, jerks, mounts the pavement. There are shoppers idling even behind the stalls. What's he saying? Something, something. *Get out of it, blast you! Out of it!* Punters shout catcalls, cheer and pull, shove and scatter. The crowd is on his side – everyone in Shoreditch loves an underdog. Laughing Boy is there beside him, an old man in dapper clothes, thumping the roof. 'Go on, my son!' he's bellowing, 'you lead them a merry dance!'

Now he's almost clear – oh, he's so nearly free. It is so close and so dear to him that he groans aloud through clenched teeth. The whistles are falling behind him. He guns the engine, risks a glance in the mirror, sees the Black Maria still unmoving on the corner.

When he looks ahead again the dark woman is in his path.

She is stopped on the pavement, one arm bent to her hip. She is looking directly at him. Her man is in the road beside her. He is at the last stall, buying flowers from Rob Tull – Christmas roses, wrapped in newspaper. They are all done up in their Sunday best,

Clarence and Bernadette, as if they have just been to church, though it is not church they come from.

Her eyes are wide. Her smile of pain has had no time to fade. Michael turns the wheel. The tyres slip. This time there is no correction.

When he opens his eyes he is alone. His hands still grip the wheel: he can feel the pulse in his fingertips. He sways in the dusty hush. It seems to him that he feels the collision only now, after the fact: the force of it shudders through him.

The crowds are drawing closer, though they no longer have eyes for him. They are gathering beside him, by a figure who lies doubled in the gutter. Policemen are ushering them back. Dick Wise is calling out to them, *Gentlemen, is there a doctor here? Hallo?*

A man begins to howl. Another asks to be let through. Iris is there, her face milk-white, her hand in the orphan boy's. Clarence is down on his knees. His hands are fluttering, patting, stroking. He is calling his wife's name as if she isn't there.

She is, still. Bernadette looks up at her man. She says, 'My baby. Oh Lord, Clarence, Sybil, my baby.'

Does she think she has lost her child? Is it a blessing that she is wrong? She is wrong. It is Sybil who will be saved. The baby – who, inasmuch as she has ever wanted anything, has never wanted to go anywhere – will be delivered, will go on. It is her mother who is dying. Even now, as Clarence smooths her face and hair, the life that has come so far is running out of Bernadette. It is leaving her in pieces, with her words, with her breath, without it.

★

1968
(THE COLLISIONS)

1. FLORENCE IN JUNE

Swimming pool colours: turquoise, azure, iridium. The shadows of ripples on the tiles, all tiger-band and giraffe-skin, their patterns gelling and rescinding in perpetual slow motion.

Florence floats, sun in her face. Her eyes are shut, spangled with lash-drops. The light still feeds into her, creeping through her lids, entering into her mind in blooms of magenta.

Oh, she thinks, you *pretty* world.

The lilo bobs: it starts to move. Florence shades her eyes and peers along her length with the hauteur of a popstar. Terence is towing her in. He frog-squats at the poolside, inscrutable in sunglasses. He lays a hand on her.

'You're hot,' he says, and Florence flexes.

'Sizzling,' she murmurs.

'Take care, baby. You don't want to burn.'

'I might,' she says. 'You don't know. I might want to try everything once, anything, even burning.'

'You're nuts,' Terence says.

Florence reaches for his sunglasses. 'Take them off.'

'What for?'

'I want to see your eyes.'

They have crow's-feet, Terence's eyes. They are warm, amused, potentially cruel. Florence likes them. Too often they are hidden behind lenses. Terence has English knees, thinning hair, a sparrow chest puffed up with curls. His eyes are the best bit of him.

'Come in the water. Play with me,' she says; but Terence stands.

'Not now, I'm going to make a run into town. You want anything?'

'You're dull,' she says.

He pauses above her, a small man towering against a faded denim sky. 'Anything?'

But Florence doesn't answer. She pushes off from the poolside. She stretches, tigerish herself. The lilo lulls her. Anything, she thinks. I can have anything, *anything*.

After he's gone she pads inside in search of cigarettes. She sits on the steps, under the trees, and watches the hand-span butterflies that float down to the rocks and model themselves in the sunlight she slowly shafts with smoke.

Terence is fun. They won't last. He's not her husband, it's not her pool. Both are as good as hers for now, but she's always been better at the finding than the keeping. When Terence is over (which might be sooner rather than later; his wife is busy mending bridges), Florence will find someone else, someone else with somewhere else where she can bask and float.

Terence is a photographer, the kind who has become as celebrated as the celebrities he shoots: the kind who invests in property, in London and here in the sun. He works mainly with women, likes women more than men, admires and flatters them, and makes a point of making love to them. Not only for the pleasure but because he wants the moment after. Florence has given him that. Having given it, she suspects he lives for that more than anything: the shutter-capture of the instant when all the guards are down, when the eyes lie open.

She finishes her drink and swims a dozen dutiful lengths before collapsing back onto the lilo. She's thirty but looks younger.

She thinks of property. She owns nowhere herself. Terence won't even tell her how many places he has. It isn't shyness or modesty, but a sure reticence she supposes comes with power. All week he's been on the phone to London. He has problems with squatters in Camden. Possession is nine-tenths of the law: that, Terence says, is just the problem.

Florence trails pool water through her fingers, willing it hers, possessing it.

It won't work. Never mind – easy go, easy come. She should leave soon, she thinks. Better to resist temptation and go while she's still wanted, while there's nothing more complicated than a honeymoonish summer to remember. She has been here since the start of June and now the month is almost out. She'll give it one more week. And then?

And then she'll be free again. Chain-free, Terence would say. She'll be scot-free and clean away.

A voice speaks in her head. It mutters up out of nothing.

Dirty as a coal miner.

This is how it happens with her. A memory will eel through her, slick, dark, muscular. This time all Florence grasps are the words, the fierceness they once inspired, and a tangle of things which are all of a piece: a ghost, an orphan boy, a black pit in a ruined world. Her mother, calling her in.

Floss?

She shivers in the heat. It's not often, now, that anyone calls her that. It's been a long time since anyone called her home. How far is

Florence from those things, here, how many years and miles? Tens and hundreds and not enough. Her childhood is out of sight, but her mind won't relinquish it.

More miles, those are what she needs. It has worked for Terence and it will for her. Keep clocking up the years and miles, keep chasing the sun, and one day she must wake to find she's left Columbia Road behind, and the girl's name with it. And the girl.

'Don't worry about it.'

'I don't worry,' Floss says, 'I just don't like it. I don't want to be remembering all that, growing up. What's the point?'

'Suit yourself.'

'It's got nothing to do with me.'

'Course it does.'

'It doesn't. I've changed. I mean, no, I *haven't* – that's what I mean. It's not just that I'm here, it's that I never belonged there. This was what I was always meant for. This, you know, somewhere like this.'

The cicadas begin, one joining one joining many. Terence goes to the kitchen counter. He starts to cook as he unpacks, taking only what he needs – eggs, smoked meat, white cheese, green leaves – unhurriedly, efficiently.

'You might never have got this far,' he says, when the eggs are going, 'if you hadn't started there.'

'That's rubbish. Sentimental hippy tosh. Either you've got it or you haven't. It's nothing to do with anyone else, or anything. It's *you*. You know what I mean. You're the same. You didn't need to live like crap to know you were meant for better. Did you?'

'Dunno,' Terence says, tasting a finger. 'I don't remember.'

'Exactly!' Florence cries. 'Exactly my point.'

He brings the food. It's not half bad. Terence cooks only three things – egg and chips, omelette, and beef and onions – but he does them well, and Florence has nothing to do with kitchens if she can help it.

'Anyway,' he says, once they've put away the omelette and only the token salad remains, 'you've scrubbed up well, haven't you, Little Miss Coal Miner? I'll give you that.'

'Fuck off.'

'Come here.'

'You dirty Bow Street bastard.'

'Come here,' he says, and she does.

There is a dream she has sometimes. In it her body is transformed. It has no shape or orifice. It becomes a hairless, sealed thing. Her new body floats in a sea so proximate to blood heat she can hardly feel it.

Nothing else happens in this dream. It doesn't go anywhere. And Florence doesn't mind it – there is even an easefulness to it – but it puzzles her. That smooth sexlessness. That has nothing to do with her: that too.

Terence prefers the beach.

'It's loony. You've got a pool like that, what do you want with this?'

Still breathing hard from the sea he throws himself down (all knuckles and knees), towels off his hair (what there is of it), and frowns down the strand, as if he's trying to square his view of it with her dismissal. He shrugs.

'I like it,' he says.

Florence needles him. 'You just like being recognised. It's an ego trip, isn't it? I think you get off on it.'

It's not true and they both know it. Terence enjoys his fame, but he has retained a photographer's gift for imperceptibility. He takes pleasure and a boyish pride in that. In London, in company, Florence has seen him switch on his famous self like a flash bulb. He dazzles, then; but not now. Here and now he is – as he prefers – a watcher in a candid world.

This place of his is on Corfu, and the island suits him. Few here know or care what Terence is elsewhere. He is one of several moneyed foreign owners of one of several bespoke villas concealed in the hills beyond a west coast fishing village. Most local interest in him stops there, and tourists are still rare beyond Corfu Town. Today the two of them share the beach with a yacht's-worth of Italians, two quiet Americans, a handful of young Corfiots, and a mad dog-pack of village boys who duck and chase along the rocks and up to the quay, where they leap in slapstick postures into the all-consuming sea.

(Nor is Florence recognised herself. There was a time she might have been, for a season or two, years ago, when her spritely face and form were sought after by the fashionable magazines. No one here would know her now. She misses it.)

'I've been thinking,' she says. 'I should be getting home.'

Terence squints at her. 'Don't be silly. What for?'

'For fun. A bit more town, a bit less country.'

'You should have said, if you felt like that. I thought you *were* having fun. You're sure?'

'Quite sure. Besides, I don't want you waking up one day and realising you don't want me here.'

'I want you here,' Terence says. 'There's nothing to realise.'

Florence says nothing. It surprises her, that her leaving gets under his skin. She lies back in the sun and enjoys the fact of it.

'It's a shame,' Terence says. 'I've got to clear off in a fortnight. You could've had the place to yourself.'

'You didn't tell me that.'

'Didn't know. Only heard the other night.'

'Where are you going?'

'The States. I didn't think you'd mind,' he says; but he has seen that she does, and Florence stiffens. *Take me with you*, she'd like to say, but it's too needful and she bites it back.

'Over the Pond and far away. Lucky you. I should still go, I'd die of boredom out here on my own.'

'Suit yourself.'

'You always say that, and I always do.'

He stretches out, propping his head on the lunch hamper. I could have stayed, she thinks. Oh well. It's true about the boredom.

She can feel him still watching her, lazily composing her. For him, Florence looks out to sea. Somewhere out there is Italy, one of the few countries she's been, years ago, on a shoot. Most of the world she only knows from pictures. She can see Italy now ... but no she can't, she's wrong. There's nothing there but clouds.

'You should try to be less English,' Terence says, and Florence breaks her pose.

'What's that supposed to mean?'

'Stop worrying what other people think. A woman like you doesn't need to. You're beautiful, Flo.'

'I know,' Florence says, 'and I don't. Anyway, you're English too, and you're not even half pretty. You should be the one who's worrying.'

'Yeah, but I'm not, am I?'

Hoots of laughter reach them. Terence's eyes drift away from Florence. The Italians are playing football, the diffident girls in flotsam goals, the boys striving to reach them. Terence sits up, opens the hamper. He takes out his cigarettes and then, more stealthily, a camera. He lights up without taking his eyes off the Italians.

'I like it,' he says again, softly, and trains the lens.

On her last night on the island they go for dinner at a friend's. The friend is Terence's, of course (Florence knowing no one here, any more than they know her), an American half-Scot, the founder-owner of a transatlantic publishing house.

Like Terence's own villa, that of the publisher is freshly built along the lines of an old Corfiot mansion, on the smaller ruins of which it stands and from which it takes its bearings and, here and there, a stone that still carries the trace of some broken relief or pattern. The older guests are in the lounge with drinks, the younger by the poolside. Florence opts for the terrace, where the generations mingle and there is a predominance of men, a group of them gravitating to the publisher himself. Florence likes male company. She is more at home with the other sex than with her own: in that, as in their beginnings, she and Terence are alike.

The men are all more or less famous. The publisher is a deft host, approaching seventy and unconvincingly retired; brisk but soft-spoken, in the manner of one used to being listened to. The younger men around him are drawn out of themselves: in their efforts to perform, their small talk exhausts itself and moves on to greater things.

'You've had protests in London, too?' an American film actor asks of an English oarsman.

'So we claim. Pretty weak tea, I'm afraid – we're not much when it comes to revolution.'

'Why be afraid? It's not like you need revolting.'

'But we don't like to be outplayed. The Continentals put on

such a show . . . all those barricades! They've shown us up, you see. These days we feel rather as if we're acquiring the losing habit. Football aside. And war, of course.'

'Perhaps it is a war,' the actor says, and an older woman at the edge of things rattles a cough of irritation.

'It's not a war, nothing like. Be glad you're too young to know the difference.'

'Tell it to the Vietnamese,' the actor says, tartly, but the oarsman is quick to smooth things over.

'It's not a *world* war, to be fair.'

'I don't know,' the actor says. 'The whole world seems to be going crazy, these days. I don't know where we're sailing, but I don't like the cut of our jib. And don't tell me London doesn't have its share of crazies, I've seen them.'

'Oh, we do, but ours are harmless. They're not *doers*, like yours. Our crazies don't knock people off. They're even worse at shooting than they are at shouting. We're not much cop at assassination.'

'Character assassination,' the actor mutters. 'I've read your critics, you're plenty good at that.'

The publisher stirs. 'Speaking of the devil, there's something I might show you. Entertain yourselves,' he says, and goes inside, reappearing soon enough with a thin cyan folder. He holds it low down against his thigh, like something best kept inconspicuous.

'That looks devilish, alright,' the oarsman says. 'What is it, the next *Lady Chatterley*?'

'It's a Verifax,' the publisher says, 'of the diary of Sirhan Sirhan.'

'You're *kidding*,' the actor says. 'May I – ?'

'Who's this Sirhan fellow?'

'The psycho who shot Bobby K. How did you get this already? Is it for real?'

'So I'm reliably informed.'

The actor exclaims as he reads. Florence is closest to him when he offers up the folder. She takes it out of politeness, angles its pages to a lantern, and reads:

> my determination to ~~eliminatee~~ eliminate R.F.K. is becoming more the more of an unshakable obsession.

> please pay to the order
> plea
>   port wine
>   port wine
> port wine
>   port wine

> R.F.K. must die. R.F.K. must be killed. Robert F. Kennedy must be assassinated. R.F.K. must be assassinated assassinated ~~as~~. Robert F. Kennedy Robert F. Kennedy, Robert F. Kennedy must be assassinated assassinated. I have never heard

> please pay to the order of of of of of of of of of of of of this or that –

'What do you think?' the publisher asks, and Florence is jolted up to find him watching her, much as Terence does. For once she doesn't like it.

'It's horrible.'

The publisher nods. 'I agree. But interesting.'

'It's not right,' she says, 'reading it. You shouldn't have it. You should burn it.'

'Perhaps,' the publisher says. 'Or perhaps I should publish it. There's a sense of the zeitgeist about it.'

'It's sick,' Florence says, her voice too sharp, too real for this company: even to her, it isn't clear whether she means their reading of the thing or the thing itself. Her hands are shaking.

'Take it, I don't want it,' she says, and the oarsman cocks a brow as he takes the folder from her. The older woman clears her throat and lights another Dunhill. Terence is suddenly there among them.

'You alright?' he asks; but before Florence can fake an answer the staff are coming out to usher them in for dinner.

She is placed some way from Terence, between an Egyptian novelist and his much younger French wife, who is a poet. The conversation shrinks again to small talk of the world of letters. Florence lets it pass over her.

The food comes all at once and keeps coming, gobbets and dollops of foreign stuff on pretty plates and stupid rustic platters. Florence is eating too much, she knows, more than she wants or needs, in an effort to think of something other than the publisher's folder. The malice in it has jarred her. It's not part of her world, that violent incantation, not part of this world she adores and has made her own. It makes her angry, that the publisher would bring the folder into it. The folder is an imposter.

Florence looks at her hands and out at the dusk. She can see trees on the hill lines – the strange tall ones that are like the columns of mossy ruins – and the lights of Perama coming on below, and other lights beyond them, fishing boats rocking out to sea, twinkling like evening stars.

Look, she thinks. Look at how beautiful it is! Don't you know how lucky we are? Don't you remember how much work it took to get here? Why bring ugliness into it? Isn't there enough wrong with the world? Aren't you satisfied with that? Leave bloodiness where it belongs; it's *easy*. Just have some faith in beauty. Just be grateful for what you've earned. Be happy to be lucky.

Laughter erupts around her, and she pulls herself together. She has missed some splendid joke. Beside her the Egyptian smokes as he eats, small raisin-dark cigars. As she studies him he meets her eye and smiles.

'You must find this dull,' he says, 'all this talk of books.'

'Oh,' Florence says, 'I bore easily.'

'You are with the photographer?' he asks, and she bristles.

'I don't see why you should put it like that. I don't see why I need to be here with anyone.'

'I did not mean –' the Egyptian begins, but Florence won't have it.

'You mean I'm not famous. You haven't heard of me, so I must be some kind of hanger-on.'

'No, I apologise, I meant no such thing. In fact I have heard of you.'

'Oh, don't.'

'It's true, we have met before. We were not properly introduced, Miss Lockhart, but indeed I do remember you. You were being photographed in one of the hotels in London. We met in an elevator . . . this was some years ago. I forget the hotel.'

But not me, Florence thinks, and for the first time all night her heart lifts with unadulterated pleasure.

She looks up at the novelist. He has a gentle, craggy face. The gentleness might make him handsome, though it's hard to tell in the lamplight, which romanticises everyone.

'Lifts,' she says. 'We call them lifts. We don't have elevators in London.'

'Lifts,' the Egyptian happily concedes. 'You must excuse me, but now that we meet again, I would very much like you *not* to dislike my company, yes? May I tell you something? It is an anecdote about elevators. Lifts! I hope to be amusing.'

Florence relents. She wants to be spoiled. 'Well go on, then,' she says.

'So I will tell you now about the lifts of Cairo, the lifts of the Hotel Shepherd. The Shepherd is magnificent, truly, second in Egypt only to the Winter Palace in Luxor. In this hotel are ten lifts, with ten lift men, in robes and turbans. You might say the work of these lift men is not rewarding, but in fact it matters. Of course it is prohibited for a guest to use a lift without its man. So, it matters for the guests. Then there are ten families, living on the *baksheesh*, the tips that come from those ten moving boxes. And, if you spoke Arabic, and if you gave *baksheesh*, very soon you would have the many stories of those men, their children and ancestors.

'The lifts, they are also grand, also very old. Wooden, made in Leeds, in your England. Often, every few journeys, one of them breaks down. Sometimes they stop between the floors. Then the lift man opens a kind of a hatch in the side of the box, and shouts down *Five* or *Six*. That is the name of his lift. And then up comes a second lift, with its man, beside the first, and you crawl through the hatches, from *Six* to *Seven*. So you continue on your way. This activity is happening *all the time*.'

The publisher's daughter-in-law laughs. She is listening to the Egyptian, as are some others, Terence among them. The woman next to Terence has a hand under the table, slanted towards his knee or lap. They all wait idly on the Egyptian's amusing anecdote. A pang goes through Florence, sharp and sweet, of jealousy and want.

'I don't believe you,' she says. 'You're making it up. Anyway, what does it matter? Don't you have stairs in Egypt?'

'Yes, we have stairs too, of course, but in the Hotel Shepherd there are nine floors. A long climb, and Cairo is hot, and the stories of the lift men, sometimes they are sensational. And also, yes, I must tell you ... As it happens, there are strict controls on the women there. You see, the lift men of the Shepherd, they will admit only wives. From the ground up to the eighth floor, when they open their doors, they ask the women for their passports, for their identifications. But when they open their doors on the ninth floor . . .'

Mild laughter on the evening breeze. The Egyptian waves his hand, blowing – *hoof! hoof!* – on his fingertips, as if they have caught alight from the little cigar he holds.

Florence nods a brittle thanks. She takes her chance and turns away. The Egyptian's wife is there, ready for her with a smile.

'My husband loves telling stories,' she says, apologetically. 'He is always trying to make people happy.'

'I was happy to begin with,' Florence says.

'Your name is Florence? A pretty name. It doesn't sound English.'

'Should I take that as a compliment?'

'Oh,' the wife says, 'perhaps. What do you do, Florence?'

'I used to model.'

The wife of the Egyptian nods, as if that much is obvious. 'And now?'

And now Florence says nothing, having nothing to answer.

Terence drives her to the airport. It's a sunstruck morning. Neither of them are morning people, even on those days when they don't nurse hangovers. Light flickers through the cypresses. They're both wearing sunglasses.

'Penny for your thoughts,' Terence says, and Florence grins into the wind, holding onto her headscarf: Terence has the roof down.

'What kind of cheap mind do you think I have? For my thoughts I'll take a ticket to London, and I'll still be doing you a favour.'

'Done.'

'I was thinking of last night. Your friend the publisher.'

'Did you like him?'

'Not much. He had this folder . . .'

'I saw. He's always pulling numbers like that. Still gets a kick out of it, showing off his latest finds. What was it?'

'The diary of some nutcase. It wasn't nice, I didn't think. You didn't read it?'

'I didn't have the privilege. He must have liked you. What wasn't nice about it?'

They turn a hairpin, barely slowing. The sea lies below them in a gulf of shadow.

'Oh,' Florence sighs, 'I don't know! Nothing really, it was just words, words. It might have been just me, no one else seemed to mind it. I don't either, today. It's hard to go on minding, isn't it, when it's so lovely here?'

There is building going on at the airport. They stand in the lee of the old passenger station, out of the light and dust. A Comet waits on a runway that juts out into the sea. Three old warplanes are lined up beyond the jet, dwarfed by it but still powerful, crouched in the sun like hounds.

Terence holds her. 'Well, here we are. Take care of yourself, Flo, won't you?'

'How do I look?'

'Knockout. You don't need me to tell you that.'

'It doesn't cost you anything.'

'Blimey, you're not crying on me, are you?'

'Don't be silly,' Florence says, but she winces, takes off her sunglasses, chuckles. 'There's actually something in my eye.'

'Shoreditch coal dust, probably.'

'Get lost.'

'Muck. There's no getting away from it.'

'Bastard. Honestly you are. When are you coming home?'

He hesitates. 'I don't know. I was thinking I might try it on with the Yanks for a while, see if I can make a splash. You only live once, don't you?'

Florence laughs. She kisses him, releasing herself. 'There's no getting away from it. Good luck,' she says, and starts towards the new station.

★

London is wet and grey, a mockery of itself. As she nears home the rain hardens, knuckling down into the byways and the Tottenham Court Road, crizzling down the windows, drumming off the dustbins.

Her flat is in Percy Street, two floors above Sieghart the Jewellers: three rooms, one of them good, in a handsome Georgian house, and the street itself not all bad, either, with a shabby Fitzrovian glamour, and only once or twice each block a building derelict since the war.

Wolf-whistles from the men sheltering by the City Tote. 'Haven't I seen you on the telly?' one calls out, and his mate, 'Can I do your washing for a month?'

'I'd rather stink,' Florence calls back, and the men chortle to one another, chuffed just to have an answer.

She climbs the dog-leg stairs, humping her case after her. She unlocks the door, goes to the window, lights a cigarette, and peers out – breath on wet glass – across the scaffolds and chimneypots and mansard roofs of the West End, her West End, as if she is anchoring herself.

She loves this view, for all its greyness. It's as much as she can afford; more, if she's honest, which often she is not, and most often with herself. No work and all play makes Florence a poor girl. Her last two jobs – small-change gigs, for hands and eyes – came over a year ago. She lives here by the grace of others, by virtue of their favours. She takes what she's given, and there is always someone wanting to give Florence something. Look at Terence. Look at her father, who sends her money twice a year, birthday and Christmas, his postal order always accompanied by a letter. Florence used to send them back, letter and order, when she could still afford that anger.

And even so, her savings dwindle. One day they'll run out ... and the Terences? Will they run too? The thought fills her with such fear that Florence never lets it occur.

Small things, each in its place: she scavenges shillings, feeds the meter, runs the bath, scrubs herself clean of the sheen and smell of transit, her hair a slick bright rope of blonde. She boils the kettle (no milk, but sugar) and picks fresh clothes (a gypsy print, Ossie Clark, given to her years ago when the makers still gave her things, warm and worn enough to be a house dress now: she hasn't changed her size). She carries her tea downstairs to borrow milk and fetch her post.

'You get so much!' says Mr Sieghart, 'and not just bills, there's invitations too. RSVPs on the envelopes. All kinds of places! Hotels! Not that I mean to look, but I can't help seeing. Well, it just looks such fun, all of it.'

'Thanks,' Florence says. '... Milk?'

'Oh yes. Hang on,' the jeweller says, and fetches a bottle from the back. 'Shall I just ... shall I be mother?'

Skinflint, Florence thinks, but she likes her landlord, lonely dirty old man that he is, and she does what she can (within reason) to stay on the right side of him. The world would be a harder place for a girl like her without men like him.

'Mother away,' she says, and he does, topping up her cup, frowning in concentration, as if he's setting diamonds.

'There,' he says, 'that's the ticket. I can't drink it black myself, can't drink milk straight either. It's just one of those things, isn't it? One's no good without the other.'

Caledonian Land
and its directors, Mr Hilary Chance and Mr William
N.J. Steele
request the pleasure of the company of
Miss Florence Lockhart
at its
Summer Dinner
in the Palace Suite
Royal Garden Hotel, Kensington High St., W.8.
on Saturday, 15th June, at 7.30 p.m. for 8.00 p.m.

Evening Dress   *R.S.V.P.*

There are other invitations. There are others for tonight, it being a summer Saturday – one for a mime performance, one for a film launch supper party – and the dinner isn't promising, even if they'll still seat her. Florence vaguely remembers a Hilary Chance, a beer-flushed business boy with no talk except of himself and nothing of that worth recalling. She knows this hotel, too: it isn't the Savoy. And Kensington is alright, but it's a trog from here in any weather.

She'll go anyway, if they'll have her. The mime is too hippy (*Pierrot in Turquoise Will Welcome Your Presence at Gandalf's Garden Benefit*: why is she sent this stuff? What does it even *mean*?), and a film launch supper is bits on sticks; it isn't dinner. Dinner is worth shifting for, with nothing in the house but cold tea and a dash of milk. Florence checks the time, weighs the card, dials the number.

She takes the Underground. She wears raw silk, bone-white, boat necked, sleeveless, thigh length, belted with a black vinyl leash.

White vinyl Courrèges slit boots. A slender velvet choker. She wears her hair up.

The clothes don't make her beautiful: Florence is that regardless. Even so, they change her. She believes in them, and so the clothes are more than physically worn. They are in her mind. Dressed, she is twenty-four again, pure gold; twenty-one and going places; eighteen and on the up, the past dwindling behind her. She lifts her chin as she crosses St Giles's. Her look is poised at the midpoint between arrogance and desire. She is her father's daughter. Oh, she is Michael's daughter, to the bone.

And someone is watching her.

She has no inkling. She buys her ticket and descends the stairs and dirty escalators of Tottenham Court Road Underground. If someone follows her – jostling, to keep her in sight – he is only one of many, leading and trailing and surrounding Florence as she makes her way towards the westbound Central line. She is too composed to notice much of anyone else, and any sense of being watched is lost in a general consciousness of eyes – the many eyes of London, taking her in, lingering and then drawn away and on.

Now she has nearly reached the platforms. She is in the last crosstunnel, checking the maps on the wall, when there is a brief disturbance on the stairs behind her.

'I said stop that shoving, won't you?' a man says, his voice raised to another, and as the other answers Florence looks back and meets his eyes.

It's only for a moment. Before a second is out she is looking back at the maps, but she is aware of him now. She is being followed. The certainty is like a pressure, like the change in the air which fore-shadows the arrival of an Underground train.

Florence steels herself. She risks a second glance. The man has stepped back upwards, and as he sees her turn he ducks into the stair-raked crowd. He's too lanky for those around him to be much of a hiding place. Florence has an impression of dark skin, wide eyes, a look of hunger that is all about her – but she doesn't want to meet that gaze again, and she turns away.

She thinks, Let him look. Let him look, it does no harm. Let him try more than that and he'll find out what she's made of. She strides out onto the platform.

She doesn't have long to wait for the train. Already the air is moving, pushing in out of the dark. Florence edges down the platform through tangles and knots of crowd. Only when the train is there, as it is thundering alongside, does she risk another look back towards the crosstunnel.

There. He is a black man, very tall, and alone. He wears some kind of uniform that means he belongs down here: Underground clothes. He is standing in the thick of the crowd, but there is a space around him – people allow him room – and his face is turned towards Florence. He looks desperate for her. The whites of his eyes catch hers.

(*is that*)

The train doors trundle open. Florence gets on with those around her. A pipe-and-crossword man offers up his seat for her and she takes it without a word. She is only dimly aware of the gesture. Her eyes have lost their proudness now, and

(*was that was it?*)

her composure is forgotten. She stares at nothing. She looks the wrong side of ordinary herself; she has gone pale as her raw silk dress in the electric light.

They come into Oxford Street. The train disgorges and engorges. At the next stop west – almost too late – Florence jumps up and pushes. She gets out – grime on her knuckles – and trots to the crosstunnel, then straight on to the eastbound platform. The tunnel mouth is dead silent.

'Come on,' Florence whispers, 'oh, come on, will you?'

Slowly the air does come. Displaced, it seethes and quickens, and Florence rocks on her go-go soles as the eastbound train pulls in beside her.

She gets off where she started. The Tottenham Court Road platforms are quieter now, as if there has been some general exodus to the dance halls and restaurants four score feet above.

Florence looks left and right. Her heart falls: she's too late; he's gone. Then she remembers – stupid! – that he was never here; he was on the other side, watching her heading west; and she runs to the crosstunnel and through, and looks, and

(*is it?*)

there he is, and it's him.

He is sitting on the furthest bench, hard against the tunnel mouth, head lowered. He is hunched uncomfortably forward, his elbows on his knees, a roll-up gone out in his hand. His face is still turned westwards, towards the tunnel which took Florence away from him.

Her steps echo down the platform. He doesn't look up once, he doesn't see her coming. She stands in front of him, and only then does he rouse himself, and the lines on his face all fall away into amazement.

'Floss?' he asks, but Florence shakes her head.

'Say it. Say it's you. Go on!'

And he wipes at his mouth. He stands up and he does. 'It's me,' he says, as soft and nervous as he ever was. 'It's Jem.'

They sit side by side, him in his steel-capped boots, her in her shining clothes. A train comes and goes. Jem is smiling and then is not. Neither of them says anything until, finally, Jem does.

'I knew it was you. Soon as I saw you. You haven't changed,' he says, and Florence looks down at herself.

'No.'

Jem hesitates. 'What's wrong?'

'Nothing,' Florence says. 'It's just a shock, that's all.'

'Yeah. You look really good.'

'Thanks.'

'Your clothes are nice. You're all dressed up.'

'Oh.'

'You're going somewhere, isn't it?'

'Yes . . . look, do you have the time?' she asks, but Jem doesn't. 'I think I must be late,' she says.

'You better go, then,' he says, and Florence looks at him, hearing the crestfallenness in his voice.

'I don't have to. It wasn't anything, I didn't even want to go, it was just dinner.'

'Dinner's alright. You better.'

'No, it doesn't matter. I'm not hungry now.'

Jem shrugs. Another train is coming. They wait for it to leave.

'I could take you,' he says. 'I could buy you dinner.'

Florence laughs. 'Oh no,' she says, 'no.'

'I was going anyway, I done my shift. You could just come with me. You don't have to eat, even.'

Florence shakes her head. 'Do you eat down here, too?' she asks, and he stares at her and starts to laugh.

It's almost a giggle, his laugh, a boy's *heehee* pitched to the depth of a big man. His laughter is infectious. Florence joins in.

'Of course you don't,' she says. 'I don't know why I said that. I thought there might be a canteen or something. Well I don't know how it is down here! I don't even know what you do. I don't know anything about you now.'

'I could tell you things,' Jem says.

Florence folds her arms. The Underground is greenhouse-warm, as it often is in summer. The air soothes her. She lets out her breath.

'Alright,' she says, and Jem beams.

'Yeah?'

Florence nods. She stands. 'Take me to dinner.'

He takes her to a narrow street not far from her own. He leads her down the basement steps to a plastic tasselled curtain under an unlit sign for *The Coronation Café*. He holds the tassels open for her, holds the chair back for her, and never stops smiling.

'I'll get some food in,' he says. 'You sure you don't want nothing?'

Florence glances around. The basement is strip-lit, bright. On the wall behind the counter three framed pictures hang: the Queen, the Guinness toucan, and a great sunlit street market. The café's customers are few and mostly old. Hers is the only white face, and she is the only woman.

'Chicken's good here,' Jem says, anxiously – he's seen her look, knows what she's seeing – and she nods and smiles for him. 'So chicken, great,' he says, and retreats to the counter.

Florence opens her handbag. She doesn't need to, but it saves her from meeting the eyes of those around her. In with all the rest of it is the invitation:

Evening Dress   *R.S.V.P.*

she reads, and the words are foolish, and their flourishes too, but what she feels is like homesickness.

'I got you pop,' Jem says. 'Or I can ask for water –'

'Pop's fine,' Florence says, and he nods, still anxious. He sets the plates and bottles down, takes off his jacket, sits.

The meat is crusted black. The rice that comes with it is mixed with beans and other things, shreds of pink that Florence doesn't understand. They could be anything. She pushes them round her plate.

'When did you start eating stuff like this?'

Foreign stuff, she means. 'It's just chicken,' Jem says. 'Try it, you'll like it.'

'You don't know what I like.'

'I do. I remember. This is spicy.'

'We didn't have spicy then. We didn't hardly have chicken.'

'Try,' he says, and Florence tries. She makes a so-so face and eats.

'At ours,' Jem says, 'we had this for special. You just never ate with us.'

'Didn't I?'

He laughs. 'What, you don't remember? You eating at ours, that would've been all kinds of trouble. Do you like it?'

She gives up the so-so face. 'Yeah.'

'Really?'

'Really, yes.'

She watches him eat. He is tucking in, enjoying it now he knows she does.

'Do you come here often, then?' she asks, and smirks when he swallows hard. 'I didn't mean it like that.'

'No,' he says. 'Mostly it's another place.'

'You didn't want to take me there?'

'It isn't near. Up Camden way.'

'Is that where you live?'

He nods. 'Work up there most times too. They don't send me down here except when they need cover.'

They order more pop. In the kitchen a radio starts up, tuned to a pirate station, and a woman bawls at it, out of sight but operatic. *'How can I cook if I can't hear myself think? You best get that out of my kitchen before I lose my patience with it.'*

Jem leans close, lowers his voice. 'The other place is better.'

'I like this one,' Florence says, and saying it realises she does. 'We could have gone, though. You could have taken me underground. I bet you could sneak me in for free.'

'I don't think so. Anyway, there's too many people know me up there.'

'Are you married?'

He shakes his head. He isn't looking at her now.

'I didn't want them talking. They'd be talking about you. There are things they say, about women like you. I don't mean —'

'I know what you mean,' Florence says. 'I know what they say.'

'But you're not that kind of woman.'

I'm a woman, she almost answers; but she doesn't. It answers too much. There is only so much they can say, so soon, being who they are. Florence can see the fear in his eyes as he asks, and the hope with it.

'No,' she says, 'I'm not that kind.'

'I had a good time.'

'It wasn't nothing.'

'Jem. I said I liked it.'

'You got a different life now.'

'So?'

'Dressing up nice for dinner.'

'So what?'

He stands in the darkness of the street. His face lies in stark shadow, lined with troubles.

You've grown so tall, she wants to say, and you're still frightened of everything. It's a kind of innocence. But it can't be the whole truth of him, she knows. It can't be true in the ways that matter. She thinks, You must have grown up fast. You must have, after, but I can't remember.

'So, can I see you again?' he asks, and Florence answers.

They meet at cafés. Canteens. Sometimes at a bistro on Great Portland Street where Florence knows the owner. A pub would be cheaper, but few would welcome either of them. Only by virtue of being together might they seek to cancel out or pardon one another, and the truth is, it doesn't work like that. There are words for men like him, and names for women like her.

Jem pays. Florence thinks to, once, but she stops when she sees the expression on his face.

'Who do you see?'

'Skinny waiters, fat businessmen. A floozy who needs to go on a diet.'

'Floss! Boy, you're rough on people.'

'I'm Florence now. And no, I'm honest.'

'I didn't mean here, anyway. I meant from back then.'

'God, no one.'

'Your folks.'

'No. I see Iris sometimes. Ever-so-sensible Iris, in ever-so-sensible suburbia. Or in town, if she's feeling brave.'

'How is she?'

'Thriving. Keeping the family going. We don't have much in common.'

'Just her?'

'Just her.'

'Not your mum and dad.'

'Not if I can help it.'

He doesn't ask her why. They don't speak of that yet. They skirt and skirt around death's flame, but it is always there, a raw, incipient pain.

Fairgrounds are good to them. Fairgrounds at night are best, when the shadows mask them, and the lights of the attractions draw eyes away from them. The thunder of the Saturn Spaceships, the music of the motorcycle speedways and Golden Gallopers drown anything that might be said behind their backs or in their hearing. And the fairground people, with their greasemonkey skins and broken Polari cant, those people let them come and go without a second glance – so long as they pay their money, at least – having seen more otherworldly things than a black man and a white woman gawping at the Wall of Death, or sharing a toffee apple, or wheeling through the sweet dark air over the Kursaal of Southend, or the ponds of Hampstead Heath, or the banks of Battersea.

'I've forgotten loads from back then. You and me and the Buildings.'

'How come?'

'I don't know. It makes me angry, dragging it up. What Dad did,' she says, and there is a bitter taste in her mouth, emetic, as if the chemistry of her feelings has leached into her saliva.

'It was an accident,' he says, as she has known he will.

'It was his fault. He robbed some poor old man. He didn't have to do it, did he? So what happened after, your mum, how is that an accident? It was all his fault. I used to think he was the best thing ever. He never cared about no-one. All he wants is money and the chance to push people around. I wanted to marry a man just like him.'

'I remember.'

'You shouldn't. You don't have to, I mean, if you don't want to. You can just turn your back on it, forget it, that's what people do. We'd go mad otherwise.'

'You didn't forget me.'

'Well, of course I didn't. That's different, you're not the same thing.'

'Why's that, then?'

'Don't fish. Anyway, you wouldn't understand. You go on like you remember everything.'

'Not everything.'

'I do remember some things.'

'You remember the time we found the knife?'

'When?'

'Late on. You found this knife, and you made us promise.'

She scowls at him; though it's hard not to scowl at everything, when you're eating toffee apple. 'You're thinking of someone else. I'm not into promises.'

Jem stops, and she stops with him. His face is a mixture of things, gravity and laughter. 'Florence, you did! You found us this knife, up in the attics, and then ... and then we promised.'

'Alright, I believe you. Thousands wouldn't. I suppose you're going to tell me I promised you'd be my first.'

'What? No!'

'Lucky, you've missed that boat. So what was it, then?'

But what can Jem do but laugh? So he laughs and shakes his head. 'I don't know,' he says, 'you never told me,' and Florence hoots.

'You made a promise and you didn't know what it was? What kind of promise was that?'

'I don't know that either.'

But, *Maybe this*, is what he thinks, in long-surrendered, renewed hope. Maybe it was something like this.

Neither of them can cook for love or money, but anyone can make a picnic. They meet halfway in Regent's Park, or atop Primrose Hill with London laid out at their feet, or by the Serpentine, where the cygnets loot their sandwiches.

'Rascals,' Jem tells them to their faces. He tears off crusts and offers ransoms, minding his fingertips. The cygnets hiss like dragons.

'Ugh,' Florence says. 'Don't feed them, you're making them worse.'

'They're alright.'

'They're rude. Ugly. Not like those white ones out there.'

'Those are the same! These just got some growing left. These are like the teenagers.'

'Get off. Really? No. Go on, what are they, then?'

'Swans! How come you don't know that?'

'Why should I? What do swans do for me? They're still ugly, anyway,' Florence says, and she claps her hands; but the cygnets are already leaving, now the sandwiches are gone. Florence lies back on the grass. She closes her eyes: she basks. When she wakes her head is on Jem's lap. He is stroking her hair.

'You were always clever,' she says. 'You went on to the Grammar, didn't you?'

'Not for long.'

'Why?'

'They hated me. I hated them, leastways. Got out soon as I could. It was better when I was earning. I get time to think, down there.'

'Iris ditched University. She worked like a dog to get in and then she met Harry and that was that.'

'She got kids?'

'Girls. And you used to make up games. You were good at them.'

'I don't do that no more. Don't play games.'

Florence sits up. 'Well, what do you do? I mean when you're not working?'

'I see you.'

'I know that, don't I?'

'I see my old man. My sister. They're both close by. Camden way.'

'What sister?' she asks, and he looks at her.

'Sybil. You don't remember Sybil?'

'I'm sorry.'

'You don't remember nothing.'

'I'm sorry.'

Later, packing away, she asks, 'What's she like?'

'Sparky, like you. Younger than us, different that way. She lives a different kind of life.'

Florence laughs drily. 'Trust me, I've seen all kinds. What does she do?'

'Just now she sells holidays, you know those places? She lives here and there. Anyplace that doesn't cost.'

'Can I meet her?'

Jem shrugs uncomfortably, backed up against the truth. 'She gets angry, you know.'

'You mean about what happened,' she says, and he nods. 'It's going to be hard, isn't it? With our families.'

'Yeah.'

'Eight years,' she says. 'That was how long he was gone, in the end.'

She looks at Jem. He shrugs, but she can see him thinking, turning it over, the time her father served for his mother.

She thinks, I shouldn't watch, it's not my place. But she wants to know what he thinks. Eight years ... was that right or wrong? Was it just, was it sufficient? Is it immaterial? She wishes she could ask. She wants to think that Jem has answers, but he doesn't say anything.

'We could see Iris,' she says, to break the silence. 'She'll be alright. I'll bet she'd love it.'

'I'd like that,' Jem says.

Later still, as he walks her home:

'Stories. There, I remember that. You used to tell me stories.'

'Yeah.'

'Do you still do that?'

'If you like.'

'But you still do them, I mean? For yourself?'

'Yeah,' Jem says, and he presses her hand. 'I still do them.'

The first time they make love. The sheer might of him; the long, dark musculature. The way he lifts her. The wet of his mouth on her tears on her face. The way he lifts her onto him. And when he lays her down. And the beauty of him.

She remembers those things. She takes care of them. She will remember them all for the rest of her life.

2. IRIS IN JULY

When Iris hears the news, her second thought (the first is *!*) is, I shouldn't be surprised. Nothing ventured and much gained; that's how it is for Floss. Nothing nurtured, nothing tended, and the best things in life – the sweetest windfalls – falling into her lap all the same. I mustn't mind, Iris thinks.

She's with Mum when Floss rings. They've been to town, but it's muggy, the weather having turned abruptly seasonable, and their plans for lunch and shops haven't amounted to much. They've come away smelling of Tube, with an unsought haul of brochures, with frustrated appetites and a carrier of frozen foods Iris hardly remembers buying, and for which she ekes out room while Mum makes the tea.

'Sugar ... where've you put it now?' Mary asks, and half to herself, 'Look, here it is. You don't need all this out, do you? You'll fatten the girls if you're not careful. Are you listening, love?'

But Mary's love is on her knees, suppliant before the ice compartment. She grubs old stores out of the rime – Bird's Eye peas, Findus fish fingers. She doesn't mind it, this. It's satisfying, digging, and there's satisfaction, too, in the throwing out of old for new, and in the thunder she makes, which lets her off an answer: for a moment she's absolved from talking to her mother.

Iris thinks, I used to be more patient. Or Mum was easier – one or the other thing, or both. These days, certainly, they find it hard to get on whenever Dad's elsewhere. Still kneeling, it occurs to Iris that they're too much alike, that it comes down to patience either way: her own with all those she cares for, and Mum's with waiting for her man. They are the women who have endured, who have stood with Dad through the years of shame and loneliness, but somehow they need him all the more for that, are querulous without him.

(And where is Michael, anyway? Seeing to business, to properties and tenancies: attending to his realm. These days the firm is legitimate, as much as any business is. There's less grind to it than there was, there being younger hands to take up the slack their seniors leave, but somehow, still, there's never much less time spent away in the company of men, and hardly fewer of the old faces: Wolfowitz may be dead and buried in sodden Shoreditch clay, but Cyril Noakes and Alan Swan are alive and well, each living decently in decent suburbia, each having kept faith with their man Michael through hard times, just as Michael kept faith with them.)

'Tea's made,' Mum says, and Iris mutters thanks, hauls herself up, helps carry. They sit by the new French windows, looking out at Harry's joy, his southern suntrap garden, with its neat beds and sheds and lawn.

'At least we got out cheap,' Mum says, more at ease now the weight's off her feet. 'Dad'll be proud of us.'

Iris smiles for her. 'I don't suppose we needed anything anyway.'

'No, well,' Mum says, 'we've his hard work to thank for that,' and she lights up and starts on the brochures. The first is full of holidays, pages of paradise. 'Look at this, *Rome*. People get born in London and it isn't enough for them. They're all like cats, they don't know where they want to be, in or out. I wouldn't mind that view but Dad wouldn't stand it. I sound old.'

'You don't, Mum. You're not,' Iris says. But the first assurance is a lie, even if the second is true. Her mother sounds as she looks. The sunlight that slants through her smoke finds Mary reduced. She isn't yet fifty, but time is overtaking her. Her health isn't the best. The doctors are talking of tests. The years of waiting have wrung half the life out of her. Mary isn't the woman she once was.

'Floss went to Italy once, remember? I've a picture, look,' Iris says, and she gets the photocube that holds the shot and watches her mother soften and brighten, finding her better-favoured daughter.

'That's lovely of her,' Mum says, but gradually her frown creeps back. She hardly sees Floss, by more or less mutual consent. The few meetings they have go poorly, their talk always turning to Dad. Neither of them can help herself. To Mary it's unthinkable that Floss can go on blaming him, unforgivable that Floss can be so unforgiving, when what he did, he did for them. As if he hasn't been punished enough. As if they haven't all been punished.

Still frowning, Mary turns the cube. 'I don't know why you keep this one. You could have more of family. I never liked that boy one bit. It all went bad after him. What was his name?'

'Pond,' Iris says, and she is reaching for the cube, reclaiming it, when the telephone starts to ring.

They meet in Golders Hill Park, the three of them together for the first time in twenty years.

'You're jealous,' Florence murmurs, and Iris tugs at her cardigan, peering after the gentle stranger Jem has become, in case he hears them talking from his place at the ice cream kiosk.

'Don't be silly. I'm happy for you.'

'Oh, I know you are, you always are. You're the saint of happiness for others. You could be jealous too, though, couldn't you?'

'Well, I'm not. Shush.'

Jem is grinning as he comes back. He has choc ices in his hands. Park-goers and ice cream-queuers look up at his beaming height: this July Saturday he is the Ice Cream King.

'They got all sorts here,' he says cheerily. 'Coming up with funky things now. Butterscotch ripple, Italian flavours.'

'I went to Italy once,' Florence says. 'The food was awful, all grease.'

'I've still got the picture,' Iris says, and her sister crows.

'You haven't!'

'Why not? I like it.'

'I don't even remember what I was doing there.'

'Advertising. They took you to Siena. Come on, you must remember.'

'I'd like to see that,' Jem says.

'You should come, then,' Iris says. 'Come for tea, if you don't mind taking pot luck. You could meet Harry and the girls. Will you?'

'We really have to get back,' Florence says, but Jem is speaking too, more eagerly, and their eyes meet as their voices jar: they have argued this over before, in anticipation of the matter arising, on the way up to Golders Green. 'Oh,' Florence relents, 'alright. Why not? I haven't seen the girls for ages.'

'No, well,' Iris says.

Unwittingly they have begun to walk, across the park's ridge of high ground, towards the bandstand. If you had to pick the older sister you'd pick wrong. Florence could be twenty-one, with her foxy gypsy skirt and her sandals in her hand. And Iris, in her shirtwaist dress and Orlon cardy, with her not-blonde hair, coils of which escape her ears whatever she applies, punctuating her face with mousy brackets or incessant questions . . . Iris is twenty-nine, and could be pushing forty. Two children – neither an easy birth – have slowed her, and slowness has thickened her. Big-built, people call her now, though she never used to be. She seems older than her older sister, and she feels it, and sometimes it seems to her that she always did, as if the past itself could be rewritten by the present.

North and west, London is clear for miles under a mackerel sky. Jem points out Wembley. 'I might bring my old man up here. He'd like it, if I could shift him.'

'Does he take much shifting?' Iris asks, and Jem grimaces.

'Takes a crowbar.'

Iris turns. South and east, the hills of Hampstead obscure anything beyond themselves.

'You can't see far that way, can you? You wouldn't know the East End was there at all. There are plenty of people who like it that way, up here. The ones who got out.'

'East End's alright,' Jem says. 'It weren't so bad for us. We had good times down there.'

Iris lifts her gaze from the curtailed view; she lays it, curiously, on Jem. 'I don't know how you can say that. You of all people.'

Once upon a time Florence was the fearless one; but times have changed, and the sisters with them. If anyone is remotely fearless now, in the uneasy silence Iris leaves, it is Iris herself. Florence occupies herself with a plaque of chocolate that is sliding earthwards from its slab.

'It was alright,' Jem says again, awkwardly persistent. 'We had some good times back then. That isn't wrong, it don't make what happened worse. I'm alright with that.'

They sit. A dog sidles up for patting, then drags its owner off to see the deer in their enclosure. The sun passes behind a scud of cloud. It's one of those summers when all it takes is a cloud for all the warmth to go out of a moment, which is why Iris brought the sensible cardigan.

'I don't know,' she says. '*I* liked it down there. I just didn't think you would. I loved the Buildings.'

'The Columbia Buildings,' Jem smiles, 'and the flower market.'

'Oh, I loved the market! And I never loved Holloway at all. That's where we went afterwards. Mum thought it'd be easier, because it was nearer Dad, and no one knew us up there.'

And what about Dad, come to that? *What about him?* Florence threw back, when Iris first asked, cradling the telephone in the private shadows of the hall. *Jem doesn't want to meet him, and I can't stand the sight of him, so it's easy, isn't it? Dad's got nothing to do with us,* Florence said, and Iris thought, You silly fool, of course he does. He's everything to do with you, both of you. You can't run away from him forever.

She pulls her cardy tight. She shouldn't have said yes to ice cream. Her beautiful fool of a sister finishes her chocolate with aplomb, eyes the bared vanilla. 'I've had enough,' Florence says. 'Jem, you have it.'

'Your sis might want it.'

'She doesn't. Iris is jealous of other things,' Florence says, and Iris blushes to her roots.

'Floss!'

'What? Anyway, it's true,' Florence says, and turns to Jem. 'Iris thinks I get all the luck. Which is ridiculous, of course, because Iris has everything.'

'Aha,' Jem says. He lies back on the lawn, closing his eyes, keeping out of it.

'This is nice,' Florence says, 'The three of us. It feels like we're the same as ever, doesn't it?' she asks, and Iris stirs.

'I'm really not,' she says. 'Jealous. I don't know why you say that.'

'You are, though, a bit. It's because of Pond, isn't it?' Florence asks, and beside her Jem opens his eyes.

'What about Pond?'

★

What about Pond?

Iris has one photograph of him. She keeps it in her photocube, along with the cropped shot of Florence (sunset-lit, sipping a long drink in Siena), recent snaps of Harry, Megan and Beth, and one of Mum and Dad, twelve years old, taken the month he was released.

The photocube lives on Iris's best, deep windowsill. The six pictures in the cube are of those who matter most to her. One picture, of necessity, is always out of sight.

Iris thinks about this. It's as if, when she rotates the cube (after Harry goes, every day), she's turning a picture to the wall. It's as if she's ashamed of someone she loves, or can no longer face them. That's how it feels to her. She doesn't like doing it.

Iris isn't needy. It's not that she *needs* to see these pictures: needs aren't so frivolous. Needs aren't frivolous, are they? Needs aren't just wishes or desires. Needs are the things you live for, and for the lack of which you sicken. Food is a need, and love might be, if love is a thing for which you live.

Who does Iris love? Her father. Her other family, according to their needs. Harry, often; not always. Iris could get by alone – she isn't afraid of solitude – but need should be respected, and so those who need her, matter to her. She is charged with them. In this way, for Iris, needing or being needed have come to much the same thing.

She thinks about the cube too often. She has weighed up solutions – taking one photo out (but which would go? Would it be Pond?), or not turning the cube at all – but even as it is, six pictures hardly cover those who matter. Losing a picture for good wouldn't make things better. It would make more sense to throw away the cube, but then Harry would ask more questions. There have been enough about Pond, over the years, and Iris doesn't want to scrabble for answers.

And it annoys her, too, that a cube should have six sides, when there are seven days in a week. It's messy, slipshod. It means that if you rotate your cube in order – as she does – someone is turned down twice each week, Monday and Sunday. Like this:

ABCDEFA

BCDEFAB

PONDDEFABPOND

Iris knows it's too much, all this thinking. She'd never mention it to Mum or Harry. She knows the cube means nothing in the scheme of things. And it shouldn't matter anyway, since it balances over time. This turning down of the loved, it all evens out in the end.

Does she love Pond, too? She thinks she might have, once. She thinks she could again, although it has been almost too long to know; and what kind of love it might have been, or could be, isn't clear to her.

And does she need him? Why would she? The photocube is full. Iris has loved ones all around her. In her dreams her family is a net, spread out on her lap (*from* her lap) and unfurling out of sight, with snarls she worries at and rents she works to mend. Iris is the one who tries to keep things together, if anyone does, above and below and around her. If Iris is starved of anything, it isn't love.

And nor does Pond need her. Iris knows it must be true. He can't need her, or he'd have looked for her; and if Pond had looked for her then he'd have wanted to be found; and if he'd wanted that then she'd have found him by now, wouldn't she? But if he has no need of her, and she has no need of him, then why does she still look for him? Why even keep the picture here, orphaned amongst her family, on the best windowsill?

Sometimes Iris thinks her thinking will send her mad.

Everyone's mad, Harry says, *but some are madder than others*. It's one of his sayings, this. Harry is full of sayings. *I'm full of it*, Harry says.

The photograph of Pond shows him as Iris never knew him. He looks fifteen or so, half-grown, not quite handsome. He is dressed in an open-collared shirt which might have been khaki in life. He is sitting outside, on a hillside, holding a kite he's made. Its tail coils on his knees. The reels and guys lie in his hands. He smiles at the camera, but his eyes are searching, as they always were.

Iris knows he made the kite because Dora told her so. It's four years since she found Mr and Mrs Lazarus. She was just beginning to look, then, and they came so easily that for a while Iris felt as if Pond, too, would be simple; that he, too, wouldn't have gone far, his presence just around some corner she'd soon effortlessly turn.

Later she looked for other things – records of orphans and bombings, trails of triplicate – but to start with it was just the name. Not Pond, the one he gave himself, but Lazarus, which he was given.

How long did it take to find Dora and Solly? It can't have been ten minutes. Harry was still at the hospital, the girls out like lights, the house straightened after them. Iris had a space to herself and she'd made up her mind to try. She sat down in the sitting room with a whisky neat (a bolster against self-ridicule) and the green phonebook — *London Postal Area, L–R* — and did the simplest thing: she looked up Lazarus. There were only eight of them, and a quarter looked like Solomon.

Lazarus, S., 124A Newling Estate, Columbia Rd., Shoreditch, E.2.

Lazarus Watches (commercial), 24 Great Eastern St., Shoreditch, E.2

'I beg your pardon? No, I'm sorry, dear, you must have the wrong number, I don't think I know ... Iris Lockhart? Iris Lockhart! Goodness, of course I do! Is it me? Well of course it's *me*, Dora! How are you? And how's your sister? How's your mother? *I'm talking, Solly! No, it's Iris Lockhart. LOCKHART. Yes! No, not that one, the other one.* What, dear? Oh, that would be lovely. Oh yes. Oh, you'd be welcome. No, you choose. You choose, I'm sure you're busy, Iris, aren't you? Thursday lunch ... no, I'm available. You'll miss Solly at the shop but never mind, I can tell him all about it later. No, don't worry yourself. How nice! How good to hear from you! I'll see you on Thursday. See you!'

She took a Dundee cake and flowers; white chrysanthemums and blue gentians. Meg needed walking to school that year, while Beth was still at nursery, and Iris left late and got the flowers in a rush at Golders Green station, dissatisfied with them but seeing nothing better.

She was halfway to Old Street, rearranging the blooms on her knees — the way Dad used to, nipping off the dead wood — when she realised what a foolish gift they were to be taking to Columbia Road. As if she'd never been before, and didn't know where she was heading.

And then she got there and she didn't. She hadn't been back, then, since she was nine years old, not since Dad was sent down and Mum moved them away. Afterwards they'd sometimes heard bits about Columbia Road – the Buildings had been demolished, the dairy on Ezra Street sold on – but to Iris they'd seemed more and more reports of another world, a place she'd read about, not real or attainable. Mum never took them back and Iris never took herself – it came to seem almost forbidden – though now and then, in Holloway, she'd see someone on a Sunday morning, laden with pots and greenery, and she'd feel her loss.

She needn't have worried about the flowers.

'Oh, how lovely! You'll spoil us. Let me find something for them. And shall I take your things? Look at you, Iris, all grown up!'

Dora looked the same to her: smallish, prettyish, foreign-ish. She had a pretty smile, too, but behind that welcome her face was waiting to fall back into a habitual unhappiness. And that was the same, too, Iris was sure, though as a girl she'd never seen it, or seeing it hadn't recognised it for what it was.

'Make yourself at home. You'll be hungry, won't you? I've made too much, I'm sorry . . . and you've bought this delicious cake . . . but I've only done sandwiches, and Solly likes them for lunches, so we don't have to finish them, we can have cake instead, what a treat. How's your mother?' Dora asked, and she said that Mum sent love, though Mum didn't, of course, because Iris hadn't told her anything. What would have been the point? Love would have been the last thing Mum would have sent to anyone from the Buildings, all of them forever tarnished by association with the death of Bernadette, all despised for having been witness to Michael's humiliation.

'Have you come far?'

'Yes. Well, just from Golders Green.'

'Oh yes,' Dora said, knowledgeably, respectfully. 'Golders Green. I expect it's nice there, is it?'

What did she answer? It doesn't matter. She had followed Dora through into the kitchenette – making herself at home or useful – and from the window she could see the clearances. The slabs of half-finished cluster blocks and rain-stained high-rises, the vista of demolitions and great empty foundations with ironwork rising overhead like rusted spears or russet saplings; and inside, through the service hatch, in Dora's boxy lounge, an upright piano, a pot of violets, and a picture in a prop-foot frame, its face turned towards the wall.

'It's changed so much,' she said (not *What is that picture?* She didn't know to ask that, then), and Dora tutted, busying herself with the teapot and cosy.

'You shouldn't look out there. I don't understand it. They say they need houses and then they knock them down. Sometimes they come and say Shoreditch has to go, all of it. I think they hate it. I don't know why, do you? What do they think is wrong with us? They promise to make it better, but it isn't better, you can see. They're too quick with their promises, that's the trouble with politicians. And you know about the Buildings? A white elephant, they said. Even the baths, all gone. Still, we mustn't grumble, that's what Solly says. At least we have this, and the shop. There, the tea. Look at this cake!'

They passed trays through into the lounge. Their talk grew smaller as they ate.

'And you're married?'

'Yes.'

'What does your husband do?'

'He's a doctor, a surgeon at the London Hospital.'

'Oh, you must be proud. My father was a doctor. And children?'

'Two girls, Megan and Beth. Megan is five and Beth's four.'

'You're very lucky.'

'Yes, I know.'

'Well, here we are!'

Then Dora was quiet; as if, with nothing left to do, she had nothing left to say. When her cup chattered on its saucer Iris saw her hands were shaking, and she had to stop herself from reaching out and stilling them with her own. She didn't know what to say herself. Dora's nerves were infectious. The flat was unnaturally silent. It smelt faintly repellant: pipe smoke, egg and cress sandwiches, and two people no longer young.

She said, 'You have a piano,' and Dora looked at the upright with unnecessary gratitude.

'Oh yes! Solly bought it for my fortieth. I learned when I was a girl. I used to play for Solly sometimes, when we met. My father was always there, of course ... he made Solly so nervous. I could play Bach, but I daren't now. Sometimes I do try Chopin.'

She got up, and for a moment Iris thought she meant to play – it might have been a relief – but instead Dora picked up the picture from beside the violets. 'And this is Henry,' she said, brightly. 'You remember Henry, don't you? Of course you do, you were always running wild together.'

Pond on a hillside, with a kite across his knees.

'He made that himself, that kite. Solly was pleased, ever so. It was something they did together. It has two strings, you see, for tricks. You like the picture, don't you?'

'Yes,' Iris said, 'I do. It's not how I remember him, but –'

'No, because he'd be fourteen there ... well, that's what we called him, fourteen. That was his official age. You could tell he was older by then, you could see it in his face. He was always small for his age. You didn't know him then. He got to be so clever. He caught up like anything at school. He wanted to be a pilot. Not an army pilot, because he was against all that. Fighting.'

She was speaking of him in the past. A chill went through Iris (the violets; the picture turned to the wall), and she searched out Dora's gaze. 'He's not —'

'Oh no, it's not like *that*. We'd have heard, wouldn't we, if it was?' Dora asked, reasonably, and all Iris could do was nod into the silence that slunk back in between them.

They were side by side on the settee. She was looking back at Pond's face, uncertain, trying to think what to say next, when Dora reached up and stroked her hair. It was a motherly gesture, an errant curl tucked back behind Iris's ear.

'So, where —' she started, but Dora went on again, as if she hadn't heard.

'He missed you, after you'd gone. You especially. He liked you, dear. There was Bernadette's boy, Jem, they stayed friends for a bit, but after Bernadette that was hard. And they went to different schools, and then the LCC men came and condemned the Buildings, and we were all moved out. We all went our own ways. I don't know what happened to the Malcolms, I think they might have gone by then. You can have that if you like, the picture.'

'Oh,' Iris said, 'I couldn't,' but Dora *tush*ed.

'It's no trouble, I've copies. I want you to have it. I've albums, too, would you like to see?'

They looked together. Pond as Iris remembered him; animal, whip-thin, all hollow and bone. Pond as Henry Lazarus, filling into hand-me-downs. Henry in uniform: cub scout, boy scout, school. On a beach, on a train, on a boat eating sandwiches (egg and cress, from the look of them). Henry eating spaghetti. Poised over a Christmas pudding and its spectral flame. On a hill, with a kite, smiling, his eyes still searching.

'Where is he?' she asked, when she couldn't bear it any more, and Dora closed the album, patted it, and pushed herself back to her feet. She went to the service hatch, where Iris's flowers stood in a cut glass vase, waiting for their right place to be found.

'I've always liked 'mums. You don't have to wonder about them, they wear their hearts on their sleeves. Some flowers are like that, aren't they? They're just pretty and that's the end of them. Do you know what I mean?' Dora asked, with such expectancy that Iris must have agreed, must have said yes out of politeness; but she can't recall. Her own voice escapes her, though the memory isn't so old, in the scheme of things.

'We don't know, love,' Dora said then. 'Henry went away. He went away twelve years ago and he never came back to us.'

Because it is unfinished. Because, when Michael Lockhart was found guilty on five counts of eight (*warehousebreaking with aggravation; stealing the contents of a safe; dangerous driving; assault on a Peace Officer with intent to resist apprehension; manslaughter committed with intent to resist or prevent the lawful apprehension or detainer of himself, the said Michael Lockhart*), being acquitted only of the attempted murder of John McEachan and two lesser charges, which malicious assault Norman Varney had admitted to his common-law wife; and when the Judge called Michael *A cold and violent man*, and sent him away out of the lives of all who needed him ... because whatever Iris felt for Pond was unformed, then, only just beginning. Because those feelings were a bright point in the bright time just before the storm. Because she wants to know the end.

Perhaps that's why she looks for him.

The names trouble her. There are too many to account for. He could be Something Pond. He could be Something Lazarus. He could go under Henry, and it still wouldn't be his real name. There were names given him and lost before Iris ever knew him. Iris has found them. Pond could have found them, too: Dora says he looked for them, in the beginning. So many names are possible that he becomes anonymous.

And what *is* he? What has he become? He might have fallen through the cracks. He might be on the streets again, or sleeping in a hole in the ground. He might be a nobody, or wealthy. Wealth might conceal him. He might be dead. He might be flying.

When they were in Holloway Iris hardly ever thought of Pond. He was part of the lost world then, the world of Columbia Road, and like the road itself he seemed increasingly unreal. Iris doesn't recall Mum or Floss ever mentioning him at home, and no one spoke of Pond to Dad on those days – rare as birthdays – when Mum took them along on visits to Pentonville (the doors and gates closing them in, the eyes of men dwelling on them, and Floss always terrible to Dad – embittered by lost faith – when she still visited at all). Even after Dad came home Pond remained one of many things never spoken of, the memories that might have lead to talk of Bernadette, and being unmentionable he faded away over the years almost to nothing.

It was only when Iris left home that Pond came back to her, or she to him. It was at college that she began to wonder, and it began with Semlin.

Imaginary friends belong to the hard chapters of childhood. They come calling when there are things which can't be said to people in the flesh, or when the flesh won't listen, or when what others say is dangerous to listen to, and only the whispers of a Semlin will drown the danger out.

Later there are real friends, and sooner or later doubt creeps in. It takes a child to make a Semlin and to go on believing in him. That's what Iris thinks, because that's how it was for her. Semlin came to her when Iris came to London, and all the friends she'd made in her first six years were left behind in Birmingham; and he left her in Holloway, where she grew out of him.

Or did she? Has she? In Holloway, Iris kept up the habit of talking to herself, a friendly to-and-fro murmur that made solitude comforting. Bit by bit, in North London, she stopped naming her comforter, but it was half-Semlin all the same, imagined at fourteen or sixteen not out of faith but with dim affection. Iris recalled her made-up friend long after she'd formally dispensed with his services; and even now, now and then, she converses with something, though it might be years since she put a name to her conversant. Iris doesn't fear to be alone because she never feels alone.

They became intertwined, those things, though Iris hardly knows it. Her faithful echo became the sum of both lost friends; half-Semlin, half-Pond.

In 1958, two years after Michael came home, the Lockharts moved from their Holloway flat to a house in Highbury, and Iris went up to Leeds. She'd worked hard at school, had surpassed the expectations of her unexpectant Secondary Modern teachers, and had offers, for History, from two Universities. Leeds was the less prestigious, but it was her choice. Before her interviews she'd looked up her suitors on the map. Leeds was further and that was enough. Iris was less sure of herself then, more willing to follow Florence in her dogged flight from Michael and childhood. All through those years she thought she wanted distance.

She didn't find it. Leeds was full of echoes. The back-to-backs, where the kids kicked rag-footballs hell for leather and played their made-up games; the covered markets, where the costers hawked cuts of meat and cloth, choice or cheap; and the forthright people, whose warmth embraced her but whose thresholds she never crossed, never being invited: none of it was foreign to her. It was intimate but faint, as though she'd lived it all herself, not only in another city, but in another life.

She liked Leeds, but not its University. She was too reticent to shine in lectures, too doubtful to excel on paper. Her tutors had no time for her. She made friends with difficulty. Her hall of residence was Moor Grange in Headingley, a Victorian conversion, handsome to look at from a distance but internally unpleasant, with disused gaslights that still leaked a residual stench in close weather, and dank parqueted corridors that echoed under the heels of girls who shopped in shops, not markets, and whose voices jostled for position, diffident or confident, but always – to Iris – seeming driven by a need to hunt out common ground, a reassuring hierarchy of grammar schools, holidays, paternal occupations, books and clothes and boys and places which Iris had never read or worn or seen or known to fancy.

The evening she arrived in Leeds: that was when she found Semlin.

Her train had been delayed, first in leaving London and again later that afternoon while crossing some interminable process of Midlands mining towns. It was dark by the time she reached Moor Grange and the porter was short with her. Iris gave her name and received her keys and dour directions, but somehow she went wrong. She missed her floor and climbed on as far as the attics, which the girls called the Garrets, where the corridors admitted little natural light, and the rooms – she heard it later – were uncomfortably low, their ceilings gathering down to filthy lattice-leaded windows.

She put down her cases to pat along the walls for light. She found a timer switch, pressed it and hurried on unhindered, peering down at her keys and up at the doors, none of which was hers and some of which were already posted with the names of eager new inhabitants. She had gone half the hallway's length when the lamps flickered, the plunger by the stairwell forewarning of its depletion, and Iris just had time to catch the name on the next door. *J. Semlin*, she read, and then the lights went out.

She stood trembling. She told herself she was wrong, but she knew what she'd seen, and as the dark receded – her eyes accustoming to the dim cast of the next window – the door became half-visible. She made herself go closer. There was the name, handwritten in inked capitals on cartridge paper, the scrap inserted into a brass slot meant for something more enduring. She could hear nothing from inside. She raised her hand to knock and then lowered it and turned back the way she'd come. Somewhere along the walls she found another switch and went on without looking back through the reinvigorated light.

She never met J. Semlin. She listened for the name, at Moor Grange, at the University and in town, but Iris never heard anyone call for her or speak of her and she never saw her. Later – years later – she asked someone about the name, a man who knew about such things, and he told her that it might be Balkan or German, that there were Semlins in the East and that some of those had gone to Canada. And once, at the end of her time in Leeds, she went back up to the Garrets, meaning to knock, but only once, and that was more than enough.

In a way it was nothing. Nothing really happened except that the door haunted her. Its name was hers, but not hers. *Semlin*. It was her possession, being her invention. It was her secret and it had no right to be out in the world. It was like meeting an abandoned friend in a new place, or coming suddenly on a mirror in an unfamiliar house. It was like seeing a ghost. She thought of the door too often, too much for comfort, and as the door nagged at her she began to think and dream of other things. Semlin led back to the street of flowers, to the hole in Long Debris, to Bernadette, and Pond.

She kept Dad from everyone. She told no one about him until she left college, and then, of those she'd met at Leeds, only Harry, and Connie, her one best friend. She met Connie in the autumn term, in Kirkgate Market, at Turner's Ladies' Intimates.

Iris was looking at the lingerie; looking without touching, because all but the most functional items were beyond her means (half the bras she owned then were still rubberised home-mades; her best were Marks and Sparks discounts, in grim melanoid flesh-tones). Close by, Mrs Turner and a tall girl were discussing stockings.

'I don't do them,' Mrs Turner said, and the girl folded her arms, bracing for disagreement.

'Well, that's a pity. I've tried the shops. Women do wear them.'

'Ladies don't.'

'How would you know? Oh look, I haven't come to argue about it. I just thought, in the markets ... I don't suppose you'd know who has them?'

'Mesh,' said Mrs Turner, and others besides Iris heard her then, the man with the dogs by Scarr's Drapery (the dogs following their master's gaze), the women by the corsets. 'You're a student, aren't you? What do you want with them?'

'That's hardly your business, is it?'

'It's my business, if I'm saying what I know.'

'Well are you going to, or not?'

The coster sucked her cheeks. The girl's face was flaming. She stood too straight for comfort, as if to draw together the tatters of her dignity. She looks like the guards at Buckingham Palace, Iris thought, like a guard in rotten weather; boylike, toylike, ridiculous.

'Try Loughton's, over there. They do theatricals,' Mrs Turner said, and close by in the roofed-in gloom a woman chuckled. Iris became aware that the people around her had become an audience, an unkind one, wanting nothing good, hungry for comeuppance; and with awareness came regret, for Iris, at having thought of the girl unkindly herself.

'Mind how you go, love,' Mrs Turner said, as the girl turned away; and then, raising her iron-flat coster's voice, for the benefit of her crowd, 'You might want to mind your manners, and all.'

'Oh? Why's that?'

'Men like young ladies with good manners. You talk with them as you talk with me, you won't be getting far with them and they won't go far with you. And then those mesh stockings of yours, they won't be here nor there, will they?'

The girl walked briskly. She had reached the market gates, was unruffling a brolly, before Iris caught her up.

'Excuse me, are you alright? I saw what happened,' she said, and the girl turned to her; on her, almost, with the shoppers shouldering around them, still market-thick in the high street.

'Did you? I hope you had a good laugh at my expense. Save some fun for your friends at Moor Grange, won't you? I'm sure they'll thank you for the entertainment.'

Her cheeks were still flushed, Iris saw, and her eyes were wet; but not miserable, as Iris's would have been. Agitated, not chastened.

'I'm sorry,' she said, 'I didn't mean to . . . I didn't laugh, anyway. I thought it was horrible,' Iris said, and before she could say anything else the girl was shrugging and glancing away.

'Well, it was my own fault. I asked the wrong woman for my sluttish stockings, didn't I? And I should have shut up when I had the chance, but I never can seem to. Still, it wasn't pleasant. I don't think I'll be back in a hurry. Gosh, I'm dying to sit down. I suppose that's the trouble with markets, isn't it? Do you think someone around here would serve us tea, or will word of me have spread already?'

Iris paid for the teas. The girl had cigarettes.

'You're very kind. You're an angel, actually,' the girl said, 'or a knight in shining armour. Which would make me your damsel in distress, wouldn't it? Or your soul in need of saving. Are you?'

'Am I what?'

'A good Samaritan, always saving Philistines. Was it Philistines with him? Anyhow, you look like you might be.'

'I don't see how,' Iris said. 'I don't know how. To save people, I mean. I don't know much of anything. My tutor seems to think I'm more of a Philistine.'

'You're lucky. Mine thinks I'm the damsel, and the story is he eats them. I'm Connie.'

'Iris.'

'Angel, then. Knights get pretty names, like Lancelot or Percival, but Iris is beautiful.'

'Is it?'

'Of course it is. Flowers and rainbows. Not like Constance. Who chose it?'

'My mum.'

'There you are. Daddy chose mine. You can tell he wasn't keen. Nothing's much fun if it's constant, is it? Miss Constance Nuisance Interruption, that's what he used to call me.'

They nursed their teas. The place was cosy, the one window drizzle-fogged. The smell of fried breakfasts, thick as lard.

'Why were you buying them?' Iris asked, 'the stockings?'

'Oh ... it sounds silly now. There's a fellow I've been seeing, at the Medical School. He said something about liking them. Not that I'm doing it for him, I don't dress for men. He did spark my interest, though. That woman was right, I do go in for the theatrical. I wanted to see Richard's face. Gobsmacked, is that what you say? Do you have a fellow?'

'No,' Iris said, meaning *Never.*

'You should come along to the Med School, you'll have young doctors swarming all over you.'

'I don't know if I want to be swarmed.'

'It's alright, they don't sting, not unless you want them to. They're gentlemen most of the time, just a bit full of bravado. I think it must be the prospect of future eminence. It's charming, in any case. Will you? Come along?'

Afterwards, walking to Connie's bike, Iris remembered the unasked question. 'How do you know where I live?'

'I've seen you around. You stand out a bit, always by yourself. It makes you look brave.'

'I'm not.'

'You look it. Women are expected to seek safety in numbers, one way or another. You don't do what's expected of you. That's bravery, isn't it? And I suppose you won't take it the wrong way if I say you dress a little differently. The grammar school girls all look the same. Like eggs. No, hens – pushy, pecky, henpecked hens. I've digs at Moorfield Lodge. We're almost next door neighbours. The Lodge is a pit.'

'The Grange is too. I don't have any friends there. I couldn't tell anyone about you, even if I wanted to.'

'You could always tell me instead,' Connie said. 'I'll laugh at myself tomorrow. I will, you wait. I've had plenty of practice.'

It wasn't common ground, Kirkgate market. Connie didn't belong there, and never went back again, but nor did she share much with the other girls (*studentesses*, Iris's tutor called them). Her father was a diplomat, twice unhappily married, and his only child had grown up with consequent unhappiness at an expensive but ill-suited range of international and boarding schools, in Manila, Yorkshire and Sussex. Connie felt as far beyond the small worlds of the Lodge and the Grange as Iris felt below them.

A fortnight after they met, Iris went with Connie to the halls of the Leeds School of Medicine. Connie had set up dinner with her man, Richard, and a friend, at an Indian restaurant not far from East Parade.

'His name's Harry. I think you might like him, but – listen – dinners can be awkward. They're a shade too obvious, and I don't want that making you nervous. We'd do better to mix it up a bit.'

'I'm not wearing mesh stockings, if that's what you think.'

'I wish you would. No, I've a plan. I bought some fizz up for the term, look here, there's still a bottle to go. We take it and infiltrate their halls. The night porter's darling, he's let me up before. We catch the men half-decent and force the drink on them. Inevitable merriment ensues. What do you think?'

'I don't –'

'Don't think. Trust me, it's ironclad. Ready?'

They were scrunched up in front of Connie's mirror, Connie dazzling in the forty-watt light, Iris all done up, unsmiling, bereft of herself.

'Connie, I think I might just go home. You won't mind, will you? I'm not like you,' she said, and Connie cocked her head at their dim, different reflections. She reached up and stroked their necks. One hand on Iris, one on herself.

'You can't now,' she said. 'You're too beautiful for home. Look at you. My angel.'

The night porter wasn't darling. Iris stood on the lamp-lit steps while Connie argued, and by the time she'd given up they were late for the restaurant and had to make a run for it, clutching their handbags and the bottle, excusing themselves through the evening crowds and the things the crowds called after them, and it was awful, but at the end of it was Harry.

He wasn't much to look at then, although he has one of those faces that gain with age. Now, ten years on, Iris finds herself – against the odds, she thinks – married to a handsome man. It seems a mistake to her, the way their looks have diverged, an error on the part of nature. It's a glitch that – bit by bit – is driving them apart. She has been hurt by Harry's looks, more than once, but she takes pleasure in them all the same. The pleasure surprises her, as hunger often does: sometimes, when Iris is looking after those who count on her to do so, she'll forget to eat until the small hours, when the pangs strike through her. She should take better care of herself, Iris. Or someone should.

In any case, he wasn't handsome then. Then, in a wet October, in a Leeds curry house, he was rising to meet her from a chair of thinning velvet, Richard rising beside him, both with pipes, both – in light of lateness – with the correct expressions of grateful concern, with giveaway eyes twinkling in insolent amusement, and Harry beardless and chinless, with nothing much to say for himself, because Richard forgot to introduce him until the glasses arrived for the fizz, just as Connie forgot to introduce Iris.

'Blast! So sorry, head like a sieve. This is Harry, my friend and accomplice. Also a genius.'

Sorry! Connie said with her eyes, and at the same time Harry said, 'Harry,' and held out his hand. 'You must be Iris.'

'What kind of genius?' she asked, and he let go of her and rubbed at his hair, which was thinning, like the velvet.

'No kind at all. I don't know what Richard's on about.'

'The top of the class kind,' Richard said. 'Harry's every teacher's pet. He can do things with a scalpel you wouldn't believe. He could be doing them now, under the table. You'll stand up to go, Iris, and find yourself with a beautifully turned false leg, and all along you thought Harry was just playing footsie.'

'Richard!'

'It's true, darling. And worse still, he's for the NHS. Harry's not in it for the money, are you? He won't touch the stuff, will you?'

'I won't say no, if you're offering.'

London, Iris thought. The milder, less flashy sound of the south or the estuaries. Not moneyed, not even comfortably off. Not comfortable at all. Impatient with himself, maybe with all of us. But here he is, all the same. He must want to be with us. Perhaps he even needs us, Iris thought, and she wondered what it was he thought he needed, besides the obvious.

He was busy with his food by then – wary of attention, she thought – but when he glanced up again it was to meet her gaze straight on. His eyes were grey, gently questioning: *Now then, what are you looking at me for? There's nothing to see here, is there?*

His eyes were always beautiful. They're still the best part of him, Iris sometimes thinks, but she keeps the thought to herself. It's not the kind of thing she'd say. It's the kind of thing Floss would say. Besides, who would she tell, now Semlin is real and gone?

By then the dreams had begun. Sometimes they started out with Iris opening the Semlin door, but not always: nor was Semlin in everything that followed, though Pond was, always.

In the first dream they were playing Troll. They were children again, but it wasn't just the four of them. Now they were six: Iris and Floss, Pond and Jem, Harry and Semlin. Iris was the troll.

I don't want to be, she said, and Floss put her arms akimbo.

Well you are. It's decided. You have to do it now.

She got under the bridge. It was cold in the echo place. Water shone down the bricks. The others were out of sight, waiting to play, even Semlin. Without him she was alone. She didn't want to be without him, but to get him back she'd have to win.

Who goes on my bridge? she called, and hearing them she leapt up and caught them one by one. Only they weren't all there any more.

Where's Pond? one of them said, and only then would Iris see that he was no longer with them. *The trolls have got him*, someone said.

Then they looked. They called his name. *We have to find him,* Iris told them, but it was never any good.

In the second dream it was just the two of them, Iris and Semlin. It was the day Bernadette died, and they were climbing down into the pit in Long Debris, looking for their friend. They'd searched for Pond everywhere else, and they were worried something might have happened to him.

The water was black where the pit had filled. Their hands sank into clay. They came to the mouth of a hole in the wall. It smelt of rats, the awful smell of dead rats, like rotten cabbage.

Don't be scared, Semlin said, *I can see in the dark*, and he took her hand and led her in, but the hole went on for a long time, down and down.

I don't think he's here, she said, but Semlin said, *We can't give up. Try calling his name*, so she did.

Iris? Pond said. *What are you doing here?*

I came looking for you. Are you alright?

Yes, thanks, Pond said. *It's alright down here, except I don't have any friends. Do you have yours?*

Yes, Iris said, *he's holding my hand.*

What's he for?

Oh, he's just for playing. What's yours for?

He looks out for me, Pond said, and that was where the second dream ended.

In the third she was making love to him. She took his hand and led him in. She wanted it so badly, so badly that even as they did it she still wanted him to hurry up and begin.

Doesn't it hurt? Pond asked, and she shook her head.

Not really.

It must, you're bleeding.

It's not bad, she said. *It doesn't matter.*

We have to stop, Pond said. *I have to go.*

And she told him not to. She always told him, but he always did.

She heard nothing from Harry for a week and then he turned up at the Grange out of the blue and took her dancing. She liked it and thought he did too. Afterwards he walked her home. It was the end of autumn.

'Bit of a problem,' he said, 'if we go on like this.'

There's someone else. That's what she thought. She didn't even know him yet. He wasn't even *handsome* yet, and there wasn't anyone else, not then, so far as she knows, but that's what she thought all the same. And she was right to think it.

'What is?'

'Neither of us being much of a talker. Connie does half of it and Richard fills in the rest. You and me, we don't get a word in edgeways.'

She asked, 'What shall we talk about?'

'I don't know. What are you thinking about, walking along there, quiet as a mouse?'

'A door,' she said flatly, and of course he laughed.

'You could put a fellow's back up, thinking about doors with him. What is it, Ten Downing Street?'

'No. When I was little, I was . . .'

'What?'

'Nothing. Please forget I mentioned it.'

'Oh no, you can't stop there, I won't get any sleep. You could have been anything. Chimneysweep. Cat burglar.'

'I was always imagining things. I had this made-up friend. There's a door here with his name on it.'

'Go on. Where?'

'Moor Grange, up in the Garrets. Someone called Semlin lives up there. That's what I was thinking about. You did ask.'

'*Semlin?*'

'It was my name. I mean it was the name I made up. It wasn't supposed to be real, I thought I'd imagined it.'

'Fancy that. Must have given you a turn.'

'Yes, it did.'

Quiet streets. The must of leaves. Harry beside her, going miles out of his way, out of need or the kindness of his heart.

'So what was he like, then,' Harry asked, 'this friend of yours?'

'I'm not sure. I hadn't thought of him in years, not until I came up here.'

'He.'

'Yes. He was mousy. Skinny.'

'Not a looker, then. Good.'

'And he was always hungry, so I used to save food for him; and he lived underground . . . no, that's wrong. I don't know, it's hard remembering him now.'

'Like a dream,' Harry said.

'Like that. But he mattered to me. He was there when I needed him and I did, a lot.'

'Where was all this?'

'Shoreditch. Where were you?'

'Catford, after the war.'

'Didn't you have someone like that? Something like that, I mean?'

'No,' Harry said, and he put his arm around her. It was a cold night, after all. 'But I wish I had.'

His hands. She remembers, after she let him – the first time – pulling his arms around her, and seeing that his nails were polished. Not just trimmed but shining, smooth. The rest of him was rough against her, wire-haired and wet, animal, but his hands were always surgeon's hands.

She remembers she could feel him smiling. It was already dawn and snow shone light up into the room. Her man was smiling, and down below a bike went past, whistling.

They were married in December, in London, in the holidays. Of the day itself Iris remembers almost nothing (Dad's gaunt hand, giving her away; a ceremony through which she moved in a Delphic trance of nerves, the answers to all questions coming to her unbidden), but in the golden months afterwards she was happy, as happy as she's ever been in the years since Bernadette. By Easter she was pregnant. Harry was in his final year, and got them a flat together around the corner from the School of Medicine. Iris thinks perhaps Dad lent them something for that.

The day she left Moor Grange, Iris went back up to the Garrets. There were girls coming down the stairs, but their conversation died away behind as she reached the top, and the corridor itself was quiet.

She went up to the door. The scrap of paper was gone, but she knew the door as if it were her own. She had to steel herself to knock. There was a scuffling when she did, perhaps of rats or birds – it wasn't a human sound – and that was all. No one answered. She never stepped inside.

At first Harry was all she needed. Harry was enough for Iris when she was enough for Harry. Before she understood she wasn't – before she knew there were other women, that the women he shouldn't have were what Harry needed most – she began to look for Pond. In that way it was like an instinct.

And then it was when the girls were small that she began. Why then? Because, Iris thinks, that was when the life she'd made was supposed to have reached fruition. She was meant to be satisfied then, to be sated by the fruits, and sometimes it was almost true – some days Harry and the girls filled her thoughts and hours – but in the end it never was. If those loved ones were enough she would have known it then, when the girls still clung to her and Harry never strayed. There is more she needs. Pond is the form it takes.

On 5th May, 1952, Henry Lazarus was up with the larks. He was never much for lying in, but that morning he was down to eat before Solly left for work. Dora made them tea and porridge. Henry had golden syrup with it. And they had the wireless on, remember? The Black Dyke Mills were playing Fletcher. Dora recalls Solly and Henry admiring the performance: Solly recalls that Dora talked all over it. Henry had a test at school, and Solly quizzed him on the Stuarts and the Tudors. They talked about Petticoat Lane, about Henry helping out on Sundays, and the chances of getting to Southend or Brighton in the holidays. No one was out of sorts, were they? Dora thinks Henry seemed excited that morning – more talkative than usual. Solly went off to the Lane. Henry kissed Dora goodbye and left for school. He never arrived and never came back.

He took no money and left no note. He was wearing his duffle-coat and uniform. He went on foot. The school was less than half a mile. His teachers were surprised – Henry had been getting on well academically, if not always with his fellows – but the police were matter-of-fact. It does occur in such cases, one told Solly. Solly asked, What d'you mean, *such cases*? Abnormal ones, the policeman said. It's nobody's fault, sir, in this kind of situation.

Pond had lived with Solly and Dora for four years. On paper he was fourteen. Iris's best guess now is that he was getting on for three years older. In his satchel, in lieu of books, were two changes of clothes missing from his wardrobe, and, though it was a warm day, a scarf, a hat, and a pair of gloves Dora had knitted for him, and into which she had stitched the name, *Henry Lazarus.*

She wishes she didn't, but Iris talks in her sleep. Her talk takes the form of questions. If Harry is awake he sometimes answers them, and his voice stays with her later, where hers alone does not.

Where are you? she'll murmur, *where've you gone? Why?* And Harry will pat her, grumbling back, *I'm here, you daft love. I ain't going anywhere.*

Only twice, over the years, has she found anything of Pond. They're only glimmers, these things, but they give her hope, they lead her on.

The first glimmer was Dora. Iris has seen her only three times, once with Solly in attendance. She makes them painfully nervous – Dora shy, Solly curmudgeonly – by which she understands they'd rather be left alone. She reminds them too much of Pond, Iris thinks, or maybe of her father, and either way of unhappiness. She misses them, misses the way they cherish one another. It wasn't the son they lost, she thinks, so much as the years of childlessness, before and after, that make them close, that draw them together.

The second glimmer was Pond's real name. That's how Iris thinks of it, though she could be wrong. In any case, it only matters if Pond finds it too, and takes it back.

Iris found the name two years ago. She couldn't have done it without Harry.

'That pet project of yours. Operation Pond.'

'Don't call it that.'

'Alright, I was only trying to help.'

'No, you weren't, you were putting it down. Meg! You're not to go in the tunnel without me.'

There is a walk they used to do with the girls, when they had more time for leisure. They would drive out to Hertfordshire and park by an old railway line. No trains have gone that way for years, and at the end of the line is the village where Connie and Richard still live, near Richard's practice; and the line was green and lovely in any season, even winter, with holly and ivy and fir bowing down around them all the way, except in the tunnel, and that never felt too long. The girls would hold their breaths until they came out safe again.

'Thing is,' Harry said, 'I had a thought. I was down in the basement, and there are all these official papers —'

'They're in the spare room. What are you on about?'

'Not *ours*, I'm talking about in the hospital. We were down there yesterday —'

'We?'

'Me and the caretaker,' Harry said, and when he went on he did so more carefully. 'Nice chap. He's been sorting it out. It was a mess down there after the war, but he reckons he's got it straight.'

So he should have. So Harry should have gone carefully. What was her name, the woman, then? Iris conveniently forgets. There's no need, now, to give her her name, or to put a face to her. She was nothing special, neither the first nor the last.

They were at the tunnel's mouth. Meg and Beth were bent double, pop-eyed goblins, gorging themselves on air.

'Alright, go on,' Iris said, and they charged ahead, stumbling, glancing back at her from the gloom.

'So,' Harry shrugged, 'these papers. There's ours, the London Hospital's, then there's the ones for the places we took in under the Health Service. Mile End, St Clement's, Bethnal Green. I looked at Bethnal Green for you. Your road, Columbia, it comes up. It's on patient records. That must have been your local, Bethnal Green

Infirmary. That or the Mildmay, and the Mildmay was a Mission, not everyone's cup of tea, that, two lumps of salvation with your medicine ... What I'm saying is, the old records for your neighbourhood, they've ended up at the London. You can look at them. I can slip you in. There's all the births and deaths they did, operations, out-patients. There are maps for the nurses they used to send out, all the names and addresses. Good, eh?'

'It doesn't help,' Iris said, and her voice echoed in the tunnel, took on a desultory resonance. 'We never knew Pond's real name, or where he came from.'

'I know, but you said he was living in a cellar. Chances are he stuck to what he knew, a little lad. I wouldn't have gone far, if I was him. What I was thinking was, I could get you in, you could look at the old maps, go back down your way, work out what street, maybe what house it was, Pond's. You might put a name to the number, then.'

'I can't. It's not there now, where he lived. They built flats on it.'

'Right,' Harry said, flagging. 'Well, I just thought it was worth a shot. They're blue-chip, these records, you won't find better. You know what hospitals are like, wanting everything signed and dated.'

The girls were twenty yards ahead, limned against the tunnel's mouth. Iris lowered her voice. 'Why are you doing this?'

'I thought I could help.'

'Why? Does it make you feel better?'

'No. Not at the moment, no.'

'It won't make us better.'

'No.'

They had stopped by then. Iris had folded her arms around herself. She could hardly make him out.

'I need it to,' Harry said.

'I know.'

'I need you.'

'I know that,' she said, and started on again. When Harry tried to take her hand she shook herself free, but when they came out into the December light they could hear church bells, the wind carrying them from Connie's village in great intermittent swoops. It's not Sunday, she thought, and then she knew they must be winter wedding bells.

She did it anyway. She tried it just as Harry said, and there had been a boy, born at the house that would have stood about where the flooded cellar was. He would have been almost thirteen when Iris first met him. That didn't seem wrong, when she weighed it up. Dora said Pond had been small for his age.

His name was Sydney Marsh. His father was Stanley, a cabinet-maker with a workshop on Arline Street. His mother was Mary, like Iris's. There were two younger sisters and a brother, less than a year older. Sydney was taken to Bethnal Green Infirmary at twelve weeks, with *Eczema on face since birth. Now generalised with marked lichenification. Healing cavernous haemangioma R upper back. Mother – mild eczema. Maternal Uncle – eczema, asthma. Treatment – weak tar paste, all but face and hands.*

None of the Marshes came to the infirmary after the summer of 1940. When Iris looked for them elsewhere she found them all dead or missing in the end-of-the-world with which the Blitz began, when the Germans bombed London every night but one for ten weeks and six days. (Iris thinks of the one night sometimes: its millions of held breaths; its silent clouded heaven). Iris was one that year and still in Birmingham. Sydney must have been five. The Marsh house was struck early on, and towards the end of the war a rocket missed the City and demolished what remained, one house

233

of thousands nearby destroyed or ruined beyond repair. By then little of the street survived, and what was left had been abandoned by all but the destitute.

It disappointed her, the name. It was a glimmer of hope, alright, but it didn't lead her to him. It didn't shout out to her. *Sydney Marsh*. It solved nothing. There it was, in black and white, but it was just a name.

★

'What about Pond?'

On Golders Hill Jem is opening his eyes. The war is long ago. A dog barks: the trees echo it. Florence is smiling at her mischief.

'Iris looks for him,' Florence says. 'Well, you do, don't you? There's no point fuming about it.'

'I'm not *fuming*. Stop telling me what I am,' Iris says, ungently, but her sister only curls down next to Jem, seeking alliance.

'She's been looking for years, and she never gets anywhere.'

'Nothing wrong with looking,' Jem says, and Florence elbows him. 'What's that for?'

'Don't encourage her. I mean honestly, Iris, what do you *need* him for? What would you do with him if you found him? I don't know why you bother. Why do you?'

'Because I miss him.'

'I don't see why. *I* don't. He wasn't ever really one of us.'

Iris doesn't answer. She stands up on the hillside, brushes mowings from her dress. 'We should get on,' she says, 'if you're coming for tea. The girls will be running Harry ragged.'

'But he wasn't, was he?' Florence says, cross with them both. 'He wasn't like us. We didn't *know* him. He could have been anything.'

'Royalty in exile,' Jess murmurs, and Florence almost spits.

'Some exile that'd be, a bloody Shoreditch bombsite.'

'I always liked him, though, you know. I liked him whatever he was,' Jem says, and he ghosts a wink at Iris. She could kiss him for it.

Now she's doing the tea. She thinks of Connie as she cooks, Pond and Jem and Semlin; her friends real and imaginary, lost and found.

When the food can take care of itself she goes through and begins to lay: dusk will hold off but the rain might not; better to eat inside. She gets the photocube and lays it out where Jem will sit, with the shot of Florence facing him. Meg beams up at her, Harry and Beth are hidden, but Iris can hear them: their voices come in with the long summer light. The sky is warm to the west, cooler above; pink for a girl, blue for a boy.

She goes to the French windows. Out on the lawn the girls are playing swingball with Jem, but Iris doesn't really see them. She is thinking of the dreams she used to have at University. There was a fourth, and sometimes she still has that one, though the others are only memories. The fourth dream is so simple that Iris hardly thinks of it as a dream at all, it is so transparent in its intent.

In the fourth dream she is back in the Garrets of Moor Grange. She walks down the corridor to knock at the Semlin door, but there's no need, it's already open. She steps through, and there is Pond.

Other doors slam behind her. Iris shakes her head clear, and then Harry is striding in – *marmalized* by the girls – with the girls themselves around his heels, Megan gabbling at him, Beth dressed up in an assemblage of battered boxes – and here is Jem with Florence swooping past, exclaiming at the snapshot that has been laid out for their pleasure: Floss in splendid isolation, in the sunset, in Siena.

Iris plucks at her younger one. 'Excuse me,' she says, 'Who are you, please?'

'The first girl on the moon.'

Megan says, 'We made her out of Daz.'

'Well,' Iris says, 'I'm afraid moon girls aren't allowed earth food.'

Beth sheds sulky boxes. 'I might not want it. What is it?'

'Haddock Monte Carlo,' her mother says, and the girls perk up.

'What's *Monte Carlo*?'

'Wash your hands and you'll find out,' Iris says, and Harry pecks her on the cheek.

'You look happy,' he murmurs, and he sounds happy himself to see it; but she is, just at this moment. The low light has escaped the clouds and is burnishing the room, and suddenly it feels to Iris like 1968, not the deadly one she lives but that which people write about. Not now but *Now*, a halcyon summer in which anything is possible: moon girls, Italian flavours, and Jem come back to them, and Pond not gone for good, but living, smiling, imminent.

3. POND IN AUGUST

Waster. Useless pikey waster. Shut your face, I've had enough of you, you're as much use as a plate of cold sick. You fucking waste of space, pikey little dole queue scum. You can take the scum out of the slum but you can't wipe the shit off a turd. You little tosser. Dosser. Shut up, you waste of space gobshite. Pot of toss. You make me sick to the teeth. Scraping you divvies off my streets. STAND UP WHEN I'M TALKING TO YOU. Scum, that's all you are. You waste of spunk. You don't deserve nothing. My God you're a job, filling my cells with your stink of piss. Do us a favour, boy. Do us a favour and we'll let you go. Do us a favour and jump off the pier, go on, why don't you? Walk into the sea, we'll let you out for that. You've no right. You've no right to breathe the same air as a human being.

Brighton came first. He wanted to see the sea again. It wasn't hard. He got on the train and no one spoke to him. He was still little then. He could still make himself colourless. No one even saw him.

He got off the train and he could smell it. Solly and Dora had taken him there once for holidays. He walked to the sea and sat down on the stones. It was sunny, the stones were warm as loaves.

There was music drifting from the pier. He had his satchel with the clothes. But he wasn't cold.

There was a draw to it. There is this draw to the sea and the ends of the lines. He wasn't the only one who felt it. The streets and parades, the prom and the beach, they were full of people like him. They were then and they still are. But he's not one of them anymore.

Brighthelmstone. That's another name for Brighton, the name it had before people grew tired of its beauty. It was on a sign. By the sign was a bench with a roof where he slept. Sometimes a hairy man slept there and then he slept on the beach. At night the stones were cold and he wore all the clothes. Sometimes at night he could hear the sea down under them. Curl into the stones and you can hear the sea breathing under everything.

Another night there was another man. He came to sleep with him and he let him. He didn't have a knife. He didn't want one. It was after Mrs Malcolm and he didn't want to see harm come to anyone ever again.

He was dirty after the sleepy man but he was dirty before. Dora had hated dirtiness but she hadn't known about him. He knew the truth and the truth is he was dirty before Dora ever came. It was the knife that made him. He didn't always know that. He started knowing it the day when Mrs Malcolm died in the street of flowers. After Mrs Malcolm he didn't want to fetch his old knife or even look on it again. So he didn't have a knife when the sleepy man came and so he let him.

Moon was angry with him. He wanted to take care of him and he wouldn't have it. It was July 1952. Moon didn't speak to him until September 1955. It doesn't matter now. Now Moon is gone, but he was there then and it was a lonely time when he wouldn't say anything. It wasn't kind of him.

Mostly the days were the same. The nights were different. Sometimes they were quiet. The best ones are so soft. There is a lull. The air stops moving. The people are all gone. On those nights he slept well and when he woke he walked along the low line where the stones end and the sand begins. The sand is the bottom of the sea and in the moonlight, when he walked, the sea belonged to him.

But at night anything can happen and you have to watch yourself. The sleepy man could come or the police, or there was fighting. It began with drink or no drink. Once there was a knife and he was no longer small but he tried to make himself colourless. A man was cut and the next day he came back down with stitches in him. His flesh opened up warm and deep and they went and shut it up. That's what the cut man told him. He wasn't happy about it. They went and stitched me up, he said.

In the days he ate and lazed. He was fed by God. To get the daily bread you had to hear the good news and the cut man never listened but he did. It was fair enough. Or some days they didn't go to God but mostly it was the same arrangement. You listened and ate, you ate while you listened. Sometimes it's best if you nod. An old lady told him odd things. The burned child is not the sinner. Cities give us collision. The blade itself incites violence. Other things he didn't like but she had food so it didn't matter.

He didn't ask for the room but the old lady gave it. She had nine of them but none for the cut man. She only wanted him and once a woman who wept and later a black woman who made him think of Mrs Malcolm though really she was nothing like. She wore only white and ate only white food and drank milk. She powdered her skin with anything white she could get her hands on. They gave her flour because with that she could do no harm to herself. He stayed with the old lady for four hundred and ten days, four hundred and eleven nights. She had *Tales of Arabian Nights*. She had books and he could borrow them. Some of them he could read but some were French or half in Japanese or Russian. She had two rooms just for books and one for newspapers. She liked the crosswords. Sometimes they did the ones she'd missed. They had to dig for them. Or they just played games with words. He made them up for her.

They were washing up. He said, 'A Go ace went north, always tending seawards, homewards, triumphant.' She liked that. She made him say it again and the next day she wrote her answer and left it on the hallway table. It said, 'O, if you only could listen! Nothing whatever surpasses tenderness.' And that night he said, 'I do, but when other people cluster together, listening dissipates.'

Some nights they listened to recordings. There was one piece she had which was so beautiful he covered his ears because it was unbearable. Other nights they drank strong drink and those nights she came to him. Her flesh was warm and deep and he found he wanted it.

Her name was Alice and in the end she died. It was night and he packed his things. He didn't want to be with the dead. That was his last time in Brighthelmstone. He went down to the sea and it was a good night, soft. He sat down on the stones. The sea was hardly breathing. It was like a pond, and in the pond, a moon.

He walked inland. He knew about the countryside but he hadn't lived in it. He had read books but not enough. The weather was turning and it was colder than he knew. If it's warmth you want you need the places where other people live. There's a warmth you only get where people come together. You can't kindle it in your-self. You can't do it alone. That's what the cities are for. That's why people huddle and hug and touch, for the warmth it brings. Cities give us collision. They strike the fire out of us.

He thought he would harvest apples and sleep in hay as his reward, but it wasn't like that. He slept in woods under leaves. What people there were there were poor, with nothing to spare for him. Once he went too close and their man shot a gun at him. *Run now*, Moon said, *run*, and he hadn't moved but then he did. He went into the woods and lay under a broken tree, and for days he kept on running and sleeping wherever the days left him.

He was hungrier than he had ever been. He followed the slots of deer and found them but he couldn't kill them. They looked him in the eye. He knew not to eat the mushrooms. He drank puddles if the rain was fresh and groundwater where he heard it gibbering out of the earth. He broke the awns from the last corn and cooked them over embers. He made fires from flints and lichen, but their warmth never got into him, he couldn't get enough of them.

He came to Crowborough and asked for the London road. He went across the Weald. He followed the roads but didn't walk them. Alice was dead and he was afraid the police would come for him. At Tunbridge Wells he saw them waiting and he went away over the fields.

Winter was coming. He looked for holes, but the animals were small and jealous and he wasn't strong enough to dig anything better for himself. He wondered if he had the strength to live that way again. He had grown older and softer. Moon was looking out for him but still, he didn't know.

He went closer to the roads. One night a lorry stopped for him. He asked for London but the man was only going east as far as Canterbury. He got down where the lights began. The man said Whitehorse Lane and when Wednesday came he found his way. He listened to the news of God and ate as much as they would give him.

He heard about people like him who had died. The Sally Army First Lieutenant told him. The cold can take you just like that, the First Lieutenant said, and he snapped his fingers. His other name was Hughes and he had been all over, Newfoundland to Africa. He was older than Alice. It worried him that Hughes would die. He didn't want to see that again but he needed a place to last the winter and Hughes offered one.

It was alright, that place. There were steps that pulled down with a hook. The bloody old banger lived at the bottom and he lived at the top. There were boards across the beams and they made an attic. There was a camp bed up there with old tyres under broken springs. There was a round window, quartered with cobwebbed panes, and on clear mornings the sun was caught in it. It was alright except you couldn't stand up in it.

They had a bargain. His side of it was: one, to keep himself presentable; two, odd jobs; three, to be in at night, to put the wind up the burglars. It was a good bargain. There were never any burglars. Hughes's side of it was: one, the roof over his head; two, breakfasts and suppers, and if there was hoarfrost or night frost he could eat them in the kitchen. Afterwards he could sit by the range and read for half an hour.

Most days he did the odd jobs. Wednesdays, Hughes put on God's armour and they went to Whitehorse Lane to give out soup, soap and salvation. Sundays too, and then he laid out the books and chairs and took them in. The harvest songs frightened him and he was glad he had missed them.

This is the field, the world below,
In which the sower came to sow;
Jesus, the wheat; Satan, the tares;
For so the word of God declares.
And soon the reaping time will come,
And angels shout the harvest home.

Saturdays he had to wash in the tin bath by the kitchen door. And he had to shave. Hughes taught him. He lent him a razor but his hands shook. He didn't like to use it. They were only safety blades but Moon laughed when he read that. *Hide one*, Moon said, but he never did. He knew about the blade itself.

There were books but only true ones. There were no crosswords because Hughes took no newspapers. Hughes didn't hold with printing lies.

We believe that our first parents were created in a state of innocencey, but by their disobedience they lost their purity and happiness, and that in consequence of their fall all men have become sinners, totally depraved and as such are justly exposed to the wrath of God.

That was what the true books said and they made sense to him.

There was no drink, except there was. Hughes hid it from himself like filth. Sometimes he could smell it on him and those nights Hughes made him drink and wept in the armchair beside him. He told him about Ricks and Hendry who had gone down like Vikings. They were good men who had looked to him. He hadn't known what he was at. Those are pearls that were their eyes.

They were drinking. Hughes said, 'You do know there is no God? It's the worst lie there ever was. All we have is us. It's only us and we have to make a bloody fist of it. You know that, son, don't you?' And he said he did although he hadn't, not until then.

They had a bargain. He had kept his side and Hughes had kept his, but still, he left in the spring. Hughes was sorry to see him go. He said so and he meant it. And he didn't say but he was sorry too. He didn't say that he was afraid Hughes would die. 'It's for the best,' he said. Hughes didn't see it, but it was. It is. It's for the best to leave before your sins catch up with you. They come like cloud shadows, they race across the land behind you, and you do well to run. That's why he left Solly and Dora. He misses them more than anyone, but the memories he has of them are still pure, wheaten, golden.

He went towards London. Hughes put him on the train but at Chatham he got off. He had clean castoffs but the guard was watching. And it was April and fresh and he wasn't in a hurry. He followed the estuary to the river and he walked inland beside its coombs and downs of mud.

From Hughes he had money and the castoffs. They were suits and shoes. They were too big for him but the old clothes were too small and anyway he liked them. They smelled of Hughes, of his house, and on his lapel Hughes had pinned a Sally Army badge. *Blood & Fire*, it said. Hughes said he'd grow into them but he thought he was done with that. He was smaller than other men but stronger than they thought and smarter. Small and smart is useful things. You shouldn't bet against them.

In Erith he stopped for three years. The shoes were chafing. He sat by the memorial and watched the people come and go into and out of London. There were drinkers and they welcomed him. There were dogs too but they didn't mind. Library Mary, Little Mary, Yorkie and Arnold were the drinkers' names, and Arnold said they would be friends and that the place to go was King's. He found it by the drinking fountain and paid a night up front. They had room for him but no rooms, it was only cubicles. In the washroom there were basins and you could ask for soap. You hung your clothes in front of you so as to keep an eye on them. The orderly said they had no fishers but he didn't know what that meant. He thought it was to do with meals. He said he didn't mind but the orderly laughed at him.

He never slept well at King's. You could hear the other men tossing and turning in the dark, each within his own partitions. Sometimes they cried out or moaned into their bedding. But you always slept in the end. It was warm, it was spring, and by day the drinkers were kind to him.

Arnold taught him something:

> *There are men in Erith*
> *That no one sees or hears,*
> *And there looms on the marge of the river a barge*
> *That no one rows or steers.*

'That's us,' Arnold said. He'd never seen the barge but he'd met a man who had.

King's was a dosshouse. Some men could never settle in them. Yorkie said he couldn't breathe indoors. Other men had other names for King's, they called it The Royal or The Crown. If they expected letters they called it The Eighth House. The postmen knew what was meant. Most people knew most of the names. They were old and worn and they didn't hide much, but some men were always ashamed and so they went on using them.

The tenth night when he woke his castoffs were gone. It wasn't all of them. It was the trousers he had used and the jacket he had saved, but in that jacket was all the money Hughes had given him. Arnold said he had been fished. You did it with a hook and line over the cubicle partitions. They all knew which fellow it was but by the time they looked for him he was long gone himself.

You were to pay each night up front at King's and he couldn't. He spent a fortnight rough. He went with Arnold and begged for the shillings for King's. More often than not the wind came inland off the estuary and brought a sour haze of dust from the cement factories. People fretted about the dust and there were slim pickings then, but sometimes, if the wind was clean, they did well enough to drink. The Lord provides a man with bread but precious little wine. It was a long time that he begged in the end but he didn't feel it pass. The drink made the days run together, riverine. They were his days, but their surface was placid and he never felt their current.

He had never begged on purpose. His first mum had hated beggars. She had called them bad men, had said they were not fit to love. He hadn't ever wanted to become the thing she'd hated. He wasn't any good at it. He wanted to be colourless, to be one of the Men of Erith, but that was no use for begging. You needed to be seen. To beg you have to prove yourself, to be the proof of what you lack. You have to leave yourself open to the sidelong glances; and when you do you see your state reflected in the eyes of others.

A man stopped in front of him. He looked him up and down and dropped a shilling on his jacket. He said, 'What are you thinking?'

He said, 'I'm thinking it will rain tonight. That will buy me something to keep me dry. Thanks for it. I'm grateful.'

The man with the money frowned at him. He looked let down, as if he'd been shortchanged by a fairground slot. Not shortchanged by much: one coin was no great loss to him.

It was a lie, about the rain. What was he thinking? Sometimes it was why he didn't go on into London. Sometimes it was the kites. Solly at his shoulder and the strings drumming in his fingers. Sometimes he tried to sing the songs that Dora sang for him. Often he thought of Mrs Malcolm. The time she stood up for him against the man who took her life, and the time she died in the street of flowers with the flowers all around her. It might have been one of those things, but this was years ago and he really can't remember. Whatever it was, it wasn't something you sell to a man for a shilling.

All that time he was on the threshold of London. In Erith he was close enough to see the lights and feel the warmth, and he wanted to go in to them but he didn't. Moon said *Wait*. Moon was always careful as an animal that smells a trap.

Was there a trap? He thought he'd stopped because his shoes had hurt, but no. It was the trap, and the trap was home. The old places tugged at him and they were dangerous. He wanted to revisit them, Shoreditch and Bethnal Green, the Buildings and the land where the house had stood where he was born, but Solly and Dora would be there. He wanted to see them most of all, but not to be seen. He didn't want them to know what he was or what he had become. It does no good to go back. That was what he thought, and that was why he lingered in the half-lands where London goes out into darkness.

One morning before throwing-out a subbie came into King's. He was from the Cement Combine and he wanted a dozen men for Swanscombe. There was cash in hand for the day and a hot meal if it went late.

Arnold was leery. He said he'd done it once and that was once too often. He warned him off but he didn't listen. He'd had enough of begging. He got on the truck with the other King's men and it took them downriver, past the pits and ponds, towards the Swanscombe tower.

They worked at the tip wagons. A train of them had gone over a way short of the kilns and the limestone had to be hauled back on. It was blasted quarry rocks. Some hid sharp edges and it took two men to cradle them. It was bloody work if you weren't careful. He was careful enough, but there was nothing you could do about the dust. They shouldered through it and it turned them into weary ghosts. It lay like snow on the scrub and along the telegraph wires. It settled in their hair and on their necks and faces and he thought of the woman Alice had let in. Long afterwards you tasted it and sweated the smell of it.

Four of the King's men left at noon, but he didn't. He saw it out and got his cash in hand. Vicars the subbie doffed his cap, slapped it clean and put it on him. 'That for an honest day, son,' he said. He told him to come back if he wanted more of the same, and he did.

For two years he was casual at the cement works. Often it was Swanscombe but sometimes it was one of the others, Kent or Johnson's or Bevan's. The times were not good for the works and they were all pulling together. Mostly he had odd jobs – shifting, sweeping and shovelling – but later Vicars taught him to light the kilns and mill the hard clinker that was dragged out of them. That was better. The dust lay more peacefully inside and it was warmer in the winter.

He stayed on at King's. He hid the money that he saved. On days when there was no work he lazed with Arnold and the Marys. Yorkie had gone away and no one knew where he lived or even if he did. He had enough to buy them drink and he was eager for it. The dust leached him dry and he always had a thirst on him.

He drank more towards the end because there was less to do. Vicars sat him down. He said, 'Now look here, Henry. You never heard this from me but listen. People round here are changing. They all want jam today but they won't get their hands dirty for it. It's going to be different from now on. You'll have heard some of the works are closing. You're a young fellow and a young man needs to keep busy. You keep your hand in and you'll stay out of trouble. What I'm telling you is this isn't the place for you. You're best off away from here. Are you listening to what I'm saying?'

He was. It was all true. The half-lands weren't right for him any more than the countryside was. Moon had said to wait, but he didn't understand the way the drink could fish away the days. The drink had made him wait too long, and for the first time he saw that Moon didn't know everything. It was Vicars who knew about the drink. When Vicars said trouble it was the drink he meant and all that followed from it. He thanked Vicars and shook his hand and that night he slept better than he had in all the years at King's. The next day he said his farewells and walked on, westwards, into London.

He always thought he would meet Solly or Dora, but he never did. The city gives us collisions, it throws people together just when they least expect it, when they've lost hope or when their guards are down. You never know who it'll be or whether you'll be glad to see them, and it might be people or then again, it might be other things and you no more than an onlooker. Hopes or songs, architectures, parades or bicycles or hungers. But all these things start with people and sometimes all it comes down to is two strangers, say, in a crowd. Once he was in Bermondsey, in lodgings by the railway, and he saw the man who used to make the dogs fight in Petticoat Lane. They were in the smoking room, where the lodgers gathered to wait for supper, and aside from them the others were all travelling salesmen, but the dog man didn't know him. He was old by then and he was older himself.

It was 1959 when he came back to London and since then it has been ten years. There has always been work for him. At first he took whatever the subbies were offering. For a while he lived south of the river and now it is Rowton's, in Camden Town, but everywhere there were subbies wanting men. Mainly it was putting up buildings or tearing them down. 'You,' they said, 'you and you. You're with Ridout today,' or, 'You're with McGuire.' It was rough work but it was ready money and more than enough to meet his needs.

Through one winter and spring he worked at a yard in Somers Town. It was scrap metal mostly. He was a wrecker and repairer. He learned something. Most things, you strike them and they break, but not all. Heat iron, hammer it, and its substance draws strength from your own. Beat at it, burn it or douse it, iron only hardens. Most things are weakened by what they endure, but some are tempered. He wondered which thing he was like, and whether you could ever know or have any choice in the matter.

There were days he didn't want to work and others when he couldn't. It was four years before he put the drink behind him. At Rowton House throwing-out is nine o'clock and if he wasn't working then he used to walk until they'd let him in. From Arlington Road he went west to Primrose Hill or north to Hampstead Heath or south as far as the river. He never went far east. He always had his own room at Rowton's and he paid by the week, but sometimes he couldn't face the house itself, the din of it, and then he slept a night or two in the parks or under the arches or bridges. It is no bad thing to find a place where you can be alone in London. Sometimes it would be lashing rain and then he only walked as far as the National Central Library. The Central is on Store Street now but it was a little nearer then, off Gower Street, on Malet Place.

At first he read anything. He didn't know how it worked and he didn't like to ask. He took down whatever was to hand, it might be a telephone directory or a map or a dictionary. The dictionaries were alright. He learned French from them. He asked Moon if he remembered what was in the French books Alice kept, but he no longer could. Moon was forgetful because often he lay forgotten. He was becoming faint by then.

There were porters and assistants and then there were librarians. There was one called Miss Collins. Her Christian name was Kitty. He didn't like to look at her because she was beautiful. He would never have spoken to her if she hadn't started it.

They were in the last aisle of History. She was up a ladder. He was on a chair. She leant off the ladder to whisper. She asked if he was after anything in particular.

He didn't know how to answer that. He thought he might mention that she should mind the ladder. Instead he found himself asking whether they had any names. He was sorry when he'd spoken because her smile dimmed.

'Well, I'm sure we could find you some. Did you have any preference? You know, famous beekeepers, Scottish kings?'

'It was mine,' he said. 'But it doesn't matter.'

'You're looking for your name,' she said, and because she waited he tried to explain. He said that he wasn't. He told her that he had but it had done no good, that he had never got it back, and that she had asked and it had just occurred to him. It was awkward talking so much, he wasn't used to it, and all the time he went on Kitty just looked at him. She didn't smile again but when he was done she came down the ladder and touched him on the arm. Probably he flinched because she said, 'It's alright, I want to help. I can, if you'd like. Come with me.' Then she led him away and she did.

It took them three years. There were other names they found with his, those of his family. Other facts. His birthday, his age. That his father was born in Kent, not far from the estuary, and his mother in Ireland. He was glad to know all of it. He wrote everything down in the notebook he keeps with the other things that matter, which are his savings, Dora's gloves, Vicars's cap and the Sally Army badge. Some of the facts he half recalled, but most were long buried or else he never knew them at all.

Kitty is married now, but they can still be friends and colleagues. He doesn't know how it is they're friends, but they're colleagues because they work together. Kitty made it happen. At first he was a bureau porter and on paper he still is, but most of the time they prefer him up in the library. He's good with its systems, and he is so quiet, Kitty says, that he might have been born a librarian. It's a good library, the Central. They have a motto: *Any book to anybody anywhere.* You can order from the regions and they send it to London for you. Anyone can do it.

There is a pattern to his days. At seven he wakes. He does his teeth and shaves and makes his sandwiches. He has a cup of tea at Sampson's in Inverness Street. At eight he walks to the library. He takes his lunch with Kitty. If it's not too wet they share their sandwiches in the square. At five he's all done. If Kitty can they go for tea but mostly she can't any more. If not he always tries to take a book home to Rowton House.

After reading he gets into bed. He sleeps better now, but some nights he still wakes from dreams. There is one. There is this one of the man he killed when he was small. In the dream it all happens afresh: the man all over him; the knife. It is always terrible, but there is no God to pray to, neither for the man nor for himself.

If he has no other book he sometimes reads his notes. He likes to look over the facts, but he doesn't do it often. They make him dream too much.

He dreams that he wakes. He is small again. It's dark and Mum is dressing him. Together they are counting buttons. Whisper five, whisper six, and he's in his siren suit and cloak, when suddenly there's uproar. The floor upheaves, the world is burning. He tumbles and gets up and runs. He can't see anyone to save him. Find a safe place, Dad would say, so he looks and he does and he hides in it. Outside there's noise but he stays still and it doesn't last forever. It's raining and he's glad it does, because rain keeps the bombs at bay. Even once it's quiet he can hear the rain, still coming down.

He wakes again and night has fallen. He crawls and stands under the stars. He calls, but no one hears. Everything he knows is gone. Where his home was there is nothing but ruins and mud and water. There is nothing but a pond, and in the pond, a moon.

★

The first time he sees Mrs Malcolm he gives no credit to it. She is walking down Tottenham Court Road under a big scarlet umbrella. It is the rush hour, but the umbrella forges space for her. There is a young woman with her, a girl with false blonde hair: the false blonde girl is laughing, though Mrs Malcolm is not. She looks youthful herself. She is younger than him and very much alive.

He doesn't believe his eyes and so he does nothing about it. He turns away and walks on towards Store Street. For a while, on the way, he thinks of Mrs Malcolm: brave, generous with her strength, powerless against harm. There weren't many who stood up for him back then, but Mrs Malcolm did. It was just the once, but once is enough when you're that hungry for kindness. And then he was there when she died, and there was nothing he could do, nothing anyone could do for her, though the child might be saved. That was what the doctor said, the one who came out of the crowd and knelt down by her side, and he was right.

Still, by the time he gets to work he has put her out of his mind. It isn't her. It is someone who looks like her. It is August 1968, and Mrs Malcolm has been dead for almost twenty years.

He thinks nothing more of it until it happens again. This time Mrs Malcolm is alone. It's the evening of a fine day and she doesn't carry the umbrella. They are at the traffic lights, waiting to cross the Euston Road, and in the crowd with them is a man in a sandwich board, banging his corners into people and shouting about the end of time. 'No more of your debauchery!' he yells, but the boards say *NO MORE OF YOUR DEBORTUARY*, front and back, and Mrs Malcolm gives the man such a look. He knows the look. He knows the face and he has time to be sure of it. When the lights change she crosses with the sandwich man steering clear of her, but he stays where he is. Mrs Malcolm is dead and he doesn't want to walk beside her.

His sleep is disturbed that night. The next day he feels no better and Kitty notices. They're having their sandwiches in Bedford Square and she prods him. 'What?' she asks, and he says, 'Pardon?', and she says, 'You can't fob me off, Sydney. Look at you, you're all goosebumps. Aren't you going to tell me what's wrong?'

As best he can he does. Kitty thinks about it. She is eating one of his sandwich paste sandwiches and her blue eyes are on the trees. 'Well,' she says, 'it certainly isn't poor Mrs Malcolm. There's no such thing as ghosts. You know that, don't you?'

He thinks of Erith, of the barge that no one rows or steers, but 'Yes,' is what he says.

'Well then, you needn't be afraid of her. If you see her again you must ask her. You're not such a bad looking chap, I don't suppose she'll mind. I'll bet a round of cheese and celery she's nobody you know. Or you can choose the filling.'

'It's not just looks. It's how she is,' he says, 'they're just the same,' and Kitty shrugs. She has finished eating. She's winnowing crumbs from her skirt.

'Perhaps it's a relation,' she says. 'Did anyone survive her, your Mrs Malcolm?' Kitty asks, and he doesn't reply, because at once he knows.

He is impatient to see her again. It's a week before he does, but when the chance comes he takes it. It's another morning and he follows her. He worries that he'll be late – he never is, for the library – though in the end he isn't, because Mrs Malcolm's daughter doesn't take him far.

She is with the false blonde girl again. He is quick and neither of them notices. They go down Tottenham Court Road as far as the Tabernacle. Mrs Malcolm's daughter treads out her cigarette and the women go into a shop together. The shop is called *Donald Fisher Travel*. He doesn't enter it.

He learns the times to walk and linger, the spaces in which their paths might cross. Often he gets it wrong. It upsets him to miss her. Once he is close enough that he can hear her talking. With the false blonde girl she is discussing strangers, a Tess, a Charles, a Don. Mrs Malcolm's daughter doesn't have Mrs Malcolm's voice. Hers has more London in it, less of the sun, more of the gloom. One day Kitty is off sick and he spends his whole lunch hour watching. He loiters by the tobacconist's at the dark mouth of Alfred Mews. Across the Tottenham Court Road he sees Mrs Malcolm's daughter inside Donald Fisher Travel. She eats her lunch at her desk, she takes two sugars in her tea, she smiles for her first customer of the afternoon.

He imagines she is good at what she does. She always smiles for those who go into the shop. When she smiles she is transformed and people buy from her. She is selling them holidays. She smiles for the customers and sometimes for her friends, but not when she thinks no one watches. Not once in his sight does she smile for herself.

He no longer takes books home with him. Instead he sits by his window and watches dusk fill Arlington Road, down from the sky and up from the cellars. He thinks of Mrs Malcolm, shrunk into a victim, and of her daughter, born one. She was delivered from a dead mother in the back of a Black Maria. She must be nineteen years old. He is thirty-three. He would seem old to her, and strange. To most people he is strange. He doesn't want to frighten her, but he wants to meet her.

He wants to talk to her. Or . . . what? He wants to do something. He doesn't know what it can be. He works at knowing, day by day. And then one night he wakes in the dark from the dream of the fire, and he grasps it.

4. SYBIL IN SEPTEMBER

Before Uncle Neville died, on the days when he was well, he sometimes gave Sybil lessons. What were the lessons in? Nothing that has yet led her to a better life or place; but Sybil adored the lessons, as she adored her uncle.

He taught her the history of Jamaica, through the mingling of its peoples. The long-lost Ciboney and half-remembered Taino. The Spanish and the English, and with them the slaves of Africa, the Congo and Igbo, Ashanti and Fanti. Then the Maroons up in the hills, with Taino and Ashanti blood still running in their veins – like Queen Mother Nanny of the Windward Maroons, who fought the English to the end. And then the Scots, who Cromwell banished halfway across the world; and the Indians and Chinamen, who bought their freedom through their service; and the droves of Irish, the long-lived Jews, the red-nosed Dutchmen and red-necked Germans; and the small islanders, sailing from pitiful places no bigger shore to shore than Camden Town, some of them; but all of them, in turn, finding good harbour under the blue mountains and green hills of Jamaica.

Neville taught her about Glasgow, Westmoreland Parish, a place as far from anywhere as maybe anyone could go. The

Glasgow Estate, way back, its puncheons of rum and hogsheads of sugar going to the wharves of Green Island and from there to an Empire always in need of sweetening. The church where your father once found a yellow snake in the font. The fruit trees where you can help yourself: the children who walk country miles to school and breakfast as they come, cane joints in their pockets and mango on their fingers. The view from Mount Cromwell: the highlands to the east, and north and south the miles of cane, the telltale cloud above the Frome sugar factory, the Green and Newfound Rivers losing their ways in the Great Morass; and west, the rooftops of Green Island, where your mother went to boarding school, the first Glasgow child who ever did so well, the finest student I ever had the privilege to teach. The shining sea beyond, and after dark the Negril Lighthouse, lighting sailors to their beds.

The names of places. Rock Spring and Mint, Jerusalem and Paradise. The strong names the Maroons gave their country far up east: Me-No-Sen-You-No-Come and the Land of Lookbehind. The way the Trade winds carried inland the presence of the sea – and the evening wind, the Undertaker, bearing down from the hills the smell of orange groves and pimento barbecues. The nights, sounding of paddy frogs, smelling of cookfires and paraffin in cork-wick bottles. And then the warmth of the mornings, sinking in to the bone.

Neville told her about her families. The Malcolms with their Scottish blood, the Jarretts with their property. The mothers and grandmothers: Millicent Malcolm – Aunty Centy – Aunt Yam in the marketplaces – who raised Neville and Clarence mannerly, who saved the packets her daughter-in-law sent from the promised land of London, bought a higgler's truck and higgled yam to Lucea and Savanna-la-Mar and as far as Kingston right until the day she died; and Mrs Jarrett, who might never die if she has a say in it, with her bloodhound jowls and the face of a Roman Senator. Her twelve acres, cattle and cane, out on the highland road, and at the dim-lit heart of them the old manse with its drive of flametrees, its rooms dark as caves but airy as coves; and just as old, the stories of Mrs Jarrett's great-grandmother, Cooba – a Maroon name – born a slave and made a mistress, who lived like a white lady. You should have seen your father sweat, the day he went up that long drive to ask for Bernadette Jarrett! She knows how to stare a man down, your namesake, Sybil Jarrett – but always Mrs Jarrett – who returned with cold regards the first and only packet your mother ever sent. But that's where the fight in you comes from. That's who you should be thanking, any time in your life it comes down to fighting.

When she was seven, Sybil said goodbye to everyone. She told them she was leaving London. Her family were moving to Jamaica, to the house where her mother was born. She had convinced herself and so she was convincing: even the ladies at chapel believed her. When Clarence put the record straight Sybil burst into fierce tears. She hated London. She hated Dad. 'Your uncle only tell one side,' he said, when she had cooled to sullenness. 'You ever hear of anyone going home?'

There were other lessons, too. The love of books, the reading of them, and anything and everything they contained. The rules of the Shakespearian sonnet, the roll calls of prime ministers, the ruined dream of Rome. The wonders of architecture: the proportions of cathedrals, the spun-stone glory of the windows of the Saint-Chapelle and Chartres.

'The men who built these towers,' Uncle Neville said, his scarred hand framing the picture, 'they used to make up nets. Come dusk they fished for their suppers, up on the towers they raised.'

'Flying fish,' Sybil whispered, but she was wrong, like she always was.

'Birds. Those men fished for swifts. Caught them clean out of the air. The world was full of wonder, then,' Uncle Neville said: but afterwards Sybil told Jem, and Jem told Dad, who shook his head, laughing without really laughing, the way he has always laughed in the lifetime Sybil has known him. 'Man do anything for hunger.' was all he said.

★

It's Monday morning, and it's raining as if God stirred and thought, What's that infernal noise down there? Since when did I tell those wretches they could make a place like London? It's time I put an end to summer and drowned the sorry lot of them.

Sybil wakes. She thinks, I hear you, raining. Don't think you humble me, you up there. I don't expect better from you; I don't need your charity.

It isn't far to work. She dares herself to walk: *go* on. If she was still a kid she would. If Trudi were here they might, for kicks. But this isn't just umbrella weather, it's not the kind of rain you sing in, and besides, Trudi isn't here, she's been home to see her mum, she'll come to work from Somers Town if she makes it in at all, and so when Sybil sees the bus she does what anyone would do; she waves her free arm like a schoolgirl – *Me Miss, Me Miss, Me* – and runs towards the Hampstead Road as if her life depends on it.

She has to push aboard. In spite of the crowd there's one seat, right up by the driver's box, beside a black woman. More fool the lot of you, Sybil thinks, and presses in. No one begrudges her the place.

The woman turns to her. She is old and broad and her eyes are red. As her voice starts to rise the passengers nearby shift away as best they can, and they haven't gone far before Sybil is on her feet, cheek by jowl amongst them, shivering in the damp: ashamed, and angry at herself for feeling such a thing.

'So you want to sit by me?' the woman calls after her. 'What you want me to do, girl, split myself in two? Cut me in half. I worked *hard* for this seat. I come from a better class than you. Cut me in half! My parents send me to school. Asking for my seat! I can smell your *pouch*, girl. I clean your pouch in hospital for fifteen years. What you going to do? Cut me in two? I *know you, girl,*' the woman shouts, though Sybil is beyond her reach, stepping down into the rain beside the wet dark edifice of Whitefield's Tabernacle.

Donald Fisher is keeping watch. He stands at his window, hands tucked back, like a captain or a lighthouse keeper.

'Look at that,' he says to Sybil. 'You might call that rain, Billie, I call it free publicity. All those poor mugs getting soaked, stuck here when the sun don't shine. Eh?'

'Yes, Mr Fisher,' Sybil says.

'Look at it,' Don says, with relish. 'You can't get that for love or money.'

'Yes, Mr Fisher,' Sybil mutters, and edges towards Trudi, who has made it after all, and who is miming Sybil in nodding caricature.

There are four women at Donald Fisher's: Sybil, Trudi, Tess and Phyllis. Don's Dollies, the men call them, and now and then it's what they call themselves. Some things, you just put up with them, don't you? And then you get used to them. Familiarity breeds consent.

In the old days (as Don says, to any cornered listener) the back-bone of the business was business: Paris and Rome for the small fry, long-haul for the same old blue-chip flyers, paid for by the same old blue-chip firms. Now times are changing. The Tottenham Court Road office is placed to catch the passing trade, and has framed pictures of wonders (Corcovado, the Taj Mahal), exemplary souvenirs (hats of various shapes and sizes), complimentary beverages, and a less businesslike class of chair (upholstered in two-tone yellow) to accommodate the backsides of the civil servant put out to clover, the widow with her affairs in order, the homesick émigré, the whizz-kid who means to flaunt it, the well-endowed honeymooner – all those who might be rich enough to fly the world for pleasure.

It's just work. To begin with Sybil did find enjoyment in it, of a vicarious and jealous kind, and Don was always full of talk of trips and junkets he had known. She should have known better than to hope. She has been lured by hints of promises: she isn't going anywhere. There is no escape for her. Her work is to sell to others the thing that she herself desires.

All day the rain keeps up, but still the punters trickle in. Donald Fisher knows his business: people shake their brollies, look at the wonders and over their shoulders, as if they never mean to set another sodding foot in London.

'Omelettes,' says Trudi's customer. 'I'm particular about my food. Omelettes, see, they're easy on the old carburettor. My wife used to do them. Would they have omelettes, there?'

Trudi rearranges brochures; the dusks and dawns, noons and nights of a dozen paradises. She looks as if she has a headache.

'What we've got,' she says, 'is packages. They're very popular. All your meals taken care of, no bother with anything –'

'That's all very well,' the customer butts in, 'that's very nice, I'm sure, but do they do *omelettes*, dear? That's what I'm asking.'

From the corner of her eye Trudi can see Sybil. It's Sybil's turn for mime: *My wife used to do them*, she mouths. She's keeping her face businesslike, keeping herself looking busy. There's no one queueing, though for some time a small man has been stood by the door, advancing no further, as if he's sheltering from the rain. Cap in hand, peeking at the souvenirs, the salesgirls, the pictures, as if he expects to come on one that says *Trespassers Will Be Prosecuted*.

Trudi swivels. 'Billie?' she says, crisply, 'this gentleman would like to know if they can make him an omelette in Brazil. Could you make some calls? Start with the Copacabana Palace.'

'Hang on,' says the customer, alarmed, 'no need to telephone *international* –'

Sybil picks up the phone. The customer watches her warily. 'Who's paying for that?' he asks.

Sybil says, 'It's courtesy.'

'Oh well,' the customer says, sitting back, 'if it's like that.'

Sybil ignores Trudi's sanitised mirth. She holds the phone to her head like a weapon. In passing she notices that the man by the door is leaving: he glances back at her as he steps into the street. 'And how do you like your omelette, sir?'

The customer ponders the question, and Sybil with it. 'No foreign muck,' he says. 'No monkeying around. That's what I'm looking for, see? I want them done just the way my wife used to do them.'

Don't count on better. Count on worse, then nothing going to let you down. The words are Clarence's. Sybil takes them to heart. She tries to live by them. They've never disappointed her: they leave no room for disappointment.

But nor do they allow her hope. There are too many days like this, with no good to be got out of them, in which everyone she meets contrives to shame or anger her. On days like this it's hope you need. She wants it. She does hope, when she thinks no one is watching. Despite the words that knot her heart, Sybil knows she hopes too much.

She takes the bus home with Trudi. Charles is up and making curry. Tony's keeping him company, reading out choice bits of news. The four of them live on Mornington Terrace, facing the arched cliff of brick that cuts down to the Euston railway lines. It's a decent squat. The owner is an artist, a celebrity photographer who hasn't the heart for aggro, or perhaps for the aggravation of attendant bad publicity. The heavies came round just the once, cut the power and cleared them out, but Charles (who is older and knows the form) shimmied back in and tapped the wires, and that was a year ago. There's been no trouble since.

There are nine permanent residents, but most of them are nomads. Charles is on the dole and Sybil and Trudi work close by, but Tony is only home on off days. Tony's a flight attendant, as are three of the absentees, all of them pretty boys (and all of them straight, as all are too quick to add when asked their business), all of whom spend stretches in the air, or overnighting overseas in jetlagged five-star hotels, from which they liberate – in seasons of one-upmanship – treasure troves of bad taste houseware: mismatched faux-silver cutlery; hewn rock-effect glass ashtrays; monogrammed dressing gowns; pea-and-princess stacks of towels; golf umbrellas; heated blankets; scented soaps; doll's-house jars of marmalade and honeycomb; four yards of Hollywood red carpet (now muddied in the hall); a hookah pipe shipped from Damascus; and once (Tony's finest hour) a throne-like kingsize armchair, with *Excelsior, Penang* impressed in its jade leatherette.

Sybil has been here since spring, when a girlfriend married away and left a room to her. Even now, in these September nights, she can feel how cold the place will be when the weather turns, the way the wind comes prying in where the old house has worn away. Come night she'll curl into her blankets and try not to lose sleep over it. She's seen worse and shouldn't count on better.

When Tony is tripping – as he means to tonight – he talks about their generation and the great things they're doing. The wealth they'll share and share alike, the end they'll bring to war, the men they'll put on the moon. And Sybil says nothing, but she has none of it. What are they doing, except living? What has changed and what is changing? Nothing to do with them. The moon is for dreamers; it lies beyond her reach. Sybil doesn't aim for it.

She trudges upstairs. By her bedding are the books she owns. Most are tatty paperbacks she's scrounged; two mean more to her. The first is her Confirmation Bible, the second a Shakespeare. There are two book-plates in the Shakespeare. The first is addressed to Uncle Neville: *On His Appointment as Principal of Glasgow Elementary School, with Felicitations from His Affectionate Predecessor, Miss Hilda Shearer, Glasgow, Westmoreland Parish, Jamaica, 3rd February, 1935.* The second is a pale imitation of the older, braver blessing. *To Sybil, from Dad, Happy Birthday 1962*, is all it dares say.

Tony says, 'This is the Age. This is the Age of the Man in the Moon. We're going to put him there, just like we said we would. We're the ones who do as we say, we're the generation who aim for the moon and *reach* it. We're going to change the world and nothing can stop us. Billie, we have to make a flag for ourselves. We make it blue, and the face of the Man in the Moon, silver, placid, smiling down on us ... won't that be beautiful? Can we make it, Billie?'

'I'm here,' Sybil says, and Tony reaches for her hand.

'Good,' he says. 'You are good, looking after me. Watching your hapless flock by night.'

'I said I would, didn't I?'

'You did, and you always keep your word. You're a friend to your friends, Sybil, and God help your enemies. You're the lion who lies down with lambs. I should make more of that, a girl as fierce and true as you. Really I should take advantage. Promise me something.'

'What?'

'Let me in your knickers tonight.'

'In your dreams,' Sybil says, and beyond her Charles harrumphs and turns a lamplit page, and Trudi ratchets up the television's brassy theme: no spirit of the age will ever wholly overcome their English priggishness.

'Oh well. At least let's do the flag. We can fly it over the railway. We can make the moon from milk tops.'

Sybil squeezes his hand. 'Hush,' she says. 'Tony, you need to chill out now.'

Tony moves in slo-mo, like a frogman or a spaceman. 'I know, but I choose not to. I choose to boldly go where no man has gone before. I choose to trip and do the other things, not because they are easy, but just because I want to. Many years ago, the great British explorer George Mallory, who got high on Everest, was asked why he wanted to do such a thing. He said, *Because it is there.* Well, now greater highs are here, and we're going to do them, and the moon is there, and splendid flag potential. And therefore, as we set sail we ask for God's blessing on the greatest trip on which man has ever embarked. Who am I?'

'JFK,' Charles says, from the depths of the jade armchair. 'You're misquoting, and he's history. You might show him more respect.'

Trudi says, 'Too right. You shouldn't take the piss out of the dead.'

'Piss? Trudi, you do me wrong. Truly, Trudi, you misgrok me. My worship of JFK is unsullied by the taint of urine. The man was wise and beautiful. Also a good Irishman. Don't you agree, Charlie?'

'Top drawer,' Charles says, and Tony beams and rushes on.

'JFK and Jesus Christ, there's nothing to choose between them. Both handsome devils with the best lines. Both good with women, both gorgeous pin-up martyrs.'

'Wash your mouth out,' Trudi whispers, but Tony doesn't hear or care.

'Verily, I believe in the pearly wisdom of Jesus Fucking Kennedy,' he says, and his eyes drift shut. His free hand fibrillates, as if he is dreaming of pianos.

★

When she wakes the light is grey around the half-loose dustsheet curtain. Tony coughs awake beside her. He is skinny as a boy. His hair sticks up in squaw feathers. He croaks an oath at the day and burrows back into her.

'Leave off,' Sybil chides.

'You're warm, though. Any chance of tea?'

She doesn't bother with an answer. She gets up and washes at the handbasin, props her mirror on the chair, takes her work clothes from the hanger. Tony rolls a cigarette and picks through her books as he smokes, pausing only to read the Bible, dour as a prophet.

'*They were stoned, they were sawn in two, they were killed with the sword; they went about in the skins of sheep and goats, destitute, afflicted, ill-treated – of whom the world was not worthy – wandering over deserts and mountains, and in dens and caves of the earth.*'

'Don't mock,' Sybil says, though God knows she does herself.

'*And all these, though well attested by their faith, did not receive what was promised*. As if I would. Do you think it's talking about us, mind? Destitute, stoned *and* too good for the world? Don't tell me that's coincidence.'

But Sybil won't rise to the bait, and Tony rifles on, muttering at the paperbacks. 'Incontinent fucks,' he says. 'They write such shit, these people, and they just can't keep it to themselves.'

Tony aspires to be an author, come the day when his saleable looks are gone. You can't fly the skies forever. You can see too many new horizons; so Tony says, and he'd know.

Trudi's wireless *wah-wah*s through the wall. 'At least they're doing something. At least they're writing,' Sybil says, and Tony lets the book fall.

'Firm artistic sphincters. The world would be a better place for them. I'm doing something.'

She doesn't ask. He'll have a ready answer. She imagines him as a boy, limber with excuses, as she stands to clip her bra. Behind her she can hear him stubbing out his cigarette, and she feels him watching.

'You're beautiful,' he says, and Sybil meets his mirrored eyes. Her own are imperious.

'You best be saying so, this morning.'

'Marry me.'

'In your dreams,' she says again, like a mantra.

'I'll share them with you, my dreams.'

'You share them with too many girls.'

'You're different. Marry me.'

She turns. This is new. Tony lies naked on the mattress, the blankets tangled with his ankles. His body is ludicrous, but his eyes are grave. She says, 'You don't know me.'

'It's been a summer.'

'On and off.'

'I'm on it now. I'm serious. You're my charm, you don't take any of my bullshit.'

'I did last night.'

'Come on,' Tony says, 'that was the real deal.'

'No,' Sybil says, 'I'm saying no. I'm not waiting around for you.'

'And where would you be off to?'

'Somewhere,' she says. 'Anywhere.'

Tony relaxes. 'Ah, come on,' he smiles. 'Billie, Billie, fly me to the moon, why don't you? You belong here, love, you've nowhere else. Born and bred, you are, not like some. Not like me. You need old smoke in your veins, you'll never stray far from London. Besides, there's me to think of. You'd always come back,' Tony says, 'for me'. And he opens his arms on the sheets, palms up, like a martyr or a conjurer. *Nothing in this hand, nothing in this hand.*

The rain has softened overnight. Trudi and Sybil walk, as they do most days. It's not like they're made of money, and it's not like they don't have umbrellas.

'Hold this a sec,' Trudi says, and Sybil takes her brolly, the gaudy hemispheres (*Toronto Sheraton* and *Tel Aviv Carlton*) bumping bellies overhead as Trudi deploys cigarettes.

'Give us one then,' says Sybil, and Trudi lights them both and puts Sybil's in her mouth, smirking at the filmstar gesture; but when they start again she winces.

'This effing rain.'

'What is it now?'

'My heels. Honest, I think I'm bleeding.'

'Stop moaning, silly cow. Come on, here, chop chop,' Sybil says, and Trudi obeys, leaning on her friend and walking like a wounded trooper on towards Mornington Crescent.

'Tony was a state last night,' Trudi says. 'It's getting on Charlie's wick, you know. We don't want the neighbours complaining, that's what he says.'

'It isn't Charlie's place,' Sybil says, but Trudi pouts.

'More his than ours, he was there first. Anyway, Tony does go on. All that rubbish last night.'

'What rubbish?'

Trudi gropes at her, her voice a mocking Dublin whinge. 'Billie, get your knickers off, Billie, put the kettle on.'

Sybil roars with laughter. 'Is that supposed to be *Tony*? Lord, you better start running, girl, you need to keep your day job.'

Trudi lets her go. Her face has pinched. 'It's not right, though, Billie,' she says. 'He shouldn't talk to you like that. Are you and him going steady, then?'

Sybil takes a last breath of fag, crushes it out underfoot. 'No,' she says, and then, 'Tony's alright.'

Ffft! goes Trudi, as she hobbles. 'Swanning off round the world or high as a kite. When he's not flying he's on something. He's hopeless and he wasn't always. I'm not being rude, but you're not doing him any favours. He needs someone sorting him out, that's what Tony needs.'

Sybil's smile has faded, too. Her face – so lovely when she laughs (she has her mother's face, high-brown, queenly, darker and finer than her father's) – those features have composed themselves into a sculpted mask, the muscles setting hard; and Trudi sees the change and quails.

'I'm not having a go, Billie, really I'm not. I'm just saying.'

'Yeah? Well now you've said it,' Sybil says, and that shuts Trudi up good and proper. Being friends with Sybil means knowing when you're beaten. Besides, Trudi's feet are killing her, and who else is she going to lean on?

They limp on, conversationless. The crowd is hard going, a bog of damp backsides and brollies, and it's only as they near the shop that Sybil sees someone waiting. Now and then he glances in, as if Don hasn't opened up: but Don is never late, Donald Fisher loves the early bird, he marks its footsteps well and forever sings its praises.

'Him again,' Trudi mutters, and the loiterer turns. His face clears as he sees them. He says nothing, but takes off his cap and steps back for them to enter. It's only then, as he follows, that Sybil remembers him as the man who sheltered from the rain.

'Late!' Don barks, tapping his wrist. 'Punctuality!'

'Sorry, Mr Fisher,' Trudi says, and with game girlishness, 'Patience is a virtue, sir.'

'I don't want your bleeding virtue. You look a shambles,' Don rumbles, and then, noticing the early-doors customer, lowers his voice and nods sidelong. 'Go on. Work your women's magic.'

In the drab back room they share a lipstick by the mirror.

'Who is he, then?' Sybil asks, and Trudi makes a face.

'Some dirty old man. He was in and out last week.'

'He was here yesterday, too.'

'He never buys nothing,' Trudi says. 'Never even asks, just looks. I know that's what Don wants Dollies for, but still. They give me the creeps, voyeurs.'

Sybil regards herself. 'He's not that old,' she says, 'I don't know about the dirty.'

Trudi is easing off her shoes, wedging in cotton wool. She looks up wickedly.

'Marry or shag or throw off a cliff?' she asks, but Sybil shrugs. There's nothing about the man that makes the game worth playing. Already she finds it hard to picture him. He's nothing, no trouble, not flash. Dressed for some discreet business, though Sybil can't place what that business might be.

'Maybe he's an undertaker,' she murmurs, but Trudi is packing away, smacking her lips, all done.

'Frankly, my dear, I don't give a shit. He's all yours if you want him,' she says, and blows a farewell kiss.

Sybil trails after her. The man is where they left him. Phyllis and Tess are at their desks, Trudi is settling, and they're all doing their best to look right through him. Nor does the man look at them, though he meets Sybil's eye. She smiles, meaning little by it – it's what she always does – but the man smiles back, and then he ducks his head and comes and sits.

He clears his throat. The girls are listening. Sybil sees that he knows it. 'I'd like to book a holiday,' he says, eventually.

'Well,' she says, 'you're in the right place.' She leans forward and adds, 'It's alright, it's not like the dentist,' but the man just blinks, as if he doesn't get it or thinks the joke's on him.

She tries again. 'Did you have somewhere in mind, sir?'

The man nods. 'No,' he says. 'I hoped you might advise me. I'm Sydney.'

'There you are, then. Go there,' Sybil says brightly, and regrets it as she does. Trudi chortles at her post and the man's head drops. He fiddles with his cap. You can't but feel sorry for him.

'I don't know about that.'

'Forget it. I'm Sybil,' Sybil says, and is relieved when he stops with his fiddling. She gets out some papers. 'How about I give you some choices, you tell me what you like. Alright, ready? Mountains or sea? City or surf? Beach or Botticelli?'

The questions are Don's and loathsome, but on she goes with them. The man answers a couple but he's hardly listening. He's staring at her, as if searching her for something. He looks like he might be hard of hearing, or as if the words she reads don't matter to him at all, because what he hears her say is something else entirely.

'I've always wanted to fly,' he puts in, and she has to laugh, but it's alright, he smiles. 'That must sound strange to you.'

'No,' she lies, but of course it does. He is strange, the way some people are. He's one of those who aren't quite at home in the world.

'I know,' he says, 'I've got it. The trip of a lifetime.'

'That's what you'd like?'

'That's it. What would you recommend?'

She recommends the cruises. She lays out the bumph for the five-star liners, the garish floating palaces of the Atlantic and Pacific, the excursions by seaplane. She tries the deluxe packages, the gaudy extravagances, the grand hotels of the New World and the Old. She lays them all out on the desk and talks them up, while he sits in silence.

'If you were me,' he says, 'if you were in my shoes, what would you choose?'

She smiles properly. 'But I'm not, am I?'

'But if you were.'

'Well, if you're really asking *me*, Jamaica.'

He asks her why, and so she tells him. As best she can she describes the blue mountains and green hills which she has never seen. The congregated peoples, the hay-warm smell of cane and the trees where you can help yourself. The towns with names like sweets or cocktails or happy-ever-afters. The fresh warmth of the mornings and the name of the town where her mother was born. She tells him too much, but there is a freedom even in the telling: once she's started she can't find it in herself to stop. She smiles again when she does.

'I don't know what's up with me. Talking your ear off!' she says. 'Anyway, that's just me. That's my dream trip, not yours. You need to think about yourself.'

He stands and puts on his coat. 'I will,' he says.

'Are you leaving, then?'

'I'll come back. Thank you. Goodbye,' he says, and just like that he's gone.

You don't know Sybil. Don't think you know the daughter just because you met the mother. There are likenesses of look and gesture, but those things are innocent. An infant might have those things without knowing what it has or does. Sybil never learned how to be her mother's daughter.

Bernadette aspired to dignity. At best Sybil musters pride. She takes pride in knowing how to fight. She fights for herself, most of the time, and if there's time to spare, then fuck it, she'll fight for anyone who can't stand up for themselves. Even Sydney: Sybil would rather fight for him than pity him.

If she had known her mother then she would grieve for her, but she didn't and cannot. She can only imagine grief. What she feels is less realised. It is loss that drives her, and – on the many mornings when loss is insufficient – anger.

On better days, as today, she doesn't go straight home. She buys groceries and walks up through Camden Town, through the no-ballgames courts and the wealth-of-Empire terraces, to the flat on St Mark's Square, where her uncle used to tell her stories of swift-catchers and safe harbours, and where her father now lives on, alone in his brother's place.

Someone needs to clean for Clarence. Someone needs to see he eats, someone needs to talk to him and let air into those hollow rooms, and if Jem does more than most men, still, it does Sybil good.

She presses the bell and waits. The rain has run itself out. The sun is on St Mark's ragstone, though shadow quarters the churchyard. The door opens behind her.

274

'You're late,' Dad says. 'It been raining?'

'Yeah,' Sybil says, 'so you going to let me in or what?'

She follows him up. The building never seems to change, and the flat, too, is much as she always remembers it; underlit, smelling of mice, bare as if untenanted.

He sits by her while she cooks. From somewhere – Jem or the dole office – he has a crossword over which to grumble. 'Neville was the one with a head for these things.'

'No one making you do it. No one making you do anything,' she says, sterner than she feels. At least he's sitting, and without drinking. On the worst days he lets her in, goes back to bed and waits until she's gone.

She fries potatoes, lights the oven. 'You get that from Jem?'

'He came by some time.'

'He still with that girl?'

Clarence bends over the crossword, meek and gigantic. 'No one asking you to like her,' he says, and Sybil laughs, bitter and easy.

'They wasting time if they trying. Do you?'

He hides in the puzzle again. '*Do* you?' she persists, and he sighs.

'The way I remember she was a good child. Not like her old man. Never cold. Besides, Jem don't bring her here. It isn't any of our business.'

She turns potatoes, cracks eggs, shirrs them. *Whose business, if it isn't ours?* she thinks, but she keeps her mouth shut. She has said enough and heard enough of Florence Lockhart: talking will only spur her anger.

'How's that work? They treating you right?' Dad asks, and Sybil relents.

'This man came in today looking for the holiday of a lifetime. Wants to know all about Jamaica.'

'Better lifetime here,' Dad says, refractory and loyal always to the mother country, and fetches salt as Sybil brings the food to table.

After they're done she washes and dusts. There's one bottle in the cupboard and she leaves it where it is. It will do no good to take it. 'Maybe something on the wireless,' he calls, and she puts it on. The cricket has been rained off but they're talking it over anyway. Clarence sits in the lounge, half listening, half watching her. The lino is worn patternless in a patch around his feet.

'You look like her just then,' he says.

'Sweeping up after you?' she asks, but he smiles, shakes his head. 'Talking about that girl.'

'You look like an old man,' she says, straightening, 'And you ain't. How old are you?'

'If you don't know I don't.'

'You're not old,' she says, and goes to him, kisses him.

★

Sydney. It's one of those names that no one calls kids anymore. Sydney has gone bad with time. It smells of old men, of rooms where someone in the corner goes on about the war like a vicar with a dog-eared sermon. It's an old name, and old means poor. Sydney is someone born into another time, a place of jam tomorrow and tomorrow never coming.

He doesn't come back for two days. Trudi wonders if they've seen the last of him, but Sybil has no doubt. She thinks, He's summoning his courage. It'll be easier next time. He was afraid before, scared of sitting down and saying something to my face, but now he's done it once and that's why he'll be back, because the worst is over with.

She thinks, It's me that he's afraid of. There's no sense in that. It's me he fears and wants to see, and why? Why do I matter to a stranger? You should run a mile, girl, you shouldn't mean a thing to him. You shouldn't talk to him again, she thinks; but she knows she will.

She wants the measure of him. It vexes her to have no answers. She isn't scared of him. Sybil prides herself on fearlessness, and he isn't some dirty old man – whatever Trudi says – or not just that. There's always sex, but it's more than that with him. It was more like family, the way she found herself talking. For all his awkwardness she found herself at ease with him. And she'd never tell Trudi, but she might even fancy him, enough at least not to kick him out of bed, if it ever came to that. He's alright looking, though she has Tony to remind her that looks aren't everything.

It's Thursday noon and busy. Sybil is making calls when Phyllis stops beside her. Phyllis is the office gossip, a sponger of pleasure and grief. 'Don't look now, dear,' she murmurs, and lingers as Sybil does.

Sydney is in the queue. It's almost funny, watching him. He's at the front, but each time a salesgirl comes free he stands aside, letting another in before him. He peers Sybil's way in cornered exasperation.

'Would you like me –' Phyllis begins, but Sybil cuts her off, fobs off the voice on the phone, and is hanging up as Sydney seats himself.

'Hello,' she smiles. 'I was wondering when I'd see you again.'

'I was thinking,' he says, and she thinks, No you weren't, Sydney. You did all your thinking before. It was nerve you needed and you must have found it somewhere, because here you are.

'So?'

'I'd like to do it. What you said.'

'The trip of a lifetime, you mean.'

'No. Well, yes. I mean Jamaica.'

They sit looking at one another. She hasn't been speaking the way you should with customers. Her voice and look are franker, more clandestine, more cautious. Why cautious? Because whatever's happening here matters, she thinks, and I still don't understand why.

'Sydney,' she says, 'if all you want is flying, you don't have to go far. It costs, you see what I'm saying?'

'Oh, I have money,' he says, and reaching into his coat he brings out a brown envelope, fattened, misshapen. He sets it on the desk carefully, as if its freight is new to him. 'I've been saving,' he says.

'Put that away,' she says, and he does while she gets out the forms, the necessary triplicate. She feeds the typewriter. 'Montego Bay or Kingston?'

'I don't mind,' he says. 'You decide.'

'Montego, then. You'll want somewhere to stay, as well.'

'I hadn't thought,' he says, and she laughs.

'You planning to sleep on the beach? And you need to give me dates.'

'I don't know,' he says. 'You might choose.'

'Sydney, I can't do it all for you,' Sybil says. 'You got to decide these things for yourself.'

'I'm sorry. I'd like two tickets.'

'For your wife?' she asks, though the question makes no sense: she knows there is no wife for a man like Sydney.

'For you,' he says, wretchedly.

He doesn't meet her gaze. He has dropped his head again. Later she's glad of that. She must have looked so thick just then.

And she was angry with him, too. She thought he was playing with her, being cruel with her, and her look must have been vicious.

'What are you talking about?'

'I'd like to do something for you.'

'Why?' she asks, and when he doesn't reply, 'I don't need charity. You don't owe me nothing. You don't even know me.'

'Please don't shout,' he says, and Sybil hears that she is. Everyone is looking. She bunches her hands and shuts herself up until they all go back to their own shop-soiled businesses.

'You don't know me!' she hisses again, but all he does is shrug.

'Hardly. Even so.'

She thinks, I had him wrong. He isn't a nothing man. There's something about him, under the skin. There's something in him you don't see or hear, a strength and intelligence. She thinks, Girl, he's brave as you are. He comes from somewhere dark and goes along on his own way, like water underground, and there's no stopping him.

'I ain't going with you,' she says, and he looks up.

'I don't mind. It can be just you.'

'You're crazy,' she says.

'I don't mind, really,' he says. 'I just wanted to see it.'

'Why?'

'You made it sound nice. But I can stay here.'

For a long time, then, she stares at him. He doesn't like it, he flinches and fidgets. He puts up with it for as long as he can, then says, 'I'm not asking for anything. It's a gift. I want to do it.'

'Flying me halfway around the world. You want to do that.'

'If it's what you'd like. I thought perhaps you would.'

'You're mad.'

'I might be,' he says. 'I couldn't say.'

She looks at the triplicate. Where it says *Route* she has entered a flight path's cipher, *BOAC-Cunard 707, LHR-JFK-MBJ. Passengers,* is the next open question. Sybil aligns the page, hovers, types, *2.*

No one believes her, obviously. 'I don't believe you!' Trudi cries, but she's happy, of course she is — Sybil always knew — to have Tony to herself.

'I don't believe what I am *hearing*,' Clarence roars, slapping his long thighs with his long hands — and it's not the kind of thing he says, it's something Neville might have said, but she's glad he roars it all the same, just to see the light in his eyes, to hear him thundering.

'What is it, then,' Trudi asks, 'some kind of honeymoon? What is he, your sugar daddy in mufti?'

'Piss off,' Sybil says. 'You telling me you'd say no?'

Pssh, goes Trudi. 'You wouldn't see me for dust, love. Lie back and think of England and never see London again, I wouldn't need asking twice. I just can't believe it, him walking in, you saying yes. It'd be romantic if he was normal. You'll look after yourself, won't you? You never know, with men.'

'You're away, then, I hear,' Tony says, but he believes her even less. His eyes are still laughing as she packs what little she doesn't mean to leave behind, the tickets in her Bible, pressed between prophets like flowers. *You'll be back*, the eyes say. *There's no escape for the likes of you.*

'So you leaving us,' Clarence says, and this second time he has Jem there, the three of them around the table, now loud and hard, now soft and tender, like drinkers at a wake. 'Is that it?'

'I never said that,' she says. 'Anyway, you left.'

'That was different. I was coming *here*. We was coming to a better place.'

'Is that what you call it? This?'

'You don't know. You was better off raised here. I blame Neville, always with his stories. You belong here.'

'How come you know that, if I don't?'

'So how come you don't? You don't know worse than this, that's why. You could show your parents some gratitude. And who is this fellow? Who is this Sydney? He should be sitting here at my table with his cap in his hand.'

'He's just a bloke,' Sybil says. 'He won't be no trouble. Look, I'm not going for him.'

'Dad,' Jem says, 'it's just a holiday,' but none of them believe it. Clarence's hands are shaking.

'Is that all it is? Sybil? You tell it to my face.'

'Stop laying it on me like it's something bad! *Accusing* me. I'm not planning on never seeing you again. It's not like I'm going off to war. I've got this one chance, you want me to turn it down? You think I won't regret it? This is what I've always wanted, don't pretend like you don't remember. You're not changing my mind.'

They nurse their drinks like wrongs. Dad shakes his head, he sighs. 'You need money?'

'No,' Sybil says, and then, reluctantly, 'I might need something.'

Mrs S. Jarrett,
Highland House, Lucea Road,
Glasgow,
Westmoreland,
Jamaica.

Saturday 21st September 1968

Dear Madam,
Please excuse my writing unexpectedly. My name is Sybil Malcolm. My mother was Bernadette, your daughter.

My father (Clarence) says you know you have a granddaughter as my mother wrote it to you. I don't know what else you could know. I am 19 years old now. I am sorry to say I don't know too much about you. When I was little, my uncle (Neville) used to talk about you often, but that was a long time ago and I suppose things have changed. My father doesn't talk about you except to give me this address which I hope is still correct so this will reach you.

I am writing because I have been given a chance to visit Jamaica. I leave here this Thursday and by the time you get this I expect I will be in Montego Bay. I don't mean to impose on you, but if you would see me I would like that. I will be in touch as best I can,

Yours sincerely,
Sybil Malcolm.

The truth is she doesn't believe herself. Even at the post office, sending airmail to an old woman who may be in her grave, and counting out seven and six for her Visitors Passport, and then saying her last goodbyes, and waiting for the shuttle bus at the West London Air Terminal; even as she and Sydney Marsh advance awkward and inchmeal down the cabin, the passengers around them all dressed as if for dinner – all the time it's as if she's walking on water.

I can't believe I'm doing this. As if it hasn't been said enough she is about to whisper it again when they breast the clouds. 'Oh,' she says instead, 'Sydney, look. Aren't they beautiful?'

'Yes,' Sydney murmurs, and Sybil remembers what he said about flying.

'Do you want to sit by the window?'

'No,' he says, 'no,' but his eyes still creep back to the unearthly plains and tors that now stretch like Heaven below them. 'Could I?'

'Course. Here,' she says, and as the light goes off (the stewardess announcing that they may smoke if they wish, that soon they shall be served cocktails and lunch and afternoon tea), they clamber out of their places, over and around the aggrieved stranger in the aisle seat, who seems to Sybil much less strange than either of them are themselves.

They leave at noon and arrive as sunset catches up with them. Sydney is sleeping. Sybil watches over him as they swing across the bay. A headland, dirty wharves, a market square. The lights of paradise coming on along the strip. White sand, green sea, and inland in the distance, mountains, dark and rising.

'First time, Miss?' asks the customs man, and Sybil allows that it is, disliking the gaze which weighs and measures her. 'Visiting family?'

'I might,' she says, and he raises an indulgent brow.

'Long way to come for might,' he says, and waves her on into the twilight.

Sydney is out ahead of her. Other arrivals part around him, trailing after porters, exclaiming at the heat and tugging at their ties. Sydney's eyes are closed. 'What are you doing?' Sybil asks.

'Smelling. It smells different.'

She stands beside him, shuts her eyes, smiling. 'Yeah,' she says, 'alright.'

'The dust is made from different things.'

'Now you're too mad for me. Come on.'

Sydney sighs. He opens his eyes like a hampered anchorite. The road is lined with flowering trees and rental lots, Avis, Chelsea, Dullum's U-Drive. A jet ascends out of the dusk into red light: Sydney's gaze follows it. 'Perhaps we could stay here,' he says, and Sybil has to laugh.

'Sydney, this is just the airport! You come all this way, you don't want to see what else there is?'

'I don't know. This is very nice.'

'But I've got family. We should go and stay with them.'

'In the town where your mother was born.'

'Yes.'

'Is it far?'

But Sybil doesn't know, their leaving having thrown all planning into disarray. They have to stop at Information, where a winning-smiled boy issues them with a map (*Courtesy of ESSO, for the more Discerning Driver*) and hunts with them for Glasgow, a pinpoint at a three-way crossroads, and not so far as the crow flies, south-west across inlets and mountains.

It's only on the off chance that she asks for the island phone-book. In her dreams there are no telephones in Glasgow, nothing new to break its timeless spell; but her dreams are old and suspect, and there are three listings after all, for the P.O., the police, the inspector of sanitation.

'Good night?'

'Hello? Is that Glasgow post office?'

'What time it is?'

'Sorry? I can't –'

'You too late, dear, we closed.'

'I don't want – wait – hello? I'm just looking for a Mrs Jarrett.'

'A who you say?'

'*Jarrett.* Is she still . . . do you know a Mrs Jarrett?'

'Surely.'

'So she still lives there? In Glasgow?'

'Man was in yesterday.'

'I need to get a message to her. Can you help me? I need to let her know I'm coming. This is her granddaughter. Her granddaughter, Sybil Malcolm. I've come from London, England. I wrote to let her know. Hello?'

'I'm still here, child.'

'I'll be there tomorrow, afternoon or evening. Could you tell her?'

'I'll send up word.'

'Oh, thank you.'

'Never you mind, she'll hear of it.'

'Thank you so much.'

'Walk good,' the voice says, and is gone.

They rent a car. Sybil drives. Montego Bay is coming alive with evening crowds, *Yellowbird* and *Sundowner* picked out in neon above them. The first hotels are plush, all red carpets and uplit fountains, and Sybil and Sydney pass them by in silent agreement. For want of a plan they have nowhere booked.

The sea opens alongside them. The moon is rising. Sybil draws in under the palms. 'Look at the beach.'

'Yes.'

'Want to get out?'

'Can we?'

'We can do anything,' she says, but still their voices are no more than church whispers as they leave the car behind, as Sybil kicks off her shoes and wades through sand and surf while Sydney sits and watches. To him she becomes a moonlit silhouette, her progress slow and dancelike. He doesn't see her face when she looks up at him and smiles.

Afterwards they eat. Sybil drinks. Around them Americans order daiquiris and doubloons. The breeze is cooler now: it catches the rich foreign laughter and carries it out to sea.

'Sydney Marsh,' Sybil says, and he looks up at his name and down from her gaze. 'Who are you? Where did you come from?'

'London.'

'No one's just from London.'

'My mother was Irish.'

'Was she soft like you? Giving strangers favours?'

'You're not a stranger.'

'No? What's my favourite song? What's my favourite food?'

'Jerk chicken?' he hazards, that being what she's having, and she laughs.

'Sydney, it wasn't a real question. You don't know me, I don't know you. You could be anyone. I could.'

He stops eating to think it over. He starts to speak and stops. He says, 'I've never done anything like this. I wouldn't be here if it wasn't for you. I don't think it's foolish. I don't think you're anyone.'

What about you? she wants to ask, but a waiter is beside them, is asking if he might suggest a fresh drink for the lady, a pick-me-up for the lucky gentleman, a toast for a honeymoon, and as he speaks the charm of the moment passes. They leave quickly, like failed imposters, and drive on.

Downtown there are guest houses. 'Two rooms,' Sybil says to the proprietress at Dadlani's Blue Moon Inn, and the woman shakes her head as if two rooms are a scandal, and once she's shown them up she bustles back with a tray of rum-and-lime and just-cut flowers, as if to bring them courage. They sit on their shared balcony and wait until she's gone.

'You're not drinking.'

'No,' Sydney says. 'I used to.'

'Oh.'

'I don't need it any more.'

'My dad does. Maybe if he was back here he wouldn't.'

Sydney moves carefully in the dark. As if to slake his thirst he draws a line in the wet on his glass. 'I don't think it helps,' he says, 'to run away.'

'Is that what we're doing?'

'It's what people do,' he says, and Sybil feels her hackles rise, her hope tested.

'We could be running towards something. People do that too.'

'Towards what?'

'Something better. Isn't this better?'

For a while he doesn't answer. He is looking at the inland stars, which are ardent, unpolluted by anything but moonlight. 'This is beautiful,' he says.

She wakes once in the night. It is so hot. In her sleep she has pulled off the sheet and lies naked to the air but for a satin of sweat.

Unbidden she is thinking of Sydney. Their conversation, the day he offered her more than he had any right to give. *You don't know me*, she told him. *Hardly*, he answered.

It nags at her, the memory, but she is too tired, she drifts. She thinks again of running. Her elders and betters, long ago, though not so far from here. Neville, Clarence and Bernadette, leaving home for the mother country and all that awaited them.

When she stirs again it's late. For a moment she is placeless. The shutters are ajar: between them, when she turns her head, she can see two great black birds wheeling in a sky as blue as touch-paper.

She folds away the shutters and looks out on Jamaica. It still seems a dream to her, and this morning a disquieting one. What is she doing here? She knows no one but Sydney, a man she hardly knows at all. *You never know, with men.* She has the name of the place where her mother was born, the name of her grandmother, and neither is real to her. They're like coloured plates from Uncle

Neville's books, larger than life and brighter: they're stories an old man told a needy child in rainy London.

She goes down for breakfast. Sydney is there before her. The sight of him is unwelcome: dimly, she recollects having drunk and said too much last night, and anyway he looks so English, so forlornly out of place, still dressed in what might be his only clothes, his small concessions to the heat a chair in the dappled shade and his jacket hung on it.

The proprietress is sitting by him, as if she doesn't mean to let him go until he has eaten everything. 'This is Mrs Dadlani,' Sydney says. 'This is my friend, Sybil.'

Mrs Dadlani looks at her like a cat disturbed at its meal. 'You breakfasting, Miss?' she asks, and goes sulkily when Sybil says she is.

'So I'm your friend now?' Sybil asks, and isn't sorry when he blushes.

'What should I say?'

'Friend is fine. You're making more of them.'

'We were just talking. There was a bird as well. It sat up here, but it went . . . somewhere. I think you might have missed it.'

'I'll live,' she says, sitting, and he looks at her hesitantly and goes back to his food with what is today a satisfying awkwardness. Mrs Dadlani comes out with a fresh haul from the kitchen.

'Mr Marsh tell me you leaving so soon.'

'Mr Marsh is right,' Sybil says. 'I don't want all that.'

'Ackee and saltfish,' Mrs Dadlani says, laying dishes like penances. 'Bammy bread, that's fresh, you eat it up. Callaloo, plaintain, pawpaw.'

'It's a fruit,' Sydney says, and Sybil glares at him.

'I can see what it is.'

'You two keeping company,' Mrs Dadlani says, benignly dictatorial, 'and not even breakfasting together. You want anything else, Miss?'

Oh, she does. Sybil wants more coffee and less talk, more pawpaw and the bill; and everything she wants, she gets.

It's Sydney's turn to drive. Sybil takes the top down, mans the map and the radio. The breeze and music soothe her. She is still tense, the way she gets before a fight, but it isn't Sydney's fault, she was wrong to blame him. It is what lies ahead that is a worry to her, the vital unknown that steels her, and all that is lessened here, out on the road, between places.

They go west along the coast. Boulevards and limewashed palms give way to wharves and breakwaters, golf links to gas containers. An inlet of white sand crescented with flotsam, a river mouth criss-crossed with mangroves. A woman at a stall, by Hopewell, who lifts her hand to them and makes the sign of the cross in blessing or aversion.

At Lucea they stop for a lunch of fried fish and plantain chips, parcelled up in pages of *The Jamaica Gleaner*. Afterwards they sit on the beach, digging their toes into the sand, making the most of it: the road ahead tends inland. Sydney dozes in the sun.

'Fish and chips,' Sybil says, 'just like home. We could be down in Brighton.'

Sydney cracks open his eyes. 'It'd be raining there.'

'Too right! Soggy newspaper.'

'Soggy chips.'

Sybil guffaws. 'Look at you, wind in your hair. You should be in a film,' she says, and he combs his fingers through his thinning strands: he is no good with teasing. 'Sydney, I'm sorry about this morning.'

'Oh no, it's alright.'

'I was just worrying,' she says, and Sydney looks out at the surf, the glitter beyond, as if puzzling at what there could be to worry about. 'I don't know about my family here. It's just my grand-mother. She could be horrible. I don't think my dad ever liked her. To tell the truth I think he was always scared of her.'

Sydney nods. 'But you're not.'

'Why wouldn't I be?'

'Because you're not scared of anything,' he says, and she leans back on the sand and laughs again, freely.

'At least I've got you,' she says, 'to believe in me.'

'I do.'

'I'm not complaining.'

'Tell me about her,' he asks, and so she does, the way that she was told it. Mrs Jarrett, who she should be thanking any time it comes down to fighting, who returned with cold regards all that was sent from England. Who might return her granddaughter, if that is how she is.

They drive south. Bit by bit the signs of habitation thin: a last stallholder; a last house where men sit smoking in the yard; a figure in a field, bent-backed, bare-chested, cutting, cutting; then nothing but the fields themselves and the road shimmering between them.

The hills rise but keep their distance. They are into forest now. Sometimes it comes down to the road, only to draw back again around some tended acreage like a vast, cautious animal. The road follows the valleys but rises imperceptibly, so that now and then they catch flashes of the sea, westwards and far away through trunks and canopy ... and neither says so, but they miss it. You know where you are with the sea: you could be looking out at

Brighton. The forest brings home to them how far from home they've come, and how little they belong. Sydney fidgets at the wheel. Sybil mutters at the map, which is a playful tourist thing, showing an island of hotels, highways and waterfalls, cocktail hours and parasols, and not these crags and clefts and unpeopled inland valleys.

They crest a rise. Below them, by the road, an old man sits in the shade. He is cotton-haired, shirtsleeved, alone, working something into a bucket between his feet. He stands as he sees them and waves them down unhurriedly.

'Miss Malcolm?'

'Yes.'

'Mrs Jarrett expecting you,' the man says. 'This way,' he says, and where he points they go.

They turn along an unmarked track, under an avenue of high dark trees. The man is walking up behind them, coming on but dwindling, and when Sybil looks round again there is the house ahead, already looming up, the manse of her uncle's stories. Sydney is turning in between lawns of Bermuda grass, a row of Spanish jars, a raised ironwork terrace. There is a porch above them, shadowed with bougainvillea, and a figure stepping out into those shadows at the sound of them; a woman, straight-backed, dressed in mourning, shading her eyes at their coming.

They sit in the drawing room. Sydney has been sent to put the car away, to take their cases to their rooms and Sybil doesn't know what else. It is just the two of them. The man, Cornelius, has brought them lemonade.

Sybil thinks, She's not that old. The way Neville told it – the way she heard it – her namesake was a crone, a witch out of fairytale. Here in the flesh she's handsome. She can be seventy at most.

'Sit up straight,' Mrs Jarrett says, 'no. There, in the light. Let me look at you.'

Her eyes are healthy, steady. For a long while all she does is look. It would make anyone nervous.

'You take after her some,' her grandmother says at last, and Sybil murmurs thanks – though it's hardly a compliment, the way Mrs Jarrett says it. It's more like something the customs man might have said. *You'll do. You can sit there on my chair, for now.* 'You wear no ring.'

'No.'

'Who is that man outside?'

'Sydney.'

'You make no mention of him.'

'When would I –'

'In your letter.'

'Oh, no. He's just a friend.'

'You keeping company with him?'

'People here keep saying that. I don't know what it means,' Sybil says, but Mrs Jarrett moves her mouth, as if probing meat for shot, and waits her out. 'I don't know. No, alright?'

That makes the old woman grin, at least. She barks wholehearted laughter. 'Ha!' she says, 'ha! Ha! You got her temper, too.'

'I heard that.'

'Talking back just like her! You remember how she talked?' Mrs Jarrett asks, and for the first time it occurs to Sybil that her grandmother is older than she looks.

'She died when I was born,' Sybil says, and the old woman's smile fades, her eyes going flinty again, as if she expects no better from the world than such folly and wilfulness.

'What do you think? That I don't know how my child passed?'

'No. I didn't mean to –'

'I'll have some lemonade now.'

Sybil pours. Her hand trembles, as if her grandmother's vigour has taken something out of her. A perilous silence falls between them. Outside a bird starts singing. There are cages on the terrace, hanging from the eaves like lanterns. Mrs Jarrett drinks her drink and pouts at its sourness.

'Well,' she says, 'here you are. Flesh and blood, no doubt. You planning on staying long?'

'I don't have plans exactly. I just wanted to see –'

'This man of yours, he works?'

'He's a librarian.'

'He can put his hand to things?'

'I don't think he minds what he does.'

'Cornelius could do with help. He be getting on,' Mrs Jarrett says, and then, 'You do be like her, except the hands. You have your father's hands. Workers' hands,' she says, and as Sybil clasps them, 'I never thought much of the Malcolms. White collar folk when they tried. Most of them never did. The schoolmaster, your uncle, he was the best of them. He still teaching?'

'He died, too.'

'The men do that.'

That's it. That's enough of you, Sybil thinks, or feels; there's not much thought in it. 'I didn't come here,' she says, 'all this way, to listen to you disrespecting my father.'

Her grandmother gives a rougher laugh. 'It *respect* he wanting now?'

'He earned it.'

'About time he earned something. He never did earn my daughter.'

'You don't know nothing about him.'

'I'll speak my own mind in my own house,' Mrs Jarrett mutters, and peers out from under her brows. 'You sure you won't remember her?'

'Of course I don't!'

'Girl, don't you raise your voice to me. Not anything? Folk must have told you things.'

Sybil takes a slowing breath. 'She looked after us. She chose my name. She didn't like London, didn't get on with it. She loved my brother. She was big-hearted. Brave, that's what people say. They say how she was ready to stand up for us ...'

Already she is trailing off. Is this all she has to share of her mother? It is too awful to think so.

Her grandmother is still leant forward, avid. 'I don't know,' Sybil says, 'I'm sorry,' and at last the old woman's gaze slackens, idling around the gloomy, polished room.

'You'll be tired. Cornelius has made up rooms for you,' Mrs Jarrett says, and with that Sybil is dismissed, to retreat out of the dark into revivifying sunlight.

Out front the car is gone, and Sydney with it. Sybil thinks, He's left me here. It isn't true – she knows that – but as she steps into the light there is a moment when she fears it.

What would I do? Walk, she thinks, as she goes in search of him. I'd start walking right now and I wouldn't stop until I saw the sea again. No way would I stay here alone.

She finds him sitting in the car, parked up beside a garage. Cornelius is making room, reversing out a flatbed truck. Neither man sees her. There is a clearing down below – across a narrow valley – in which a figure is at work. When the truck stops, the

sound of an axe comes clear across the wooded distance. Sydney is
watching, listening, and his face is peaceful.

'Where did you go?' she says, and he jumps.

'Just here. How was it?'

'I don't know. Come on.'

'I should put the car away. Cornelius –'

'He can wait, can't he?'

'But where are we going?'

'I don't care. Just walk with me, will you?'

They cross the lawns into the woods, lifting a bough, a latch.
Overgrown, under the trees, are ruined storehouses, a dry mill-race,
a cane press left to rust.

By the press they sit. Yardfowl pick at the dirt. The house is out
of sight behind them. Sybil lights a cigarette.

'Everyone was right,' she says. 'They all told me not to come. I
should have listened. I don't know what I'm doing here. You were
right and all, weren't you?'

'When was I?'

'Saying we should stay at the airport. I wish we had!'

'I didn't mean it, not like that.'

'I don't belong here. And you! You came all this way for
nothing.'

Sydney glances around. 'I don't think this is nothing. It doesn't
look that way to me.'

Sybil stamps out the fag. 'Look,' she says, 'give us a hug.'

He does. It is awkward at first; then he relaxes, and it becomes
effortless.

'She doesn't want me here.'

'Did she say so?'

'She didn't need to. It's my mum she wants.'

'Don't you?'

'So what if I do? She isn't here, alright? So I can't have her either, can I?'

'No,' Sydney says, 'but you can have this.'

Stay the night, at least, he says, and Sybil says alright, alright. At table there is nothing but the smallest of small talk; the car, the roads, the post office, the busybodies of Glasgow town. No one asks again how long the two of them might stay. No one asks how long they might be given welcome.

Sydney is a silent third. What passes, passes over him. His eyes meet Mrs Jarrett's once, and hers are sharp, but that is all. He is at one remove from the bone-china conversation. If anything is settled – if anyone is reconciled – it seems nothing to do with him. Despite his place between the women he is closer to the man, Cornelius, who brings them in what they might eat and takes away what they do not, snuffing the candles in their wake without a word.

The next morning, and the next, Sybil is woken by the birds. The hills are full of cockerels which crow all night at dogs or lamps or moonlight – Sybil doesn't know – but there is something else that has made the house its territory. Sybil comes to know its song, which is shy and fine. It starts before first light, when the hills are at their quietest: aside from the cockerels it's the first singer, and it's the best. Every day she listens, drifting in and out of sleep, and in that state it seems to her that it must be a lucky thing, that something beautiful watches over her here. She wishes she knew its name.

Once she asks Cornelius – she tries to sing the song – but it's no use, she can't do it right, and all he does is beam. 'We are blessed,' he says, and goes on about his business.

Her room is her mother's room. It comes to her only when her mind has resolved the fact: she knows nothing, she knows nothing, and then she has no doubt.

There are pictures on the walls: English ladies and their lovers, walking arm-in-arm through a London that never was. There is the Marble Arch, the Embankment, the Monument, each of them precisely drawn and nothing like itself. There is a dressing-table at which she sits, looking at her three reflections. Roses are painted on the glass, bordering her with English buds and blooms.

She goes to the window. In the yard Sydney and Cornelius are leaning, talking. They have been working at the car. Tomorrow they will drive to Montego Bay and take the truck back home together.

'Might be you could fit her dresses,' Mrs Jarrett says.

'You kept them?'

'No doubt. Don't ask me where. Cornelius will know.'

'I'm not her. Are you listening?'

'No one asking you to be.'

'That's not what it feels like, sometimes.'

Mrs Jarrett looks her up and down. 'You'll do, child, as you are. You'll just have to breathe in some.'

She does. Her grandmother helps. The dresses are beautiful.

The cagebirds are bananaquits. The great dark ones are John Crows. The morning sentinel she never finds – later she thinks she must have dreamt him. She studies hummingbirds instead, the mango, vervain and scissorstail. Even the yardbird cockerels demand attention, strutting their dusty finery.

She never knew she cared for birds, but here they are so bright, like flowers. She paints them with a set she finds in her mother's chest one evening. It's a child's paintbox, old, pre-war, and the brushes have dried hard, but bit by bit she soaks and kneads them back to suppleness. Sometimes, when she paints, she licks the bristles while she's thinking, forgetting what she's at, staining her tongue with tinctures.

She thinks: everything is brighter here. Even the nights – which frighten her at first, plunging her into darkness – even they have a clarity. You see cars passing miles away, beyond the reach of sound, and on clear nights the wash of stars.

In Mrs Jarrett's albums every other picture shows their daughter, their mother. In one, lights hang in swags along a nighttime promenade, though Bernadette herself shines brighter, her dress surf-pale and surf-fine, her smile flashing.

'Kingston,' Mrs Jarrett says. 'We were dined at the Liganea. Afterwards she danced. The men you can imagine. She had that dress made up. It did look fine on her.'

Across each page of photographs a ghostly second lies, imprinted with faint designs – cobwebs, forget-me-nots – which sigh and lisp as Sybil's grandmother lifts each of them away.

Bernadette in a crêpe dress, hardly more than a child. A handsome man stands just behind her, smiling, one hand on her shoulder. 'Your uncle,' Mrs Jarrett says.

'His finest student. That was what Neville called her.'

'He was fine himself. My child was never taught better.'

'I wouldn't have known him,' Sybil says, and then, shyly, 'I wouldn't have known her.'

'Well,' her grandmother says, 'leastways you know her now.'

One day – it is her idea – they walk up Cromwell with a picnic, her grandmother staunch and stiff, the chair they bring for her turned west to look down on all she owns – the fields let to Glasgow men, Kendal and Cessnock men. And beyond the Jarrett acreage – see the roofs there? – Green Island, where Bernardette was schooled; and beyond that the gleam of the sea, out at the end of things.

'I like it here,' Sydney says, and Mrs Jarrett says, 'I'm glad' – first to him, then to Sybil. She grabs Sybil's hand in her own (which hurts, the old woman's being all rings, skin and bone). 'Thank you for coming,' she says, and Sybil gives some awkward answer she mutters and forgets. 'Thank you for having me.' That's what it might have been.

The days pass so easily. The sun at six: the sun at seven. Cutlassfish for Friday supper. Sydney and Cornelius, clearing land beyond the lawns, playing dominoes at night, pruning the pepper trees with their leaves like burnished leather. The downpour that comes on them all just as September ends, rain hemming the eaves. Four days of October breeze in which the young trees buck and sway. Then clear days again, like a bounty, the earth still warm, the nights like velvet.

The night she goes to Sydney's room for the first time. He opens the door. There she is, barefoot, blue-lit, her lamp guttering.

He shivers when she touches him. He sweats and sweats under her hands. Ssh, she says, ssh, but still he is abject, grotesque, not to her but to himself. He breathes so fast it is as if he might be drowning.

Then the hunger takes him. Thought leaves him, and leaves him graceful. He is strong and sure as he has always been, alone, in the darkest places. His skin smells of smoke and resin.

'I have to tell you something,' he says afterwards, and he does. He tells her everything. Her head is on his chest. Sometimes she weeps. Later she sleeps and wakes to find him still talking of things she has never known. Her brother playing made-up games, her mother in the street of flowers, the songs men sing in Erith. There is no end to what he needs to tell, nor she to hear from him.

Letters come from London. *When are you coming home?* they say, and Sybil writes back. *Soon*, she says. At first it is the truth, and later it is still a truth, but not one they will understand until, given time, it sinks in.

Here is something you could know, Clarence writes, his script crabbed like his fingers by the wretched English winter. *This is from when I was younger than you. I was working nightwatch at Frome sugar factory, which maybe you can see it now. It used to be we hitched down and walked back if it came to it. It was five miles. It was three fellows together.*

Coming home it was still dark but getting on for dawn. It was the morning after I asked your mother for her hand. I saw her from a way off and when she saw me — how she smiled!! She was standing at the Glasgow crossroads. I saw that and I knew, how she smiled to see me come, that she meant to be mine. There she was, waiting for me, shining like a firefly.

She is on the terrace, fixing washing. Inside her gran is pottering, singing badly to herself some buoyant old island song. Down the drive Sybil sees their truck rattling home to them, its dust and flashes through the flametrees. Sydney is bringing up supplies, ice and fish and bottled gas and no doubt something small to make her smile from Green Island: there are always treats with him. Letters from England, too, if her luck is in.

But then it is in any case. Sybil needs no letter, no reminder to count her blessings. You make your own luck, alright, but you better cherish it. Maybe it comes in now and one day it draws out again. Sybil means to mind her blessings, to make the best of each of them.

Soon Sydney will walk on up, her gentle handsome man. He will lean into her kiss, sit and talk awhile, and when he goes from her he will leave reluctantly, as if nowhere but by her side is he at home in the world. It is a life. It is their life to come, and there is good in it.

5. DORA IN OCTOBER

She is thinking of happiness. Happiness, Dora thinks, isn't at all like joy. Joy grasps you so fiercely, catches you up and sets you down before you know what's happening, as if there has been some mistake and joy was never meant for you. You're too fragile to live with joy: you bear it for no more than seconds. Joy feels as if it must be meant for angels, or animals.

And happiness? *You must be happy*, people tell her, and Dora wonders, must I be? Am I to be happy, then?

Joy, you know it when it grips you, you feel it so palpably that you might die of it. But happiness . . . to Dora, it's less a feeling than a thought. There are days when she wonders if she even believes in it. She doubts it as others doubt love. It's what people are meant to want. It's so mild and virtuous. Happiness ever after: it's the child's consolation when the story is all said and done.

What if you had to choose? What if – Dora asks herself – you could have only one thing forever, what would it be for you, would it be joy or happiness?

★

She's in Rantzen's Fashions – not to buy at Dudley Rantzen's prices; she only stopped to spend a penny – and there is Mary Lockhart, from the old days, from the Buildings.

Hide! Dora's body says, and it doesn't give her time to argue, it's creeping crabwise back along the aisle towards the changing rooms – rump swishing through the coats – but it's too late, Mary's waving.

'Dora!' she calls, 'Dora Lazarus? It is you, isn't it?'

'Mary,' Dora says, emerging weakly. 'I didn't recognise you. Except you haven't changed a bit.'

'Oh, don't,' Mary says, and it's true, the lie is clumsy. *An English rose*, Solly used to call Mary, *with the thorns left on*. Dora wonders what he'd call her now. Certainly she's still handsome, still lovely in the bone . . . but there's too much bone on show, too little softening flesh. As she leans in for a kiss Dora flinches at the smell of her: an evening perfume, the cloy of too many cigarettes, and something nastier beneath their musk and ammonia.

'Are you in a hurry?' Mary asks. 'Could we go for tea?'

'I'm sorry, Mary, I have a meeting of the residents . . .'

'Oh, that's a pity,' Mary says, and it's peculiar, but she sounds as if she means it. *Did we ever once sit down together?* Dora asks herself. *So if not then, why now? We made strange neighbours then, and now we are only strangers.*

'Everything else has changed,' Mary is saying, 'around here, I mean. I'd heard, but it's another thing to see it. I suppose it's for the best. The Buildings were dreadful, weren't they? Where are you living now?'

'The Newling Estate,' Dora says, and, pride making her unguarded, 'We have a little garden.'

Mary smiles keenly down at her. 'Aren't you the lucky one?'

'Oh yes,' says Dora, 'ever so.'

'How did you swing that, with just the boy? Or did you have your own, later?'

'No, none of our own. And you, Mary? Where do you live now?' she asks, though she already knows.

'Highbury, for our sins.'

You have no shame, Dora thinks, *to speak in the same breath of your family's sins and success*; but 'You've done well for yourselves,' is all she says.

'We've worked for it. Well, that's Michael, there's never been any stopping him.'

'You won't come this way often, then?'

'No ... I was just passing,' Mary says, and some of the air seems to go out of her, her gaze wandering across the winter-dressed mannequins and the clientele, who thumb Rantzen's wools and furs as if they are still marketgoers, testing meat for tenderness. Mary frowns, as if puzzled to have ended up amongst them. 'I had a call to make in Whitechapel. My son in-law, you know, he's a surgeon at the London.'

'Yes,' Dora says, 'I did hear that. You must be proud,' she says to Mary, as she said to Iris four years ago; but what she thinks is, *Hospitals. That's the smell, the one she hides.*

'Well,' Mary says, fussing with her bag, 'I suppose this is goodbye, then,' and smiles with a sadness Dora never thought she could possess.

She's old, Dora thinks. *And sick. You wouldn't know we're almost of an age. Of course she has had children, too*: and then, the thought vindictive, *Michael must still love her very much.*

'Goodbye Mary,' she says.

She is herself still pretty, in her way. Solly says so. Other men, too, with their looks and words. Once that would have made her shy and it remains a surprise to her, a thrill, half-anticipated, half-disbelieving.

She is uncoarsened, unsatisfied. Still hungry, still slim and firm, her flesh filling her skin. There is still a glow to her. She walks with her chin up. She is happy with Solly, happier with him than with anyone. But there are other things than happiness.

She takes the long way home from Rantzen's, enjoying the autumn sunshine. The estate children have come out to play. Dora calls their names and they run up, larking at her heels, breathlessly chattering. 'There's eels in Lee's all in a bucket!' cries Ria Isaacs. 'We put our hands in them!'

'Well, aren't you brave?' Dora says. She remembers Ria before she was born. The flutter and butt of a babe in the belly. The elder sister, Bessie, six years old and grimly determined, sitting out in the road with a handscrawled sign until her mother Sarah heard of it and hauled her in: FOR SALE, GIRL BABY, 2d.

> *Will we would we*
> *Can we could we*
> *Might we may we*
> *Kiss the baby?*

Dora, Dora, Solly always says, Why is it always not enough? I have far more better things to do with my time than watch my wife being sad. Watching her being happy – that would be a better thing. I could be listening to her singing. Why be sad, dearest? Nothing in life is perfect. Look at what we have.

What do we have? she will ask, and he will take her hand, press it, rub it between his own as if to kindle warmth in her.

'We have us,' he says.

But why can't things be perfect? Some things almost are. The delight of infants. Music. There are Bach sonatas – those she dared play as a girl – which seem to Dora so transcendent, so unbridled in their brilliance, that only in performance are they anchored to the earth. A man made them. What man can make, cannot men live?

There is no residents' meeting: she was invited to one once, but was too timid to attend. Not that Mary will ever know that. Dora walks through Newling's titanic shadows, opens her front door, locks out the world behind her. She sees to her face and makes Solly his tea. Two rounds of salted dripping, the fat studded with scratchings; two of chopped liver. She cuts the crusts and lays them out: tomorrow they'll be crumb for schnitzel. Sun floods the dusty windowpane, illuminates her nimble hands, the hatch, the piano's treble end. It is October and still warmish, though the long days are drawing in and people stay outside, making the best of it, basking and brooding on winter. In Market Square, Jack Harrow's Staff bitch lies on her back, nipples bared for all to see, and barks at the afternoon, on and on, like a silly girl with hiccoughs. *No dogs*, the Market Square signs say, *No ball games, No hawkers.*

'Solly?' Dora calls, 'dripping or liver?'

No reply. Dora makes up a plate. In passing, on her way, her hand reaches to touch the wall-turned picture on the piano, as if it were a talisman.

Solly is snoring in his deckchair – bought on impulse in the spring – the wireless beside him talking about Apollo and the dark side of the moon. Dora looms over it, picking at the sandwiches, then glances at her neighbours' curtains, sets down the plate, turns off the wireless, kneels.

He's a well-made man, her one. Not tall and not what you'd

call handsome – not that she's ever told him so – but stocky and hard-wearing, like a thing you'd be sensible to buy. He'll be fifty-four this year, but he could be almost anything, thirty or seventy. His arms are big and freckled and sunburned from the elbows down. Under his string vest his chest is thick with red hair. When he sleeps he isn't gentle, the way some are: the dozing Solly frowns. You can see the animal in him. He's a bear, an ape . . . or what? An orangutang, that's it. *The Times* is crushed protectively against one hairy armpit. From his free hand his pipe droops: his knuckles graze the lawn. As Dora bends to look, a single ant climbs up his thumb, pausing in the unruly hairs, rearing, sending messages: *we are entering unknown lands.*

She takes another bite of sandwich, then reaches out, weaves her fingers through the vest, into his hair, and grips him, waking him with a start.

'We're closed,' he says, 'no! Mmn, what? Oh. I didn't hear you come in.'

'You snore too loud,' she says, and he catches her in one fore-shank, swings her down onto him. 'Don't! Look, it's tea time, I did you dripping.'

'For dripping,' Solly says, 'a fellow would forgive you anything,' and he leans down for the plate.

You'll never guess who I saw, she wants to say. But she shouldn't. There is no good at all to be had from raking up the Lockharts.

'Ah,' he sighs, munching. 'How do you always know what I want?'

'I put my ear to your head,' she says, 'and listen to your dreams'; but Solly is starting to frown.

'Wait. Don't move.'

'What? What is it?'

307

'Look at that,' he says, 'will you? I'm telling you, these ants. They're in for the high jump now, see, they've eaten half my sandwiches.'

'Oh,' she says, '*Solly.*'

Some dawns, as she wakes, she finds herself thinking, *I'd like to go home now, please, can I?*

She doesn't mean Shoreditch, nor the Buildings, though she does miss them. It's Danzig she really wants. To start again, to have another run: that's what Danzig would mean. But it's no good, Danzig is gone. Even the name has been effaced. There is no going back, however much she yearns for it.

She is forty-eight, only forty-eight, and so often thinking of the past. She dwells on it. Dwells *in* it, almost, lingering over its attendant happinesses and unhappinesses. And its joys too, of course. Like this.

★

In the Columbia Buildings square the LCC men are talking. Each one steps up to say his piece, clambering onto the tailboard of a public information van which has been parked up for the purpose: his colleagues nod and tamp their pipes until they're called upon. There are three of them, all younger than Dora, each with the oilskin confidence of local government. They're not shy to raise their voices: they might as well be costers, with lungs on them like that. The second man totters as he gets down, one arm windmilling, and laughter eddies through the crowd ... but the truth is it's muted, with no proper malice to it. These days the Buildings can't muster much in the way of a public gathering. Most got out years ago, all those who had the cash or chance for something, anything, elsewhere. It is March 1957, and the Buildings are being condemned.

'A few of you,' the third man says – he is the most senior of them – 'a few of you may have heard rumours that portions of the Columbia Market Buildings would remain habitable for awhile. Let me hit such speculation on the head. You should all of you be making alternative living arrangements today, if you have not done so already, whether with us or through your own enterprises. By this time next year the tenements you see now will have been demolished in their entirety. In five years this land will be occupied by brand new homes, designed, as Mr Laing has told you, by the best architects, to the highest modern specifications, with conveniences and space to suit the needs of the twentieth century family, and with planned occupancy comfortably exceeding that afforded currently. I will be frank with you. You know as well as I do that your habitations here are damp, cramped, poorly ventilated, badly plumbed, inadequately lit . . . I could go on, and no doubt so could you. Our ambition is to make these slum defects things of the past –'

'You won't be touching *my* plumbing,' Hullo Evans calls, to desultory hoots and applause, and he winks at Dora, who stands beside him with Solly's hand gripped tightly in hers. Through his grasp she can feel her husband's trembling, nervous ire. 'What are you calling a slum?' someone else shouts out – and there is a wider murmur, the first stirrings of a defense of the place they call their own; but the council man won't be brooked.

'The structures that surround us now put us all in danger. The war did them grave damage – you may not see it, sir, but I assure you it is there, in the retaining walls and in the foundations. Who will be responsible, if some part of your home falls and does a person harm tomorrow? Will you? No, you will not, because the council is your landlord. We take on ourselves that responsibility, and as responsible owners we have made the surveys that prove what we've all known for years – that these antique buildings are no longer fit for purpose. Our purpose, therefore, is to see them cleared and replaced with safe and proper dwellings.'

'Where are we to go, then?' someone asks. It's John Remnant, Dora sees, the spindlemaker who has lived and worked in the Buildings longer than anyone remaining. John's voice is mild with some faded country burr, but others take up his question; younger, more forceful tongues. The council man waits them out, leaning to chat with his colleagues, straightening, raising a hand.

'Some of you, I'm sure, will want to return here – to new homes – when the estate is finished. You will be happy to hear that those who wish to put their names down on the housing list today, may do so. You will not be given special treatment, but you will be getting in "early doors", as it were. I would urge you all to apply, the housing situation being what it is. In the interim, provision may be made for the elderly and for families with children who find themselves with no recourse elsewhere. The county council is able to relocate those in most need to prefabricated housing in East Ham, Catford and Epsom. Yes, Miss, Epsom is quite far. I would ask you all to remember that this is all in the short term. Our view is the longer one, and I am sure that you, too, once you have considered the issues fully, will come to see things the same way. It is your children you should think of. Well then. Are there any questions? No questions? Mr Laing, here beside me, will be taking names ...'

'*Catford!*' Jack Harrow spits. 'I wouldn't walk my shittest dog down there. I'm down the Birdcage, who's with me? Solly, you'll have one.'

'Oh,' Solly says, cleaning his spectacles, peering around as the crowd trails off, 'no, you wouldn't want me, Jack. The taste in my mouth, you'll end up carrying me back. I'll save us both the trouble, head straight home with Dora, if you don't mind.'

'Right you are,' Jack says. 'Enjoy it while you can, won't you?' And off he heads towards the arch, his hounds skittering around him.

Half the night Solly paces, his footsteps starting up and stopping, kitchen to lounge to kitchen, like a timepiece he has taken apart and can't see how to mend.

Dora, nightgowned, in the doorway. 'Come to bed now,' she whispers, and Solly stops in the dark and lifts his head.

'I'm thinking,' he says. 'Can't you see?'

'What do you need to think about now? Think tomorrow.'

He isn't having it. 'Those jumped-up boys,' he spits, 'they should kit them out in jackboots.'

'They're doing what they think is best.'

'For who? For us? Not likely. Putzes, they think we are, the way they look down at us —'

'Solly,' she says, 'don't talk like that.'

'They don't do this for us. For their long views, is why they do it. If we wanted five-year plans we could clear off to Moscow. We were *happy* here.'

'Not always,' Dora murmurs, and he huffs, puffs himself up.

'Who is happy always? We never asked for different. Do they ever ask us what we want? Someone should teach them manners. I wish ...'

'What?'

'I wish Jack had set his dogs on them,' Solly says, but he is abashed, he can't bring himself to mean it, and Dora laughs.

'Come to bed,' she says again, and he does, then, but he isn't finished: in his sleep he goes on tossing and turning.

What *I* wish, Dora thinks, is that Bernie were still here. Bernie would have known what to say to council men and their long views. She'd have stood up for all of them. But Bernie Malcolm is nine years dead, and Clarence and his children long gone out of Dora's life. Dora wishes them well wherever they are, though Bernie is the one she misses.

Henry? Solly mutters, once. Other things too, mumbled pleadings and entreaties. The name aside it is all incomprehensible, but Dora needs no gloss to understand. That they have nowhere to go is only the sharp end of it. The keener edge is Henry, five years gone. What will Henry do, when he comes home and finds no home, finds them vanished and the Buildings with them? He'll turn his back. He'll walk away just as he did that bright morning, when he kissed them goodbye and never returned.

One day he will. Of course he'll come, when he's ready, when he's done whatever it was he had to do, out in the world. Because what kind of life would it be, if they never saw him again?

Fred and Sarah Isaacs nab a place down on Grey Eagle Street. 'No point waiting for council favours,' says Fred. 'It's basement, but there's two rooms, see? And it wouldn't hurt us to share the rent. There's a courtyard, Solly – you could park your barrow. Don't get your hopes up too much, we're not talking Claridge's, and Sarah says to say we'll want the space back when the baby comes. Fancy a look?'

Two rooms is mostly all it is. There's a tiny pantry by the yard door, and a queer dead corner to the hall with a kitchen grate and an oven, a lampblacked, hunchbacked beast that looks as old as the house itself. In the room which would be theirs a window gives a chink of light and a mole's-eye view of ankles passing. There is a privy in the yard and a toilet upstairs with the Irish, and the first floor is Irish, too: on the second lives Mr Barnard, rent collector for a dozen Spitalfields lodgings.

'Well?' Solly asks, 'what do you reckon?'

They're talking at the mole's-eye window, shoulder to shoulder, hush-hush: Sarah is perched on the stairs, taking the weight off her feet, while Fred scurries around, fag in hand like a dowser's wand, searching out draughts and mouseholes.

'We might not find better.'

'Or worse. Fred wasn't joking about Claridge's. What's that *pong?*'

'Cabbage?'

'If you say so.'

'We can keep looking once we're in. I can do it while you're working. And this isn't far.'

'No,' says Solly, perking up. 'We could nip back sometimes, see how they're getting on up there, could we?'

'Of course, dear,' she says.

'Right,' he says, giving himself a shake. 'Better get our skates on, then. Better get packing.'

They're in before March is out. Barnard likes the easy life and is affable enough when he comes below stairs each week, marvelling at Sarah's bloom and girth, not saying no to tea as he counts their rent. The Irish, though, don't want them there and make no bones about it, hats on tight and fists in pockets when it comes to introductions, dour on the landings, brooding in the courtyard over the affront of Solly's barrow.

'This is a Christian house!' Mrs Powers throws open her window to yell, one night as he gets in, and Solly goggles up at her, dead on his feet and at a loss for the words that all come later, in the mole's-eye room with Dora: what's unchristian – if that's your poison – about a man with a barrowload of watches?

At County Hall she waits in line, for a ticket, for a form, for her turn with the pens chained by their blotting pads and inkwells. 'I've been here *hours*,' a woman hisses to Dora, as they scratch away, 'Have you? Some people seem to go straight through. I'd take the war over this. At least when you were queueing then it felt like you were all in it together.'

'Cheer up, love,' the man behind them says, making them both jump, 'it'll all be over by Christmas,' and the woman blows on her form, ever so cool, and says she won't be holding her breath if it's all the same to him.

The waiting room is high and wide as the house on Grey Eagle Street. Dora still has on her winter coat, but it's cold all the same, the seats by the radiators being all taken or reserved with hats or caps or warning glances. Now and then a bored factotum comes and calls a ticket number. In the corner furthest from his door a family have brought out a thermos and are eating saveloys with their fingers off a sheet of newspaper.

At last she is seen into an office where a fair-haired man sits writing. 'Make yourself at home,' he calls, head down, and Dora takes the chair that has been set out in front of him.

He is scribbling on her form. She wants to crane and look, but hates that he might see her do it. Instead she tries to still herself: hands not to wring themselves, teeth not to knead her lips. The man's writing is busy as ants. On his little finger he wears a ring. The left hand is all he has: down the other side his jacket sleeve is pinned, angled towards the pocket.

'Sorry if you've been kept waiting,' he says, sitting back abruptly. 'It's a jungle out there these days, we hack away for all we're worth but we never see the end of it. Miss Lazarus, I presume?'

'Mrs,' she whispers, and the man peers back at the form.

'So you are. Well, you wear it well, I'm sure you won't mind me saying. The moniker, I mean.'

His eyes are pale and kind. 'Are you the officer I should speak to about council accommodation?' she asks, and he smiles.

'Well, yes. One of them, at any rate,' he says, and taps the form with his pen. 'Your English is impressive. May I ask if you studied, in Germany?'

'I am not German. I have been here for twenty years,' she says, tilting her chin. 'I am a British citizen.'

'So I see,' the man says, 'an English *hausfrau* in need of a homestead.'

'Yes,' Dora says. 'We would be so glad of somewhere. Please.'

Scritchscritch, goes the man's pen. His forehead is creased. He is frowning even as he smiles. There is an edge to his voice, a forced civility that Dora does not quite hear or comprehend.

'You understand, I'm sure, that we can't provide for everyone. We build what we can, but I'm afraid that often we are forced to disappoint. It's the war, you see, it does have a habit of raising people's expectations beyond what is strictly practical. To the Pyrrhic victors, the spoiled ambitions. Unless you are in acute need, the list for council housing . . .'

'We must be patient,' Dora says. 'I understand.'

'Patience is a virtue,' the man says, 'but we don't provision on grounds of saintliness. You have somewhere now? Rented quarters, it says here.'

'In Spitalfields. Until September only.'

'Is it very far from your husband's work?'

'No.'

'Do you find it unaffordable?'

'No, it is not expensive for us.'

Scritchscritch, he goes again. Through the window Dora can hear gulls, severe and free, as they scour the river.

'Clean?' the man asks. 'Do you find yourself capable of keeping your quarters sanitary?'

'Yes, of course.'

'You are neither of you infirm? No. Do you have dependents, Mrs Lazarus?'

'I don't –'

'Children, perhaps.'

'No.'

'No children,' the man murmurs. 'Pity.'

Dora thinks of eyes. Eyes can lie, of course. People can lie with their looks, if they are those kinds of people.

'We were in the Buildings,' she says, more urgently, and the man glances up.

'I beg your pardon?'

'The Buildings in Columbia Road. You are knocking them down.'

'Oh, goodness,' the man says, 'the market buildings. How on earth did you end up in those old piles?'

'We can put down our names, for the new estate. We were told so. You said we would be early doors.'

'Not personally, I shouldn't think. *Early doors* indeed. If only my colleagues spoke English as well as you do, Mrs Lazarus! We'd all be on a clearer footing, then. Of course you can put down your names for the Columbia Road development, but nothing is assured. In the meantime –'

'We have only five months,' she says. 'Where we live now.'

'So you've said. You don't strike me as incapable of finding somewhere under your own steam, however, nor can I honestly describe you as in grave need. Do you have enough space? For the moment, I mean?'

'No,' she says, but his kindly gaze is on her.

'How many rooms?'

'One.'

'One room to yourselves?'

'Yes.'

'And you are married, and childless.'

'Yes,' she says, and bites her lip at last as the man's left hand reaches out, the little gold-ringed finger raised to tap-tap-tap at Dora's script.

Saturdays, they walk up to Columbia Road. They do some shopping, show their faces, then go and see the Buildings. Some weeks it feels like sightseeing, others like calling on a friend who has been unwell for years and is coming to the end. The hoardings go up promptly, but there's no hastiness to the business that goes on behind them: nothing is torn down for months. It's as if the council have decided to save themselves the effort and let nature do its work.

Nature does well enough. Emptied of people, the Buildings suffer. At first it's just the shabbiness of everyday abandonment, but soon the decay gathers pace. One day they come and every window visible is smashed, as if a small army has gone round with hammers and a vengeance. Another morning – a gusty one – the hoardings have blown down all along the eastern side, and by the time Solly and Dora arrive others have already picked their ways in, to look at what was theirs, to gawp, perhaps to steal. They find the entranceways fumy with cats and vanished men, the chapel spire leaning, the brickwork everywhere extruding greasy growths of moss and mould. Great slubs of concrete have hardened on the flagstones of the square, where the counterweights of the wrecking cranes lie waiting, the Buildings housing their own incipient destruction.

Mr Barnard broaches his tea. 'Ah,' he says, 'that does it. It never tastes the same upstairs. I'd blame the pipes if I wasn't such a bodger when it comes to cooking. That's what you get, you see, with a public school education.'

Mr Barnard spent his childhood at a boarding school in Wiltshire. It made him what he is. So he tells his tenants, and he wears the tie each day to prove it.

'Won't you have something to eat?' Sarah asks, half-rising, but Barnard waves her down.

'You sit down, Mrs Isaacs, look after yourself.'

'I'll go,' Dora says, 'cake?', and Barnard beams and says he doesn't mind if he does.

She heads to the pantry, cuts and butters slices. In the Isaacses' room she can hear Sarah and the rent collector making the best of things. Barnard isn't troublesome, but there's no parlour for him, he likes to sit and chat, and so it is a bedroom or nothing. The Isaacses have good furniture – better than Dora's – but still: it is too intimate, to have a stranger sitting in there. Probably, she thinks, he sees worse in other places. There was a week when he came early, and after awhile Dora found herself smelling the warm straw musk of piss, and saw the Isaacses' chamberpot, unemptied under the bed.

When she gets back Barnard has their rent out. 'And you, Mrs Lazarus?' he asks, 'how are things in the hours and minutes business?'

'Dora has been looking for somewhere else to live,' says Sarah. She is not unkind, Sarah, but she can seem hard, the way she ploughs straight to the point. 'Because, the baby.'

'Um,' Barnard says, frowning through the cake. 'I'll be sorry to see you go. I hope you and Fred stay on, Mrs Isaacs. The only thing worse than losing good tenants is watching the dodgers move in. Any luck, Mrs Lazarus?'

'The council,' she says, and tries to shrug away the scorn that creeps into her voice, 'they are no use. I saw a man. He wasn't kind. He said they have nowhere for us, not now, maybe never,' she says, and Mr Barnard clears his throat in a fierce kind of way.

'Now look here,' he says, putting the rent down, taking up his accounts book and pencil. 'I've nothing against good government, except I've never seen it yet. You go to the LCC, you're talking to the wrong people. Just because they tell you they don't have a shoebox between them, that doesn't make it true. They're mealy-mouthed up there, it's all queues with them, and the thing about a queue, Mrs Lazarus, is that someone's always on the VIP list. This is my head office, there are some gents there you should talk to. I'll tell them you're coming, put in a word on high for you. We'll see if we can't do you better than the jobsworth socialists, shall we?' Barnard asks, and tears off the foot of a page with a flourish that brings it to her hands.

S.N.L. Holdings, Barnard has written, and under the name an address out on the Holloway Road. Dora takes the Underground, emerging cautiously, stopping where the crowd deposits her, like an unseasoned traveller setting foot on foreign soil. She is light with hunger, though too ill at ease to stop and do anything about it. The shops – grimy, gaudy, windblown – don't look much different from those at home, but she barely knows North London, doesn't know which way to turn so that, if her gaze could travel as the crow flies, home would lie before her.

Barnard's headquarters is above a memorial masons, its waiting room reached by way of an unlocked side door and a poky ascent. There are two secretaries, one smoking and typing, one filing and eating a chocolate orange. 'Can I help you?' the filer asks, and before Dora can reply, 'Would you like some of this? Go on, there's nothing wrong with it, I'm on a diet, that's all.'

Dora takes a segment. 'I don't have an appointment. Mr Barnard told me to come, just as a favour –'

'Oh, *Bill*,' the filer exclaims, 'him and his favours! He could warn us sometimes, couldn't he?', but the smoker chips in wearily. 'He did say something. Hang on, I'll see who's in.'

'If you'll have a seat, Mrs –?' says the filer, and Dora gives her name and obeys. *laitnediseR & laicremmoC*, says the window behind her, as if Mr Barnard's employers are strange foreign gentlemen. There are magazines on the counter, but she's too impatient to read: nor can she face the chocolate, which grows greasy in her fingers, until, when the receptionists aren't looking, she slips it into the plant pot beside her. Then there is nothing to do but stare at the fish tank in the corner, its denizens brighter than life, ornaments distracted by their own ornaments: a sunken galleon; a ruined castle; a treasure chest on a bed of doubloons.

Lucky fish, Dora thinks. Someone looks after you.

'Mrs Lazarus?' the smoker calls, 'you can go in now,' and Dora proceeds, through a ribbed glass door and down a gloomy corridor, towards the warm light of the room which lies open at the end of it, where a man sits at his desk, speaking on the telephone.

'No,' he says, 'leave them be. Give them enough rope, we'll see what they do with it. You'll wait for my word.'

His face is lowered. It is his voice Dora recognises. The soft, measured command of it. The lilt, and the effortless menace.

'Michael,' she says, 'Michael Lockhart,' and at his name he looks up, and it is as if the light has changed, the atmosphere; and his face with it.

He makes to stand before he speaks. It takes only that moment for him to regain himself. 'Please,' is his first word, with a gesture of admittance. He eyes her as she enters. Quite suddenly she is sweating: she can feel the cool shame of it under her arms and on her lip. She stares at him and can think only one thing: *I am here with the man who killed Bernadette Malcolm.*

He has remembered the phone, still in his hand. 'Oscar? Keep me posted,' he says, and hangs up. His startlement has ebbed, perhaps as hers has become apparent.

'I didn't know,' Dora says quickly, as if she is the one at fault. Is anyone? She'd like someone to be. 'Mr Barnard told me to come, he didn't say it was you.'

'Good old Bill,' Michael says. 'Talks for England, never says much. Sit down, won't you?'

She arranges herself, not looking at him. She is in her best worsted day dress, but it is no defence now. 'You'll have to forgive me, I've forgotten your name,' he says.

'It's Dora.'

'Dora. The watchmaker's wife. Solly Lazarus.'

'Yes.'

'You had a boy. The one who lived wild.'

'Yes.'

On the desk a carriage clock apportions seconds. She is braced for the enquiries which must follow. They don't come, but all the while –

she can feel it – he goes on watching her. When she has finally steeled herself – when she looks up to meet his gaze – his eyes are curious.

'So,' he says, 'Bill put you onto us.'

'We are in Grey Eagle Street.'

'Bill's place. You're on our books, then.'

'We can't stay. Bill said – Mr Barnard said –'

'He told you we'd help.'

'Can you?'

'Do you want me to?'

She runs out of words. She has had no time to think about this. How can she want Michael Lockhart's help? He has no right. She wants to be away from him: it has only been fright which has kept her in her seat, first fright and now pride. It is all wrong, it is disgusting, that he should have the privilege of offering her anything. She should have nothing to do with him. And who is he, to be putting his finger on her feelings? How is it he thinks to ask what she should have asked herself?

She remembers Bernadette. A picture house, the four of them squashed up together in the dark, sharing potato crisp sandwiches. Henry and Jem, side by side, their eyes lit up: angels watching angels.

She is about to stand when he does so himself. 'I was on my way to lunch,' he says. 'You're welcome to join me. Will you?'

'No!'

He glances at the clock. 'You're not hungry?'

'Yes,' she says. 'No.'

'Come, then,' he says tersely, picking his hat from the stand. 'Or don't. It's your choice,' he says, and so it is.

It is the first time in her life she has eaten an Italian meal. Only later does this occur to her. At the time she is too nervous to notice, too angry with herself for going, with Michael for asking her.

The trattoria is four doors down. There are red carnations in mismatched vases and a window table waiting. Michael orders for both of them: minestrone, veal parmigiana, beef ravioli, no wine. The owner sends them aperitifs in tiny wasp-waisted glasses.

They begin in thorny silence. Outside a mother goes past in an apron and cardy, three girls merry-go-rounding around her.

'You can talk to me,' Michael says. 'I don't bite.'

'What do you want me to say?'

'You could tell me what you want. Or if you don't want my help, you could be civil for a minute. You might as well tell me about yourself. What you've been doing these last nine years, you and your husband and the lad.'

'It is not your business, what we do.'

He shrugs, tends to his soup. 'You got out of the Buildings, leastways.'

'They are knocking them down, they don't give us a choice.'

'I heard. Can't say I'm sorry.'

'You should be. The Buildings were special.'

'They were old. The new estates are opportunities. Livelihoods and living space for thousands. Like you.'

'Not like me. They promise us nothing. And what is so good about these new places? Will they be beautiful?'

'Beauty comes at a price we can no longer afford.'

'Will they last longer than the Buildings? A hundred years?

'Probably not.'

She savours the point, pushes home her advantage, glad to give better than she gets. 'It should make you happy. Every block they knock down, it must mean more rent for you.'

He has the courtesy to meet her eye, to measure her, and not to smile. 'There is that,' he says.

'What about you? What have you been doing? Getting rich and fat.'

'I've been poorer and thinner. I've done well enough.'

'You must deserve it,' Dora says, the acid of the words cutting the sweetness of her dish. Then she realises. He is handsome as he ever was – the lopsided quirk of his mouth and all – but Michael's features are no longer striking in their gauntness. There is a puffiness around his eyes, and his frame, too, has filled out more than he might like. He is in his thirties, she thinks, as she is herself, but he could pass for older. It is an easy mistake to make, to look at his good suit and shoes and think that he has dined in restaurants all these years. Only he can't have done. He is a man who has consumed what he has been given, who has been told when to eat, and who has exercised only as permitted by the rules of his confinement.

Good, she thinks. *I wish he was still in there. If he is happy it has not been enough.* She is blushing, though, the flush spreading contagiously, and she bows her head and works at her meal.

'Your husband, still down the markets, is he?'

He is carrying on as if he has noticed nothing, and despite herself Dora is grateful. 'He has a good pitch on the Lane,' she says.

'You know, our business started in the markets. We do a fair share of housing now, but on the whole we're still commercial. Pitches, lock-ups. Shops.'

She glances up into the pause he leaves, snorts ridicule. 'How nice for you. You are suggesting we could afford a shop?'

'You can afford what your business earns. Yours is sound: people will always want the time on them. Get them inside, put them at their ease, you'll find them less thrifty. Your husband might find it easier, too. He never struck me as a barrowman by nature.'

The owner's slender-waisted glass still sits untouched beside her. Dora takes it, sips from it, for courage or forgetfulness. 'Mull it over,' Michael is saying. 'I could set you up with a premises here, shop and top, get you out of Shoreditch –'

'No! We want to be close to the Buildings ... to where the Buildings were.'

He is looking at her too much. 'Alright. I'll see to it. Shall I?' he asks, and she can't help but meet his eyes as she says that, please, he will.

'Any luck?' Solly asks, as he creaks into bed that evening, 'Placewise?'

It isn't luck, she wants to say. You shouldn't think it's that, Solly, it doesn't feel like that. Not for you.

'Mr Barnard's company are looking.'

'That's good of them. Don't give them anything up front.'

'They talked about a shop.'

'Talk's cheap.'

'It wouldn't be a big place. You'd like it better in winter.'

'Wouldn't I just?' Solly murmurs, and Dora listens to him, nursing his bad back in the gloom. 'No harm dreaming, I suppose. It's about time we got on in the world. Good chap, Mr Barnard. Good girl, you,' he says, and pats her flank, rolls over the sag in the mattress to nuzzle her, abruptly falling asleep in her arms.

That night the man she dreams of is not her husband.

Friday they meet again. Barnard gives her the address – on Great Eastern Street, by Old Street – but she's not surprised when it's Michael who comes for her.

It's raining as he parks. 'Hop in,' he says, and she does. The car bears his smell and that of women: Mary, she thinks, or his girls. She almost hopes it is them, though it can do her no good to be right.

Beside them is a small parade – a rope merchants, a veneer work-shop, a barber-cobblers and a pub. The fifth front has a *to let* sign above the furled awning. It's a neat place, set back with its neigh-bours from the greater eastwards march of tenements and ware-houses. 'Is that it?' Dora asks, and he nods, eyeing it through the splotched window.

'Close to home,' he says, 'as ordered. I'll have keys next week, but what you see is what you get. You should bring your man down, have him try it on for size.'

'Is that the flat, above it?'

'No, not for want of trying. There's a fellow in there won't shift till they carry him out in a box. I've a place on Old Street. We'll drive, if it's the same to you.'

It isn't far: walking distance. He is ungainly in climbing from his seat, and it is only then Dora remembers he ever needed a stick. He shakes out keys, leads her into the stairwell of a tenement. The rain is too unforgiving for niceties, or for her to stop and think what it is she's doing.

Four flights up and he bends to unlock a second door. 'After you,' he says, and Dora steps into the gloom, feeling him close behind her, brushing past her to open curtains and scuff at dust.

'I lodged here myself, a long time ago. It hasn't changed much.'

'You have,' she says, 'you became the landlord,' and he shrugs, not modestly, she thinks, but as if he is too sure of himself to care, his gaze still moving critically over the walls and ceiling.

'There's not much to it. Front room, bedroom, privy. I'll keep looking, but you can move in here whenever it suits. It's the best I can do for now.'

She walks to a window, lets out a gasp. 'You can see for miles!'

Michael moves to stand beside her. 'Depends on your point of view. From where I'm standing it looks like a hundred yards of East End rain,' he says, but drily, and she is smiling herself.

'It's much better than where we are now.'

She crosses to the second window, comparing the greatness of the sky, the fantastic landscape of rooftops. 'If it's views you like,' Michael says, 'I've some dealings with the fellows at the Buildings. Six storeys they'll be putting up, if they stick to their guns. I could –'

'No.' She turns. 'A garden, that's what I'd like. A garden where I can grow things, and I want a tree in it, an elder.'

'I'll do my best.'

'Why? Why should you even try?' she asks, and his smile ebbs.

'Why shouldn't I? You asked me to.'

'I know,' she says, 'I'm grateful. Michael, before, in the Buildings, I was nothing to you. You never looked at me. You were never kind. No kinder than you had to be, not to strangers.'

'Is that what you want of me, unkindness? Because you expect it of me?'

'No,' she says, 'of course not. I just need –'

'I don't know,' he says, under his breath. He has drawn in, hands gathered into pockets, head bowed, and a weariness has crept into his voice that draws all definition from his words.

'What does that mean? You don't know what I want of you? You don't know why you're doing this?'

'Don't raise your voice to me,' he says, and Dora understands then that she should be frightened, that she is frightened, in fact; and that she doesn't care. I am alone with him, she thinks. I meant to be alone with him, and there is no helping me now.

'It doesn't make it better.'

'What's that?'

327

'It doesn't make you right. I can't forgive you for Bernadette.'

'Who are you saying?' he whispers, and the anger in his eyes is rising, inflammatory; and then she is kissing him.

As if he means to shove her away his hands go to her shoulders. Then he is kissing her back, his fingers climbing to her hair, into it, fiercely cupping her skull. She is moaning into his mouth. One foot jounces on the boards as her legs begin to go. Michael is hoisting up her dress.

'Little skipjack,' Fred Isaacs says, patting at his wife's belly. 'Little bumpkin, are you dancing for us, in there?'

'Gently,' Sarah admonishes, and then, 'Congratulations, Dora, Solomon. You must have friends in high places.'

'We don't,' Dora says, 'just Mr Barnard.'

'To Barnard,' Solly says, cheery as a Buddha, refilling glasses. 'No, scratch that – why should he get all the credit? To my wife, my pertinacious, perspicacious, pretty wife, who needs another top-up. I don't see who else I should be thanking.'

They're in the Isaacses' room, the men both half-cut, and Dora tipsy, too, in the hope that it might soothe her nerves. 'We shouldn't celebrate,' she says, 'not until we have something in writing,' but Solly isn't having that.

'You deserve a medal, that's what ... and look here, all we've got is sherry. You should see the shop, though, Fred, you'll want Sarah out there, too, doing the business.'

Only Sarah is sober, and quieter than the rest. She is an attentive woman. Dora can't hate her for it, it's the way she is, but Sarah is the one who sees when she comes and goes, sees what little she has to show for the hours she spends away; who hears – if anyone does – when Dora fills the basin and washes her parts, crouched alone in the mole's-eye room. Sarah's gaze is gentle, but Dora shivers when it lingers.

Her hours are spent in joy. They meet in the gardens by St Paul's, where no one who knows them would have any business being, and walk apart, like strangers, to the car. Michael is the man with the keys to the city, to unlet Soho attic flats and disinhabited Southwark railway terraces, though once, in Woolwich, the place he brings them to has been taken up by squatters, and he leads her off without a word, the muscles ticking in his cheeks, and drives until they find waste ground, and fucks her there in the noon-hot shadows of a derelict. It is summer, and the smell of the place fills her as her pleasure overtakes her. The sweetness of the estuaries, the candied semen of balsam, and the rankness of old elderflower, soiled, unharvested.

How does she dare? She has never been brave, but she is proud, and she is owed joy. Isn't everyone?

In July they move to Old Street. It's Barnard who deals with them, who gives them the tour and the salesman's spiel, as if the flat were fancy or they in any need of convincing. Michael's name is never mentioned. As Solly signs the contract Barnard's eyes meet Dora's, and she understands that his discretion is exercised according to instructions.

Mrs Walkling, their new neighbour, is a widow with no time for women. She is capricious with Dora, full of malign misinformation, but takes a shine to Solly and bakes him Eccles cakes: the first has two hairs in it, one ginger, one tawny, neither Mrs Walkling's. She has nine cats, all mollies. 'They don't vie with me,' she says, as she scoops them from their stairwell lairs. 'They don't talk back. My girls know better,' Mrs Walkling says.

One evening she looks up and Solly is watching her. She is darning their old curtains, and – she knows it only now – has been singing as she works. 'What?' she asks, and he shrugs.

'You're on top of the world.'

'Just happy,' she says, 'I must be happy. Can't you hear me singing?'

He smiles for her, but the dimple of his frown remains. 'I can stop,' she says, 'if it bothers you.'

'No,' he says, 'why should it? I'm happy when you're happy.'

Another night he falls asleep over his reading. Dora goes to close the book. It's something from the library: history is Solly's thing, or essays – Orwell if there's nothing better – but this is poetry, she sees, and she turns the page and reads.

> *I am in love*
> *And that is my shame.*
> *What hurts my soul*
> *My soul adores,*
> *No better than a beast*
> *Upon all fours.*

Old Street makes things no simpler. The cats follow Dora around, in and out and up and down, like inscrutable informants, and their mistress loiters on the stairs, leaves her door ajar, and barters her half-imagined rumours with the railwaymen's wives downstairs. The walls might as well have ears. And then the shop is close, so near that Solly can be home when Dora least expects him, looking for a kiss or company, a working for a watch, mustard for a sandwich.

On the City Road, by Moorgate, there are four telephones, the boxes all lined up like soldiers. On Friday afternoons – that being when Solly works late, hoping for the weekend crowds – Dora dials, pays, gives a name that is not hers, and waits to be put through. 'How are you?' she asks, and if Michael says, 'very well,' or 'never better,' her chest tightens, because it means he'll come; but if he says, 'Busy today,' she hangs up and walks homewards with her lying heart in tatters.

Christmas, he buys her pearls. *Learn from my weaknesses*, her father told her once, in Danzig, near the end; *Don't put your faith in things*. But her father is long gone, him and his treasured possessions, and it seems to Dora now that her lover's gift is more than just an object. As she lifts the rope against herself its lustre takes her breath away; then, 'Michael!' she exclaims, and he laughs and settles back to watch her.

She wears them only that winter, with him. For years, afterwards, she takes them from their hiding place, wherever it is she lives, whenever she is missing Michael and sure to be alone. Not to put them on again – because there is no one to share them – but to recall that Michael once gave her such things. They are dark, the pearls, and their hues alter, ashen in one light, burnt umber in another; and Dora, when she looks at them, sees what she suspects Michael did not, at least in any way he might have admitted to himself: that their colours recollect those of Bernadette Malcolm.

It is sex with them, or argument. There is no middle ground, nor are the two things so far apart. Each is heartfelt, gut-felt. Fighting with Michael is nothing like arguing with Solly. They never quibble, she and Michael; they never bicker.

'You don't make love to me.'

'What do I do, then?' And when she turns her head away, 'If you can do it, you can say it.'

'What would you do with her?'

'I don't know what you mean,' he says, but he does, he knows all too well that she means Bernadette. That she means, Do you care for me because you never cared for her?

'You can tell me. *Tell me*. What would you do?'

He laughs. It is a cruel laugh, but the pitilessness is all for himself. He sits up, lights a cigarette. 'You're mad,' he says. 'You must be mad, to be jealous of the dead.'

In January he stops taking her calls. The first time it happens she understands that Mary must be with him, or someone else so proximate that he doesn't trust himself to speak. He is busy with family, she knows – he has been moving himself, from Holloway to a bigger place on Highbury Fields – but the next Friday it's the same, and the week after.

'Mr Lockhart is in a meeting,' the secretaries tell her, 'perhaps you might call back tomorrow?' They are prim and tart, or so it seems to Dora, as if they've come to their own conclusions.

On the first Saturday in February she goes with Solly to Columbia Road. The new estate is going up, and whatever their misgivings or allegiances there is a thrill to the scale of the ascension. They buy kippers at Lee's and tobacco at Shaw's, and a dozen freckled market eggs, because they look so pretty and they can afford them, now. It is crisp and bright, and Solly too is sunny, full of plans, prodding his pipe at the dreams that lie mid-air before them. They're almost home when Dora sees Michael's car, its muzzle jutting from the narrow shadows of Boot Street.

'Oh, milk!' she says, once they're in, 'Solly, we'll need a pint for the kippers, I don't want the stink of them frying. I'll just run out for it,' and she does run: flees, almost, before Solly can offer himself.

The car still lurks in Boot Street. Michael sees her coming, leans to get the door. Already her eyes are tearing. Before he can speak, before she can think to stop herself, Dora has slapped him.

There is silence in the blow's wake. The slap is her question and she waits for his answer. He could hit her back, there are men that would. Part of her hopes he will, but she isn't surprised when he doesn't. He doesn't have that in him, despite Bernadette or because of her: Dora knows him, now, and is sure of it.

He raises his hand to check his face. One side still bears her fingers' imprints, with a deeper bloom where her rings have caught his cheekbone.

'Are you done?'

'No. Yes. Do you hate me?'

'I wish I did, it would make things easier.'

'You don't want to see me again. That's it, isn't it? Why don't you?'

'Your husband knows.'

For a while she says nothing. She is lost for words: she gapes like the fish he keeps in their ornamented tank. She sags back, holds onto his gaze. Later she wonders if she faints: certainly, when she comes back to herself, she has lost the sense of what he has been telling her.

'. . . Last week, too,' he is saying. 'You never looked my way. I wanted to tell you to your face. He came by the office three weeks back. Might have been out there all day waiting, he looked cold enough. He saw my face and I saw his. He knows, I saw it in his eyes, he made sure of it. You never mentioned me?'

'No,' she whispers, 'no, of course not, never.'

'Your man's no fool, though. He twigged to something. He can put two and two together.'

'But he never told me. Why wouldn't he?'

'That's between you and him.'

'Because he wants me,' she says as it comes to her, 'and he won't let me have you.' Michael broods on that, nods. 'Don't you?' she asks, 'want me?'

'Dora –'

She raises her chin. 'I don't care. Let him know. Michael?' she asks, but what she is asking she hardly knows, and besides, his expression has drawn in.

'I won't have Mary finding out.'

'What if she does? What does it matter?' She laughs. 'Oh, Michael, don't tell me I'd be the first.'

'It would be hard on her,' Michael says, 'it being you. You're part and parcel of the worst of it for her.'

'I don't understand,' she says, and he scowls. He would rather speak of anything than this. 'The Buildings, the Malcolms. The dead, Dora. Mary would take you badly. I won't have that.'

'But she won't find out. We'll be more careful, and Solly would never –'

'Are you sure of that?' Michael asks, and she knows he's right. What does she know of Solly, who has gone on all these weeks as if nothing has changed between them?

'Dora,' he says then, as gently as he is able, 'we were never built to last. We both knew it from the start.'

'I didn't. Don't you tell me what I know.'

'I'm telling you we're done. I'm sorry. Look, I've fixed the other place for you, up at the estate. It won't be much of a garden, community spaces are what they're all about now. You'll hear from them – Dora!'

She is out by then. She is running again and doesn't stop till she's home. She forgets the milk, of course, though it hardly matters. Solly doesn't mention it. They have the kippers fried, the curtains reek of them for weeks, and nothing is said between them, not then, not once, not ever.

It ends then. It doesn't end when she finds out where he lives. She doesn't go to Highbury Fields, one chill March evening, to ask for the Lockhart house. She never waits under the plane trees, watching the lights of his windows for hours until she sees his form: nor does she edge closer, lurking on the green, until he comes out to her. What if she had? What would he have said? But she would have stopped him, she would have stopped him with a kiss, and when he told her no she would have bitten him, fastened onto him with her teeth. When he shoved her away she would have wiped the blood from her mouth, her eyes shining with the taste of him.

You stay away from me, he would have hissed, *you stay away from me and mine*. Then – had she done these things – she would have gone. And after all, would it have been worth it? To be sure of the end of it? But it can't have happened that way. Only a woman with no pride would go so far. Only a madwoman would do those things, and afterwards go home to her husband with the taste of her lover still on her tongue.

What kind of husband would let that pass? Hers would look up from his pages, his eyes still wanting. He'd kiss her a welcome. *How are you, dear?* he would ask her, and she would answer, *It's so cold outside. Never mind,* he'd have said, *never mind. It's warm in here.*

★

Besides, it never ends. Days might pass at a time, but then something will bring him back. A woman will laugh like Bernadette, and she will pity Michael all over again. Or it will be the back of a man's head in a crowd, or Solly's touch as she's sleeping: or Iris, when she used to come; Iris's eyes, and the remnant of his accent in hers. How frightened she was, the first time Iris rang! She thought that she had been found out, that Michael's daughter had come to bring her to book.

She'll always love him now. It is 1968, the end of autumn. The days are shortening. The nights are lit with harvest moons, even here, where nothing waits for harvesting. Dora rises from Solly's lap and goes in. She hears the radio start up again, her man humming along. She goes into the bedroom, opens her dresser, draws out a box. From it she takes the black pearls. She lifts them against her neck. She looks up into her eyes.

★

1988
(The Fisher King)

1 . DAWN

London, dark and early. No light yet except the moon, that and what the city gives. Clouds the size of motherships, their bellies urbilucent rose.

In the Hotel Ibis, Euston, Michael Lockhart lies alone, half dressed in evening clothes. His breath is rank, from age and from the drink he failed to hold last night. He sweats soured vintages. His breath comes haltingly, apnoeic: a watcher or intruder might think him dying in his sleep. Only his pulse still moves, and his eyes, under their lids.

One arm lies thrown out, like that of a suicide or singer. Gold gleams dully at his wrist. How far Michael has come from the Columbia Road Buildings, from his days of cutthroats and carnations! Still, there's a hunger to him, a needful severity. Even asleep, he has a look which says, *Don't touch my plate, I'm not yet done with that.*

In his dreams he shrugs off years: they come away so easily. What does a man like Michael dream about? The same as anyone. Michael dreams of Michael, every night, in one skin or another. Asleep, he's selfish as a child, as rooted in himself. Of others he dreams only of cobbled forms he fears or craves. Sometimes it might be Dora, and then he'll groan at the clench of her teeth in his cheek, but most nights he dreams of family; more nights than not, of Mary.

This morning it isn't her. Instead it is the Lockhart men, the company of his childhood. Michael's stroke is still to come – the war itself is still to come, and the years of punishment – and he is a boy again, cocksure, fifteen, without impediment.

'*How about a song, Dad?*'

'*No, I'm not in the mood.*'

'*Oh, aye? Look out, lads, the old man's got the hump.*'

'*You'd have one yourself, Mickey, if you ever bothered with the news. It don't turn a fellow on to singing. Who's took my apron?*'

'*Jerry, I shouldn't wonder.*'

'*You can laugh now.*'

'*So I can and so I do. How about a story, then? Christy, you'll have one.*'

'*Nothing mild enough for your tender ears. Besides, a song's better for shop.*'

'*Graeme?*'

'*I'll work to either.*'

'*To neither, more like. Go on, Dad.*'

'*I'm thinking.*'

'*Hold the front page!*'

'*Will you not prattle on? Alright, now. There was a man like the three of you, by which I mean still half boy where it mattered most, up here –*'

'*– So says you!*'

'*– Strong of arm and thick of wit, and his mother called him Percival. Percy aimed to be a knight, so off he went to make his name. One evening he was riding and he came into a barren land. In its hills no tree put on its green, in its valleys no flower bloomed, and its fields lay unsown, because no seed would flourish in them.*'

Now Percy came to a river. An old man was fishing there, from a pinch-beck little boat moored up on the other side, and he had with him two boatmen. One was busy gutting fish while the other held a lamp, and this one saw the rider and tugged at his master's sleeve.

Who's that, the fisher calls, trespassing in my lands?

Lord, Percy calls back — thinking himself very civil — I am Percival, and I seek to cross your river.

Your luck's out, lad, says the fisher. My little boat won't do, nor will you find bridge nor ford, not here nor elsewhere in my kingdom.

Now, Percy knew little of the world, and of its kingdoms only Arthur's — that being the isle of Britain — and he didn't think he could have strayed so far as to have left that behind. Still, not wanting to offend, he knelt before the fisher, as a knight would to a king. Sire, he says, if there's no way across, I'll beg a night's boarding.

The fisher gave him a hungry look and pointed with his rod. My hall lies on your bank, says he. You'll have shelter of me there. Ride upstream and I'll follow.

So Percy went upriver, into the woods where the trees put on no green, and the day was between the dog and the wolf, the sun was almost set, he was picking his way and losing it along the dusky bridle paths, grumbling all the time that the old codger had played him false, when up ahead he saw a light, and there was the hall of the fisher king.

A big place it was, but a sorry one, too, just like the lands around it. The walls were overgrown, and what had grown no longer grew, but lay dead as if struck off at the roots. There was no banter in the yard, no hounds to start up barking. Percy banged at the door. Out came men for his horse and arms and in they led him. Gloomy, they were, and inside stood a lily-white girl as maudlin as her men, who washed Percy's hands and feet and showed him to his place at table.

Now in at the door came the fisher king, hollering for his supper. The boatmen were at his sides, and by the firelight Percy saw their liege was lame. He weren't that old when it came to it, he still had all his hair on him, but he was houghed, which means hamstrung, and his legs couldn't bear him.

Up to his throne limped the fisher king, and at his word the meal was brought. First came soup, in a gilt tureen that made the trestle groan. Fish soup, it was, and the fisher king drank it up through his moustaches, but Percy only played with his, because it hardly hit the spot, a soup, after a long day's riding.'

'You can't get your teeth into soup.'

'So Percy thought himself. Still, he held his tongue, as he felt a knight would in company.

Next came gruel, in a fine cauldron it took two men to bear. Fish gruel, it was, and the fisher king wolfed it down and mopped his beard, but Percy couldn't help but think, fine crockery's all well and good if you've something worth putting in it. What kind of king eats gruel? I could murder a pie, he thought — but he kept his mouth shut, because his mother always said to mind his manners.

After that three men came in, carrying an iron spear. Blade to butt the weapon was as long as the three men were tall, and in the hearthlight Percy saw blood shining down its haft, and the men themselves were downcast. What's happened now? thought Percy. He saw the king was eyeing him, as if eager to tell his tale, but still the young man held his tongue, as he thought only proper.

Last the lily-white girl came in. In her hands was a golden bowl that seemed to turn her hands to gold, and as she stepped across the hall all the king's men wept and groaned. What now, Percy thought — more fish? For something was in the bowl, bobbing in dark wine or water, but only as the girl approached could he peer in at its lip. It was the king's head, floating, with hair around and eyes upcast.

Percy jumped up from his place. There sat the king beside him, head on neck, neck on trunk, though his gaze was keen and waiting; but Percy

342

asked nothing of him. He didn't know what to ask, or how to ask, or where to start, the supper having turned so strange and inhospitable. He was a callow boy, one who'd been raised gently and who aimed at being a gentleman. So the girl passed on and the king arose, and off they all went to their rest. Come morning Percy thanked the girl for his bed and board (such as it was, what with the fish), and took his leave of her.

He came to the woods and he came to the river and what did he find in the light but a ford. So the old man tricked me after all, Percy says to himself, but there being no harm done he spurred his horse across. Soon enough he found a road. By it grew ripe orchards and down it was a city that looked British as Birmingham. Percy rode up to the gates where a beggar sat, whistling birdsongs, and Percy threw him down a coin, because a knight shows charity.

Thanks for a kindness, the beggar says, and safe journey, Percival, flower of warriors, candle of knights, though you're a callow boy and leave troubles like weeds behind you.

How do you know me? asks Percy, and what have I left behind?

A wounded land, says the beggar, a wounded king, and you who might have healed him.

Me? says Percy. What do I know of wounds or healing, bleeding heads or bloody spears? What was I meant to do?

Don't ask me, the beggar says. You should have asked the man who knew. You might have saved the fisher king and your lily-white girl much suffering, but you'll never help them now. You rode on none the wiser, and onwards you'll ride the same, for that's the lot of callow boys, who prattle on when they should listen, and gawk when they should ask, and one day end up wounded men, waiting for their own salvations —'

As Michael wakes his eyes go wide. He heaves in breath just as, five hours ago, he heaved out Scotch and claret; as if he is or were about to drown on lack or excess. He hunches up on spine and elbows and peers, as if there might be someone there, a watcher or intruder, in the dark geography of the room he doesn't know.

His father's voice comes back to him. Michael sinks down. He thinks, I'll be in Birmingham, then. The old man has come to sit, is napping in a corner. The curtains are still drawn, the way they were after the stroke, all day. Except they don't look right . . . they look like blinds, the slats kinked wide, with deep tiers of night sky behind them.

Besides, the old man's long dead.

Michael thinks, Where am I, then? Not home; not Cyril's either. The sky has the blacklight tinge of darkness on the edge of dawn. There's a feel to the room that makes him think of hospitals. Unwillingly he reaches for his heart. Its beat is turgid, less comforting than the shirt and tie which clothe it. No physician has undone the garments Michael couldn't work himself, last night, and with that thought the night comes back to him.

He's in a second-rate hotel, in the slagheap neighbourhood that clings to the railways of Euston, King's Cross and St Pancras. Tenners for the night porter, small change spilling from his pockets. He'd walked there all the way from Mayfair – heading homewards, if not home – through Soho and Bloomsbury and their throwing-out-time crowds, their parting shots and furtive gropes and boozy, flagrant kisses. And before the walk there was his own crowd, upstairs at Crockford's Casino, in a private, wine-dark room: the company of men again, the brotherhood of old companions, all drinking to Mary. Cyril with an arm around him, mouthing nonsense in his ear, and Oscar with them on the steps, sober and faithful as a hound, ready to drive him home. He hadn't wanted that. *I'll stretch my legs. Don't go worrying, it's a fine night for a stroll, I'll get myself home when I'm good and done – I'll just walk this off a bit, this . . . Look, look here, how much I've here, you all got the rounds in, didn't you? What did you think you were you playing at? I've cash for a ride to John o' Groats, let alone Highbury. Go on, I'll see you all tomorrow . . .*

So he said. He didn't mean it, that about home. He hadn't wanted to go back alone to the empty house.

Now he rises in the dark, fumbles at a light cord, pisses. He ducks his head to a tap and drinks, crabwise from the neck up. His feet are still chafed from the walk and his skull aches from the water's cold and from the toxins in his blood. A scrap of dream comes back to him – *hair around and eyes upcast* – and he shuts his eyes and drives it down.

He can't get enough of the water. He walks to the bedroom's window with a cup brimful in his hand. Down below, a sweeper machine is crawling up Cardington Street, its rotors scrubbing, busy-busy, cleaning up after London. Two men in donkey jackets come along behind like mourners.

'You could clean me,' Michael says.

He has never liked hotels, their smell of loneliness. Those forms they have you filling in with name, birthplace, passport, address. Michael knows what they mean, those questions. Bad things happen in hotels. They're careless, loveless places. If hotels were halfway honest they'd ask you for your next of kin – and who would he give them, then?

Was he dreaming of family? The Lockhart men, in Birmingham. What was that his dad was telling? Something about a crippled king . . . the rest's already fading. Did Dad ever tell such a story? It stands to reason he must have – else how could Michael dream it now? – but it isn't something he remembers, now he's himself again. He doesn't like it much, either, now he has the wits to judge it. It makes no sense, the story of the wound; it has no point or end. *You can't get your teeth into it.* Michael wills it to be gone, to be as faint as his own ghost in the window's doubled glass.

345

The sky is lightening. He has no business waking early. Later there'll be enough to do. Later he'll be needed and he'll need to be up to it, but he has no use for these small hours today. It's habit which forces them on him. It's time or work, take your pick. Time does it to you, certainly: both kinds. You learn to sleep when the lights are put out for you. You're taught to wake early and never forget the lesson.

He turns back to the room. The bed looks torn apart. Around it – on bureaux, in corners – sit the modern conveniences, the Corby, clock radio, TV and phone, all of them overly familiar but in the half-light altered, foreign. Michael tastes bile in his throat. He drains the cup he holds and swallows hard to seal the deal.

He'd like to call someone. *Mary*, he thinks, but there's no mod-con for that. Iris, then – Iris as the next best thing, the surrogate – but no. Let her sleep, good girl. He won't go troubling her.

Cyril. It's too early, but there's no one else. He picks up, dials, waits, waits. Cyril's missus kneeing him, grumbling him out of bed, packing him off down the stairs, out in suburbia.

'Noakes,' the receiver says, the name like an oath in the face, and Michael grins his crooked grin.

'Slept well, I hope.'

'For fuck's sake, Mickey. Fuck off back up north, will you? What time is it?'

'It's light.'

'My arse it is. Mickey ...'

'How's Trish?'

'Needing her beauty sleep. Tell you what, you get some too, then you can ask her later.'

Michael sits. One leg lies straightened, less out of need than habit. Though his face still bears a slant he has no stick, has had no

346

need of one for many years. It's Cyril who walks with one now, whose breath is heavy from the stairs. 'I fancied a talk,' he says.

'You can talk in your sleep. Go back to bed, will you? Your car ain't till eleven.'

'It'll have to find me first.'

'Right,' Cyril says, without surprise. 'Where are you?'

'King's Cross, thereabouts.'

'Got company?'

'You.'

'Not really the day for it, is it, for the local variety.'

'I hadn't thought about it.'

'You'll need a shave,' Cyril says, 'clean schmutter.'

Michael reaches for a brochure, leafs through its offerings. 'They've laundry service.'

'Overnight, always is. Besides, it won't be right, will it? You'll want to look your best.'

'I could do with the right shoes.'

'I'll send one of the boys round yours. Jack'll do it. The car too. I'll fix it. Where do I tell them?'

'Ibis, Euston,' Michael reads, and Cyril laughs, *hur hur.*

'You're a rich man, Mickey.'

'No point spending it all at once.' On the clock radio, numerals shift: five on the dot. 'Cyril, I was thinking you might happen to know a story. There's a knight who's still a boy, and a fisherman who it turns out he's king . . . do you know that one?'

'Not ringing any bells.'

'He was houghed.'

'You what? Who was what?'

'No one. It doesn't matter.'

'Not really my department, dreams. Trish was reading something about how they don't mean nothing. All that stuff they talk about, doing your mum up the chuff, it's all wrong, they're saying now. Brain cells ticking over, that's all it is, electricity. Sometimes a dream is just a dream. Mickey ...'

'I'm keeping you.'

'You're entitled. You know I'm not forgetting that. Anything you need –'

'I know.'

'– You've earned it, Mickey, always. But get some rest. It's a long day you got coming. You sit there thinking, you'll do your head in before you get started.'

'Wise words.'

'Get out of it. You alright, son?'

'Never better. Go to bed.'

'I'll see you there, then, shall I?'

'You will.'

He listens until the line goes dead. The room reasserts itself. Someone is stirring through the wall, or else something is stirring in it. A TV comes on midflow: Mrs T on the morning news, muted but immutable. *Mr President, as someone once said, the people had nothing to lose but their chains. They had a world to win. And they are winning it* . . .

There's a throwaway razor in the bathroom. Michael sheds his shirt and tie, wets his face and tends to it, listening to the rooms around him, the telephones and televisions coming alive one by one, the crowd of early morning wallahs and Midlands commercial travellers waiting for their trains back home. The smell of fried toast from the kitchens.

Yesterday there were crowds out. It was the weather, they'd have said, it's the summer coming, we love summer, but Michael looked at them and thought: What is it you're all doing? What do you think's the point of all your comings and goings? What *is* it? By the

Union Chapel there was this girl on a step, dreadlocked and dishevelled, feeding a burger to her kid, stuffing his teeth with reconstituted meat.

There was a show Michael saw once: Mary will have had it on. When it all got started – people – no one had the time for anything much more than food. Killing it, eating it, keeping it from decay. Then some bright spark got farming going and bingo, there was time to spare. Not much, though; not enough to go round to just anyone. Time to think, like this, to stare back into the mirror – that was the privilege, the greatest luxury. The kings had it, and what, the priests. The rest went on as before. Their work was the stuffing of mouths, their own and those they served. And that's still it, Michael thinks, looking back at his eyes (which are blue as they ever were, undimmed in fierceness, aquiline). That's all there is to it, that's all they're ever doing, people – it's all we really want. Give us all the time in the world, we won't know how to spend it. It scares us, we hate it, time, it bores us, so what we do? We stuff ourselves and one another. We get our heads back down, chop chop, the way it used to be, like animals, like blind things, stuffing, licking, blow-jobbing, troughing . . .

Often, this last week, he's caught himself dwelling on strangers. Always they're young. Mainly they're girls, like the young mother on the steps. His thirst for them seems unquenchable. Sometimes they catch him looking. *Dirty old man*, their eyes say. He disgusts or amuses them: at worst they pity him. A few of them take stock of what he drives or what he wears: *you can have it, if you pay for it*, their looks say, or they dare him: *come and have a go, if you think you're hard enough*. The youngest are afraid of him, walk on more hurriedly or run. None of them know better. They mistake his intensity. They imagine their plush eyes and skins are all that he could want, that only lust could move an old man to stare after them.

They don't know how he hates them, how their daring to exist fills him with loathing and amazement. None of them has an inkling that he begrudges them their lives. It turns his stomach to see them, so wasteful and rich in years, when those of his own wife are spent.

His hand is trembling. Carefully he sets down the razor. He's nicked himself – there, on the neck – but a spit and a lick and the blood is gone. 'No harm done,' he says, and though his eyes are troubled it's only the truth. The wound is so slight, and the blade so fresh, that he hardly feels it.

2 . NOON

The hearse is punctual, as hearses somehow always are. In it comes Jack, as promised, with Michael's mourning suit and shoes. He's a decent boy, Jack, quick all round and grateful for a chance in life: a Swan, with Alan's zeal for business but less malice in his bones. The hearse makes him nervous, though, makes him overly familiar, searching after small talk well past the point when a grown man might understand his master wants nothing more than the car's cloistered, meditative silence.

'I've a mate does this, the driving part of it. They're top notch, these, Daimlers, all the best fittings – you wouldn't believe the sound they've got, sir. Quadrophonic in the back, see. So my mate says, when he's finished a job, when he's driving round the lockup, he looks out for couples. Like he cruises up, gives them a sound track, a love song, you know, a serenade. Lionel Ritchie, Hot Chocolate. They love it. Makes them laugh, he says. Brightens up their days.'

They're navigating the snarl of traffic east of the King's Cross terminus. Michael sees why they make good time, now: drivers give them a wide berth, wave them by, as if their vehicle were a person touched by harm.

'I believe in miracles,' Jack says, and Michael turns to stare. 'Do you?'

The boy flushes. 'No, it's a line,' he says, 'a song.'

'I see.'

Jack ploughs on. 'Nice day, isn't it? Hot. The weather said for rain but they're always wrong half the time. Sure to be a good turnout.'

Dimly, it occurs to Michael that the boy is trying to make an impression; that this journey is, to him, not essentially funereal, but rather an opportunity, a chance to get ahead. You snooze, as they say now, you lose. 'Is it?'

'Oh, you can count on it, I would have thought. I mean it's as nice as it can be, considering. I wouldn't mind some air,' Jack says. 'Sir, could I –?'

The undertaker meets his eye – Michael's – in the rear view mirror: Jack's window sheathes itself in the body of the door. In another time or place it would gratify Michael, this small exchange. The unspoken understanding, and the tacit recognition of their places – the Swan boy's, the driver's, his. He is a man men look to, still, as he has always been. On another day he would warm his hands on that.

They've done well out of him, the Swans. Since Alan died, twelve years ago, it's Michael who has run the business, managing the Swan concerns and Cyril's alongside his own. The street markets are dying – are pale shadows now of what they were after the war – but Michael foresaw their demise and got out of them years ago, moving capital off the streets into the shops and flats above them. They are all landlords, his people, now, and property developers. He has made money out of money, as he always knew he could, and the Swans, Noakeses and Lockharts are all free of Shoreditch, gone forth and multiplied to the ends of the Tube lines. Their fields bloom, Michael thinks, his own, Cyril's, dead Alan Swan's. Their seeds are sown, and so they reap.

They come up Pentonville to Angel. On the corner, by the bank, a foreigner is hawking tat from a blanket at his feet. What's he selling? Yellow plastic, formed into the shapes of birds. The man is filling one with water, cupping it to his lips, dancing as it sings.

'Come all, buy my wares,' Michael murmurs, and feels the Swan boy shift beside him in his ill-fitting, ill-suited suit.

'Sir?'

'It's just a rhyme. I used to be a coster.'

'What,' Jack says, startled, 'like that?'

'More or less. Flowers and razors. Not round here, East End. You should ask your folks about it. You ever go down the markets, Jack?'

'Not much,' the boy says, unable to feign enthusiasm even for his gaffer. 'My nan does her shopping there.'

Michael nods. 'They're not what they used to be,' he says. 'There used to be more life in them. It was my wife's, that rhyme. It got the girls to sleep. They used to beg for it. *Come all, buy my wares. Come buy my nuts and plums and pears. Here's the Devil and the Pope, and here's a little girl, just going on a rope. Here are the booths where the high Dutch maid is, and here are the bears, that dance like any ladies . . .'*

He stops. Already it is too much, this small recitation. Cyril was right: it's a long day coming, and he is faltering too soon.

They pass through Highbury and Archway, Highgate and East Finchley. By the gates of Islington Cemetery and Crematorium, Cyril is waiting for them. He leans by Michael's window, all seamed face and sovereign rings.

'I'll walk you up. Jack, good boy, you drive on and lend a hand,' he says, and pats the roof as Michael gets out beside him. They watch the hearse move off. Cyril shakes out cigarettes.

'Thought you might need a breath of fresh air,' he says, and Michael takes one, bows to the flame. They start after the car. The path meanders, cutting off within its loops dense banks of shrub and cedar, in which, as he and Cyril walk, Michael glimpses hidden structures: chapels and columbaria, outhouses, furnaces.

'There's a crowd down there. Your girls arrived.'

'Both of them?'

Cyril stops, puts out his smoke. 'I thought you'd want to know.'

He does, is gladdened by it. He hoped Floss would show, for Mary's sake, or for appearances. Not since her childhood have he and Floss been on speaking terms, and Mary always took his side. Not even in the hospice, when Floss visited, did one forgive the other, or the other him.

'Who else?' he asks, and Cyril glances up from his trodden butt.

'No one from the old days.'

'Good,' Michael says, and on they go.

Their allotted chapel isn't far. Around its pocket portico stand relatives from London, Birmingham and north of the border; from Elvanfoot and Muirkirk, Musselburgh and Edinburgh. Faces turn his way, with his features or with hers, the more open of them both pitying and relieved — and why relief, he wonders? Do they think he might not have come? It's as if, with Mary gone, some mishap might have befallen him, some fatal symmetry; or as if he might have left her here, waiting at her last altar.

Oscar trudges up with Jack in tow. 'All set?' Cyril asks Oscar, and the man nods, sour as ever. Oscar never changes: it's a certainty they all rely on. Oscar's main claim to fame these days — it is typical of him — is having kept all his hair.

An uncertain silence falls. Jack was right: it couldn't be a better day, considering. Sunlight falls warm through the cedars. The air is scented, sedative. Jack is waiting on his word, Oscar and Cyril too.

Needing orders, Michael thinks, though just now he has none to give.

'As you were, gents,' he says, his voice carrying awkwardly, and then Iris is there, with the young priest at her side.

'Dad,' she says, and takes his arm, kisses him. 'You look tired,' she whispers, and he is, for he almost growls at her *What do you expect?* or *What else would I be?* – but in the nick of time he stops himself. Under her makeup, his youngest looks as worn as Michael feels himself. I should have called you, Michael thinks. You would have been there, sitting up, and Cyril and his missus could have had their beauty sleep while we kept vigil.

The priest is hovering, but Michael's gaze wanders past them both, searching for Floss. There she is, with her fellow, Jem. She's fifty this year, Michael's eldest, though her looks knock off a decade even on a day like this. There is a boy, too, fifteen years old, though Michael has never met him, neither Floss nor Mary having had the stomach for such a meeting. Iris says he's growing tall, like all the Malcolm men. Their eyes meet his: in Jem's, but not in hers, he sees what might be compassion.

'Well,' says the priest, 'shall we?' – as if inviting them to dance – and Michael and Iris follow him, her hand still on his arm, with all the rest behind them.

Inside the chapel feels too small, and dark after the sunlight. Iris leads him to his place. There is a rustling around him, the unnatural sound of many people moving, voiceless, to the places that fit them. There is a bier, still coffinless. Michael fixes his eyes ahead. Somewhere out of sight – he could swear he feels it, his hairs rising – Mary is coming.

Abruptly the organ begins. They sing – Michael hardly knows what – and then the priest's voice fills the hall, modulated, not unfeeling, though neither eager nor sepulchral. Michael watches his face: he isn't so gone with grief that he can't appreciate skilled work. It's a point Mary was firm on: her celebrant would be Catholic, and properly ordained, and Scottish. *You'll be lucky to land a Cockney altar boy*, Michael told her – neither of them ever having been much in the way of churchgoers – but she wasn't having that. *Don't mock me, Michael. Luck won't come into it, because I've you to look out for me. I want the right man for it. I'll have the proper words said.*

The crowd behind him stirs. Mary comes in, transformed. For so long she was sick, on and off the chemical and radiation therapy, in and out of hospital as the tumours came and went. Michael thinks, I should be glad she's freed, glad to be freed of that myself, but all he can do is look at the strangeness of the box, the inhuman mass of it, as the priest cleanses it with water and incense.

'We commend our sister Mary to you, Lord. Now that she has passed from this life, may she live on in your presence. In your mercy and love, forgive whatever sins she may have committed through human weakness . . .'

Michael shuts his eyes, rests them. He has done right so far, today. Out of nothing he thinks of their first car, bought to surprise Mary. *It's too much!* Mary is saying, in the street of flowers. *It's what we deserve*, he answers. And so it was, or so he thought – though no good came of it, that car. And still he thinks the same thing now: nothing is more than we deserve.

'*You have prepared a banquet for me in the sight of my foes. My head you have anointed with oil; my cup is overflowing.*'

Behind them someone coughs, coughs, snorts down a third slap-stick spasm. There is the sound of hurried rising, the fit running its course outside. Michael thinks, our own bodies betray us, and our minds too. There's no end to what they feel they deserve. Nothing is promised us, but our hearts don't know it or don't care. We are our own worst enemies.

Not that he supposes there's any malice in the cougher's indignity. Michael has no foes here. Mary and he are amongst friends . . . or at least friends and family. By no means are they the same thing.

'You love truth in the heart. Then in the secret of my heart teach me wisdom. Oh purify me, then I shall be clean. Oh wash me, I shall be whiter than snow. Make me hear rejoicing and gladness, that the bones you have crushed may thrill. From my sins turn away your face, and blot out all my guilt.'

Over knuckles clenched in prayer, Michael frowns in puzzlement. It isn't right for Mary, this talk of guilt and sin. What did she have, to be guilty of? The sin of waiting for him? If there's guilt to be felt for the harm done them, or for the harm that led to it, that's Michael's business. Mary needed him and stood by him. He trusts that he was worth it.

Unforgivingness. Is that a sin? He thinks, I'll ask the Father, after. If so, then that was Mary's. She blamed Floss for her faithlessness, and Alan, too, until the end, for putting Michael in harm's way – as if he himself had no choice in the matter. She never forgave the Malcolms, not Clarence or Bernadette, nor their children, nor the grandchild they have come to share. What would she forgive them for – for what could she withhold forgiveness? Michael has never understood it. Still, that was how it was for Mary, for forty years, and he never begrudged her it. Her unforgivingness was laid at his feet, a gift of faith to the man she loved. All those touched by the woman's death were complicit, except him.

When he looks up again Mary is gone. The coffin has been spirited away without his noticing. Around him the Lord's Prayer is being said. *Forgive us our trespasses, and all those who trespass against us.* The sibilences seem to echo on after the voices fall silent. The priest says more, but it is soon done: they are all leaving, and Michael and Iris rise and go along with them.

Outside the crowd is louder now, voices unbuttoned, the speakers happy to have the sun back on their faces, and with the sense, too, of obligations met, the dead put in their place and a drink just around the corner. 'I should go ahead,' Iris says, 'to see it's all set up at yours. My lot will go with you, Dad, is that alright? The driver who brought you – where is he? He's meant to be looking out for you . . .'

'Don't you worry about me,' he says, and she manages an anxious smile as she kisses him goodbye. The crowd closes in on him, full of handshakes and thoughts that are with him. Michael edges through their wellwishings. He can see Floss, checking her watch. She looks harsh in the light: still beautiful as ever, but with nothing spare on her, no softness, no give, any more than there is on him.

'You came,' he says, and she glances up.

'I'm here,' she says. 'Where else would I be?'

Michael nods and averts his eyes. The priest is doing the rounds, a smallish, florid man, circulating platitudes. Michael is disappointed by him. There seems less to him now the prayers are ended, the power gone out of him.

'You look well,' he lies. 'How are you?'

'We're fine,' she says. 'What about you?'

'I don't complain.'

'No,' she says, 'you don't.' It could almost be a compliment. It's how she is, after all, taking life as it comes. 'You've been drinking, I can smell it on you.'

'Can you? The boys saw to it. A send-off.'

'You never used to.'

'I don't now. I haven't the head for it. They'll have me out again tonight, no doubt.'

'Poor Dad,' Floss says – and he is braced for it, but still he flinches at the curl of her voice, the temper of her. She is his daughter, his of the two, the one who took after him. It is that likeness that has turned against him. She is her own person, he knows, but her stubbornness, and her bitterness . . . always, when they meet, it feels to Michael as if he has turned against himself.

Whatever I did, it was for you. That's what he wants to say, but there is never the right time or place for it. Nor is it honest, and he recoils, now, from the thought of angering her.

'I was wondering if we could meet up. I had in mind it might be all of us, Iris and hers, you and Jem and the boy,' he says, and she smiles with false mirth.

'The *boy*. Do you even know his name?'

He does – Iris has told him it – but it escapes him, now, when he needs it most. 'You know how it'll be,' Floss is saying. 'It doesn't all go right again, just because Mum's dead.'

'It was just a thought.'

'Have it your way, it's your own funeral,' she says, and then her man is there, none too soon, a giant with grey in his hair, looming up between them.

'Mr Lockhart,' Jem says. 'I'm sorry for your loss.'

Michael takes the proffered hand. 'I was just saying to your wife,' he says, the words sounding oddly, 'We could see more of one another.'

'Sure,' Jem says, carefully, 'we could do that.'

'Will you be coming on?' Michael asks, though he might have saved his breath, he knows their answer.

'We're late,' Floss says. 'Not for you. Can we go now, Jem, actually? I've had enough of this.'

'Another time,' Jem says, and Michael echoes that – its promise or apology – as they move away.

Others are departing, too, making for the reception. Harry comes up. 'Mr Lockhart,' he says, and sneezes like a dog barking, all teeth. Faintly, Michael recognises the voice of the cougher. He has never warmed to Harry, has never seen the point of the man or liked what marriage to him has done to Iris, over the years, but there it is, here Harry is, still, and it isn't any of his business.

'Sorry,' Harry says. 'It's the trees that do me. Ready for the off?'

The hearse awaits. Megan and Beth are already inside, with their men and Megan's girl, Alice – his daughter's daughter's daughter – who can't be more than six. To Michael's way of thinking it's no place for a child, this, but the thought might be old-fashioned. He winks for her as the men budge up, and Alice smiles, lily-white in the shadows.

They start through the cemetery, still stately but no longer solemn, the Daimler being crammed with people, all knees and foggy breath and voices. 'You alright there?' Harry asks him, and he says he couldn't be better, though the truth is he feels out of it, out of place amongst them all, as if he should be somewhere else, with someone else: with Mary, of course. His gaze is drawn away, across mourners leaving afoot, the graveyard gates, the world beyond still going about its business in terraced maisonettes and shops: his gaze lets it all slide, then locks.

It's his daughter he sees first. Floss and Jem, hand in hand, walk-ing south towards the station. He catches sight of them just as she does the same, though it isn't him she sees. A smile of recognition is brightening her face, her unclasped hand is rising, waving to someone up ahead. Michael's eyes follow hers.

By a café, by the station, sit and stand a knot of people. Gathered together as they are he would know them anywhere. Waving back at Michael's daughter is Dora Lazarus. It has been thirty years since he has seen her. She was bonny then and still is now, as full of joy as she ever was in his company. By her stands the orphan boy, done up tight in his duffle-coat, slight and pale, with his hand in hers. At his side, at the café table, sits the watchmaker. He has a chessboard in front of him, but his glare is on Michael: *I know your kind*, it says. And there, facing Solomon, is a second man, older still to look at, with his trilby in his hands, his hair snowy against grey skin, and his eyes drifting from the board, away on their own weary path, until they catch Michael's, and hold.

Smoothly the hearse picks up speed. Michael shoulders himself some space, peers back, but Clarence Malcolm's regard and Dora's brightness are already lost to him: the knot is out of sight. He thinks, I might have made them up, the lot of them, like bloody ghosts. But ghosts are lonely things, aren't they? And no one in that gathering looked in need of company. It's Michael who sits apart from those who prattle on around him, closer to the dead than to his kin, while those who are left in his wake go on together, living, loving.

3 . DUSK

All afternoon the mourners linger, the old men on their best behaviour, the gossips eking out their news of turns for the worst elsewhere, the kids still frocked or jacketed and playing French cricket in the garden, or exploring upstairs rooms which smell to them of dead people, while nieces Michael hardly knows offer help he has no wish for, and in-laws he couldn't name answer his door and telephone, and ask him what the house is worth (guessing at it themselves, as if it were a jar of coins), and cadge fags on the patio, or loiter at the cold collation, helping themselves to a last glass, to drink to old acquaintance.

At one point, seeking respite, he comes on Alice in the hall, arranging flowers in a Tupperware. 'What's that you've there?' he asks, and she peers up at him gravely. 'Misteria,' she says, 'they're for you,' and gives him the bowl before wandering away. The flowers are heaped up like grapes, bruised by the child's ministrations.

Wisteria: Mary's favourite, loved for their dusty elegance and air of property, of old growth and suntrap walls. He remembers her excitement, long ago, the January day they were shown the house. *Oh, Michael, you won't believe — it's got its own wisteria!* Bashed about as they are, he isn't sorry to have the flowers. He never would have thought to have noticed them himself.

Afterwards, the last guests gone, he drags a kitchen chair outside, wrestles off his tie and sits. Late light cuts across the lawn. Iris, Harry and the boys are clearing up inside. One of them – Jack, no doubt – is experimenting with the hi-fi, finding something to work to. Oscar comes out with tea.

'Nothing stronger?' Michael asks, and Oscar shrugs, as if to say it isn't his idea, nor would it be his preference. He walks out onto the grass and rolls a cigarette, neat about it, quietly offering Michael his quiet company. People have dogs, Michael thinks, when what they need is Oscars. Any other day it would put him at his ease.

'Oscar,' he asks, 'my daughter, Floss. She's a son I've forgot the name of.'

'Grant,' Oscar says, letting the lapse pass without comment, and Michael nods, relieved. Grant Malcolm: it's one thing off his mind. 'Mr Noakes was asking where we will go tonight.'

'Cyril,' Michael says. 'You can call him Cyril, speaking of names. You've been with us long enough, you're hardly fresh off the boat. You don't have to doff your cap.'

If he's too harsh, Oscar doesn't waver. He nods at the tea. 'I can find you stronger.'

'Later.'

'Later, where?'

'You can work it out, can't you? Somewhere quiet, members only. I've had enough chat for one day.'

'Crockford's,' Oscar suggests, and Michael thinks it over.

'Call them, see if they can fit us in. That room upstairs again.'

Oscar studies him. 'Afterwards, maybe girls,' he says, 'Raymond's, the second show.'

'Not tonight.'

'Or fighting.'

'Fighting?'

'York Hall.'

Boxing, he means. York Hall is Bethnal Green, their old parish. 'Too far east,' Michael says, 'we'll want brighter lights than that.' But Oscar has him bang to rights. All afternoon his thoughts have circled the gathering by the station. Clarence Malcolm, Dora Lazarus and his Floss, the whole sorry lot of them. Why were they there? To celebrate? To gloat? To go on where together, and raise a glass to what? And him the outsider outside his own wife's funeral, not at the centre but the margin, watching the world move on without him ... Yes, a fight would do him good. He wouldn't say no to one himself. He'd like to hit and to be hit, to be jarred free of all this thought: to feel nothing for awhile but the black, viscous pleasure of violence.

It's past eight before they're ready for the off. 'Coming, Harry?' Cyril asks, but Harry has done his bit, he should be getting home with Iris, so that it's just the boys – Cyril, Oscar, Jack and him – who head on into town.

Michael drives, being sober. The light is going around them just as the promised rain begins. The precipitation is so fine as to be almost imperceptible, the pavements darkening, oily, as if London is sweating out its inexhaustible pollution.

'Well,' says Cyril, 'that's that. I never much liked funerals, but I thought it went off alright.'

He glances Michael's way, and Michael nods, though it's just for form. *They were all there*, is what he thinks, *all those from the old days. You never saw them, Cyril, but they were, and there was no goodwill in them.*

'What's the verdict, then, Oscar? Dinner first, drinking later?'

Oscar shifts in the back. Michael can feel his eyes on him.

'Dinner,' Michael answers for him. 'After that we'll take it as it comes.'

They come down into Mayfair. It's Friday night, and parking's scarce, so that they walk the last leg to Crockford's. The manager

364

welcomes them back, shows them up to their room, opens the doors onto the terrace.

Michael orders red meat, rare, and eats it hard and fast. Abruptly he is ravenous, as if, with Mary put to rest, he has a void to fill. There's a waitress there to pour the wine, and Jack strikes up some banter with her, a flirt to cheer them all. 'Jack,' Cyril says, 'ain't you got a girl these days?' And off Jack goes, cock of the walk, full of his own woes and wonders, with the rest of them half listening, like workers by a wireless.

'So, what's the occasion?' the waitress asks, showing willing. 'It must be something special for you all to be let out tonight,' and Jack gulps on his spiel and falters.

'It's a sending off,' Cyril says, and the waitress screws up her face. 'What, like in football?'

Not exactly, dear, he tells her, and they share a laugh about it, insomuch as it can be laughable: the waitress does her best.

'You should have seen her,' Cyril says to Jack, 'when she was your age. Mary. My God but she was something. Best luck Mickey ever had, wasn't she, Mickey?'

'She was,' he says, and then, 'I didn't always know it.'

'Mickey,' Cyril says, but the warning is halfhearted: it isn't the night for them.

'I always wanted more for us. You,' Michael says, to Cyril, 'you were happy with what you had. I never used to trust that. I thought you were complacent. I didn't see it for contentment.'

'Well,' Cyril says, 'you got what you wanted, though, didn't you? You made your fortune; hers, too. We all make mistakes, but here we are. It worked out for the best in the end.'

'I don't know,' Michael says, 'I don't know that it did,' and Cyril's gentle, seamed face hardens.

'There's no point dwelling. You were young and hungry. You set out for more of everything and bingo, here you are with it. You couldn't ask for more than this. You came out on top, you did alright, and you did alright by her. Look at us, we should all be grateful. We're bloody *kings* compared to what we were! Up the West End, drinking wine, and this nice young lady to pour it for us. Come on, let's have a toast: to Mary. Will you have a taste yourself, my love?'

They raise and drink and fall quiet. There is the clink of thick club cutlery on heavy china. The waitress has stepped back from them, is hiding her face by the dumbwaiter, but it's alright, they're almost done. 'Jack,' Oscar says quietly, 'you'll know a place to go on to.'

Jack does. Michael gets the bill. For the waitress he asks for an envelope, folds in a fifty for her. Oscar and Jack have gone ahead. Michael follows them out with Cyril at his side.

'Alright?' Cyril asks, and when he nods, 'Almost there now. Tomorrow it's onwards and upwards again, the way it's always been for us.'

They're heading into Soho, where the evening crowds are denser, clustered around pubs and bars, peep shows, clip joints, encounter parlours. The vice business is past its prime, these days, is dying one by-law at a time, though there's no shortage of custom.

'I saw them,' Michael says, and Cyril glances around inquiringly. 'Eh?'

'The old lot, from the Buildings. Not here. They were meeting Floss, it was outside the cemetery.'

Cyril has slowed, is peering at him, one hand waist-high to steer the crowd. 'Why didn't you tell me?'

'I'm telling you now. It was after the service, there wasn't much you could have done.'

Cyril shrugs. 'I could have had a word, asked for some respect. Who was it? What were they doing, all the way out there?'

'I didn't wait around. Drinking champagne, for all I know, they had that look about them. It was Dora, the watchmaker's wife, him too, and the orphan boy they took in. Them and Clarence Malcolm.'

'What do you mean, the *boy*?' Cyril asks, 'he must be, what, fifties by now. The world's moved on a bit since then, ain't it?' he says, and Michael grinds to a halt. He raises a hand to wipe his mouth, staring at nothing or the crowds, who stare queerly back at him.

'Fuck me,' he says, softly. 'I must be wrong in the head. Am I mad, Cyril? I've been seeing things. I saw them clear as I see you.'

Cyril has a hand on him. 'Easy,' he says, 'come and lean a minute, I'll run in here and get a chair.'

'No – leave it, Cyril. I'm alright.'

'Sure, now?'

'I'm alright,' Michael says, more strongly.

'Course you bloody are,' Cyril says. 'You're right in the head as the rest of us. It's a long day, that's all, it's a lot to take in, it's just got tangled up, that's all. It's the grief of it, Mickey.'

They start off again, snail's pace: slow as hearses, Michael thinks faintly, or Chelsea Pensioners. Half a block ahead stands Oscar, looking back, his head cocked. Like a hound, Michael thinks, who scents his master's worries, and he laughs. 'Good old Oscar,' he whispers, 'good boy.'

'Let's see the inside of Jack's place,' Cyril is saying, 'have a drink and a sit down.'

'Alright.'

'One for the road and we'll get you home.'

'Alright. It could have been worse.'

'How's that?' Cyril asks, but Michael shakes his head. *It could have been her I saw*, is what he thinks, but he daren't say the words: the thought alone is terrible enough.

4. MIDNIGHT

Glitterball-spun light. Spirit on the rocks, the glass pressed into his hands, its sweat icy between his fingers. Arms around his shoulders. 'One more, Mr Lockhart?' his embracers ask, and he says go on, then, keep them coming. They laugh and pat him on the back. 'You still alright there, Mickey?' they ask, and he says oh yes, never better.

Up above them and their shadows, in the densest whirl of light, girls, so young and beautiful it breaks his heart to look at them. Flash cash in the gloom around them, young bloods and silver foxes with their tongues and wallets out. A split-second in the mirrors when he catches one girl's eyes. There is no disgust in them, only the deadly boredom of her simulation.

His ears ring with the din. He can't hear himself speak. Jack Swan is shouting in his ear, so shatteringly close that he can smell his breath. 'This is the life, sir, isn't it? This is the way to do it! The stories it could tell, this place!', and he says, but I don't want them. I don't want stories, Jack, I've had enough of them for one day.

The spirit courses in his blood; his temples thrum with it. It's true, he's never felt better. The girl is still dancing above him, by him, for him alone. Her skin is dark and plush as mink, black as the pearls he once gave Dora Lazarus. Oscar is there at his right hand. Oscar, he says, tell me something, the woman who died, the one I killed, do you ever think of her?

'We all do,' Oscar says, and he is so grateful he smiles, as he so rarely does, it seems so generous that anyone should answer him.

Listen, he says, Oscar, listen. Did you ever hear this story? There's a knight who's still a boy, and a fisher who's a king . . . do you know that one, Oscar? Can you tell me what it means?

This time there is no reply. When he looks, Oscar is gone. A stranger is there in his stead, an old man with stone-grey skin who turns and becomes Clarence Malcolm.

He rises. Hands try and hold him down. A table turns, its freight of glass cascading into darkness. Leave off me, he says, I need air, and then he's stumbling free, through the mass of seated watchers, up the stairs, into the night.

Where is he? Some alley, a chink of stars immured above. He leans against damp brick and vomits into the rankness, backhands the last spool from his lips. Behind him, by the alley's mouth, someone laughs and jeers, and he turns – his hands already fists, his knuckles grazing on mortar – but there is no one to be seen, only a car's brief passing, out under a shimmy of neon.

He pushes himself upright, walks out into the street. Which one is it? Brewer or Wardour or Old Compton. 'They all look the same to me,' he says, and hears himself for what seems the first time in hours, his voice thick as that of any pavement drunkard. Abruptly he wants nothing so much as to be home, out of sight of the city's unremitting judgement. Where is his car? Somewhere the wrong side of Crockford's, and too far for him, now, even if he could trust himself to sober up behind the wheel.

He straightens, steadies, starts to walk again. It feels better to be moving, though his heart is going double time, he can feel it in his breath. He grins as best he can and shakes his head at it. 'Get back to work,' he says, 'you've years left in you yet.'

At Air Street he turns south. Ahead of him he can hear the perpetual motion of Piccadilly, and as he comes out by the circus he sees, in the oncoming coil of traffic, a black cab's molten-copper beacon.

'Last orders,' the driver warns, kerb-crawling in beside him. 'Might not be you, depends on where you're heading.'

'North,' says Michael, 'Highbury,' and the man hawks, phut and into the gutter it goes.

'Can't do it, can I? I'm for Romford. Try Trafalgar Square, you'll still catch someone if you're lucky ...'

He's already starting away when Michael grabs the open window. 'Shoreditch. You can do me that,' he says, and when the driver glances down at his hand, 'I'll make it worth it.'

He gets in, leans back into leather. Eros wheels above him. In the blissful dark, as they start eastwards, he closes his eyes. He'd like to drowse, but his thoughts still nag, as if he's forgotten or neglected something. He thinks of those he has left behind, Dora, his boys, his girls.

'Long day, sir?' a voice asks, and he opens his eyes to see the driver's slot open, his face streetlit, in profile. 'Not exactly the same thing, Shoreditch and Highbury. Got friends down there, have you?'

'Good friends,' Michael says, 'good family,' and the man peers back, one-eyed, measuring: it isn't any of his business, so long as he gets paid.

'Where am I dropping you, then?'

'Home,' Michael says, and the man laughs, none too kindly.

'So where's home, when it's at home?'

'The Buildings.'

'Listen, I'm not being funny, but if you can't tell me somewhere proper I can't take you anywhere.'

'Columbia Buildings,' Michael says, scowling to remember, 'Columbia Road.'

'That's more like it. You see, that wasn't so hard, sir, was it? Now we're both getting somewhere.'

He gazes out. They're passing from the Strand into Fleet Street, Fleet Street to Ludgate Hill, leaving Westminster behind, entering into London according to the old boundaries, shadowing the unseen, guiding permutations of the river.

Southwards, between the buildings, the air is thickening, acquiring luminosity. It takes him a moment to realise what he's seeing. A tide of mist is rising off the Thames. Look at that! he thinks. It's like the old days. There was mist like that in the beginning, in the mornings, when he rose and went to work, his barrow elbow-deep in flowers.

He thinks, where am I going, now? Is it the street of flowers, then? He doesn't mind. It hardly matters. Wherever he goes, he ends alone.

'It's always the last job,' the driver is saying, eyes on the road, beyond appeal. 'Always the last one does my head in. The state I see people in, you wouldn't believe it if I told you. I mean look at you, sir. How old are you? Old enough to know better, I'd call you. Older, greyer and none the wiser. No offence, I'm only saying. People should look out for themselves, look after number one. It's not like anyone else will if you don't, is it? Not these days.'

Momentarily they pass into some overarching darkness. A face looms up in Michael's window. It is shark-like, monstrous: big-nosed, small-eyed, a thin-lipped mouth made for tearing morsels. They are out into lamplit night again before he recognises the features as shadowed burlesques of his own.

He thinks, am I a monster, then? The crowd outside the cemetery gates – the ghosts – they'd call him that, no doubt – and can he say for sure they're wrong? After all, no one in Michael's life has frightened him half as much as he frightens himself.

The driver is no longer talking to him, is remonstrating with the traffic. 'Lanes!' he yells, 'lanes – yes, you, you numpty! Out of it. Get out of it!'

Michael no longer listens. He is dreaming with his eyes open. It is he who is driving. He turns from the road behind to that which still lies ahead. The dark woman stands in his path, between him and his deliverance.

She is stopped in the street of flowers, one arm bent to her hip. She is looking at him across forty years. Her young man is there beside her. He is at the last stall, buying flowers. They have come halfway across the world. They are all done up in their Sunday best, Clarence and Bernadette, as if they have just been to church, though it is not church they leave behind.

She is very beautiful. Michael never saw, but it is clear to him now. It is as if, in this small, late hour, something dull and ill falls from his eyes. Even heavy with child – more than ever, with child – Bernadette Malcolm shines. She has a dignity he has never possessed and which, now, he never will; golden-rayed, unrationed, pure. Her eyes are wide. Her smile of pain has had no time to fade.

Michael closes his eyes. His heart aches in his chest. Motes of light dance on his lids – glitterball afterimages – and then even they are gone, and there is just the void again, unrelieved, unsatisfied, still waiting to be filled.

ACKNOWLEDGEMENTS

Thanks are due to the Arts Council of Great Britain, for financial support; to John Woolrich, for a place of retreat; and to Helen Garnons-Williams, Victoria Hobbs and Hannah Donat, for everything.

A NOTE ON THE TYPE

The text of this book is set in Bembo. This type was first used in 1495 by the Venetian printer Aldus Manutius for Cardinal Bembo's *De Aetna*, and was cut for Manutius by Francesco Griffo. It was one of the types used by Claude Garamond (1480–1561) as a model for his Romain de l'Université, and so it was the forerunner of what became standard European type for the following two centuries. Its modern form follows the original types and was designed for Monotype in 1929.